STORMY WEATHER

Oil is king of East Texas during the darkest years of the Great Depression. The Stoddard girls – responsible Mayme, whip-smart tomboy Jeanine and bookish Bea – trail their father from town to town as he searches for work on the pipelines and derricks, and in every small town, mother Elizabeth does her level best to make a home. When an 'accident' leaves Elizabeth and her girls alone, they return to the abandoned family farm where they pin their last hopes on a wildcat oil well ... and on the back of the late patriarch Jack's one true legacy, a dangerous racehorse named Smoky Joe.

East Riding of Yorkshire
Library and Information Service

STORMY WEATHER

STORMY WEATHER

by

Paulette Jiles

Magna Large Print Books
Long Preston, North Yorkshire,
BD23 4ND, England.

British Library Cataloguing in Publication Data.

Jiles, Paulette
    Stormy weather.

    A catalogue record of this book is
    available from the British Library

    ISBN   978-0-7505-3007-1

First published in Great Britain in 2008 by Fourth Estate
An imprint of HarperCollins Publishers

Published in Large Print 2009 by arrangement with
HarperCollins Publishers

Magna Large Print is an imprint of Library Magna Books Ltd.

Printed and bound in Great Britain by
T.J. (International) Ltd., Cornwall, PL28 8RW

For Mayme and Maxie;
who were there when I came into this world
and have been there ever since

Acknowledgments

Thanks to my agent, Liz Darhansoff, and my editor, Jennifer Brehl, for their patience. Special thanks to Donna Stoner for her encouragement. My gratitude to Gary Pogue for explanations of match-racing and betting, to Betty Nethery for personal stories of horses and match-racing in West Texas, to cable-tool drillers Pete Roseneau and Tommy Johnson, to geologist Denise Ranagan for allowing me on a drill site, to Sky Lewey for information on the mohair industry, and to the docents at the Midland Oil Museum. To Jim and Lois Webb for memories of the 1930s.

CHAPTER ONE

When her father was young, he was known to be a hand with horses. They said he could get any wage he asked for, that he could take on any job of freighting even in the fall when the rains were heavy and the oil field pipe had to be hauled over unpaved roads, when the mud was the color of solder and cased the wheel spokes. The reins were telegraph lines through which he spoke to his horses in a silent code, and it seemed to Jeanine that her father's battered hands held great powers in charge. He could drive through clouds or floods. During the early oil strikes in Central Texas he was once paid $1,250 to drive a sixteen-mule team hauling a massive oil field boiler from McAllister, Oklahoma, to Cisco, Texas. He got it across the Red River Bridge and through the bogged roads of North Texas without losing a mule or a spoke or a bolt.

Jeanine sat beside him on the wagon seat and watched the horses plunge along. They were buoyant, as if they were filled with helium. This particular morning his hands shook when he rolled a cigarette because the night before he had been drinking the brutal intoxicating mixtures that were sold because the Volstead Act was still in effect that year, 1924. After an hour they came to the oil field and her father told her to stay in the crisscross shadow of the derrick until he got his deal done because he and the foreman were probably going to sit around and talk and cuss for a while. *You can't step past those shadows, there. Don't go playing around the horses' feet. Here, read this comic book.* She sat and read from panel to panel as Texas Slim shot his way through the saloon doors on his horse Loco. She couldn't keep her mind on it and so she walked the shadows of the derrick and pretended they were dark roads leading her away to distant countries like Mars and Boston and Oklahoma.

Her father talked with the driller about pipe to be hauled and how much a load and how many loads. The driller needed casing pipe, and casing pipe weighed more than drill stem so her father was trying to get paid by weight as well as by the load. After they had agreed and shook hands, he stood up carefully to balance his enormous beating head on his shoulders and called out, 'Jeanine, come on, we've got to go.'

Jeanine came to stand against her father's knees. All the machinery was still. The oil had been found and was being held below their feet, dark and explosive, until the crew would let it up through the casing pipe.

She said, 'Let me drive the horses.' Jeanine had a low voice and it made her sound like an immature blond dwarf.

Her father patted her heavily on top of her head. 'You're too little to drive.'

'But I want to play Ben-Hur.'

He smiled. 'You can't be Ben-Hur, honey, you're a girl.'

The week before they had gone to see the

movie star Raymond Navarro playing Ben-Hur in a toga, in screenland black and white, ripping around the arena at a suicidal speed, lashing a whip.

'Yeah, but he was wearing a dress, and I'm the one that's got the pants on.'

Her father laughed and held his head. Jeanine was so relieved that her own laughter had a frantic sound and tears came to her eyes. The driller thought it was funny as well and he repeated it to the crew several times over and even after a week the driller could be heard to say *Don't mess with me, boys, I'm the one that's got the pants on.*

They started home. They lived in half of a rent house in Ranger, where they had moved as soon as there was word of an oil strike. Before that they seemed to have lived on the old Tolliver farm, but Jeanine was too young to remember it. Her father's strong hands were scarred, they had been knocked around by everything, by engine cranks and coffin hoists and the wagon jack. His cloth cap barely shaded his bloodshot eyes. All round them the horizon shifted from one red stone layer to another and down these slopes spilled live oak and Spanish oak and mesquite, wild grape and persimmon. Alongside the road were things people threw out of cars and wagons. A baby doll head lay under a dense blackbrush and seemed to watch as the hooves of the team went past. There were tin cans and mottled rags and lard pails and tiny squares of broken safety glass.

He reached under the seat and took out his bottle.

'If I have a drink now she'll never know by the

time we get home.' He took a quick drink and then handed the bottle to her. 'Hide that for me.'

Jeanine kneeled down and found the feed bags under the seat and stuffed the bottle in one of them and sat back on the seat again. She leaned against him. During the tormented shouting of the night before, Jeanine and her sister knew these were noises of pain. Their parents needed comfort.

'I love you,' she said.

'You'll be mad at me too someday, Jenny,' he said. 'Before the world is done with me.'

'But how come you threw the album out the front door?'

'Because the sewing machine was too heavy.'

The photographs of herself and her sister Mayme tumbled down the steps like playing cards, like the doll head, discarded. Her mother and father's wedding portrait spun into the dirt. Jeanine and her sister Mayme picked them all up and carefully pasted them back into the album. Before long her mother and father would kiss each other. After that her father would be paid and they would buy a case of Lithiated Lemon soda and a radio and a racehorse.

'We're going to have a racehorse one of these days,' said Jeanine. 'He'll look like Big Man.'

'Oh baby baby baby. These here are draft horses. We want something little and fast and wound up like an eight-day clock.'

Jeanine stood up in the seat. 'I want to ride on Big Man.' She had made him laugh, all was well, she would now ride in triumph into the wagon yard.

'No. You'll fall off. When those big hooves get done stepping on you you'll look like that doll's head back there.'

'I don't care.'

'All right, all right. This is so you don't tell.'

'About what?'

'My whiskey.'

'I never seen any whiskey.'

He threw her up on the near leader named Big Man and she held on to the collar knobs. She waved at cars passing by in the sovereign confidence that she was beautiful and special and her father's darling. The child of a unique destiny. She had a new pair of homemade overalls and a new short haircut. Her hair was an icy blond that would soon darken but for now all the arguing and the torment was over and the day was full of light. The high dray wheels of good fortune sang on, revolving behind her, and her father slapped the Y-lines on the horses' backs and said she was a pistol.

In 1918, the year Jeanine was born, the oil strikes in north-central Texas, at Ranger and Tarrant and Cisco, were places of astonishing chaos. The towns became hives of workers and freighters with four-horse teams and drugstores and ranked lines of Model As at the curbs, and gamblers and prostitutes and the wretched of the earth and lease-hounds with dubious paper. Homemade alcoholic drinks were sold at the back doors of the drugstores.

Crude oil sprang up out of the earth in fields that had been recently abandoned to the drought and the boll weevil, and town populations jumped from 400 to 15,000 in a matter of months. A young man named Conrad Hilton borrowed money to buy a hotel in Cisco and packed in cots so tightly you could step from one to another. He said the place was a cross between a flophouse and a gold mine.

Jeanine and her father and mother and sisters moved again, this time to Tarrant, and things started going seriously downhill. Jeanine's mother, Elizabeth, had seen the world change so rapidly she was in a state of anxiety. Women's clothing had changed in ten years from floor-length dresses and big hats to little narrow skirts that stopped above the knee, and the women who wore them drank whiskey and smoked. Her husband had taken her away from farm life to the oil fields, and she had become a mother three times over. Like so many others who followed the oil strikes, they left behind not only the place where they had been born but the Tolliver farm and their kin and the local doctor. They left behind a community where their family names were known and the graveyard under the cedars, whose stones were carved with those same names.

When they lived in Tarrant, Jeanine's father was gone every weekend to the brush-track races. When he came back, sometimes he had money and sometimes he didn't. Often he had too much to drink and then for a while he was as much fun as people on the radio. He was tall, dark, and handsome and Jeanine believed everything he said. He let her light his cigarettes, her small

16

fingers cautiously lifted the flaming kitchen match in the dark of the front porch, in the heat of a summer night.

He said someday when he made his money in the oil fields they'd have horses, they would have something fast enough to beat Harmon Baker, faster than Ace of Hearts. He sang to her the old race song about Molly and Tenbrooks. She was too young to know he was drunk and had gambled away the last of the McAllister boiler money. *Molly went to California, she done as she pleased, come back to old Kentucky and got beat with all ease...*

When they moved to the next oil strike at Mexia, in 1927, her mother packed up the photograph album and the quilts and the five Tolliver silver spoons and dishes and the buckets and her framed print of a little girl sitting alone in the woods. The little girl was listening to a bird that sang some unheard melody from the branch of a white tree and it seemed to Jeanine that the girl was dangerously alone in an alien, watery forest.

He took her with him to the brush-track races around Mexia. She held her father's bet money and watched as the horses were led up to the score line. She was only nine and the men thought she was charming, she waved her straw hat and cheered as the horses and jockeys roared down the quarter-mile straightaway track with the jockeys up in the irons, their caps turned backward, suspended over the horses' necks. They flashed past the prickly-pear flats when the cactus fruit was ripe and stood up in bloodred

17

crowns. The jockeys fought against one another in an avalanche of red dust and radiant hides, the horses hurling up clods and rocks behind them, their nostrils big as boreholes, always running on the edge of disaster, for the Texas brush tracks were poorly graded and the footing was treacherous. Betting was illegal in Texas but the money that changed hands sometimes amounted to a man's monthly wage or half the cotton crop, and often enough the bills were stained with crude oil. At that time incomparable horses ran on the Texas brush tracks: Old Joe Hancock, Red Buck, Flying Dutchman, Hot Shot, Oklahoma Star, My Texas Dandy, Rainy Day, and the beautiful earless Red Man.

CHAPTER TWO

He brought her with him down to the blacksmith shop in Mexia; an abode of men and fire and iron and cars in various stages of disassembly. He backed the Model T into the open shed and called out to the men sitting beside the forge fire and pulled the hand brake.

'I'm just going to see what the boys are up to,' he said. He slapped Jeanine's arm in a comradely way. 'You sit out here in the car and watch for the law. If you see a Texas Ranger, you say, 'Cheese it, the cops.'

'I seen that movie,' said Jeanine. 'Why do I say cheese it the cops?'

'They don't like us playing cards. They get into people's private business.'

The men all went out to the yard behind the shop and cleared a worktable. Cards spun out to each in turn. Jeanine didn't want to sit in the car. Instead she stood at her father's elbow and looked at his cards. She listened to him talk in fragments of sentences with a younger man across from him at the worktable; he was talking about selling the team. Her father said he needed to buy a truck, comes a time when you got to face facts. I'll save an hour a day not having to throw a harness on them. Cigarette smoke drifted over their heads in gray planes.

'This here fellow is Ross Everett,' he said to her. 'You wouldn't mind if he bought our team, would you? He ain't but nineteen years old but he says he's figured out how to feed them.'

Jeanine was nine now, and she knew better than to plead and besides it was not in her nature. She would bargain, try to salvage something, fix things.

'I guess you can,' she said. 'But I want Big Man. He can have Maisie and Jeff and Little Man.'

'Pistol, Big Man would be lonely,' her father said. 'He'd cry every night, he'd get drawn down.'

The talk drifted to racing, to bloodlines and quarter-mile and eighth-of-a-mile times and what the Cajuns were going to run in Louisiana. They got that mare named Della Moore, they're coming over to get into Texas racing. One man said he'd never been to Louisiana; he said it just for the record. Another man with his front teeth crossed one over the other said them boys are

19

hot. They turned that stud San Jacinto loose at 350 yards in Eagle Pass and he ate everybody up.

Jeanine lifted her square face and smiled anxiously.

'But, Daddy, didn't you say Red Nell was the one to beat at 350 yards?'

'What did I tell you?' He looked around at the other men. 'What did I tell you. She knows more than Ott Adams.'

The younger man didn't laugh. He glanced up from his cards at her. She wasn't supposed to be here. She already knew this, that her father took her places that girls weren't supposed to go. She turned away and went to poke sticks into the forge fire. There was a pack of old playing cards burning. They were used up, the men had thrown them away, and the queen of clubs dissolved into flame. Maybe he would get so drunk he would forget about selling the team.

After a while she fell asleep in the Model T on top of the groceries; bags of flour and sugar and a jug of kerosene, soup bones and bologna wrapped in brown paper. When she woke up the blacksmith's shop was silent and dark. She couldn't hear any voices. Everybody was gone. For a few terrified moments she could not remember what town they were in. Mexia, she thought, we're in Mexia. She did not know what hour of the night it might be, or what could have happened to her father.

She waited for a while and watched the last gleams from the forge fire run over the walls, the coals were a deep gemlike red and seemed like something you could hold in your hand. A cat came out from behind the quenching vat with a rat in its mouth. Jeanine sat there for a long time and was perfectly still, like a small animal in the face of unknown dangers.

She grasped the lever handle on the passenger door and opened it and stepped down. He had been out in the back. There had been a lot of laughing and talking and drinking but they must have all gone home and possibly her father had gone too and forgotten that he had come in the car and that she was with him. The floor was crusty with hoof shavings and bits of metal. She walked by the last light of the fire toward the back bay doors. She heard a noise beyond the wall, it sounded like something was dying. Long snarling groans.

Jeanine eased herself through the doors. By the remote light of the street gas lamps and a quarter moon she saw a man sitting upright in a kitchen chair with a cane in his hands. He turned his head in her direction.

'Who's that?' he said. 'There is somebody there.'

'Yes,' she said. She kept her eyes on his cane.

'Well, who is it? It's a child. Who are you?'

'Jeanine,' she said.

'What are you doing here?'

'I'm looking for my dad.'

'Is it dark?' he asked.

Jeanine put her hand to her mouth in confusion. 'Is what dark?'

The man was heavy and fat, his shoes were not at all worn but his coat and pants were threadbare. The inhuman noise came from

21

beyond a wooden wall, on the other side of the open space.

'I'm blind,' he said. 'I'm just sitting up here all night until people come in to work. In the morning. They forgot me.'

Jeanine said, 'They forgot me too.' She saw that his eyes moved and jittered, they were never still. 'Do you know what happened to my dad? Jack Stoddard?'

The blind man said, 'He's asleep, honey. He's passed out. Over there.' His eyes roved and trembled in their sockets and their movement seemed to have nothing to do with where he turned his head or the gesture he made toward the coal storage shed beyond the wall. His eyes seemed to have some secret life of their own.

She slipped past the blind man and took the latch of the shed door in both hands and pulled it open. Her father slept on his back atop several bags of coal. His handsome face was slack, his dark hair sprayed across his forehead, and his shirt stained with coal dust. He sounded like something being slaughtered in a lonesome dirty pit.

She shook his arm and said Daddy several times but he did not wake up. He jerked his arm away from her and thrashed one way and then another on the coal and then started snoring again. She started to cry but crying only made her feel worse. She went back to the blind man.

She said, 'Sir, can you help me get him home?'

'I don't know what I could do to help you.' He cleared his throat. 'You should wait until morning and some people will come. George

Dillard, he owns this place, he's the blacksmith. He'll be here about seven.'

'I have to get him home,' said Jeanine. 'My mother will be worried. We don't have any food or anything. I have to go to school.'

'How old are you?'

'I'm nine. Is there anybody close by that could help me?'

'Well, if you want to go get the town constable.'

'No, I better not.'

She cried noiselessly. Her mother and father were supposed to love each other but they yelled at each other so much, and these things kept happening. Now it was the middle of the night and she was abandoned here in a blacksmith shop with the old Tin Lizzie and the meat going bad in the heat.

'Well,' he said. 'Can you drive?'

Jeanine wiped her face on her dress. 'Yes,' she said. 'Yes, I could drive. Daddy has let me drive. I think I know where we live.'

The blind man leaned on his cane. 'Do you know how to work the pedals?'

'Yes. But I don't know how to start it.'

'Well, I'll tell you how.' His fingers wandered up and down the cane like white caterpillars in the dark. 'Do everything I say.'

Jeanine went over to the old Ford and stood waiting for the blind man to tell her what to do.

'All right, turn on that lever on the tank. That opens the gas line to the engine.'

She turned the tank lever, and when he told her to, she reached into the driver's side window and pushed up on a left-hand lever. She found the

23

hand brake and skinned her knuckles setting it.

'Your dad ought to be jailed,' he said, 'for getting drunk and leaving you in the car. There ought to be a law.'

'Oh no,' said Jeanine. 'Don't tell anybody. I can take him home.'

'Can you see over the dashboard?'

'I can!' she said. 'It's easy, I can see over it good.'

'Turn that coil box key,' he said. 'That's your electrical system.' The fingers of his right hand waved in the air as if they were independent of him or he did not realize he was doing it. 'I could take one of them Tin Lizzies apart blind. They won't let me. I could do it easy.'

Jeanine turned the coil box key, and then he told her shove up on the lever on the steering wheel that retarded the spark. She turned the key and pressed down with her heel on the starter. The motor purred smoothly, the lights came on and the blind man sat in the beams with a smile on his face. He was illuminated like an actor on a stage.

Jeanine said, 'I got to get him in the backseat.'

The blind man followed her voice in a slow shuffle, his feet like small boats sprayed aside bow waves of straw and dirt and coal ash. She tried to wake her father and after a while he wobbled upright.

'Ahhh bullshit,' he said. 'Iss juss bullshit.'

The blind man took Jack Stoddard by the ribs and lifted him.

'Guide me,' he said. 'Hey, girlie, point me at that car.'

Jeanine took hold of his sleeve and then opened the back passenger-side door and the blind man felt along the rim of the door while he lifted Jack Stoddard through it with surprising strength. She saw her father grope around and claw his way onto the torn upholstery of the rear seat and slump down again saying, 'Well what the hell is this? If this isn't a way to do a fellow.'

Jeanine said, 'Thank you, mister. I sure appreciate it.'

The blind man walked back toward his chair with sure steps, in an upright posture with his head drawn back, as if he were afraid something might strike him on the chin and as he came to his chair he put out his open, white hand in an elegant gesture, letting it fall until it touched the chair back.

'Children driving around at night,' he said. 'There ain't words to describe it. He should be arrested.'

Jeanine climbed in the passenger door. She reached down and took up a heavy twenty-five-pound flour sack and somehow got it onto the driver's seat and sat down on it so she could see over the dash. The world was now full of obstacles and pieces of metal on the ground that would reach up to pierce one of the narrow tires. She stepped on the pedal and fed gas to the engine and released the brake and drove out of the blacksmith's yard into the midnight town.

The streets were paved with brick and the tires made a flubbering noise passing over them. It was a town in the middle of the night, something she had never seen before. The daytime had receded like a tide and left all the buildings comatose, all the signs that said GROCERIES and MEXIA DRUGS and BARBERSHOP had nobody to speak to. Jeanine passed by one street after another, looking for the sign that said BRICK YARD ROAD, afraid of waking up somebody who would come and arrest her father. If she could just get home she would be all right. The headlights glared back at her from storefront windows and behind those reflections were town constables and sheriffs looking for a nine-year-old girl driving without a license with a drunk daddy in the backseat.

She came toward the railroad station. A man in a broad western hat stood beside a team of four horses. He was waiting for the train to come and he would load them up and take them away to his ranch. It was Maisie and Jeff and Big Man and Little Man. Her father had sold them that very night. Their pale straw-colored manes and tails were like lifting flax in the midnight glare of the streetlights, they nodded to one another and shifted their enormous feet.

Jeanine felt that her heart was broken but she dared not try to stop and say good-bye to the team. She felt that they were on their way to some good place and were leaving her behind, it was as if she had been deserted by some roadside. She had not yet passed Brick Yard Road. They lived down that red dirt road somewhere in a two-room rent house alongside other rent houses thrown up at the height of the oil boom and now dwindling back into mere lumber.

She gritted her teeth and held on to the wheel; the old car wavered down the street. Maybe there was such a thing as stars in the heavens coming down to guide you somewhere and she knew there wasn't. A dog darted out at the car and peppered the night with explosive barks as he ran alongside. *Shut up! Shut up!* She leaned out the window and hissed at the dog. For a few moments she felt savage with rage. All her emotions were too big for her.

The man stepped out of the light of the train station and walked into the headlights and so she jammed at the brake with both feet and killed the engine. He walked up to the driver's side and bent down to look in, his face in the shadow of his hat brim.

'You're Jack Stoddard's girl,' he said. 'What are you doing driving this car? In the middle of the night?' He glanced at the backseat to see her father lying there snoring, so ugly and wasted.

She said, 'Oh, he'll be all right in the morning!'

'Where do you live?'

She held on to the wheel as if she were afraid he would take it away from her.

'Down Brick Yard Road. Mister, do you know where it is?'

'Yes,' he said. 'Get out so I can drive.'

She didn't know if this was worse or better. She could have driven slowly up to the house, she could have killed the engine and glided silently into their littered front yard. She could still fix everything by herself. And maybe he wanted to steal the car.

'I can drive,' she said.

'You probably can but I am not going to let you.'

Jeanine got out and stood by the driver's side, and reached in to turn on the ignition coil for him when he jerked the crank around. He seemed very angry.

'You're not allowed to steal my dad's car,' she said.

'I know that.'

She stood on the brick street as he angled his long legs inside. He picked up the sack of flour and dropped it on the floor and seated himself at the wheel.

'I can turn the crank,' she said. 'I'll turn it for you if it dies again.'

'Get in,' he said.

They passed the train station and then went in among the oil rigs that had invaded the very town itself, a dark army marching among the houses and empty lots. The horsehead pumpjacks groaned and sighed with a sound like great warm rocking chairs patiently creaking in the night. With a kind of helpless terror she saw their house and the coal-oil lamp shining in the front window.

'My mother doesn't care if I drive,' she said.

'I'll wager she cares if you drive home with your dad passed out in the backseat at one o'clock in the morning.'

Jeanine wiped tears from her eyes, quickly. 'They're going to fight,' she said. 'She doesn't even know he sold our team.'

Ross Everett started to say something and opened his mouth and then cleared his throat and was silent. When they pulled into the front yard she jumped out of the passenger-side door like a small acrobat. She would tell her mother that her father just now went and fell asleep in the back. Her mother came out onto the front porch. Everett climbed out of the passenger side after her and said good evening to her mother and took off his hat and then put it on again. From the next yard a hen made an interrogative, crawling noise and in the remote distance an airplane bored through the night sky. Jeanine gathered up as many of the brown paper packages of groceries as she could.

At the last minute she remembered to jerk the sack of flour from the front. It landed on the gas cock and the sack tore open and flour poured out onto the floorboards. Jeanine turned to her mother, standing at the open door with the lamp in her shaking hand.

'Thank you, Ross,' she said.

'It's my fault for keeping him out so late,' said Everett.

Her mother nodded. 'Jeanine, don't lie for him,' she said. She put the lamp on the step and walked toward her daughter and took her hand. 'Just don't lie for him.'

CHAPTER THREE

They shifted out to the Permian Basin in far West Texas when the big Yates field came in. By 1928 the north-central Texas boom had played out and settled down to the sedate business of production. Wells had been driven in whatever place seemed to show even the least promise, including a dry hole on the old Tolliver farm itself. The Tolliver well had been drilled by a producer named D.H. Sullivan who was known as Dry Hole Sullivan. He just kept on drilling one dry hole after another and nobody knew how he managed to raise capital for his hopeless ventures but there's a sucker born every minute and most of them have at least some cash to part with in order to buy one one-thousandth of one one-thousandth of the price per barrel that might come from a future or nonexistent oil well and generally these people lived in Chicago or Baltimore or someplace like that.

They moved into a section house in a town called Monahans. The section house had been left there by the Texas and Pacific Railroad and then afterward used as a chicken house. Then during the strike it was rented out to themselves and another family. They each had a room, and the other family asked them to turn up their radio at night so they could all hear KBST out of Big

Springs. Broken egg-shells littered the corners. Her father drove a saltwater pumper; the producers injected brine into the formations to keep up the pressure when the oil was pulled out. Then her father took to driving nitroglycerin. He drove a brand-new 1929 Ford half-ton with EXPLOSIVES painted down the side in silver letters and in later years Jeanine came to understand that he also delivered bootleg whiskey with this vehicle and got away with it because the various law enforcement agencies did not want to stop him or to get anywhere near him.

There was no wood to burn in their stove in that remote desert. Coal came in with the tankers that roared into Monahans to take on oil; the coal cars were always at the end of the string next to the caboose. Jeanine and her older sister ran down the line of tankers with buckets to collect coal at five cents the bucket. It was a dirty job and they hated it. They stood and watched in the cold desert mornings with other children as the coal was shoveled out in heaps into the back of coal trucks. It had a slick repellent shine to it. The men shoveling it out onto the trucks could see that some of the children had come to pick up fallen pieces. These were children in thin sweaters and busted shoes, with anxious looks on their faces. The men shoveled big scoop-loads down to them and everyone stood back and let them collect it.

They learned about the crash of 1929 at the salt well. Jeanine had heard about the salt well and wanted to go see it and one day she said she would go by herself if the others didn't want to come with her, she would walk along the highway and out into the desert alone. She was not afraid of the empty spaces. She wasn't afraid to skip school either and she wasn't afraid of a whipping, since all their mother did was wave a homemade flyswatter at them. Jeanine was eleven now, she had developed a square face and a firm jaw and long gray eyes and dishwater blond hair. She and Mayme and another girl picked up stray pieces of coal that had fallen from the coal cars as they walked. They carried flour bags to collect it. They walked out into the immense flat stretch of the Permian Basin where it stretched without variation like a single note played on a wind instrument, on and on without end. The sunlight shone stark and unforgiving on the twisted brush. The blackbrush and creosote were short and drawn up into wired armatures with brief, hardened leaves.

They came to the derrick and a wellhead that was gushing salt water. The brine was ancient fossil seawater from two thousand feet below, it spouted into the air like a plume and all around it, the engine shed and the derrick itself and an abandoned car and pieces of rope and broken bailers, tin cans, crushed pipe, severed bolts, loops of cable, all were coated with crystallized salt. The fine crystals gleamed like minute gems and every piece of discarded trash shone like the jewels of the Romanovs.

Beside the well was a 1927 touring car with a lot of seismographic equipment, but it was turned off and the geophone needles were dead on their pegs. A man sat in the car with a radio on, and a man in chaps sat beside him. The man in the chaps took off his broad hat and wiped his head with a bandana. The salt water roared.

'Jesus Christ, they're going down like ninepins.' The men bent forward to the crackling radio. 'U.S. Steel and all of them.'

They said hello to the seismograph man and he said, Good day, girls. Mayme asked what was it that they were listening to on the radio.

'The stock market has crashed,' said the seismograph man. He turned up the volume. The announcer said that Montgomery Ward was falling from 83 to 50 and Radio was hurtling down headlong from 68 to 44. 'Are any of you heavily invested in stocks or bonds?'

Jeanine said no, they were not.

'Good. If you do, put your money in oil.'

'All right,' said Jeanine, brightly.

Mayme said, 'He's kidding you, wise up.' They talked in this way because they were very young and had seen various movie stars in films, the starlets who were cynical and smart and tossed their heads at everything. They said wise up, and tell it to your old man, and made the fashionable gestures of shrugging and lifting their chins. The girls stood by the car with black hands, holding their coal, listening.

It was in June of 1931 that the Lou Della Crim came in outside of Longview, near the Louisiana border. The Lou Della roared up in a gusher that took the drilling pipe out with it and threw the twenty-foot, two-hundred-pound joints of pipe into the air like jackstraws. The blowout of oil hurled a three-cone roller drill bit the size of an alligator a full two hundred yards. Men ran for their lives. It cost a crew ten days' labor to shut it down. They had hit the biggest oil pool in the history of the world and it was sweet, high-gravity oil so pure you could almost pour it straight into your gas tank, it was the color of honey. The wildcatter who drilled the discovery well reached the oil-bearing strata with an ancient cable-tool rig and a decrepit wooden derrick and second-hand equipment. The driller and his crew were so broke they were throwing old tires into the steam engine for fuel.

'There's going to be some wild times out there,' her father said. 'They hit it at only fifteen hundred feet, Liz. It's coming in at nearly twenty-two thousand barrels a day.'

Jeanine came to stand by him at the table and peered carefully at the exclamatory headlines of the *Longview Daily News*. She was shelling peas. Strands of desert wind sang at the top of the stovepipe and her mother read a Hardy Boys book, *The Great Airport Mystery*, aloud to Bea, on the other side of the table.

'Those boys are going to need some pipe hauled,' Jeanine said. She tossed a handful of fresh peas into her mouth. Her low, boyish voice made her father laugh so hard he dropped the paper.

'Listen to the girl,' he said. 'Ain't she a pistol.'

And so they left the Permian Basin with great hopes, the summer when Jeanine had just turned

34

thirteen and Mayme was fifteen and Bea was six. Their father bought a Reo Speed Wagon flatbed, and on this they loaded all their possessions and left the desert for East Texas. Jack and Elizabeth and Bea rode in the cab and Mayme and Jeanine rode on the flatbed with their trunks and boxes. They spent six days on the road and had eleven flats. Her father poured Karo syrup into the front tires and it made the inner tubes hold out longer. The terrible drought of the early 1930s had reduced Central and North Texas to a country of hardpan and drift and abandoned farms. They saw other people headed east along with them, loaded with mattresses and chickens and children and washboards tied to the tops of Tin Lizzies, all of them journeying toward the East Texas strike where there was work to be had.

The country near the Louisiana border was heavy and green, pine trees sagged under drapes of Virginia creeper vine that had turned the color of rust in the fall air. They came to the town of Arp. Under the black-on-white ARP sign a redheaded woman with a flock of guinea hens pecking at her feet sold boiled peanuts from a two-gallon pail. The peanuts tumbled in the smoking water. They were the color of snuff and looked like eyes gone bad. Jeanine and Mayme tried to make Bea eat them to see if it would kill her or not. Bea was, at that time, an obedient and amiable child.

Arp was where the railhead lay, a town of stacked casing pipe and barrels of drilling fluid, piles of cable and whipstocks and food supplies. The trains off-loaded equipment and canned

35

goods and then took on the high-grade East Texas crude into tanker cars. The field had developed so fast there weren't even enough pipelines. Trucks churned their wheels in the scarlet mud, hauling material to the drill sites throughout Rusk and Gregg counties. Locomotives came through at the rate of thirty a day, fifteen going north and fifteen south. There was almost no housing to be had. A city of tents had grown up around nearly every town in the area, and people lived among the forests of pine like an army of cheerful refugees. Boxcars and tankers arrived behind their engines, screaming out of the pine forests, down the unsteady roadbeds. Boxcars that said INTERNATIONAL AND GREAT NORTHERN, TEXAS AND PACIFIC, GULF COAST AND RIO GRANDE. Trains became the sound of Jeanine's memories of East Texas, the steam engines with their hoarse and violent and distant singing.

Her mother said they would not live in a tent even though Jeanine and her older sister were about to say they wanted to live in a tent more than anything. They imagined looking at the crashing loud oil strike world from under the ballooning fabric, it would be just their own family together under canvas. But their mother said if there was no house for them, she was leaving. She would take the girls and go home, back to the Tolliver farm, and he could make his own way as best he could. Elizabeth Tolliver Stoddard made a dramatic gesture toward throwing the skillet in a cardboard box and folding up Mayme's overalls. Jack Stoddard reached out to touch Jeanine's hair and said, *No, Liz, I couldn't make it without all of you. I'll find us something. Don't go, Liz.*

They were lucky to get part of a house on the north side of Longview. It was a farmhouse whose farm had been devoured by the oil fields and the tents and the little board-and-batten rent houses. It had been added onto many times; the old farmhouse was a confusing jumble of rooms and closed-in porches and windowless additions. Over everything the thin hundred-foot East Texas pines bent in the wind and sang.

They had three rooms in the back, looking out onto the well and the hard-packed dirt of the yard. There were at least three other families in the house but it seemed like more than that because there were so many children running rampant in the day and the night. Some people from Illinois on the second floor screamed at one another about whether or not a one-dollar bill the wife had received for three hens and all their chicks was counterfeit. Another family consisted of a set of parents and two ratlike boys with wide bare feet who attacked each other with china berry shooters and screamed and pretended to die. Jeanine helped to unpack; the girls would sleep in one room and their parents in another and they would eat and talk and cook and listen to the radio in the third. They stuck the stovepipe out a window. The sisters called it the Crazy House.

After school they ran down to the railroad tracks and placed things on the rails for trains to run over; sometimes a penny, although pennies

37

were precious. The trains did peculiar things to metal; nails flattened and shone, hairpins turned to steel ribbons. Men in tattered clothes jumped out of the freight cars and ran for the trackside weeds, there were so many of them that the railroad police just stood back and watched them and let them go. They were men who had seen the economic structure of the nation suddenly disintegrate without warning, and they felt they had become citizens of some strange country without knowing it. It was a nation they no longer knew. A wasteland without law or order, and they had taken to traveling through this wasteland almost like tourists.

But there was work in the East Texas oil fields. Jeanine's father drove loads from the railhead out to the field at ten dollars a load, and then fifteen dollars and then twenty dollars as the drilling became more intense and the immensity of the oil strike became apparent. The excitement of it gave him a merry, lunatic air. At one drill site, gas came up out of the mud of the slush pit in bubbles the size of baseballs. Jack Stoddard and the crew amused themselves while he waited for his load by throwing matches at the bubbles and watching them explode. He told Liz and the girls it wouldn't be long before they had them their racehorse. He stopped drinking. He said he did not have a drinking problem, the problem was the hangovers. So he moved on to gambling instead and lost money stone-cold sober.

While they lived in the Crazy House their Tolliver grandparents died within days of each other from pneumonia that many people said was caused by the dust, and Uncle Reid ran off and left Aunt Lillian and cousin Betty. He went north somewhere, maybe to the Oklahoma field, and nobody ever heard from him again. Jeanine realized people you love could disappear. This opened a hole in her universe, some illusory backdrop had torn away and beyond this an unlit waste and she could not see into it. She had a difficult time putting this into words to herself and so she sat with her fists against her eyes as they drove back to Central Texas, looking at the sparks against the dark of her eyelids.

They buried their kin in the old Tolliver graveyard, standing among a crowd of neighbors with heads bowed to hear the Methodist minister say *I am the resurrection and the life* while his tie fluttered in the hot, dust-laden wind. Little Bea was not allowed to come to the graveside because children should not be burdened with these things more than necessary or maybe the thinking was that if they were exposed to such things at a tender age they would become indifferent. Bea and a little redheaded neighbor girl had to stay inside the house where they sliced up the funeral bread and ate all the sugar and butter.

The older children gathered on the front veranda afterward to get away from the grownups who were suffering through emotions that the children could not help or allay and so they all sat and fooled around with telephone line insulators. There was a boy named Milton Brown and he was not related to her but to some neighbors. He wore a suit and steel-rimmed spectacles. He stuttered so badly he sounded as if he were trying to speak in Morse code.

Jeanine turned up one of the glass insulators and put it over her nose and her cousin Betty laughed and then stopped laughing and cleared her throat.

'We went to school t-t-together,' Milton said to Jeanine. 'I sat in front of, uh, you and stuttered.'

'I don't remember you,' said Jeanine. She said it in a mean nasal voice around the glass insulator.

'How could you forget!' He seemed to speak better if he shouted. 'I'll remind you of it someday.'

He got up in a jerky way and went inside; he left Jeanine and her cousins feeling bad about themselves in a way that was not repairable at the moment. Jeanine turned to her cousin and then didn't say anything, but got up and walked into the silent house after him. Milton Brown was sitting in the parlor in front of the Atwater Kent radio and watching the little balls inside the glass battery drift up and down while the Carter family sang 'I'll Fly Away.' He sat in a chair backward, his chin was on his forearms.

'B-border radio, Jeanine,' he said. 'Hundred thousand watts, you can get it in your bobby pins in Del Rio. Yow.'

Through the nine-foot parlor windows she could see to the veranda where her cousins sat and turned the blue-green glass knobs over in their hands and the glass glinted in the hot air. *When I die, Hallelujah bye and bye, I'll fly away.* From beyond the central hall she heard the sound of a man walking across the kitchen floor, and the tick of a dipper lowered into a white enamel water bucket. For one second she thought it was her grandfather, but it was not, nor would it ever be again. She suddenly remembered one slow, dark evening when she and her grandfather and her father and Uncle Reid had walked down to the barn lot to see the work team. She did not remember when it was, or why they had come to visit, only that it was the most peaceful memory available to her. She had felt safe and secure with her hand in her father's, and the men talking, the work team calling out to her grandfather in low tones, the warm good smell of harness and grass hay. The tears poured from between her fingers and she began to cry with quiet, strangled noises. Milton Brown sat absorbed in the radio noise and did not hear her.

It was the last time she saw the old Tolliver farm for many years. It remained in Jeanine's imagination a kind of lost kingdom far to the west of them, the old house guarded by Spanish oaks and one great live oak and the Brazos River running green and twisted far below. The scaling bark of the peach trees that had been left unpruned and uncared for, birds' nests in the chimneys. The land shriveled in the dry heat. She was left with the confused idea of her grandparents, now buried in the Tolliver graveyard, as sailing away in the strata below them to a place of great joy, buoyed on underground streams of oil.

It was in East Texas that her father began to gamble with intent seriousness, there in the

41

outwash of people who had come seeking work in the oil fields as the Depression bottomed out. Jack Stoddard was like a juggler tossing up jobs and dice and racehorses and ladies of the night. Sometimes he caught them all in order and sometimes he forgot where they were or that he did not have enough hands.

They moved twenty miles south to Kilgore. Her father made up his mind to move the way birds made up their minds in midflight, wild, startling shifts that sent them spinning away through the vagrant airs to yet another oil field. They carried their cardboard boxes through a piercing cold norther into another tiny rent house of board-and-batten. Close by was the chugging of a ditching machine biting through the dirt to lay a line of narrow production pipe. Some other family that lived there before them had blocked the holes in the walls with old corsets and underpants, and Mayme said whoever it was must have abandoned the place stark naked with their tits flopping loose and she and Jeanine laughed until they could not catch their breath.

It came to Christmas Eve of 1932; next door to them, another family lived in an abandoned engine shed. They were a foreign people and they sang *Quanno nascette ninno a Betelem me, E rannote pa vea meizo journo...* There was no money for presents so Jeanine and her older sister Mayme and Bea, who was eight, decided to sing to their mother and father. This would be their Christmas gift. In those days most people could sing unaccompanied, and the greater part of the time they had to. The sisters meant to sing

Christmas carols or comic songs, but the songs that occurred to them were old melodies of terrible sadness, songs that came to the girls without thought. They sang *O Shenandoah, I love your daughter* and *If I had the wings of an angel, over these prison walls I would fly*. They could not stop themselves, they were caught up in a descending chute of music that mourned aloud for all the Christmases unattended and wandering people who could not find their way home. They sang 'A Shanty in Old Shanty Town' and at last they slid into the atonal hills song 'The Three Little Babes,' this last a most terrible ancient lament as old as Scotland itself. It was a Christmas morning, when everything was still, and the ghosts of the three dead children came running down the hill. Jeanine could not finish it. Their father was attentive and silent over his coffee and their mother put her hand to her face and wept.

That night Jeanine could not sleep. The girls were crowded up in their one bed, wadded in quilts. They had made their mother weep on this night of the archangels and shepherds in the fields, when they were supposed to be joyful. She got out of bed and went to the window to stare out into the night, and as she wiped angrily at her eyes with a corner of the quilt snow began to fall. It was the first snow Smith County had seen in thirty years. The tops of the pine trees disappeared in a foam of descending snow. It fell on the needles and lined them with spines of white and built up on the wires of the fence lot, and burdened all the sounds of the town and the derricks with a deep, submissive hush. It was a

43

swansdown welcome for the new year, a confetti and ticker tape parade. All over the oil fields and through the overcrowded towns, each person had some small reason that the snowfall was for them alone, a sign that their lives were going to get better.

She watched as the flakes struck the window-pane and traced them with her fingertip down the cold glass as they slid and melted out of their ornate and classical designs. Far away the derrick lights shone into the columns of radiant drift. It was just before the bank failures of 1933, and the rest of the nation paused, dumbfounded, in their party clothes and tinfoil hats, in Chicago and New York and Los Angeles and New Orleans, while money fell like hot ashes out of the bottoms of their pockets.

CHAPTER FOUR

They were photographs that people took of one another with their box cameras, the old Kodaks, not the documentary photographs taken by the Farm Security Administration. People appeared at their best and kept their secrets to themselves. Elizabeth carefully pasted pictures into the album with its black paper and kept the album in a tin trunk to safeguard it from being thrown out again. There was a picture of Uncle Reid Stoddard and some other unidentified men grasping the tongs on a rotary rig; whoever took

44

the picture must have been a friend, a fellow worker. Reid and his fellows are posing boyishly, their caps tilted. In the background are canvas shields around the drilling platform to baffle the cutting wind. They are all smiling. This was shortly before Reid left in the middle of the night for Oklahoma and pinned a note to the front door with a shingle nail.

Also in the album is a picture of the three girls sitting on the flatbed of the Reo Speed Wagon carefully posed in starched dresses with their arms around one another and Bea in the middle between Jeanine and Mayme, and they all have enormous smiles. The kitten in Bea's clutches was soon lost in some move or other. There is a blurry shot of Elizabeth and Aunt Lillian at a carnival, holding fringed satin pillowcases that say EL PASO LAND OF SUNSHINE and GALVESTON. They had never been to either one of these places but you take whatever you win when you knock over the chalk milk bottle. There is a photograph of Jack Stoddard in a fedora holding a cane fishing pole with an old boot dangling on the end of the line. Who was it who took that picture? they asked themselves. They forgot, or checked to see who was missing, or tried to recall who all was there.

People at that time did not take photographs of themselves or others at gambling or drinking in the sleazy honky-tonks that mushroomed at the edges of the East Texas boomtowns and nobody with any kind of camera caught her father on film in the dance hall and bar called the Cotton Blossom dancing with a very young woman about whom he only knew her first name. The album didn't have any pictures of her mother washing clothes in a washtub in the backyard near the railroad tracks. There was no device that recorded her mother's building fear that her husband would be injured or killed in the increasing violence of the boom or that he might disappear into a life of compulsive gambling and nocturnal assignations with unknown or even known women. She had spoken of going home to the old Tolliver farm so often that it became a kind of music, a ballad. It was 'My Old Kentucky Home' and 'I'll Take You Home Again, Kathleen,' a place of noiseless days and solitude and peaches and clear water from a well, without rent, unmortgaged. Jeanine believed every word of it.

Mayme poses very carefully in a print dress, made especially for her high school graduation in Kilgore. She stands in front of a flowering crepe myrtle. The photograph does not give the slightest indication that in the town, twenty-four derricks stood within half a block of each other along Commerce Street, or that another was driven in a churchyard or that a man sitting in a barbershop getting his morning shave watched as a roughneck walked in, painted a red X on the floor and said, *We'll drill here.* Nor does the black-and-white photograph indicate the lovely dark red of her hair.

There is a photo of Bea at the age of eight sitting with her schoolbooks on a running board, she holds them out for the camera, she is proud of them. She has just finished writing a story that she very much hoped would please her teacher, the story of a princess in an enchanted forest who ate nothing but peaches. A dwarf pulling a cart had come to offer her eternal life in exchange for her golden hair. She stares at the camera while invisible stories appear and evaporate inside her skull.

The only professional photo is of Jeanine mashed in with forty-eight other children for her freshman high school picture. She turns her square face and long, bright eyes toward the school photographer, her light hair carefully curled. She is unfolding inside, leaf after leaf. She is becoming a young woman and it happens without effort.

Pictures taken at match races are hard to come by. There were no racing sheets or published bloodlines, no bleachers or stands, no guardrail, no photo finish. It was roughhouse racing, where a Stetson was dropped to the ground as a starting signal, where once a jockey killed another with a loaded bat in a race in Rocksprings and nobody was ever charged. The horses that ran on these tracks were a breed that had no official name, they were short and hardy and had a phenomenal sprint that could carry them a quarter of a mile at blazing speeds. So different from the prestigious and expensive Thoroughbred racing on distant tracks in California and Maryland and Kentucky and New York where the tall sleek horses pounded out a mile, a mile and a quarter. This was Texas, it was old-time grassroots horse racing, a colonial holdover, and enormous amounts of money changed hands below the notice of tax collectors and lawmakers.

Often the owners of these quarter-mile race-horses asked someone to take a picture of themselves with their champion in the front yard of the farmhouse or the ranch house. There are a great many of these photographs. Somebody to one side is flapping a blanket or opening an umbrella to get the horse to point his ears, to look alert, like the speed demon he is supposed to be. Many of these horses came to be famous in later years but in the Kodak Brownie photographs they always look commonplace and sleepy. If they did not win at the races they would go home and start herding cattle and dragging wood to the chuck fire.

In one photo the man named Ross Everett who had rescued Jeanine at the blacksmith shop sits on the running board of a new 1934 Chevrolet truck with his western hat at the back of his head. A roan pony stands tied to the slats of the stock rack. The pony was for his boy, who was only five, and Jeanine was in a state of acute anguish over the fact that a five-year-old kid got his own horse and she, at seventeen, had none. And so she told Ross Everett that she used to like horses but she didn't anymore, she was looking for something that talked and could sit in a seat at the movie theater and eat popcorn with its hands. She said it to be smart like Claudette Colbert. She really wanted to live in the country, married to a banker, where she could have Thoroughbreds and Airedales.

He said, *Well, that happens.* He had come all the way from Abilene to East Texas to write down the names of famous winning racing quarter-mile horses in a notebook. They had to be stallions. He thought they ought to be a recognized breed, but some people regarded them as being in the same category as bathtub gin. He was off to Louisiana here in a minute to deal with the coonasses. Ross Everett smiled into the lens and sat on the running board and pushed his hat to the back of his head and gazed out into the black-and-white world of the potential photograph. Mrs. Everett was very pretty. She stared down with deep concentration into the viewfinder to see that Jeanine had also appeared in one corner of it, looking back at her sister Mayme, her thin arms going in different directions and so she clicked it twice. She told Jeanine's mother she would send her one of the pictures. In the background a train is taking on water.

Jack Stoddard stands holding the halter of Smoky Joe Hancock, in a pressed shirt and khaki pants. The horse is blocky and ungraceful and no amount of blanket-flapping or umbrella-opening will make him look like he could cover 440 yards in twenty-four seconds. His forelock is short and frazzled, his ears flop each to one side. But Jack Stoddard has his hat brim snapped over his face and a cigar between his fingers.

This is how people wanted to appear to the world and to later generations. It is how they wished to be remembered no matter how hard life might have become. They framed themselves in their best clothes and with their most valuable possessions and smiled. Hard times and col-lapsing marriages and heavy labor was nobody's business but their own.

Nobody's business
Nobody's dirty business
Nobody's business but my own
Nobody's business, how my little baby treats me
Nobody's business but my own

So Bukka White sang in the East Texas juke joints in Houston, Conroe, Corsicana. He held the neck of the Dobro guitar like a baseball bat and wrung blues from it, and after him came Ma Rainey's Jazz Hounds. Her father lifted the dice in his fist and all eyes were on him alone until he threw and then the magical moment would be gone. The singer turned to the old 1920s song 'Red Cap Porter' and the dice moved with infinite slowness around the circle from hand to hand, manic little creatures with dots for brains. He either bought or won Smoky Joe in 1935, when they moved to Conroe, north of Houston. The Conroe field lay inside the skirts of drifting fog that came from the Gulf of Mexico. He drove up to the house shouting for them all to come out, they'd got their first real racehorse.

Smoky Joe Hancock was an own son of Old Joe Hancock, a dark two-year-old stud with a savage temper and horizontal scars on his legs where he had fought his way out of a trailer. He had stubby ears and a head like a shoe box. His mane sprayed up from his stallion's crest in short, wild tassels. He was known as a hard case. He threw his jockeys. The seller admitted he had once run off a railless brush track and tore through several

50

barbecue tables and a line of people with plates in their hands like a boxy rocket before they could get him to the score line. It was why her father got him for a low price.

Bea said, 'He's had a hard life.' Little Bea had been assigned the novel *Black Beauty* in her reading circle at the new Conroe Elementary and the book had taken a fixed grip on her imagination with its injustices and its defiantly happy ending. 'He used to belong to a rich widow, and she had her coachman to beat him with a bumbershoot until he fell to his knees.' Bea paused and then said, in a low, dramatic voice, 'On the hard cobblestones.'

He turned the stallion into an abandoned brick yard down the street from their rent house in Conroe. Smoky was both defiant and lonely in all the trash thrown into the oil-soaked earth, alert and suspicious among the broken toilet seats and greasy paper sacks.

'We got our speed demon, Jeanine,' he said. 'We're going to run the competition around here into the ground. He's blazing hell at four hundred forty yards. He just needs a hit over the head once in a while.' He said this carelessly, as if it were a matter easily taken care of with a two-by-four or a section of pipe. 'I think he can stay the longer distances. We can win some money with this horse, Pistol. And I don't want you trying to handle him. He's dangerous.'

'I don't want to take care of him,' said Jeanine. 'I got other things to do.' The brightly printed flour sacks were hard to get. Many other girls had figured out the place to get them was at the bakery or the big hotels in Conroe, where bakers and cooks emptied them and then piled them in the storage rooms. It took six flour sacks to make a dress, and you had to get them all matched. Jeanine was at present working on collecting a pattern in aqua and dark blue. It had a risque slash of red in it.

She tossed her new short bob in a way that made the blunt ends fly up. She made astonished gestures at herself in the cracked mirror.

'Either that or he starves.'

Whatever her father took up it was bound to go wrong. They would move and leave Smoky Joe behind somewhere. They would lose him. He would die of sleeping sickness, he would break one of his legs. It was the same for everybody. The feeling that things were falling apart and that nothing worked. Bonnie Parker and Clyde Barrow had been killed over in Louisiana, a hundred miles away, and for ten cents you could see the tan Ford V-8 shot all to pieces, it still had blood and the stain of brains all over the seats. The baby son of Charles Lindbergh was kidnapped and murdered. Not even rich and famous people could protect themselves from alien beings creeping in during the dark hours and destroying your life. Even if you were virtuous. Nothing was stable or safe. Even the earth itself lifted into the sky of the high plains of Texas and Oklahoma and blew into dust storms as thick as airborne petroleum.

Jeanine had a sample tube of lipstick in a harsh red and with it she made herself several new kinds of lips. She was interested in young men.

Young men were attracted by good hair and open-toed shoes with inch-and-a-half heels and dresses with the new drooping shawl collars, fall fashions of 1934. They wanted to go places and see things; you could see a demonstration of how they faked the play-by-play ball games in front of the Conroe radio station, where a man knocked two pencils together to imitate a base hit. That was free. *Play ball!* the announcer shouted into the microphone, and a man spun crowd sounds on a record. She understood that her father slid from addiction to addiction, a shape changer, and nothing would hold him in one place for long, and she knew this with a childlike combination of disillusion and forgiveness.

'Horse, you are in for a hard life,' she said. 'Hope you like potato peelings.'

She and her father walked away and Jeanine turned back to see the dark horse staring after her with his ears up, a frightened young stallion only two years old, who did not know where he was nor who had bought him nor what was to happen to him.

CHAPTER FIVE

At a race outside of Conroe they made the immense sum of fifty dollars. Jeanine began to think of how she could keep a part of it for herself. Her Conroe High School boyfriend had just abandoned her in favor of a girl who was from Conroe and had always been from Conroe. Jeanine did not know why. This was the worst of it. And in other places people had no idea why. On the front page of the Conroe newspaper that morning was a strange photograph of the cold black dust storm of April 1935 that turned the Texas and Kansas plains dark as night and buried entire towns. Nobody knew how to stop them, or why there was a Depression. But Jeanine felt at the moment reasonably safe in Conroe on the humid coast and with twenty-five dollars in bet money.

Smoky Joe ran against a Houston horse named Cherokee Chief.

'Don't hit him,' Jeanine said to the jockey. 'Maybe once. But you don't get a second.' She bent forward and held up one finger in case he was deaf or had water in his ears. 'One hit is all you get. Okay?' Her body was slim and taut beneath the cotton dress, she had the gestural vocabulary of a mime.

'I know how to ride,' said the boy. 'I ain't taking advice from no girl.'

Jeanine hurried out among the crowd of men to place bets. She wrapped dollar bills around her fingers for each separate bet, she was intent and serious. She was one of the few women in the crowd but she carried herself in this male territory as if she had special privileges. Smoky beat Cherokee chief by a length. Jeanine had clambered up the stock racks of a truck with the agility of a monkey to watch the dark stallion charge past the finish-line flag as if he were running down some enemy and suddenly it was

54

a wonderful day and here she was in her new dress in the aqua print. She jumped down and ran to the horse's owner to collect her money. He wore a suit and tie and his hat tipped back, he had a new Buick and a drink in his hand. His car radio was on. The announcer was talking about the first overnight transcontinental flights and that Generalissimo Franco was besieging Barcelona.

'Hand it over,' she said. The young man laughed and held it high above his head where she couldn't reach it.

'What's your name?' he said.

'Jeanine Stoddard,' she said. She took hold of his tie and said in a gangbuster's voice, 'Hand over that money, Pretty Boy, and nobody gets hurt.'

He held it out to her in his closed fist. She unbent his fingers and took the bills, and then stepped forward and kissed him.

She turned into the hot, noisy evening before it faded into dark, before her father came looking for her. Before he found out she had been kissing strange men. The amount of money she gripped in her hand made her nervous. Andrew Jackson's severe, drawn face stared up from out of the center of the wadded banknotes. She was afraid she might lose it or it would be stolen, or her father would come lurching out from behind a trailer and demand it from her. Then he would gamble it away on a blanket somewhere. It would end up as a wad in somebody else's pocket.

Jeanine ducked around the late-model Ford truck and trailer and nearly crashed into a man.

Half his face was white and frothy. At first she thought he had a white beard or was foaming at the mouth, and then realized he was shaving. He grasped her arm to stop her.

'Here! You're going to make me cut my throat,' he said. He shook soap from a straight razor and then let go of her. He looked at himself in the truck's side mirror and continued shaving.

It was Ross Everett.

He said, 'Is this the entire extent of your social life, Jeanine?' he said. 'Kissing strange drunks at horse races?'

Jeanine's face flushed hot. 'Mr. Everett. You were spying on me.'

'Well, it was kind of public.' He ran the razor down his cheek and flung off the foam. 'I was just standing here shaving.'

'You're going to tell my father.'

'I expect he's too goddamned busy.'

Jeanine put out her hand. 'Don't tell him. I mean it.' She kicked one of his tires. 'You are going to tell him. Because you are rotten and evil.'

'Don't tell me he's developed some fatherly instincts all of a sudden. What would he do about it?'

'He'll tell my mother.'

'Good.' He stroked the razor down his throat and slung the soap to the ground. He rinsed the blade and folded it. Splashed water onto his face from a basin sitting on the fender, wiped his face on a pink towel. His face was made up of flat planes, a square mouth. 'At least you've got one functioning parent.'

'Promise me you won't tell him.'

'All right.' In his trailer, a gray horse shifted and tapped at the floor planks. 'Well, since I just won my race, I'd probably better cut my luck and go.'

'Good.' She walked over to the trailer and peered in through the slats. A gray mare, tidy and clean-legged, shifted around on the floorboards. On the fender was a good racing saddle and a saddlecloth. 'What have you got? This is a good-looking horse.'

'Her name is She Kitty.' Ross Everett buttoned up his shirt. 'Out of Krazy Kat. I got her when old man Carruthers gave up. They shot all his cattle. He was overstocked.' He wiped at his face with one hand. 'You wouldn't know him. Your dad drags y'all around the world like a gypsy.'

'I know it.'

'You quit school?'

'Yes, sir.'

'I've been on the road three days from Comanche and made three races. Bought a horse. Now I have to go to a meeting in Houston and then head home again. My wife puts up with all this and the least I can do is show up shaved.' He pulled a tie around his neck under his collar and tied it. 'In all three races this is the first time I've seen a young girl running around by herself. If your daddy wanted a boy to be his running buddy he should go hire one.'

She wasn't his running buddy, she was his daughter, but on the other hand there he was, dancing openly with the woman in the green satin dress in the middle of the afternoon in front of everybody like a fool.

So she said, 'He couldn't keep me away if he tried.'

Everett took out a sack of tobacco and rolled a cigarette, lit it with a silver lighter that flared up several inches. He squinted his eyes against it. 'You all still got that Reo Speed Wagon with the trailer?'

'Yes. And I'm going to drive it home.'

'I guess so. You started hauling him home drunk when you were nine.' Smoke from the cigarette ran up his nose. 'And so you better do it.' He flicked off the ashes. 'I'll keep my mouth shut this time.'

She found her father at a tailgate. It was a new truck and he was dancing around in the grass to the music of 'Dinah' from a car radio. Dancing with the woman in a stained green satin dress and heavy lipstick.

'Well, Jeanine girl. How's my Pistol?' He was somewhat drunk. 'Let's see what we won.'

The woman said, 'Does she always collect your winnings for you?'

'Yeah,' her father said. 'She's my buddy.' He took the thirty-five dollars from Jeanine. She kept fifteen in her pocket and said nothing. He handed her a cold Dr Pepper. 'That's so you don't tell.'

'You're cute,' the woman said.

Jeanine ignored her. 'I'm going on home, Dad,' she said. She tipped up the ice-cold soda and it tasted like heaven.

'Go on. Tell your mother that I'm dickering about a new horse or something. Make something up. You're good at making things up.' He laughed and wiped back the lock of dark hair that fell in his face. 'I'm going to be gone for two weeks here in a little bit. Up to Central Texas. So I got to stay on her good side.'

She ran to find Smoky Joe and came upon the jockey walking the dark stallion back and forth in the grove of pines, along with other handlers and their horses. Smoky's veins stood out in his hide like coursing liquid ropes and he was still sucking air hard into his wide nostrils. She threw the soda bottle into the shadows.

'All right, I'll get him home now.' She took the lead line and patted the stallion's hot neck. 'Ain't you a rocket?' She held out a five-dollar bill to the jockey.

He snatched at it and jammed the five in his pocket. 'I should charge double for riding this goddamned maniac,' he said.

'You're going to hell for swearing,' she said.

'So's your old man.'

She led Smoky back to the trailer. He jumped in and turned to face backward. He always rode backward, he wanted to see anything that might come up on him from behind. When she pulled the headlight knob the interior light came on and shone in her face and when she lifted her head she saw Ross Everett with one boot up on his running board watching her. She leaned out of the window and stuck her tongue out at him. He blew smoke from his nose and lifted a hand.

CHAPTER SIX

At the time when Jack Stoddard was felled by sour gas, few men were required to wear gas masks on the rigs. It was impossible to wear the bulky gear and get work done because it was hard to see or talk and your own breath fogged up in your faceplate. The occurrence of hydrogen sulfide gas is capricious and unpredictable. H_2S is often precipitated out of the oil itself and gathers in half-filled tanks, seeps into low places beneath the rigs, suddenly appears along with the sweet gas without warning. H_2S knocks people unconscious at 300 parts per million, and at 600 ppm it is fatal within seconds. It has a distinctive taint of rotten eggs, but the gas also has the peculiar quality of destroying the sense of smell after the first inhalation, as if designed by the devil himself to draw the unsuspecting into the odorless world of brain injury and death.

Two other freight haulers brought Jack Stoddard home in the back of a truck, in a warm September rain straight off the Gulf of Mexico. He was laid out on a stack of blankets somebody had scooped up from the engine shack; he was covered with a slicker and awash in rainwater. His face and hands had the obscure, blue color of someone with cyanide poisoning, and although he was not conscious he floundered with vague shifting movements. Jeanine and Mayme told

Bea to stop crying, he was going to be all right.

He lay on the bed with blood running from his nose and ears. A young company doctor folded his bag together and said in a thin tenor voice that Mr. Stoddard should avoid any strenuous activity for the next month or so, and he could not say one way or the other whether Mr. Stoddard would ever regain his ability to drive a truck. The effects might show up in the lungs, but on the other hand, did they know whether or not somebody hit him over the head? The doctor bent down and looked into Jack Stoddard's eyes and said, 'Did? Somebody? Hit? You? Over the head?' He was a tidy young doctor. With a quiet and efficient gesture wiped up the blood trickling from Jack Stoddard's ear and said this was the result of a concussion of some kind, not sour gas. It was impossible to get the company to pay the medical bills because Mr. Stoddard was a contract worker and not a Shell employee.

Jeanine and her sisters watched as her father sat up straight in the bed and stared at them as if they were strangers. People completely unknown to him were gathered together in this small rent house with the ancient wallpaper and the lamp beside the bed in the gloom of the torrents washing down the windowpane, the iron bed-frame and torn quilts. His two oldest daughters about to leave home, oddly grown to adults. A person wonders how it happens. His wife sitting with her head in her hands like somebody's mother from the last century. She lifted her head and smiled at him.

'You're going to be all right, Jack,' she said.

'I know it,' he said. 'As soon as I get that horse in training.'

The young doctor said, 'Mr. Stoddard, do you know what day it is?'

'It's the day they asked me to fish out a wrench from the tank. One of those tanks. They thought it was a joke. That's what day it is.' Jack Stoddard ran his hands over his blue face. He seemed to be checking to see if it was still there, on the front of his head.

A long pause. Then the doctor said, 'Who is the president?'

'Franklin D. Roosevelt,' he said. 'I voted for him.' He fell back onto the pillows. 'Tell these people to get out of here.'

Their mother sat in the bedroom with him, reading aloud from newspapers or magazines, playing the radio. She was trying to reawaken him and make his brain work. He stared at the wallpaper and occasionally turned to look at his wife as if she were an intrusive busybody, a neighbor he knew only faintly.

Smoky Joe had been turned out into one of the sweeping coastal pastures where red cattle grazed and egrets in formal white garb tiptoed behind each cow with grave, worried gestures, darting their heads one way and then the other. Jack Stoddard had been offered three hundred dollars for him by Ross Everett, but her father had refused to sell for no reason other than the pleasure of saying no. Smoky Joe tore up the grass with great fervor. He was always hungry. From time to time Smoky charged forward into a long gallop across the pasture, scattering the domestic cows, running for the hell of it. He was now four years old and neglected, hairy, unshod, and only knew human beings as occasional visitors with food. He should have been sold long ago.

They had moved from Conroe to Wharton. It was in Wharton they heard King Edward was going to marry Wallis Simpson. Mayme couldn't believe it. They had acquired an old Emerson radio and several neighbors came over to sit in their small kitchen with its kerosene stove to listen. It was an intense evening. In the distance they could hear the noise of the big water pumps, as the rice fields were flooded. Their father lay quietly in the back room regarding the wall, which had been plastered over with newspapers. Maybe he was reading the advertisements. Elizabeth had just that morning spent fifty cents out of their stock of coins to buy beans and potatoes and lard, and the potatoes were frying as they listened to the fading newscast.

Jeanine shifted from station to station to find a clear reception and finally got a Shreveport station. The king said it was impossible to carry the heavy duty of responsibility and to discharge his duties as king as he should wish to do, without the help and support of the woman he loved. Jeanine was on the king's side but Mayme said what did he ever see in a skinny parasite like Mrs. Simpson and their mother said there wasn't much to choose between them. There was something frightening about it. A man abdicating a throne for an arid woman, men in general surrendering to loss, to an absence of rain, air, money, love, kingdoms.

In Wharton they had found another rental house near the Colorado River. The river was dark red and alluvial and not many miles away it poured into the Gulf. The house was full of junked farm equipment and stacked paper bags that had held Paris Green arsenate for killing boll weevils. They worked for two days to clear it. Five blocks away a Hooverville had grown up on the banks of the river and at night there was the glow of fires and shouting and sometimes singing.

Mayme had acquired a boyfriend in Conroe who worked for the Conroe-Lufkin Telephone Company, his name was Robert Faringham. He continued to write her even when they moved to Wharton, down to the gas country where new gas wells were being drilled by independent operators. Jeanine's father said there were all kinds of opportunities for a man who had connections. Humble was going to start up a cracking plant not too far away, to refine the wet gas and wring hydrocarbons from it. Engineers and the chemists would toss up molecules of methane and propane and butylene in a dazzling display of new modern technology, they would make aviation gas and synthetic rubber and nylon stockings and plastic telephones and cow feed from it, everything but candy kisses. He was going to leave off freighting and somehow find the means to study pipe fitting. There was good money in it. To Jeanine this meant they would go and live in some graceful country house and there would be green fields for Smoky Joe, and passionflower vines, and silence. But now he walked with careful deliberate steps around the house staring at things. He put a match to a piece of old telephone cord to see if it would burn. Elizabeth took it away from him and stamped on it and hid the matches.

Bea said, 'Jeanine, were you and Mayme talking last night about leaving?'

Jeanine said, 'We were, but we're not now. Since Daddy's got brain failure. Somebody's got to stay and help Mother get him in a straitjacket.' She closed her hands around a chair back. This throttled life had to end sometime, it had to.

'Where were you going to go?'

Mayme said, 'We were going to get an apartment back in Conroe. Stay there in one place. But Robert can just write me here.' The rain fell all over Wharton and the Colorado River ran as dark as wine. 'I'm twenty-one, Bea. Jeanine's twenty. We're old maids.' Not too far away the river spilled out into the Gulf in tangled red currents. 'Looks like we're going to stay that way.'

'Would you have just left me here?' said Bea. 'With them arguing and fighting all the time?'

The two older sisters glanced at each other.

'It's all right, Bea,' said Mayme. 'We aren't going to leave with Daddy like this. It's all right.'

'You would have too,' said Bea. 'You would have gone and left me here.'

Jeanine said, 'Nah. We'd have kidnapped you.'

They did not notice her bowed head and her heart burning in anguish. She would have been deserted. It was possible that her sisters did not love her except in the most dutiful and per-functory way. They didn't even read her stories.

Her pretty young teacher at the Wharton Elementary had just printed up one of her stories on the mimeograph machine and had tacked it up on the bulletin board. She had so much admired Bea's tale of the orphan girl and the abandoned puppy. Bea was sure that nothing good would ever happen to her except in books. When she was sitting on the back steps one evening a half-grown cat came out of the collapsing shed behind the house and sat down and mewed at her. Bea took him up gratefully and named him Prince Albert.

There was no money. They had to wait it out. They ate corn bread and grits, salt pork and cane syrup and told themselves things would get better after Jack got well. They cooked on a little kerosene stove that stank of fuel. They walked holes in their shoes looking for jobs, any job, but men with families to support wanted those same jobs and nobody would hire a single girl, even to pop the popcorn in a movie theater or sweep up at the barbershop. Fifteen million able-bodied men were out of work. Jeanine and Mayme made do. They could not face the social stigma of going on relief. They joined other women and children scavenging for soda bottles along the roadsides and lived on what was left of their father's last paycheck. They were adrift. So were millions of others and no one could figure out why the economy had ceased to function, not even the banker J.P. Morgan. He said as much on the radio.

They tiptoed around the house so as not to disturb their father and then went out into the streets of Wharton to look in the shop windows, and stand under the great live oaks and their Spanish moss by the river. They walked by the transients and the bums in the Hooverville. It was like visiting a zoo.

Then, finally, Mayme got temporary work at the cotton gin writing labels for the bales and shared her five dollars with Bea and Jeanine. She treated them to a movie; sword hacking and high seas in *Captain Blood*.

Silently Jeanine made herself a dress from material she bought at one of the Wharton dry-goods stores. Nobody else would buy it so it was cheap. Nobody wanted it because it was printed in black-and-white tiger stripes. But she had seen a picture of a tiger-stripe pattern in a secondhand *Good Housekeeping* magazine and it didn't look too garish. She would black her shoes with stove polish to match. The package of material thumped on the table.

'Shhhhh!'

She cleared the table of the fruit jar full of knives and forks and slid the scissors through the crepe. She sewed it by hand. The Singer would raise the dead with its creaking treadle. They kept the radio low.

Hitler marched into the Rhineland and made all other political parties illegal in Germany. He invaded when the crops were ripe in the fields; tanks plowed through the rye and oats and wheat and any human beings who stood in their way. Jeanine's father listened to the news broadcasts with his hands in his lap, nodding, saying We'd better not get into this. Stay out of it is what I say.

At night Bea sat with her striped cat at the kitchen table with her schoolbooks and her reading. The cat was not content unless he was with her and at night he slept on her head with a roaring purr. Her teacher had given her a book of poetry, *The Family Album of Favorite Poems*. She sat in front of the coal-oil lamp and read. Books contained speech without noise, human voices that spoke as loudly and as freely as they wished without being told to hush, hush. Mayme wrote to her young man in Conroe who worked for the Conroe-Lufkin Telephone Company. The letter was very long. Her pen made loud scratching noises. Jack Stoddard developed a strange, haughty air and spent the hot evenings sitting by the door, looking at something out in the night. He stared at his still-handsome face in the mirror on the back porch and shaved himself with slow strokes. He sat at the table in silence leafing through the women's underwear section of the Sears Roebuck catalog until Jeanine took it away from him to use in the outhouse.

Bea came in from the girls' bedroom with Prince Albert in her arms and her journal tucked beneath her elbow. The striped cat jumped down onto the kitchen floor and then into Jack Stoddard's lap. Bea watched with an open mouth as her father snatched Albert up by the scruff of the neck, the fur wadded in his fist, and drew back and punched the cat directly on his nose. Bea threw down the journal and screamed. Albert made a gasping, snorting sound. Jack released him. He laughed when the cat thrashed in snakelike motions on the floor as if its back were broken. Albert gained his balance somehow and fled, weaving, toward the door and their father kept on laughing.

Elizabeth came running in from the back porch, asking what was the matter in a controlled voice. Jeanine threw open the kitchen window. Albert bolted through it.

Bea sat in the old shed for hours that hot September night calling over and over in a sweet, enticing voice. Finally Albert crept out of a corner toward her. His nose and mouth were crusted with dried blood. He crawled into her lap and blinked up at her with furtive glances, as if he were begging for forgiveness. Bea held him and told him she would protect him and that pretty soon her father would have a brain hemorrhage and die. Bea stared into the dark of the shed and felt they were all in mortal danger and that nobody cared and they were alone on the earth.

Jeanine slept on the floor to keep cool. It was much cooler on the boards than on the bed next to Mayme. She walked through intense dreams each night and she remembered them every morning before dawn. She dreamed of her father in a shining new truck and his eyes were as red as rubies. He was holding his head aloft so that everyone would look at him and he could look at them out of the crude scarlet of his eyes. He was saying *eye eye oh eye* or maybe it was *I I oh I*. Ross Everett sat unmoved in a burning building with an onion in his hand. Smoky Joe stood in the middle of a pasture of brown grasses, his ragged tail flying in the wind, and he was speaking to her. She woke up. It was near midnight and the air had turned cool.

Mayme said, 'What are you doing, Jenny?' And then rolled over and went back to sleep.

Jeanine pulled on her striped dress and went to the window. She saw smoke rising in the chilled moonlight. It was coming from the shed. The shed was on fire.

She took up the hosiery rug from the kitchen floor and ran down across the wet grass. At the entrance to the shed she came upon her father. He was sitting on a nail keg with a dangling oily rag in his hand setting fire to it with matches. A heap of straw was on fire but it wasn't burning well, since the straw was old and moldy and wet with the dew. She called out to him and threw the hosiery rug onto the sparkling straw and stamped on it. She kicked a smoking wad onto the gravel and ground it out.

'Well, daughter,' he said. Smoke rose around him. He dropped his arms on his thighs, flapped his hands. 'Jeanine,' he said.

'What are you doing?' She stamped on flying sparks. She took a stick and lifted the glowing oily rag into the grass.

'Setting the shed on fire,' he said. He stood up. 'I wanted to get your mother's attention. I want her to know that I am crazy and dangerous.'

'I'll call the sheriff,' she said. 'I'll run over to the neighbors' and call the sheriff. They have a telephone.' They faced each other.

'Good for them.' He walked in a circle and

70

hummed a popular tune. Down on the Colorado River there was a burst of laughter. Jeanine could see the reflection of a fire on the high branches of the live oaks that drooped over the water. He had the cardboard suitcase beside him.

'Dad, come in the house and go to sleep.' She made shoving motions at him. 'Please. Please.'

He said he would go away if that was what they all wanted. Thrown out of his own home. He said for her to find for him those few little things that were still his own. His voice was that of an orphan abandoned by the roadside.

He took out a cigarette, a package of Old Golds. The smell of cigarette smoke and his Clubman's aftershave brought back memories of the good times of match racing and the awful times of moving and misery, and also the time when he had been the handsome father who had loved her. Her throat hurt it was so tight.

'Well, daughter.' He smoked and looked around himself. 'Jeanine. You were always my favorite.' He nodded. 'You were. What the hell is that piece of crap you got on? A tiger-striped prom dress or something.'

'I'll be awake all night for the rest of my life, wondering if you're going to set the house on fire.'

'Good.' He slowly turned his head to her and regarded her. 'I think I'll leave, Jeanine.'

'Dad, you're not well. You can't just leave.'

'Give me a picture of you girls.'

He crushed out his cigarette on the ground. He patted her arm and she knocked his hand away. He said all he wanted was some pictures from the

71

old album, to take with him wherever it was he was going which he didn't really know where it was. But Jeanine ought to quit living like a Wild Man out of Borneo. If she would fix herself up she might get a man. If not, not.

'Dad, you and Mother have got to settle things. Please.'

'Jeanine, Jeanine,' he said. 'Don't take sides. I was a man never meant to be married, I'm a rambler and a gambler and a long way from home. Some men can't be tied down. We've got to be free. I might come back. I might not.'

'Why did you get married, then?' She pawed at her eyes.

He said, 'Wisdom comes with age. When you're young you don't think about consequences. You meet somebody and get married and then you girls came along.'

'We just came along. You just found us wandering down the road.'

'Now. Ask me anything.'

'Ask you what?'

'Anything. Ask me anything.'

Jeanine thought of him only as a father but he had been a child once himself and he knew all children were confused by the mysteries of their lives, and he was offering her the answers, inside information. Where certain songs came from and the names of lost dogs, what your grandparents were like when they were young. Here at the time of parting when he would leave his favorite child with her long gray eyes and his own square jaw and the name of Stoddard. The sour gas had ruined some synapses in his brain and oddly joined others. He fought his way through the fierce thorns of his own cynicism, trying to reach somewhere else, but he did not know where that somewhere else might be. What was the alternative. 'Give me a picture of you girls to take with me.'

Jeanine tiptoed into the house and went to the tin trunk where the old photograph album lay and began flipping through the pages. All a child wants to know is if their parents love them and wanted them to come into the world. That's all.

Ask him anything. Jeanine wanted to ask him, Why was I born? But instead she walked back out into the humid dark and handed him a photograph of the three sisters sitting in the back of the old Reo Speed Wagon.

'Who was it took this picture?' he said.

'I don't know,' said Jeanine. She wanted to ask him, when was *he* born, and when did Grandfather Tolliver buy the land in Palo Pinto, and why did they leave? She wanted to ask him when he had first seen her mother and why he fell in love with her and what magic had brought herself and Bea and Mayme into the world as whole and entire people. It could not have been so ordinary. A dove must have appeared overhead. Or rather a redbird for Mayme and a white-wing for Bea and for herself the scrub jay who was so talkative and flashy in blue and rust. But she didn't.

He shook his head. 'You weren't brought up right, Jeanine. Dragged around from town to town. Was nothing I could do about it. Your mother was never satisfied. Always had to go someplace new. Had to have a radio.'

73

Of course it wasn't her mother who had wanted to move all the time. What was the point of arguing? It could have been *Life with Father* or *One Man's Family* but he loved his dark unspoken life more than radio scripts, didn't he.

He smiled down at the photograph. He pressed it against his coat with one hand. He was having secret thoughts. He loved having secret thoughts that nobody could see or penetrate or think about but himself. It made him inflate and grow very important and very large. Since he had swum up out of the deep underwater world of H_2S some kind of barrier had given way and he could think anything he wanted. The banisters on some internal stairs had broken with his weight. It was very good to have secret thoughts that nobody else knew about. Jack Stoddard smiled at the night and loved his own silence.

Jeanine clasped her hands together and tried to think of something good to say. Tried to make some gesture toward him.

'We had some adventures together, didn't we? At the races.'

He said, 'Yes. We did. I wanted to tell you, I learned about horses from Ab Blocker's old foreman. A black man. Best cowboy on earth. He used to run down mustangs himself alone. He used to visit the grave of Nigger Britt Johnson. Now there's a story if anybody would care to tell it which they don't as people are too caught up with stories of Bonnie Parker and the Vanderbilts and Ava Gardner. Went off alone to the Comanche and got back the women and children.' He glanced at her with a childish expression of anticipation. From inside the house she could hear the old Hamilton clock bong out the midnight hour. 'But people like reading about the Vanderbilts.'

'Okay,' said Jeanine.

'And...' He thought about what more he could tell her. He motioned with his hand and then the hand fell into his lap. He had grown up on the land that was now Camp Wolters in Central Texas, near Mineral Wells. He had grown up there when it was open country covered with the wind-torn pelt of native grasses. Once he had come upon the skull of a Comanche with a bullet hole in the cheekbone and after some exploration he had found the thighbones and ribs and tangles of buckskin fringe. During high school in Mineral Wells he had memorized Travis's last letter from the Alamo and declaimed it at graduation. He used to ride the Mineral Wells street railway to Elmhurst Park where there was a racetrack and a casino and the wind made women's long dresses fly up so you could see the black stocking garters with the red marks they made and it moved him in inexplicable ways so that he laughed and elbowed Chigger Bates. He had seen Yellow Jacket run the 880. He shifted his feet and smoked and said that we all want our parents to be better parents. We want them to be heroic even if we are cowardly, and well dressed even if we go around looking like Ma Kettle in a homemade dress and they should all be steady and true to one another.

He said, 'I bet you remember the song about the three little babes.' He wrapped up the photo

75

of his three daughters sitting and smiling in the bed of the old Reo Speed Wagon in his handkerchief. He put it in the overcoat pocket. 'You girls sang it for us at Christmas that year. Jeanine, you were so pretty, people just turned to look at you on the wagon seat, you were full of life, and you were a gutsy little kid.' He stepped on his cigarette butt. 'Tell Bea and Mayme I sure do love them.'

'You tell them.'

'You got some lessons in life to learn, girl,' he said. 'You better think about some serious changes in your attitude. You'll never get a man. Men want somebody with a heart.' He jerked up the suitcase by the handle.

He said, 'Bye, Pistol.'

And he turned his head toward his other, unfathomable life.

CHAPTER SEVEN

A week passed. Jeanine's mother waited up until late into the night. She sat at the table with the coal-oil lamp burning its amber oil until sign-off and the national anthem at eleven and then until midnight and beyond. She was waiting up for Jack, and if not for him, then the sheriff or the coroner.

Mayme complained in her sleep about the barbed-wire crisscross of her bobby pins. Bea slept against the wall with its faded paper of milkmaids and silvered wreaths, with the striped tomcat purring under her chin. In the distance thunder rolled over the lifting waves of the Gulf of Mexico. It was early October and the nights were cooler but there had been no more rain even here on the rainy coast and the entire country was shrinking in drought. Jeanine felt the rent house sailing into the untrustworthy night with themselves as passengers and no one at the helm. She pulled the quilts up tight around her neck and turned to lie against her older sister's back.

Sometime in the late windy hours her mother blew out the lamp. The flame lit her face for the brief moment before it was extinguished and it made a fire of her hair and then it was dark.

The sheriff drove in at five-thirty in the morning.

Even in her crowded dreams Jeanine heard the car stopping in front of the house. Jeanine sat up in bed. Her hair drifted into her eyes and she felt trapped in the twisted flannel nightgown. She came up out of a dream in which she had been charged and overcharged with straightening everything out and she could feel her angry frustration from the dream tumbling inside her like sand grains in a current. Mayme sat up as well and turned to the window; she pulled aside the rice-sack curtain and tried to see into the dark.

The two older sisters and their mother got up and struck a match to the lamps and dressed themselves for whatever was going to happen. A black-and-white Ford pulled up at the front gate and then the motor shut off. On the door was the insignia of the Wharton County Sheriff's Department.

He knocked on the front door and when it was opened to him he stepped into the light of the coal-oil lamp and took his hat off. He was a tall thin man in khakis with red-rimmed eyes and a revolver.

He said, 'Mrs. Stoddard?'

'Yes, I'm Mrs. Stoddard,' Elizabeth said. 'Come in.'

She turned and walked into the kitchen and he followed her. The deputy sheriff glanced around the kitchen, at the stockings soaking in a basin and the oaken icebox dripping into a pan. Curtains made of feed sacks printed with dancing orange pigs. A flesh-colored rug on the floor made of braided discarded hosiery. Jeanine's mother sat down at the table as if her knees had become disjointed.

She said, 'Is my husband in jail?'

'He's in custody.' He took a handkerchief from his back pocket and blew his nose. 'Sorry. Came down with a cold.'

'Is he shot?'

The deputy hesitated and looked over at the girls. He said, 'No, ma'am. I better speak to you alone.' He put the handkerchief back in his pocket.

'No,' said Jeanine's mother. 'Say what you have to say.'

'Your husband is charged with statutory rape. An underaged girl.' A long silence drew itself out and Jeanine saw her mother frown, as if she had been confronted with some unaccountable

78

puzzle and then she put her hand to her mouth.

'Where is he?' Elizabeth Stoddard lifted her head.

'The county jail.'

'This can't be true,' she said.

'Mrs. Stoddard, your husband has been accused by a young girl here in Wharton. She's fourteen. She ought to be charged as a juvenile delinquent but they ain't going to do it.' He turned away and cupped both hands over his nose and sneezed violently. 'Sorry.' He took out the handkerchief again.

Jeanine crossed her arms and stalked to the window where the aged glass distorted the lamp reflections. She had pulled on the tiger-striped dress, the first thing that came to hand.

She said, 'We'd be better off if he were dead.' She buttoned the neck of the dress. 'Graveyard dead.'

'Jeanine, be quiet.' Elizabeth Stoddard wadded the tea towel in her hands. 'Are you sure you have the right family?'

'I'm very sorry, Mrs. Stoddard.'

Bea came out of the girls' room. Her mother said, 'Bea, go back in the bedroom.'

Bea turned and they heard the door slam.

Elizabeth got up and went to the bedroom door. 'I'll get dressed,' she said. She came out again in her Sunday dress and hat and white gloves. Then she walked to the door and the deputy held it open for her and they left.

Everything had changed. It was as if they had been bombed and their hearts pierced by random splinters. Jeanine sat down and stared around the kitchen, so strangely intact. The water bucket and its dipper and the crashing noise of the clock's ticking. She and Mayme stared at the fruit jar full of knives and forks and spoons, none of them matching to any other. Bea came back in dressed and she carried her Big Chief writing tablet with her.

'Did you hear?'

Bea stared at them. Tears were running down her face but she did not seem to notice them.

'Yes,' she said. 'At first I thought it was a radio program. I thought Mother had the radio on.'

'Where was he?' said Jeanine. She hugged her faded plaid jacket around herself, the lines of the plaid seemed to vaporize in soft, blending lines. She wiped her eyes. 'Where did all of this happen?'

'You'd be the one to know,' said Mayme. 'You were always covering up for him. You were always lying for him.' She wiped her hands on her jeans. 'Bea, stop crying.'

'You stop,' said Bea.

'Get ready for school.'

'I don't want to go to school,' said Bea. 'I don't ever want to go again.'

'No, go on.'

'What good is school?' Bea gripped her writing tablet to her thin chest. She and Mayme were both weeping again. 'Everybody will know. What good is going to school?'

'I never covered up anything,' said Jeanine. 'This ain't my fault.'

'Yes it is. You encouraged it.'

'I never did any such thing.' Jeanine wiped tears

80

from her face. She put the two ends of the jacket zipper together and with a tearing noise she zipped it up. The kitchen had grown cold. The fire in the cookstove had burnt down. The thought of her father laying hands on some young girl made her feel cold and diminished.

'Would you two quit bawling?' Mayme put the coffeepot on the kerosene stove to boil. 'I should have left home when I turned eighteen.'

'And gone where?' said Jeanine.

'Just stayed in one place longer than y'all did.'

Bea's lips were shaking. 'This is going to be in the papers,' she said. 'In the newspapers.'

Mayme wiped her eyes and started taking the hairpins from her hair. 'Yes, and Jeanine's going to testify at the trial. She'll be in the newspapers. She'll be famous. Like Bonnie Parker.'

Jeanine reached in her coat pocket for a brush and drew it furiously through her short, light brown hair.

'Stop it, Mayme.'

Bea said, 'Mayme, don't lay your bobby pins on the kitchen table. That's disgusting.' Bea hugged her striped cat with the broken nose close to herself but he writhed out of her arms and dropped to the floor with a padded thud.

'Well excuse me, Your Holy Cleanliness.' Mayme put the hairpins in her jeans pocket. She wound up her long hair in French rolls on both sides of her head, which gave her head a square look. Her nose was red from crying. 'Maybe she's a liar.'

Bea said, 'But who would lie about something like that?' She looked up wonderingly. 'And how would she even know Daddy? And who is she?'

Mayme turned to Jeanine. 'Got any answers?'

The wind danced through the faulty window frames in thin and merry whistles. The coffeepot gurgled with a laughing noise like some small kitchen spirit calling to them that it was going to be all right, everything was going to be all right and it puffed animated, tiny clouds from its nose.

Then Bea opened her diary or journal or whatever it was. The blank book in which she wrote down everything of note that happened. She took up her pencil.

Mayme said, 'I was about to get engaged. Get married and get out of here.'

'I didn't know he proposed,' said Jeanine. She watched Bea write down *Will Robert break the engagement?* And then lay down the pencil and put out her hands toward the kerosene stove with its odorous yellow flame. The flame reached up to the coffeepot on the stove lid and the Hamilton clock said it was six-thirty in the morning. Outside it was barely light. Whatever kind of life they had been able to cobble together despite the Depression and the oil fields and their father's love of good times and gambling was collapsing all around them.

Jack Stoddard died in his jail cell, sitting on his bunk with a copy of *Black Mask Detective* in his hands. It was October 17, 1937. Outside the windows of the county jail a parade filed past with several high school bands playing 'Our Boys Will Shine Tonight'; his half-shut dead eyes were fixed on the window bars. A cleaning woman named Myra ran down to the office and said there was something wrong with a man in cell seventeen. The coroner said it was a brain hemorrhage brought on by the concussion and the sour gas. He couldn't imagine how the man had lasted so long.

Jack was buried in the Wharton city cemetery. It was a bright sunny day. Jeanine saw her mother upright and calm. Then Elizabeth began to shake, as if she had been stricken with convulsions. *I can't stop shaking,* Elizabeth said, *what's happening to me?* Mayme took hold of her mother with both hands. Jeanine ran to the truck and sat there for a while, crying so hard she could not lift her head from the steering wheel. It was pity as well as grief, pity that her handsome father should be confined in the cold and the dark beyond the sound of human voices. She dried her face on her skirt hem and started the truck engine. They drove away and left him to both the apparent and the invisible world.

The landlord came to their door and knocked lightly. He rapped his knuckles like a man who wanted his money but on the other hand the women were recently bereaved and he was fat and what he was doing appeared to be a scene from a Charlie Chaplin movie, or something from *The Perils of Pauline,* orphans being thrown out into the snow by an overweight rich landlord, which he was. The streets of Wharton were dusty. The Spanish moss that hung from the live oaks was dusty. He was throwing them out into a drought, into bank failures, into the national economic emergency. He wore white and carried a cane. He rapped again with the cane and cleared his throat of the dust and spat.

Mrs. Stoddard opened the door. She wore a clean print dress with a red belt. Behind her in the kitchen he could hear the radio. Maybe she would offer him the radio in lieu of the rent. He wouldn't accept it.

'I don't have the rent,' she said.

'I want to say how sorry I am about your husband,' he said. 'But it's just as well. We don't need perverts here in Wharton.' He tipped his hat to her. Then her three daughters came to stand behind her. He tipped his hat to them as well. 'Sorry about your father,' he said. 'But the rent is ten dollars. I know Mr. Stoddard was a gambler and my bet is he has something hidden away somewhere.'

One girl stepped forward and put her hand on her mother's shoulder.

She said, 'We're going back to where we have our own farm.'

'Where's my ten dollars?' He banged the foot of the cane on the flat dirt of the yard. Down on the river some of the hoboes were calling to one another in raffish, joking shouts. 'Pay up or you leave right now.'

'We're going home,' said her mother. She sat at the kitchen table and moved the salt and pepper shakers around. 'We've got to get packed up.'

'Yes, Mother,' said Jeanine. It was so hot she felt faint, as if she would melt and flatten out.

'You hid things for him,' said her mother. 'I

found two hundred and fifteen dollars in his toolbox. He always hid money.'

'I never hid that money,' Jeanine said. She sat with a cold cup of weak coffee in her hands and blinked repeatedly. Then she turned to her two sisters, but Mayme only stared back at her with her arms crossed and Bea turned the flatiron over on the stove. Mayme's boyfriend from Conroe had sent a sympathy card and his signature and no more. Mayme held it in her hand.

'I guess that horse is yours, Jeanine,' her mother said. 'We could try to sell him.'

'Not yet,' said Jeanine. 'Not just yet.'

'Promise me you won't gamble on the races again.'

'I won't. I promise.'

Jeanine and Mayme moved around the kitchen, packing up the lithograph of the little girl and the portrait of their Tolliver grandparents. They broke down the four-ten shotgun and stored the barrel and stock and shells behind the seat of the truck. They shut the lid on the Singer and they jammed blankets and quilts into tow sacks. They were going back to the old Tolliver farm because there was no place else to go. It was the only place where they didn't have to pay rent. If they went back to Central Texas maybe nobody would know what had happened. Jeanine washed every dish and utensil they owned and handed them to Bea and when Bea had dried them Mayme packed them in newspaper, and laid them in boxes. The five Tolliver silver spoons went into their Johnnie Walker whiskey tin. Bea worked for hours at constructing a box for Albert; it was like a wooden cell from which he gazed out with his broken nose and his jailbird stripes. They would have to pull Smoky Joe behind the truck. They had a '29 Ford ton-and-a-half now, Jack had sold the old Reo long ago.

It took them all day to make it from Wharton to Palo Pinto County, and all that day the countryside shifted and shape changed from the humid coast to the sharp, cracked red hills of north-central Texas. The windows on the truck were clouded and on the horizon was a haze of some distant dust storm. They passed men out in the fields, some with bedding plows and others with horse-drawn stalk knockers shattering the cornstalks into flying blond fragments and you could see the column of dust that they raised for miles. Sunset came as they were making their way through the limestone country of Glen Rose. Burma-Shave signs dotted the roadside; THE WOLF IS SHAVED – SO NEAT AND TRIM – RED RIDING HOOD – IS CHASING HIM. On Highway 80 they saw overloaded cars with mattresses and wash-boards tied to them, going west to the cotton harvest or to a new oil field, to the orchards of California. People searching for work, as if it were a thing, a metal in the ground or a place. They passed men walking silently with suitcases in one hand and a thumb stuck out. As they came into Central Texas the evening sky glowed with the red dusts carried down from the eroding Panhandle on a northwest wind. Elizabeth drove without speaking.

By the time they got past Dallas it was dark and

the headlights of other cars shone through the windshield on Elizabeth holding the steering wheel with both hands and Bea collapsed beside her asleep. Mayme and Jeanine rode in the truck bed wrapped in quilts. Smoky Joe shifted and stamped in the trailer, facing backward, with his tail flying up over his back. At midnight they drove up the driveway of the old house, gravel bursting from under the narrow tires.

The truck engine cooled down with minute pings sounding slower and slower and then there was only the night wind. They were on a ridge looking out over the heavy darkness of the Brazos River valley, the old Tolliver house adrift in a sea of starlight. They sat in silence. Something was tapping at one of the windows. One of the front double doors was off its hinges and it moved slightly with a raking sound. Far across the valley a cow bellowed in a long series of urgent calls after some lost calf gone astray in the night.

'Well here we are,' said Elizabeth.

There was a half moon up, and they could see that many windows were broken and the entire yard was grown up with plants that seemed willing to do anything to take over the front yard and the porch. A deer flagged its white tail and went bounding out of the barn. They got out cautiously.

Rather than walk into the deserted house in the dark they slept that first night in the truck. Smoky Joe was let go into the pasture, where he galloped from one fence line to another, calling out across the valley, asking if there were any other horses left in the world.

CHAPTER EIGHT

Mrs. Joplin ran the store at Strawn's Crossroads, a mile from the Tolliver farm. The original Strawn family had never called in their debts, so they became very poor and went off to pick cotton in Oklahoma. Mrs. Joplin always called in her debts and there was a big hand-painted sign in the front window of the store that said THIS IS NOT A BANK. Mrs. Joplin used to be a flapper but had ceased to flap after age twenty-five because of the unintended consequences. A person can't flap forever.

She watched Jeanine and Mayme and Bea come through the double screen doors into Strawn's Crossroads store. The brass bell jingled. They were oil field girls, you could tell that right away because of the bold way they carried themselves and the way they talked to one another in voices of normal volume, as if they were at home. For people dragged around from one town to another their whole lives, everyplace was home, or maybe no place was.

'You girls finding everything all right?'

'Yes, ma'am,' said Jeanine.

'Y'all are the Stoddard girls,' said Mrs. Joplin. She inclined her head in a polite, Victorian way when they introduced themselves. Mayme the tall one, the oldest, with auburn hair. Jeanine the skinny one in the middle, and the youngest, Bea, with a heavy braid down her back like a well rope.

'Do you have bobby pins?' said Mayme.

She must have got that red hair from the Stoddard side. None of the Tollivers had ever had red hair. It was such a deep winey red she might have dyed it.

'That shelf there is personal hygiene items,' said Mrs. Joplin. She led them to the wall shelves. 'And if y'all need something else of a more intimate nature for ladies, I keep it behind the counter and I'll wrap it for you.'

The three girls stood in front of the shelf and inspected the Prell shampoo, bath talcum, hairnets, and tooth powder. They didn't buy any of it. They were in trouble. That's why they had come back to that wreck of a house and the fields cooking down to hardpan in the relentless drought. They knew now what was in store for them. A can of trouble, a pound of misery, yards and yards of work to shore that old place up again. Deemie Miller came in, jangling the bell, and sat down on the Jell-O rack and she told him to get off of it.

After whispering and arguing together for a few minutes the middle one, Jeanine, walked off to another shelf and picked up a big bar of Sunshine soap. Mayme said, 'Well who put you in charge?' but she picked up a jug of vinegar by the handle. Mrs. Joplin knew this was to start cleaning everything. They also bought pinto beans and a twenty-five-pound sack of cornmeal and salt pork.

Mrs. Joplin had heard Jack Stoddard was dead.

She remembered him. As long as she could recall he would sit around and watch people with his eyes half shut. Now somebody said he'd got into sour gas at a rig out near Houston and spent three days in a coma. When he woke up he said he had seen Lucifer himself and that he liked the look of him and that he'd struck a deal of some kind with him. And then was arrested for something unmentionable and died in a jail cell. That's what Deemie Miller said.

Jack Stoddard used to come to this very store when the Strawns still owned it and buy jelly beans to take to Elizabeth before they were married. Mrs. Joplin lifted the lid on the jelly bean jar and poured out a quarter pound into a paper sack. They had come home to that collapsing old house with its windows busted out and the doors half off their hinges, a place where the noises of dinners and card games still echoed, many of which Mrs. Joplin had herself attended after her flapper days were over. After she had married. The house had been empty for years now, ten years, except for Elmo the Dwarf, who lived for a while up in the second story with a corn-shuck mattress and horse blankets until somebody found him a job in Fort Worth at the airplane factory where dwarves were needed to get up into the tail and finish the rivets. They didn't know about Elmo and she wasn't going to tell them.

Jeanine asked about oats and what quality they were and how much was a fifty-pound sack and Mrs. Joplin told her. Crimped oats, they weren't mill sweepings. Clean, good quality. She asked them if they had a horse, as if she didn't know.

'Yes,' said Jeanine, and her older sister said, 'It's her horse. He's crazy. Two of a kind.'

'Ha-ha,' said Jeanine. 'Why don't you can it, Mayme. We just met this woman and you're making fun of me.'

'Sisters fight, don't they?' Mrs. Joplin turned to Bea. The girl smiled and looked down. She, more than the other two, had the appearance and ways of a Tolliver. Sweet natured and timid.

'Yes, ma'am.' She held a red Big Chief notebook to her chest. 'I've got to have this for school.'

'We'll get it, Bea,' said Mayme. 'And pencils.'

Bea dropped the notebook on the counter and ran back to the school supplies shelf to choose two new, beautiful yellow pencils. She inspected each one carefully, as if they were not all alike. So much like her grandmother. Everybody is related to millions of people going back in time. Sometimes in the scriptures children were fathered by giants who were in the earth in those days, so you never knew. They had come back to find out who they were. They were like people whose images had been cut out of photographs so that the background was gone. She had done that herself in her flapper days. She pasted cute clippings from magazines under them; *Ooo la la!* And *I Wish I Could Shimmy Like My Sister Kate,* and then often wondered who it was who had taken the photo, but it was something people always forgot or didn't think about. Now she ran the store and managed her husband, who was twenty-five years older than she was and at

91

present very forgetful, so it was important to Mrs. Joplin not to forget anything on his behalf. Old Mrs. Tolliver whose maiden name was Neumann had been related to some of the finest families in southeastern Missouri.

'Well, I need some field corn,' said Jeanine. 'How much is it a bushel?'

'Cracked, it's ten cents the bag.'

'I'll take a bag.'

'Do you want some old newspapers to take with you? For cleanup?'

'Yes, please.'

Mrs. Joplin knew the genealogies of everybody in two counties and wrote it all down because of the way things were lost and confused during the oil strikes and washed over by the immense army of people who had poured down into Texas looking for work in the oil fields. People from Delaware and France and Kansas City traveling through a wrecked and untrustworthy land, as if they were in some country they had never heard of before, had come from another world called the 1920s. Mrs. Joplin was a dangerous person to be around if you were figuring on running from your past. There is no past; it is always an accordioned present consisting of compound interest accruing every second. She of all people understood this from her bathtub gin and Charleston days. Their grandfather Tolliver had been a forbearing old man who kept his fields free of cedar and the house painted white. And now the fields were grown up in cedar seedlings and burrs and the house was the color of gunmetal with a few chips of paint here and there.

Mrs. Joplin could see his face in Bea's deeply serious expression. The Tollivers and Neumanns had come from Missouri, by way of Hot Springs, Arkansas, and they had at some time in the past married into the Armstrongs, which is where the red hair might have come from. Mrs. Joplin's grandson Timmy Joplin was out in West Texas, at Big Spring. He joined the CCC and they had them out there slaving away on some public parks project. He had to go and see what he called 'the world.' He was engaged to one of the Armstrongs. He hadn't yet realized that wherever you are, that's the world. Mrs. Joplin wished Tim would come home.

Mrs. Joplin's oldest son, Timmy's father, had also gone off to see 'the world.' He married during the oil strike, to a skinny woman from Indiana who was no more a mother than a cowbird, which was why Mrs. Joplin and her elderly husband had raised Tim. Mrs. Joplin told Deemie Miller to quit sitting on the Jell-O rack again and wrote up the purchases while the girls walked around the store and read the messages tacked up by the wall phone, as if they had just arrived from some uncivilized Pacific island. Mayme read with interest the notice about a dance at the Old Valley Road schoolhouse and said, 'Jeanine, look here.'

Jeanine paid for the soap and vinegar and food with coins out of her jeans pockets.

'You take this to your mother from me.' Mrs. Joplin handed the jelly beans to Bea and watched the child's face light up. She went to the front doors to see the three sisters start off down the

93

road in the dry cool wind, carrying their soap and vinegar, and Jeanine the middle girl as skinny as a yard of pump water, and yet she was carrying the twenty-five-pound sack of cornmeal over one shoulder. Deemie stood at the screen doors to watch them as well. And after that nobody saw anything of them for a long time.

They had travelled all those miles to arrive at a place of dust. Dust moved through the atmosphere and hushed the evening to a powdery October darkness. It was hot during the day and hot all night long. All they had was the wood-burning cookstove and when it was fired up it drove them out to the front veranda. The valley of the Brazos River and the hills beyond seemed green because of the cedar and the oaks but the pastures were burnt out and the harvests thin. The peach orchard was stiff as whiskers with dead limbs and scale disease, the barn had lost so many boards from its walls that the floor was striped with bars of sunlight and in the shafts of light dust motes drifted. Their furniture seemed lost in the spaces of the two-story house. The kitchen chairs shrank into a huddle around the stove, and their beds jammed themselves up in the two rooms downstairs. The chain on the well windlass jerked and squealed as the bucket was cranked up.

The hills were a range of cracking red rock, they stood out against the blue sky, a country of tabled mountains that seemed to have been forged of cast iron in ages past and now were falling to pieces in rust and shattering fragments.

Jeanine walked the entire fence line with Smoky trotting behind her. His hooves made crisp sounds on the dead grass. The fence was all standing but some sections of the wire were very low, and if Smoky took it in his head to go visit with the workhorses in the next field he could go right over it. She worked for a day bracing up the mesquite posts. She took a stick and wrapped the barbed wire strands around it and twisted them tight. It would hold for a while.

The house was saturated with red dust. It fogged the windows and leaked from the baseboards. Mayme and Bea scraped away the putty on the broken windows and pulled the glass out with little breaking sounds. They covered the open panes with cardboard. Jeanine scrubbed the unbroken panes with vinegar and newspaper, and as the glass cleared she read the headlines. Bill Boyd and his Cowboy Ramblers were appearing at the Crazy Water Hotel in Mineral Wells. The government was making an aerodrome at Fort Worth, the textile mills of the East were either shutting down or emptied by violent strikes, California police were chasing migrants out of the camps. Many of these stories were written by somebody named Milton Brown. Jeanine read his name and remembered him, the stuttering boy who came to their grandparents' funeral.

Mayme lifted a bucket of water from the old well. She leaned over the well curb and drew it up on the windlass. There was no depth of water in it and the water came up cloudy. She went in and placed it on the cook-stove, and when it boiled she cut pieces of white soap into it, and then threw it on the kitchen floor in a long wave and began to mop.

'I'm going to see if that windmill will pump,' said Jeanine. She had pulled half a ruined silk stocking over her hair and wore one of her father's old shirts with CONROE OIL FIELD HAULING embroidered on the pocket. Tiny holes from either acid or welding dotted the front. 'That well water is no good.'

She climbed up the old Eclipse windmill and found the tall lever that unlocked the blades. They turned in the wind with rusty sounds and then water came out of the pipe and splashed down into the metal tank and they hauled it into the kitchen by the bucket. Jeanine reset the hinges on the front double doors and nailed them in with big common nails. She needed to make a new frame, she needed to use wood screws, but she didn't know how to do either of these things. Her father's toolbox remained a mystery.

Then she walked in the dust down to the old barn to carry cracked corn to Smoky Joe. He paced the fence line and his pasterns sank with a loaded motion. He watched for her every evening and his outline against the rank pasture grasses was like something painted on a cave wall, a prehistoric horse frozen in flight. He drank from the old mule trough and the water dripped slowly from his muzzle so that the reflected rings of light made noiseless waves up the loose boards of the barn walls.

The blank sunlight poured through the rigid branches of the Spanish oaks, through the needles of the ancient cedar that bent over the well curb. Precise black shadows were shed by its turning limbs as it spiraled toward the westering sun as it had for more than a century. Jeanine carried water and soap to the parlor. She remembered being in that room, playing on the floor with thread spools, and seeing her mother outside with Aunt Lillian and Violet Keener. Jeanine thought of them talking and laughing together in their new flapper dresses, all three of them pretty and young and not yet worn down by cares and children and errant husbands and oil-boom towns. In their bobbed hair and bright dresses and T-strapped high heels, their waistlines down around their hips and their legs shining and pale in silk stockings, they moved forward into the 1920s, the years that came like a light summer wind all over Texas, a decade that would have a hundred years in it and would never end. Jeanine hammered in a nail to put up the lithograph of the little girl in the forest, and then hung the portrait of her grandparents in the hall, where they could stare out of their antique clothing, home again.

Bea stepped up the dusty stairs into the attic and came upon a book called *The Flight of the Silver Airships* and fell into the book as if into a well. She was hungry for print and for stories about cheerful people who overcame great odds. Within the week she started school at the Old Valley Road school a mile away. She hurried from the house every morning with her books strapped in a piece of harness Jeanine had found in the barn.

As soon as the house was as scrubbed and bright as they could manage, Mayme went to ask for a job at Gareau's Dairy and Creamery only two miles down the road. They were surprised at the appearance of a new neighbor, and a young, pretty, redheaded one at that, but they needed somebody. She would be paid five dollars a week to scald milk bottles and wipe down the bottling room and throw fodder to the cows, and she could bring home as much skim milk as she wanted. So Mayme stepped out of the silent house at five-thirty every morning, carrying the empty glass vinegar jug, and shut the screen door carefully behind her. At breakfast time Elizabeth and Bea and Jeanine turned on the radio to hear the *Crazy Water Gang,* broadcast out of Mineral Wells. They listened as if the brainless jokes and live country music contained secret messages about the people who lived out beyond their silent house and would bring them news of their home county they had so longed for, all those years in the oil fields.

The windows looked out into their own 150 dry acres, studded with red outcrops of rock tumbling down the slope. About half of their land was clear of cedar seedlings; Jeanine did not know how that had happened. The rest was grown up in cedar and other brush. In the valley below were a few cotton fields now bloomed out in white tufts of fiber, and Jeanine and her sisters could see the pickers lifting their long pick-sacks and making gestures as if they were calling to one another, but they were too far away to be heard.

Two weeks after they moved in, a high wind

started up at six in the morning and continued all day. It was a deliberate, hurtful wind. By the next morning the blowing dust was so thick Mayme could not walk the two miles down the road to the dairy. Lines of dust came in under the doors. They stopped up the cracks in the windows with rags. The wind hooted at the chimney like someone blowing across the top of a bottle. The dust was carried on gusts from the northeast along with bits of dry grass and other debris from the fields, thrown against the windows. The blow lasted another night. By dawn Elizabeth was sitting beside the cold cookstove with a wet cloth in her hand. The surface of the old stove was streaked with red dust.

'We've got to think about this,' she said. 'I don't know if we can last this out.'

That night they gathered around the Emerson radio to listen to the evening news while the wind beat at the windows. Dust poured through the ceiling beside the chimney. Jeanine and Mayme swept it up on pieces of cardboard boxes and Bea kept the fire going in the cookstove. Jeanine saw Bea staring at the radio speaker, listening as if it mattered. Everything mattered to Bea. Bea's heart was engaged with the world like a gear.

Elizabeth clicked off the radio and said they had to decide what they were to do in the coming months. The old house they had longed for all those years shunting around the oil camps, that they remembered as the good place of plenty and quiet, was in a mess. The peach orchard eaten by scale and unpruned. The roof was a leaking patchwork of composite shingles and fifty-year-old cedar shingles, the fields grown up with cedar seedlings, parasites that ate up all the good things from the soil. The south fireplace had been bricked up and its chimney blocked by leaves and birds' nests. They needed chickens and a garden and money for seeds and the wallpaper should be stripped.

Bea got up and went to the bedroom she shared with her mother and came back with her book of famous poems. All the beautiful words in their sparse print telling of great events and shattering emotions. Her mother said, 'Bea, you'd better listen to this.' Bea shut the book.

'We've got to move in town,' said Elizabeth. 'We can live better if we move into town.'

'No, Mother,' said Jeanine. 'No, let's stay.'

'Jeanine, I don't know if you have a vote here,' said her mother.

Mayme said, 'We can all move in town with Aunt Lillian and Jeanine can stay out here by herself.'

'That's mean,' said Bea. 'But it's dramatic.'

'Y'all still blame me about Daddy,' said Jeanine. 'It wasn't my fault what Daddy did.'

'No, you just covered up for him.'

'Mayme, hush,' said Elizabeth. 'You girls have lived in towns all your lives. We can't keep up with the work. We might be able to sell. And you girls need a social life.'

Jeanine said, 'I don't want a social life. We can fix all this, Mother.' Jeanine made vague circles in the air with both hands to indicate some completeness, some kind of culmination. 'Nobody's going to buy. And we'll plant things. I'm going to

100

move upstairs and set up the Singer.'

'You'll freeze in the winter up there. There's no heat,' Mayme said. She wore a white kerchief over her hair all the time now, she had made it from a sugar sack and hemmed it neatly. It made her look like a nun.

'I'll find a kerosene stove somewhere. And by next fall Bea will have a going-to-high-school party.' Jeanine said this in an enthusiastic tone of voice. They were still mad at her. They were all still confused and damaged by Jack Stoddard's death, and it seemed his long shadow remained on earth even though he was gone, and it had followed them across the country to perpetuate their conflicts and divisions.

Bea put her finger in her book to mark her place. 'Can I cut my hair? When I have my high school party?'

Elizabeth said, 'Jeanine stop that. Don't make her believe those things.'

'We can't move again,' said Jeanine.

'Then what?' said Elizabeth. She laid her hand on the table. 'Then what?'

Mayme was the only one with a job. The winter was coming, and they needed wood for the kitchen range, which was $1.75 a rick or five dollars the cord and a cord would last them, say, about a month. And coal oil for the lamps would come to $3.50 a month if Bea didn't stay up all night reading.

'Bea, make a list,' said Jeanine. 'Of what all we have. Write all this down.' Bea flipped over the pages of her Big Chief notebook and ruled out columns. She doodled at the edges. A stick man

101

sat on a block of ice, milk bottles rolled their eyes at one another. 'Listen to me, this will look a lot better when there's a list.'

They could lease the fields, maybe for as much as five dollars a month. Jeanine said she would clear fifty acres of cedar somehow. And what about the work in the house? Elizabeth said. All her life she had done nothing but keep house, she had hauled and boiled water and ran out the bedbugs with sulfur and stuffed newspapers in the cracks and wrung out clothes by hand and look where it got me. Her voice was rising. Look where it got me. Bea kept her head low and wrote it all down.

She said, 'I am not going to do housework anymore. Y'all are big.'

'But what would you do, Mother?' Mayme bit her lip. She could not imagine what her mother would do other than keep house.

'I want to go into town, and spend time with Lillian and Vi,' she said. Bea's pencil stopped in mid-milk bottle.

'Mother, you're not leaving, are you?' Mayme was alarmed.

Bea said, 'Mother? Are you going away?' She had a desperate expression on her face. Then she bent over the notebook again and drew drilling rigs.

'Y'all look like you been shot,' said Elizabeth. 'I'm not leaving, but you had better think about the work this involves.'

'How much do we have left?'

'There's a hundred and seventy-five and some change.'

'I'll do the housework,' said Jeanine. 'I'll keep up the house and cooking. And Mayme's making twenty a month.'

Mayme said, 'All right. But I better see some wash hanging on the line when I come home.'

'And don't leave it out to get covered in dust,' said Elizabeth. 'If you buy chickens you'll have to build a chicken house or you might just as well feed them to the coyotes. The minute you have hens, Jeanine, every hungry thing out there wants them or the eggs.'

'And you've got to keep Bea's clothes ironed and starched,' said Mayme.

'And throw something down the old well,' said Bea. 'Animals get thirsty, they get desperate for water and they're liable to fall down in it.' She stroked Prince Albert. 'We got to put out water in a pan.'

'And you have to learn to can,' said Elizabeth. 'We need a pressure cooker and jars. You need to can whatever you can find at the farmers' market on Saturdays in Mineral Wells.'

Mayme said, 'I'll hand you two dollars a week for groceries.'

'All right,' said Jeanine. 'If we moved into town we'd end up in some crummy rent house again. Did we just sit around and talk about this place all those years for nothing?'

'It wasn't what we expected,' said Mayme. She took off the kerchief and shook it out.

'Well what the hell did you expect?' said Jeanine. She knotted her fingers together in a tight clasp.

'Don't use that language,' said her mother.

'Can I write "hell"?' said Bea.

'No.'

'Mayme, you can do better than that dairy,' said Jeanine.

'I know it,' Mayme said. 'Just let me think.'

And so they decided to stay. They could imagine the old Tolliver place into being. The sisters could dream the unstinting dreams of young people at the edge of adult life where one makes assertions and declarations about the models of cars, the numbers of children, the colors of kitchens that one wants in this future life. Mayme wanted a telephone. It would emit friendly voices from the earpiece, maybe the young man named Robert Faringham would after all, against all odds, call her on this new modern telephone with a rotary dial, and with it would come a subscriber's book and you could read down the columns of names and find your cousins and your friends. Her auburn hair shone in the lamplight. Mayme had the ability or gift of being happy, which is not all that common. She wanted a job with smart clothes and then a husband and then a home in Fort Worth and four children and herself a chatelaine like Snow White in a ruffled collar and high heels singing 'Someday My Prince Will Come.' She had just turned twenty-two so he'd better show up fast. Bea wanted electricity so she could read until the late hours and write in her notebooks. She wanted a teacher who would understand what these notebooks meant to her, who would pick up the Big Chief and read in it, and say *My goodness, look at this!*

Jeanine wanted the house painted white, and an untroubled life. Spring would come and the fields would be the dark, dense green of new cotton plants and sweet corn. The peach orchard would bloom. She wanted a good mare to run with Smoky and then there would be increase and growth. Jeanine knew the bargain she had made with her mother and sisters to stay here depended on her, that they did not care about it as much as she did but town life would drag them down into low-wage jobs and restlessness again, they would all scatter and lose their love of one another. This would be home with curtains at the windows and voices of friends come to visit speaking in low tones on the veranda in the evenings. She wanted knowledge about the soil and how windmills worked and the mysteries of hot-water heaters. She would step out of a bath of hot water and scented foam, into a summer suit of dark blue rayon with white polka dots, she would reach into an icebox for a pitcher of cool water. If she could have all this her heart would have been so full of gladness she would have spilled over. If only it would rain.

Her mother wanted a guide or some book of advice. She was moving into a life that was lived by widows, a new, frightening place. It seemed a geography that was shrouded and without color and she was paused at the edge of it.

Bea opened her book again. Then she declaimed aloud, *'Look down, fair moon, and bathe this scene; Pour softly down night's nimbus floods, on faces ghastly. Swollen, purple; on the dead, on their backs–'*

Elizabeth said, 'Stop, Bea.'

CHAPTER NINE

At Strawn's store they received a message from Mineral Wells; their relatives were coming to visit. Mayme cleaned the lamp chimneys and Jeanine washed what clothes they had and ironed them with the sad iron, raising hot steam in the kitchen. Bea used an old piece of school chalk to whiten her tennis shoes, and they waited nervously for their relatives to arrive.

Aunt Lillian and her daughter Betty drove up in a Model A and stepped out and spread their arms. How glad they were to see them again, how good they looked! The aunt and the cousin glanced at each other and then turned back to Elizabeth and her daughters and smiled again. 'Y'all are *home!*' they said.

Elizabeth smiled and hugged her sister-in-law. 'Yes, here we are,' she said.

The sisters and their cousin walked out into the fields, through the gumdrop shapes of invading cedar. Betty was the same age as Jeanine and she had the dark Stoddard hair done in a series of close waves around her head. Her head was glossy with good shampoo and she liked to move it around on her neck in subtle head gestures.

'Why are we walking around in the field?' said Betty. 'What are you going to do with all this land?'

'Well, when the cedar is cleared, it'll be good.'

Jeanine waved her hands. 'Good land.'

Smoky stood at the far end of the field under a stand of live oak with his ears turned toward their neighbor's barn. He was searching among all the dried grasses that still carried seed heads and several strands dangled from his mouth.

'What are you going to cut them down with?' said Betty.

'With a saw,' said Jeanine.

'Don't men normally do that?' asked Betty. She stared at the three-foot cedars as if they were a fixed and eternal element of the world, which could only be altered by men. Large strong men who wielded huge tools.

'I can do it. Why not?' said Jeanine.

Betty took her arm and gave her a little shake. 'You better get work in town,' she said. 'I never heard of a girl turning into a farmer.'

'Then you ain't heard much,' said Jeanine.

'And what are you going to do with that horse?'

'I don't know yet,' said Jeanine. 'But I'll let you know first, all right?'

Mayme said, 'Jeanine, hush.'

They turned back toward the house, walking up the slope through stands of Indian grass and Johnson grass. Betty's Cuban heels turned and she said she was going to break both ankles if they kept on stomping around in the fields.

'Did Mother tell you I got engaged?' she said. 'His name is Si. That's for Silas but I think Silas is so old-fashioned. It's a redneck name.' They sat on the edge of the concrete tank, under the windmill. It stood braced and thick and cool water poured out of the pipe. 'What are y'all

107

doing for men?'

'We left them all behind,' said Jeanine. Mayme stared down at the ground.

'Y'all better come into town and come out to the China Moon here one of these days. The China Moon dance palace. Si steps on my feet a lot.'

'We will,' said Mayme. 'We will, before long.'

'Well, you all need to get out *socially*,' said Betty. 'There's a *farmer* world and then there's a *social* world.' She put out a foot shod in dark red leather. 'I get shoes at cost, there where I work. These here you are looking at are *dancing* shoes. I don't normally wear them walking around in the fields, but if you want dancing shoes, I got them.'

'We'll come in town and see,' said Mayme. Bea sat on the edge of the tank and stared at Betty's dancing shoes.

'What I am talking about is *men*,' said Betty. 'You got to hunt them down, and never let them know you're sort of *stalking* them, and you got to do it in really good-looking shoes.'

Jeanine clenched her hands together as if they were lips and nodded with an interested expression.

They took their aunt and cousin on a tour of the old house. It had been built in 1883 with lumber and glass hauled from Mineral Wells, a crowd of neighbors shouting to one another, lifting the beams. They set the foundation with red sandstones and raised chimneys at either end and the two stories filled with talk and music and disputes and children running down the staircase with a racket like falling barrels. At the age of ten Elizabeth had screamed with excitement when her cousins roped and broke in new horses in the corrals, and the big sugar-grinding stones in the barn roared as they turned on one another and juice bubbled from the spout and splashed into the boiling pans. Grandpa Tolliver's two plow horses, Shorty and George, called in loud quivering whinnies every morning for their feed and banged their buckets to wake everyone up. Every evening Elizabeth's father sat on this very veranda in a striped shirt and galluses and a vast black hat and sang cowboy songs to himself, songs about thundering stampedes. And now all was still.

They stood in the parlor with its nine-foot windows and cracked, shimmering glass and the Virginia creeper swarming over the panes so that the parlor seemed to be underwater. They peered down into the well where the old centurion cedar stood guard twisted in spirals by the daily journey of the sun. They went out to the graveyard to contemplate their mutual relatives. The graves had not been tended properly. They were grown up with agarita and cactus. The cast-iron fence was leaning in sections. Jeanine tried to straighten it and her sisters and mother said to leave it alone. Her grandfather's grave spelled out his name in ornate letters, *Samuel V Tolliver, 1860-1932* and beside him *Nannie Allen Neumann Tolliver, 1862-1932.* Two unnamed babies that had lived only a few months; her mother's forgotten brother and sister.

Betty said, 'I just feel so bad for y'all losing

109

Uncle Jack but I remember when my daddy picked up and left.'

'Hush up, Betty,' said her mother.

They went on, leading their aunt and cousin slowly and uneasily around this inherited property as if it were not really their own, as if they were squatters. Elizabeth and Lillian, the accidental sisters-in-law, sat on the front veranda and drank iced tea without ice, without sugar, and with hardly any tea in it. Lillian sipped at her glass and carefully put it down. She stared around at the weedy yard and the cardboard in the windows. She put her heavy hand on Elizabeth's arm and said, 'Liz, I want you to come into town. Me and Violet have something I want you to look into.'

'What?' Elizabeth said.

'Y'all got to do something. Y'all are going to starve out here.'

'Well, we decided to try for a while.'

'How much money do you have on hand right now?'

Elizabeth squinted her eyes against the late fall sunlight and thought. 'I've got enough to buy chickens and garden seed and a few other things. Then something for an emergency.'

'What for an emergency?'

'An uncollected note. It was in Jack's tally book. A man owed him money for hauling a boiler up to Jacksboro.'

'You come into Mineral Wells and visit with me and Violet Keener. We got something we want to talk to you about.'

110

So they began to make their lives there, throughout the fall and winter of 1937. They tried to
piece their lives together the way people draw
maps of remembered places; they get things
wrong and out of proportion, they erase and
redraw again. From the radio they heard of
people dying in the dust storms just to the north
of them, in Oklahoma and the Panhandle. That
Gloria Vanderbilt was reduced to dressmaking
for a living. Of the faraway rich with more money
than there ever was in the world while men
starved and had no work and women starved and
worked both, of strikes at the textile mills in
Rhode Island and all the people going to California to pick peas or whatever there was to pick.
But the Hamilton clock seemed to tell only of
their own long hours of labor against the dust
and the drought. They were in the midst of the
Dirty Thirties, and that decade's modish
obsession with important people in far places,
with gangsters and movie stars and oil barons
and swing bands. It was easy to feel themselves
invisible and empty of significance, to forget that
behind every human life is an immense chain of
happenstance that includes the gravest concerns;
murder and theft and betrayal, great love; lives
spent in burning spiritual devotion and others in
miserly denial; that despite the supposed
conformity of country places there might be an
oil field worker who kept a trunk of fossil fish or
a man with a desperate stutter who dreamed of
being a radio announcer, a dwarf with a rivet gun
or an old maid on a rooftop with a telescope,
spending her finest hours observing the

111

harmonics of the planetary dance.

In early November they had their first freeze. By this time in late November men had brought out the big lister buster plows and carved down the middles of the rows, with mules and horses straining in harness against the cotton and cane roots, ripping them out for the new seed, gambling against the drought.

The mailman drove a buggy with a big thunderous gray horse and when Jeanine saw him coming she raced out in the cold. The faint remains of the wind carried down the smell of the newly turned earth in the cotton fields. The mailman's heavy dappled horse dozed along in a slow clopping saunter with the two shafts to either side of him bobbing to his walk. The mailman wore a hand-knitted muffler against the winter chill that some female relative had wrought for him in manly colors of brown and green and mustard and he wore it bravely, resignedly. He drove along with the reins in his lap and read all the return addresses and when he arrived at their mailbox he tipped his hat, and said his name was Herman Dienst, and then handed her the letters stained with rain.

Jeanine ran back into the house, searching through the letters. A notice from the county about taxes. A letter from Mayme's young man in Conroe, Robert Faringham. The one who worked for the Conroe-Lufkin Telephone Company.

Elizabeth sat down and opened the notice about Palo Pinto county taxes. They owed three hundred dollars in back taxes. The county tax collector said it had come to his notice that the Tolliver farm was inhabited again and although the county did not want to foreclose because the county would have no use for the land in the present economic emergency Mrs. Stoddard would please take notice of the amount of back taxes and do something about it.

Elizabeth put the notice down and then lifted it again and read it once more.

'They'll give us an extension,' Elizabeth said. 'They're not going to throw a widow woman and three daughters off their land because of back taxes. They just won't.' But the Cunningham bank in Palo Pinto had failed and in its collapse it had taken several public utility bonds with it. Men who had good jobs at one time were now sitting around the courthouse square in dirty clothes looking for freighting work, hoping for day labor with a shovel on the pipelines. 'They won't,' said Elizabeth. 'They have to accept something less, they just have to.'

All that remained in the house to eat was the pinto beans. They were eating them, it seemed, three times a day. Jeanine longed for the smell of baking bread, real yeast bread made with white flour. She lifted the pan of corn bread from the oven and sat it on a flour sack on the table beside the beans.

'Supper!' she said, and thought, *They have to.*

Bea gathered up Albert and came to the table. He was a handsome cat, even with his poor skewed nose. His eyes were outlined with black and he was dressed in an extravagant suit of

113

stripes. He had to be dusted off every day with a flour sack when he came in. His green eyes appeared over the edge of the table from Bea's lap, like a periscope arising from a deep feline sea. He stared over his broken nose at Bea's plate of beans and searched for bits of bacon. He indicated with his tender paw which bit he would like, and Bea drew it to him on her fork. Then she reached over and turned on the radio.

Elizabeth didn't eat. She just sat there and held the notice.

'I've got to ask for some kind of arrangement,' she said.

Jeanine wiped up her plate. 'Can we turn that radio off, little sister?'

'No, don't, I like it. It's *One Man's Family*.'

'I hate the way they talk,' said Jeanine.

'But they all sound so normal,' said Bea. 'I just love *One Man's Family*. They all sound so normal.'

'They are not normal. They are rich and they talk like they're from England. Save the battery.'

Jeanine wanted to be kind and speak sweetly to Bea, like her mother, but now with the notice she herself was in deep need of somebody being kind to her. She had thought they would be safe here. No rent. None of them had thought about the county taxes. Unpaid over the years, stacking up. And there was Bea with her endless diary or journal, in which all their troubles were made into a chronicle, one misery strung out into another. Bea was only thirteen but she seemed to prefer sitting up at night and reading back through her diary and all her descriptions of

114

family trouble like an old woman. Nothing could ever be fixed, no matter how hard Jeanine tried. It all just broke again but there was no other way but to lay hands on the pieces and fit them together, make them work.

'I'm going to town tomorrow,' said Elizabeth. 'Do we have the gas?'

'Yes,' said Jeanine. 'Let me drive in. I want to look around the farmers' market. I could make us some clothes if I can find good secondhand ones.' Her sisters and mother nodded in silence. 'Don't you think?' Jeanine lifted her hand into the silence. 'Everybody that thinks so raise your hand.' She smiled brightly. 'We can go to the poorhouse in double-ruffled sleeves!'

'That would be great,' said Mayme. She slapped down a magazine in front of Jeanine. 'But I don't know what for.' She was trying hard to be angry but tears sparkled in her eyes, and finally she folded up her letter from Conroe, in which Robert Faringham said that he felt they would be better apart, given the scandal about her father, and he hoped she would meet someone else more worthy of her. She lifted the stove lid and dropped the letter into the fire.

'And don't wear jeans,' said Elizabeth. She could not remember when young women first started wearing men's Levi's around the home but they had. It was one more confusing event that had crept up on her along with adultery and widowhood and the financial collapse of the United States and these two large gangly girls who were her older daughters.

Jeanine put on her jacket to go feed and water

115

Smoky. She took the fashion magazine with her. She carried two buckets at a time and filled the trough and then poured out the cracked corn into a hubcap. She read while he ate so she could get the hubcap away from him when he was done. Otherwise he would take it in his teeth and bang dents into it as if it were a toy, and it was the only spare hubcap they had. Smoky Joe bent his head over the fence to her, solitary and curious.

'Want to see the fall fashions of '37?' She held out the magazine and Smoky took it in his teeth and tossed it up and down, the spectrally thin women with slinky draped dresses and shawl collars torn out page by page. They sat together in silence while the evening shadows flooded the valley and he made grinding noises with his great horse teeth. The light was draining away westward, and as it poured away the clear hard stars opened up one by one like rain lilies.

The next morning Jeanine ran out in the early cold to pour some gas into the tank. She lugged out the ten-gallon jerrican. Her breath smoked. The eternal wind carved its transparent way through the limbs of the oak overhead, and all around her in the Central Texas farm and ranch country the faint yellow lights of coal-oil lanterns shone from remote kitchen windows.

And in all these kitchens the whisper of radio voices spoke in staticky tones to men pulling on heavy lace-up boots with tangled strings and to women breaking eggs into hot frying pans. They listened to the Early Birds from WFAA out of Dallas and to the songs of Karl the Kowhand.

116

And in all the barns and pastures, animals lifted their heads to listen, their eyes turned with deep and patient interest to the lighted windows. Scorpio stood in the deep blue sky and shone through the branches of the oak tree and lifted its brilliant, poisonous tail over all the valley of the Brazos River.

It was eight in the morning and already the teams and plows were out in the fields alongside the Brazos. Jeanine and her mother drove north toward Palo Pinto, the county seat, a small town that the railroad had passed by leaving it with only a courthouse and a jail. As she drove, the hills took on form under the wash of light like invisible writing under the pressure of fire. The frost was melted now except in the shadows of trees, and then the sun moved on and left ghost shadows of frost on the pasture grasses. Sheep and Angora goats wandered under stripped-down trees. Mules bent into their collars, and the plows tore down through the peanut fields and the cotton-row middles, a red spillage of earth on either side pouring away from the blade. The wind was dry and bitter and drove dust against the windshield.

The courthouse was a fine stone building that belonged to a much larger town but railroads go where they will.

The county tax collection office was on the first floor. People sat on chairs in the hall outside. They were all there for the same reason. The county could not collect most of its taxes and so it could not repair roads or improve schools. Counties were themselves applying for federal

117

drought relief. Jeanine sat beside her mother and glanced at the faces around her. She wondered if she was related to any of these people, or if they had known her Tolliver grandparents. They all sat watching the door with its opaque glass and the black letters that said COUNTY TAX OFFICE.

She went into the office with her mother when their name was called. She had to watch her mother's humiliation as she asked for an extension. Saw her lay down a hundred dollars and say they would pay twenty a month.

'But the taxes will still accumulate,' said the man. 'This is November and by January another fifty dollars will be due.'

'This is all I can do,' said Elizabeth.

'All right, Mrs. Stoddard,' he said. He wore a sweater vest and sleeve garters. 'We don't want to foreclose on you.' He lifted his hands in a helpless gesture. 'What would we do with another farm?' Elizabeth said *Yes, of course,* as if she understood and stood resolutely waiting for what he would say next. 'We would have to auction off the farm and I doubt that it would be bought by anybody other than a bank.' He snapped one of his sleeve garters. 'And the banks ain't looking too good.'

'Well, no,' she said. Jeanine saw that her mother's lower lip was trembling slightly. Jeanine wanted to say something to the man but couldn't think of anything polite.

'So we'll just ask you for this hundred.' He laid his hand flat on the bills and slipped them from the table and into a tin cash box. 'And wait for the next hundred.'

Elizabeth took a firm grip on Jeanine's upper arm and they left the office.

They drove on down Highway 80 into Mineral Wells. Hotels up on the mountainside dominated the town. The Crazy Water Hotel, the seven-story Baker Hotel. They had been built when Mineral Wells became famous for its sulfur springs and mineral waters. The springs were said to cure insanity and the water was bottled and sold as Crazy Water and Upper 10 Lithiated Lemon. Even movie stars came to the baths to cure whatever it was they suffered from, nervous disorders or immoderate thirst, a desire to be seen, an unslaked curiosity about Texas. Marlene Dietrich had slunk around the halls of the Baker, along with the Three Stooges and Clark Gable. Blurred photographs of the stars appeared from time to time in the Mineral Wells newspaper. Not one of them had ever had a home sold on the courthouse steps for taxes, Jeanine thought. Or ate beans twice a day. She stopped in front of the Keeners' little house on Fourth Street and saw her mother turn at the door before knocking and wave her gloved hand.

CHAPTER TEN

At the farmers' market four children and a young mother sat on the curb with a basket of shelled pecans. They had built themselves a fire in a small sheet-iron stove. Two of the children were girls and they were barefoot and sat cross-legged with their cotton skirts pulled over their knees to keep warm and played the slap-hands game. *Down in the valley where the green grass grows sat little Edna as sweet as a rose.* A thin black man made hand-carved wooden puppets jump around on top of an orange crate. Farm women sat on the bumpers of trucks and sold eggs and very yellow butter that smelled of wild onions and a boy stood with a calf's lead-rope in his hand holding up five fingers. A blind man sang a song about waiting around a water tank for a train to take him to California, his face lifted to the daytime moon and one hand out in a dramatic stage gesture.

Jeanine bent her head and pressed past all these people until she found a man in a buckboard wagon who was selling old clothes. In the jumbled heap Jeanine found a dress of garnet twilled silk that must have belonged to somebody that weighed three hundred pounds and then either died or lost weight and didn't need it anymore. She also found something for Mayme; a dirty remnant from a bolt of juniper green tabby-weave silk, and some sheer curtains that could be used for linings. Then she paid ten cents for an old squirrel fur coat. They would use it somehow. Winter was coming.

A crazy man called Oilfield Willie stood at one end of the market calling out the demonic names of Hitler and preached on the deep strata of oil and salt water.

'I am Ozymandias, king of kings!' he shouted. His ragged suit hung on him in folds. 'I have brought my sword to bear on the Oil Kings of the netherworld and upon the arteries and the hearts of coal, and I declare war on the trains of Russia and the underwater torpedoes at sea, for the devil and his soldiers are marching as to war! My children, gird up your harps and bagpipes and play the music of the great conflicts and the great strivings or the angels of iniquity will take you all down into the places where the dead hide and are turned as dark as low-grade crude! Mussolini and Hitler are waiting with skeleton rockets. Rise up! Listen! Take heart! Be not afraid! Lift up your hearts and be not dismayed, my children. I am the oil and the truth and the nitroglycerin and none can stand before me, my children.' People dropped a nickel or a dime into his hat, which sat turned up on the pavement.

Ross Everett walked up with a young boy following him. He wore a dark three-piece tweed suit and a good gray Stetson. He had a can of Arbuckle's coffee under his arm. The boy went to stand in front of the dancing puppets and as he stood there the thin black man made a Red Ryder puppet wring both arms around and around on their pivot.

'Jeanine Stoddard,' Ross said. He lifted his hat and replaced it. 'Son, this is Miss Stoddard.'

The boy turned to her and lifted his own hat and turned back to the puppets. Now Little Annie Roonie was jigging across the orange crate. The square was crowded with people selling, and the sky over Mineral Wells was reddish with dust blown down from the Panhandle. A wind snaked around through the streets and the hotels and fluttered the skirts of the girls.

'How do you do, Mr. Everett,' she said. She was surprised to see him, she had forgotten he lived somewhere close to Mineral Wells. She wadded the sheer curtains into a ball and then snatched up the squirrel fur coat and the stained crepe and mashed it all together with frantic motions. She did not want Ross Everett to see her pawing around among old used clothing. 'How good to see you again.' Jeanine felt strangely formal and reserved toward him now that she was grown up and all of twenty years old.

He smiled as she tucked the wad under one arm. 'I heard y'all had moved back,' he said. 'I'm sorry to hear your dad passed away.'

'Well, how did you hear that?'

'Race people,' he said. He stood aslant with one hand in his coat pocket. His suit coat was worn. He looked like he hadn't bought a new suit since about 1920.

'Race people. Well.' She didn't want to talk to him for some reason. Or she did but some other time when the world had been better to her and her sisters and her mother, when they were not so desperate for money, when she didn't have a bundle of rags under her arm. 'Yes, we did, we moved back to our grandparents' old farm.'

'You still have that horse?'

'Smoky Joe? Yes, we have him.'

'Are you selling?' He glanced down at the material in her hands and then he turned to the boy and said for him to buy one of the puppets if he wanted. The boy reached for the Red Ryder cowboy figure.

'No,' said Jeanine. 'I reckon we're going to race him one of these days.' She smiled as if she were very confident.

Everett nodded. He reached into his pocket for a nickel and handed it to the boy. Then the boy said he wanted a soda and Everett handed him another nickel. 'I could buy myself a beer for that,' he said. He turned back to Jeanine. 'Good luck trying to get a match,' he said. 'Nobody's going to match up against a girl.'

'No, they'll match up against the *horse*,' said Jeanine. 'Hope y'all are doing well.'

'We're doing fine,' he said. 'Just in on a monthly trip into town. Good day, Jeanine.' The boy came after him as he stepped up on the curb and they went on with their coffee and their puppet.

Jeanine saw schoolchildren running past. It must have got to three-thirty and school was out. She wanted to go into the Oil King Drugstore and buy herself something. A Dr Pepper, an ice cream, a shaker of talcum powder shaped like a champagne glass. But she would not. The holes in her shoes were like the holes in everybody's shoes but still she was ashamed of them. She seemed to be walking on dirt. She stepped by the little girls and the tin stove with its wavering column of smoke, up onto the sidewalk and walked on past the drugstore. A man in a porkpie hat came toward her and suddenly seized her by both shoulders.

'Jeanine Stoddard!' he shouted.

'What?' She started backward.

'It's me! M-m-milton Brown!' He was a short young man in a pair of spectator shoes, flagrant

123

wingtips, and a wide tie with his hair sticking up in front and glasses so thick they magnified his eyes into unsteady blue marbles. They were round as half-dollars. 'Oh Jeanine, Jeanine, look at this face!' He stood back and threw his hands wide to present himself and his pinwheel cowlick to her. He tipped his hat and then took the wad of clothes from her arms in order to see her entire form there before him. 'Do you remember me? Have you not read my n-n-newspaper columns?'

'Give that back,' she said and took the clothes from him. 'No. Well, I did when I was cleaning the windows. But I don't remember you.'

'Yes you do yes you d-do!' He stuttered terribly. Then she remembered the boy and his hammering voice that seemed to leap into a kind of dit-dit-dah-dit Morse code when he talked, turning the knob of the radio at her grandparents' funeral so many years ago; ten years ago.

'All right, yes I do,' she said. They were walking down the street with his hand on her elbow crashing through the Saturday crowds in the torrent of his enthusiasm and goodwill.

'Of course you do! We went to school together in Ranger! And then y'all left for Mexia. All I did' – he pulled her to one side to let a woman carrying a baby go past –'was listen to your grandp-p-parents' radio. The world spoke to me! All I ever wanted to do was to talk back!'

'I remember,' she said.

'Dang, girl, your father has died. I know, I am a n-newspaperman, dammit, what a thing. I am the investigator of all that is odd and anomalous. Where are you, where are you, in short, where are you living?' He shoved his hat to the back of his head.

'We came back to the old Tolliver place,' she said. They swept past a hardware store where there was a tallest cornstalk contest, the winner to receive fifty cents. Desperate farmers had stood up their best cornstalk with their names tagged to them. 'That's where we're living.'

'All of you? Anybody else dead?'

'No, no, me and Mother and Mayme and Bea.' She laughed. 'Stop making me laugh,' she said.

'Your father has died. Your life is in shambles. You are starving on the old farm. You are in the midst of dust explosions and your potatoes have the Irish rot and the mules have all died and their bones are white-white-whitening in the sun. When can I come and see you?'

'Oh put a cork in it, Milton.' She couldn't stop laughing. 'What are you doing? When did I see you last?'

'When your grandparents died. I was out there at the graveyard because my aunt is B-Baylor Joplin and she's related to the old lady at the Strawn store, you s-s-s-see all things are tied together. Ah Jeanine, your cloudy gray eyes, your sultry voice. How are y'all staying alive?'

He drew her to the benches in front of the post office. They sat down along with farmers and ranchers who were waiting for their wives to finish shopping.

'We're doing fine,' she said. 'Mayme has a job at the dairy and I'm keeping house, Bea is in school.' She lifted the wad of secondhand clothes. 'And I'm making dresses for everybody.

125

I'm the little housekeeper. We got out of the oil fields.'

The wind was pouring through the streets. It raised dust on the pavement and along the gravel roads leading up to the mountain above. The courthouse flag stood out its full length and then the confused wind backed and doubled it so that the stripes checkered themselves against the forty-eight stars. People walked with their heads down, skirt hems scalloped and rolled. In the north a solid bank of dark blue cloud was bearing down on them, with pallid, running sails of smaller clouds beneath. He gazed at her with a happy smile.

'Jeanine, you look so good. Ah, your daddy was a man I admired. Handsome devil. Rakish. They said it was sour gas. A workingman's fate. I wanted to kill myself when y'all left for Mexia, slash my wrists with a shattered radio t-t-tube.' Jeanine bent over laughing. He lowered his voice. 'It was your eyes, Jeanine. You could sing "I Wanna Be Loved by You" all the way through and you had a yellow dress and a yellow sunbonnet to match. And then you went away. All of you. Off on the road of l-life. I think the papers all say trundling. You trundled off. What the hell is a t-t-trundle?'

'You don't remember all that!' she said. 'You're making it up!'

'I am not.'

'I was ten when that song came out. We were in...' She paused to fetch up that year from her memory but she could not recall where they were. 'Out in the Permian, in Monahans? I'll have to ask Mayme. But what are you doing? How did you get on at the newspaper?'

Milton Brown took a pencil out of his jacket pocket and held the tip up in the air.

'I went to college until the old man couldn't support me anymore and he said, "Sharpen your pencil and get d-d-d-down there to the newspaper and beg for a job, son." I was dying to get into radio. But I stutter. And I suffer from a T-T-T-Texas accent. I live in a rented room above the shoe store where people come in and try on rugged footwear to plod on through the economic emergency.' He stuck his foot in the air and she could see his wingtips were cracked and shiny with desperate applications of polish to cover the aged leather and thin soles. 'I help out at the recording sessions at the Crazy Water Hotel, cut the acetate, then they run them into Dallas and b-b-broadcast them on WBAP. I'm being paid in scrip and cabbages and dozens of eggs. Do y'all need eggs?'

'Oh no!' Jeanine jumped to her feet. 'I have to buy us a setting hen, I almost forgot.'

'Oh darling Jeanine, listen.' He stood up and took her elbow. 'Move in town and live in luxury here where there are streetlights, get away from your country estate. Do y'all have enough cabbages and gruel to survive on?'

'Bye, Milton.' She held out her hand to him. He took hold of it.

'May I come and visit?'

'Yes. Leave a message at Strawn's store.'

'I will. But you'll break my heart, won't you? You'll lead me on and then c-c-c-crush my

127

hopes.' He bent forward and kissed her cheek. 'All of you will. You will toy with me, even little Bea. How old is Bea?'

'She's thirteen.'

'And lethal, thirteen and lethal. I will be out your way because there is a huge dam going in on the Brazos just above you. WPA project. After the water is impounded Roosevelt will come out and walk on it. Prairie roses will bloom. What can I bring with me?'

'Oh ... books for Bea.'

He swept off his hat and bowed. A man in coveralls sitting next to them on a bench chewed slowly and watched without expression.

'Before long, my cruel tormentor.'

Jeanine stopped in at the E-Z Step shoe store to say hello to Betty.

Betty screamed, 'Jeanine! Y'all are in town!' She made Jeanine sit down and try on shoes. So Jeanine tried on a new pair of oxfords made with manatee leather and a pair of canvas espadrilles just to look at her feet in them and imagine herself dancing in whole shoes. When Betty was putting them back in their boxes, her cousin said their mothers were over at Violet Keener's house in a conspiracy about something, something dangerous.

'Dangerous how?' said Jeanine.

'I don't know exactly but it's about money.'

Then Betty walked Jeanine to the truck and said what Jeanine needed was shoes and lipstick and a date and a dance. Jeanine decided not to say anything more about learning to drive a tractor. She said good-bye and then found a farm wife with live chickens; she bought three brown hens in a cardboard box and started for home with five gallons of gas in the refilled jerrican. She left her mother to stay the night in Mineral Wells and whatever dangerous conspiracies she and Violet and Lillian might be hatching. She drove south on State Highway 281, past the fields of cotton now stripped down to a tangle of dried stems, as if the farmers had begun to grow fence wire. A pouring wave of sheep fled down a hillside, answering some unheard call, and the dense bank of cloud to the northeast told of a windstorm to come.

She climbed up on the roof carrying a brick on a rope, dropped it down the chimney on the south end of the house, and knocked out the birds' nests and branches. She climbed down again swept up the parlor and lit a fire in it. There was nothing like a good fire. At least they had a fire.

She moved all her possessions into an upstairs room and when Mayme came home from work they carried the Singer upstairs as well. Jeanine liked the look of the bare room, uninhabited by furniture or pictures. Hers to own, a workplace. One window was covered in cardboard where they had pulled out the broken glass. Her own spare little room was next to it with a window where she could look out on the stacked blue lines of hills disappearing into the east. Jeanine took out the dress and the material and cut them into pieces. Scraps of cloth all over the floor. She cut out the sheer curtain for linings. But she knew clothes weren't good enough. Pretty clothes wouldn't get the cedar seedlings torn down or the peach orchard cultivated. She had to go over to the neighbors, the Crowsers, and get them to lend her their tractor. They had to fix the roof or the dust and the solitary, brief rains would drip down the chimney and they would wake up one morning to a cookstove full of water or dirt.

CHAPTER ELEVEN

Abel Crowser got up stiffly out of his chair and went into the kitchen. He started a fire in the cookstove and then turned the crank on the battery charger so he could click on the Admiral radio. He had wanted to go over and be friendly but the women all seemed distracted and closed up, and who could blame them? With Jack Stoddard arrested for fooling around on Elizabeth with a young girl and then dead in a jail cell. Anyhow, that's what they said at the Strawn's crossroads store. Adultery always made for gripping stories, never failed to take your attention, look at the Vanderbilt trial. It was always a damn train wreck. The women kept to themselves and their dark stallion stood at the fence line and called out to Sheba and Jo-Jo, paced up and down, lonely and, like the rest of the world, without a job.

Abel rolled the knob through the landscape of Central Texas radio, through WBAP out of Fort

Worth and KVOO from Tulsa until he found the *National Hayride*. There was a crackling burst of either static or applause. Alice clattered among the dishes and the flatware. She sang along with the staticky tenor of the music:

I want to be a cowboy's sweetheart
I want to learn to rope and to ride...

He listened to her and outside the windows the blue night sank in, and the horses settled among themselves which one had priority at the hay bunker. The government had paid him for his underweight cattle and shot them and brought in relief labor to bury them below the house in an eroded ravine. He understood it was to prevent overgrazing but it was still hard. Now the grass was supposed to come back but you can't have grass without rain.

Alice always had something useful to do no matter what age she got to. He had grown useless. He longed to plow a field again, set in good Red Top sorghum even if he had to drag the sulky plow through baked hardpan. But his old work team was so used to being retired he doubted if he could get a harness on them without a knock-down, drag-out fight.

They sat and ate by the light of the kerosene lamps. In her reflection Alice tipped her cottony head from side to side as Bob Wills and the Light Crust Doughboys sang *Take me back to Tulsa, I'm too young to marry...*

Alice said, 'Abe, have you always been faithful to me?'

He stopped chewing. He stared at her. He swallowed and then he said, 'Well, Alice. You know I have.'

'Even when you all were out there working on the Pecos high bridge?'

'You and I were just engaged then.'

'Ha. I knew it.'

'Alice, we were living in tents in Langtry and eating armadillo.'

'Mexico wasn't five miles away.'

Abel laid his fork down. 'Well, the foreman wanted ten feet of iron a day and nobody was stopping for a quick dally with a señorita.'

'I just wanted to know.'

'How come?'

'I thought you ought to get a prize. You should get an award. We could get one up from the Rotary Club there in Mineral Wells.'

'Well, Mother!' He stared out the window. 'How would you prove it?'

'Word of honor.'

He was silent for a long time. 'Word of honor. There you go.'

They finished their supper. Alice washed the dishes and then sat down with a dress and a needle and thread. Her white hair was cut short and fluffed out in curly waves around her head. She looked like Harpo Marx. Sometimes Abel thought all she needed was one of those ooga horns.

'What are you doing this week?'

'I don't have much to do, Mother. I finished clearing them seedlings last year. It was something to do anyhow.'

'You could take up sewing.' She smiled and held the dress out to him. The needle and thread were thrust in the collar. 'I'll never tell.'

'Where would I hide the evidence?'

'I'll take the blame. I'll say it was me.'

Abel leaned back and smiled at her. 'All right, I guess it's time to confess.'

'Here it comes,' she said.

'I rode in a sidesaddle once.'

'You did not!' Alice stared at him.

'I did. It was before we were married. There wasn't anybody to home, there on Mama and Daddy's place. And Mama's saddle horse was standing tied ready for her but she was in the kitchen arguing with Fat Cissy Cramer. I knew that was going to take all day.

'And I thought, "I've got to see how they ride in them." So I got in the damn thing and got my leg over the leaping horn and went trotting around the barn lot and then I heard somebody holler, some neighbor had come up, and I about went into a heart attack. I couldn't get loose from it. I had the damnedest time getting *out* of it.' He snorted into his handkerchief and then tucked it away.

Alice began to laugh.

'It's hell to get out of them. I nearly killed myself. I thought, "If I get hung up in this sidesaddle and I'm getting dragged around the barn lot when somebody comes in, I'll have to pack up and quit the country."'

'Who was the neighbor?'

'Thankfully it has been erased from my mind. I am going to forget my own name here one of these days.' In his mind he twisted at a doorknob that would not open. It made him impatient. Then it opened. 'Everett's youngest sister,' he said. 'I think.'

They fell into silence and sat listening to a newsman talk about all the alphabet agencies that were to stem the dust storms and get the factories thumping away again. The question about faithfulness, he felt, still had not been deflected even with the sidesaddle story.

He said, 'Do you have any confessions to make this evening?' He glanced up at her and observed with interest as she stitched, and folded his hardened hands one over the other.

'Give me a couple of days and I'll see if I can match that one.' She shook her head. 'The things I don't know about you.'

The fire ate its way through mesquite wood. The two cows he and Alice still kept grazed in the harvested milo field, taking up the gleanings with their ponderous thick tongues. He thought he might go out to the barn and do something to the harness. He might put a saddle on Jo-Jo and tell Alice he had to go out and check on the salt trough. But instead he sat and watched the road for another hour as the possum-belly trucks went past carrying stock from Comanche County. They would kill them and can the good ones and the canned meat would go to the relief agencies. The cans would be placed into the hands of those who had nothing to eat but the gristly meat that the government handed out to them, and they would be grateful for it.

In Mineral Wells the wind bullied scraps of flying cotton from the cotton gin. Buyers stuck their long knives deep into the six-hundred-pound bales to test the quality of the farmers' cotton and loose bits of lint sailed into the air. There were very few bales at all. What the boll weevil had not eaten the drought had baked crisp. The men waited anxiously, leaning on the wagon wheels, talking and smoking. The crop was very poor, and when they bedded up and plowed the stalks under it had sent dangerous columns of dust into the air.

It came salting over the town, a vague snow of lint. Elizabeth Stoddard and her sister-in-law Lillian Stoddard and Violet Keener sat around the Keeners' kitchen table.

'The county is going to let us pay a hundred dollars for now,' said Elizabeth. 'And twenty a month. That's as much as Mayme makes.'

Lillian placed her reddened hands together. 'I'm sorry about Jack,' she said. 'I didn't want to say much more with Bea there.'

Elizabeth turned her coffee cup around on the saucer and then back again. They wanted to hear all about Jack now that the girls weren't here. Stories like big ripe watermelons shattered open into bleeding hearts.

'You knew about him for a long time, Liz.' Violet patted her arm. 'I always had my doubts.'

Elizabeth blew her nose again. She got up and walked to the window to see the ordinary streets with ordinary people walking down them because she was about to cry again and she was tired of crying, it made her face hurt. She was a

135

good-looking woman but it was difficult to say in what way, for her features were so perfectly regular that there was nothing remarkable in her face at all; she had a wide smile, when she smiled, and ordinary brown hair and blue eyes.

'Jeanine was always his little friend,' said Liz. 'She got better treatment than her sisters. She lied for him.'

'Don't blame her,' said Lillian. 'It's not fair.'

'It's not a matter of blaming,' she said. 'Just makes me hurt when I think of it, that's all.'

'You knew it before, Liz.'

'I didn't want to know.'

She began pacing again, to the corner shelf with all of Violet's dimwitted doodads on it, china cherubs and a Bakelite soldier boy with a thermometer sticking out of his head.

'You two said I was supposed to get my mind on something else.'

'Well yes, we thought you ought to.'

'Yes, well, now look here.' Lillian laid out a sheaf of certificates. 'This will take some figuring out.'

Elizabeth sat down again. 'I've been married since I was eighteen and had three girls. And they're going to be gone before long and I'll be alone in that place.'

Violet said, 'Now pay attention, Liz, this is exciting and risky.'

'Yes, look here.' Lillian pushed the papers in front of her. 'We could get rich or end up in the County Home.'

They held the papers in their hands as if they were sheet music and they were about to begin singing. Violet read over the notes she had written down on the back of an envelope in an attempt to understand what the producer had told them in his office at the Baker Hotel.

Elizabeth said, 'All right.' She examined one of the certificates. 'And Jack was always telling me I could never handle money.'

Lillian said, 'Well, there was never much to handle.'

'What do they do?' Elizabeth read one of them. 'It says these certificates give us twenty-five seventy-five thousandths interest in the well. Does that mean the oil?'

Violet frowned at her certificate. It had an official number at the top, along with the words THE BEATTY-ORVIEL OIL COMPANY.

Violet said, 'Yes.' She paused. 'The oil.'

The women examined their certificates with anxious care. Elizabeth moved her lips as she read the fine print. She and Lillian had endured the births of their children without a doctor, they had lived through the anarchy of oil strikes and blowouts and sour gas, they had kept house in two-room shanties, but the certificates and the mimeographed reports seemed dangerous to them. A frightening world of pro rata shares and seismograph readings.

Lillian Stoddard was Elizabeth's sister-in-law, married to Jack's brother Reid when he was there but he was there no longer, absconded at age twenty-eight and Lillian with a girl to raise. Now she folded other people's sheets and towels and ironed their shirts in a Mineral Wells laundry and her girl Betty was selling shoes at the E-Z Step shoe store. Elizabeth took a handkerchief out of her sleeve and wiped the palms of her hands.

'Well, where is it?' Elizabeth tried to remember if she had ever heard of Beatty-Orviel.

'About ten miles north, it's at the edge of that Jacksboro field. A wildcat means anything that's two miles from a producing field.'

'I know that,' said Elizabeth. 'You don't have to tell me that.'

'Have you told the girls?'

'No,' she said, and thought for a moment what it would be like if the well actually came in. If they made money. Actual money.

'Now look here, look here at this other one!' Violet Keener snatched up another paper. This too said Beatty-Orviel Oil Company. 'This one gives us one-hundredth of the leaseholder's oil royalty. Now one-hundredth is per barrel. So we got stock plus a tenth of a penny a barrel.'

'What if it came in,' Elizabeth said. 'Wouldn't that be something?'

The Keeners had left the oil fields early on. Joe Keener had gone to work for the telephone company instead. They had chosen whatever was staid and dull and predictable, so they had the kind of home that Elizabeth had always longed for. Elizabeth examined the borders of the certificates, the elaborate Victorian designs. She had put into it almost all they had. But still she thought of objections so that when they argued with her and disposed of her doubts she would feel better.

'That producer is hoping this well doesn't come in,' said Elizabeth. 'Then he doesn't have

138

to pay off.'

'But he's got a top geologist!' said Violet. She pressed her voice into the upper registers like a cheerful radio announcer. 'He showed us the seismograph reports!'

Elizabeth raised her head. 'I don't know why I did this,' she said. 'But I did it.'

Lillian and Violet glanced at each other.

'For entertainment,' said Lillian.

Lillian held the seismograph reports that had been mimeographed in sticky purplish ink. The producer Albert Spanner had extracted more than a hundred dollars altogether from the three women. Violet came to look over Lillian's shoulder and read the figures again. They had all read them several times over but the phrases *Woodbine pool* and *anticline trap* and *promising seismograph registration* were so reassuring.

The coffeepot rattled its glass topper and Violet poured them all more coffee.

'I think our twenty-five seventy-five thousandths come out of the oil.' Lillian took up her pencil and tried to figure out what her twenty-five dollars would bring her.

'Think of what-all has to be paid before we see a cent,' said Elizabeth. 'All those other people Mr. Spanner has sold certificates to, and you got to pay your driller and his crew, and people have to haul things. They got to lay pipe to get it somewhere.'

Violet said, 'But listen, what if the price of oil goes up? Y'all never thought of that.'

Lillian said, 'That's right! Are we tied to the price it first came in at?'

They bent anxiously over their certificates again.

'No, here it is. Initial production sale ... pro rata. That's what pro rata means. If the price of oil goes up, we'll get more.'

Elizabeth said, 'Come to think of it, I remember plenty of wildcats that came in. Kilgore wasn't anything but independents. They drilled a well right in the churchyard in the middle of town.' She might be able to make some money on her own, it was a surprising and happy thought. Her very own money. If the well came in. The happy thought was irresistible and warm, tranquil.

'And then the big operators come and buy you out,' said Violet.

Lillian had big, wide shoulders and did herself no favors with her crown of tightly plaited braids. There was nothing yielding about her.

'I never paid much attention when Reid and us were in the field.' She read over the report, written in stiff and legal men's language. She held it in her large hands, they were shiny and cracked from detergent and heavily muscled from lifting the ironing beams of the Sno-White Dry Cleaning and Laundry. 'I was trying to make a woodstove out of a fifty-five-gallon steel drum while Reid and Jack were hauling pipe and going to the beer joints. Burned shingles in it, that were laying in a heap from where somebody tore down a bunkhouse.'

'We had one too,' Elizabeth said.

'Yes.'

'You sat it up on Garden Valley tomato cans. For legs.'

140

Violet got up and went to the cookie jar to lay out a plate of sugar cookies. An offering of delicacies, when they spoke of the hardships she had avoided by the simple solution of marrying a dull regular guy and living a boring ordinary life in one single place.

'I'm glad Joe got out when he did,' Violet said. 'After those men got killed at the Mexia blowout, he said, "That's it for me."'

'This well is going to come in.' Lillian slapped her papers down on the table.

'Yes, it could come in,' said Elizabeth. 'It could come in at a barrel of salt water a day and them having to pump it to get it out.' She twisted her wedding ring on her finger. She looked around at the neat kitchen with its pop-up steel toaster and the bright squares of linoleum. 'I should try to get work somewhere, I guess. Maybe at the laundry.'

'Just hang on and see, Liz,' said Lillian. 'Wait and see.'

'I sort of wished we would have gone to the oil strikes with you-all,' said Violet. 'All your-all's stories.'

'No, you wouldn't have wanted to go,' said Elizabeth. And an image flashed through her mind of a man running through the streets of Ranger with a dead child in his arms and a crowd following behind and all of them screaming for the doctor and the child covered with mud, drowned in an abandoned slush pit. And how she had seized her girls close and backed against the wall of the Blue Eagle Café when he ran past, gripped their hands as if she would link and forge

141

them all together, a chain that like the circle would be forever unbroken. Elizabeth stared at the ceramic tiles of the gas heater. Thus it was they had brought oil to the cities of the East. 'You wouldn't have, either, Vi. Those stories were hard bought. Those stories come at a high price.'

CHAPTER TWELVE

Elizabeth drove out of Mineral Wells, on State Highway 66, toward the big oil field that lay just at the county line. She was driving the Keeners' car with great caution, it was a nearly new Studebaker with an ornate steering wheel. She wore her maroon coat and her hat and her gloves.

The field had been brought in by Magnolia a few years ago. Most of the wells were now in production; only a few other wells were being drilled. Making hole, the men said. The horsehead pumpjacks seemed like alien beings, lately come to the country and still confused as to their whereabouts. They worked away untended, nodding and nodding, as if perpetually agreeing with everything, with the state of the weather and the cattle strolling by and the machines and the people in the fields, white farmers and black farmers and the hired families, scrapping the fields, taking up the remains of the cotton from its clawed husks that tore the fingers.

The pumpjacks stood on an upright beam called the Sampson post, and across this was laid the walking beam. On one end of the beam was the heavy horsehead and on the other end the counterbalance, and thus like great seesaws they tilted up and down, up and down. The horsehead and the counterbalance lifted and sank with a perpetual creaking and thudding noise. From the horsehead end was suspended the sucker rod, which plunged thousands of feet into the ground and drew up the oil.

Throughout the field stood several derricks, slung with giant block and tackles, and below these, men shouted to one another. The field was thriving with the noise of engines, the rolling crash of the draw works. The oak leaves were rust-colored now with the cool weather, and along the creek bottoms the pale-bodied Texas persimmons scattered yellow leaves like coins.

Elizabeth drove through the main gate. It was only a quarter mile to the engine house and the office. She drove slowly down a good hard road of gravel between rigs, passing men carrying their lunch boxes, looking for a place to sit and eat their sandwiches, for it was now nearly noon. They laid out their food carefully, everything about them was careful, they had the gravity of men who knew they were lucky to have jobs, and food in their lunch pails. The sun gleamed off the slush pits. The gray chemical mud boiled up under the pressure of hammering pumps.

She came to the office where a man stood in front of the corrugated steel building flipping through sheets of data. It was George Lacey, the connections foreman. He wore a pale brown fedora with a pair of sunglasses tucked on top of the brim, around the crown. There was a pile of cores lying nearby, stone cylinders four inches across and a foot long, drawn up from the deep strata by the core bits. She shut off the Studebaker's engine and got out and walked toward him.

She said, 'Mr. Lacey?'

His head jerked up. He was startled by the sound of a woman's voice. A woman dressed in heels and a suit and a hat had no business whatever in an oil field. He was also struck by her quiet and simple good looks and her careful small steps across the stony ground.

After a moment's pause he took off his hat.

'I'm Mrs. Stoddard,' she said. 'I was married to Jack Stoddard.'

'Mrs. Stoddard,' he said. The sunglasses fell off the hat and he bent down to pick them up. 'I was very sorry to hear about your husband.' Elizabeth nodded. He had probably heard quite a lot. 'How can I help you?'

'Well, Jack said you owed him money. For hauling a load of acid for you-all.'

'Come in.' George Lacey opened the door of the office for her, walked in after her, and stood at a desk until she had seated herself in a wooden kitchen chair against the corrugated wall. In the corner was a pile of turnbuckles and somebody's oil-covered boots. The ceaseless noise of the oil field came through the unlined wall.

'I'd appreciate it if you'd give me his pay.' She folded her gloved hands on her lap in a soft, formal gesture.

'Yes, I am more than happy,' he said. 'I didn't

know what to do about it.' His hands were raw and big. He took up a checkbook and a pen. He said, 'I can make it out to you if you want.' His hand held the pen suspended over the check, he was about to place her name on the paper. He would learn what her first name was.

'Well, cash would be better.' She tipped her feet forward and back.

'Yes, of course,' he said, and then opened a safe, rolling the tumblers over quickly, then counted out fifty dollars, a month's wages for freighting.

Elizabeth took the bills and shut her purse on them. Part of the money should go for food and gas. And then every cent of it that was left would go into the well.

Lacey said, 'You know, there's another man owes your husband some money. I don't know if he said anything.'

Elizabeth lifted her eyebrows in surprise and her mouth opened. Then she shut it. Good, more money for the well. She smiled again.

'Really? Who's that?'

'A driller named Crowninshield. He's come up from Louisiana for a drilling job for the Beatty-Orviel Oil Company, a little outfit. He's got an old cable-tool rig and contracts out.'

'Oh yes, I know about that well.'

'It's a wildcat, Mrs. Stoddard. I hope you haven't been talked into investing anything in it.'

'Oh, I bought one share.' She smiled and lifted one shoulder in a slight shrug.

The connections foreman picked up several tungsten drill-bit teeth, they lay in a heap on his desk. He rattled them back and forth in his hand

145

and then he dropped the drill-bit teeth on his desk. He felt a powerful urge to protect the woman, to ask her to let him look at what she had bought from Beatty-Orviel.

'Mrs. Stoddard, everybody is in a bind for money what with the bank failures. A person could hope he would hit something and pay off. But don't buy any more shares in it. They're selling shares to suckers for twenty-five dollars each. Don't let them talk you into buying shares. It's a wildcat well. Isn't that a dry hole? I've seen it on an old lease map. They drilled there before.'

She pushed at her jaunty hat and flushed and tucked back the little veil. 'I wouldn't let anybody talk me into buying any more. They already drilled there?' She developed an innocent expression and put a gloved forefinger to her bottom lip.

'Yes, ma'am, and they didn't hit nothing. I understand there's a new producer, and he's selling blocks of shares. He's had a fortune-teller and a water-witcher and a carny barker and I don't know what-all. Everything but a seismograph crew.'

She shook her head. 'I know, it's such a fraud.' She did not say *But he does have a seismograph report!* And she knew she would tell this to the girls, and they would get them out and go over the smeared purple ink yet again. 'Well. And how much did the driller owe Jack?'

The connections foreman reached in a desk drawer and handed her a note. The date on it told her it was from when Jack had been gone for two weeks last year, and now she wondered where he had gone besides hauling the boiler for Crowninshield. Two weeks was a long time to haul a boiler over from Louisiana. She wondered if he had been somewhere else as well. Who he had seen. Staring at the note she understood how suspicion had begun to shadow every past year, every past hour of her marriage, and the wild and improbable thought occurred to her that he could even have another family somewhere, like H. L. Hunt, like old Dad Joiner.

'Fifty dollars. Your husband hauled a derrick for him up to Jacksboro. Crowninshield was out of money and gave him a note.'

'This will be very welcome,' she said.

'I guess he thought he'd mislay the note, so he asked me to hold it for him.' He smiled and was glad to do something for her, anything, a good-looking woman. Prudent and dignified.

'Well, thank you.' She folded the signed note. She had fifty dollars in cash now, and fifty in a promissory note. 'I appreciate it.'

'I'll just indicate here in my books that you took possession of the note. I don't think I know your first name.' Mr. Lacey whisked up a sheet of Magnolia Oil notepaper and took up the pen again with a neutral expression on his face.

She hesitated. She should say *Mrs. John C. Stoddard* and that her first name was no concern of his. After a couple of seconds she straightened her shoulders and said, 'Elizabeth.'

'Very well.' He wrote quickly. 'Just an indication here to myself that you took possession of the note.' He paused. 'You've got three daughters,' he said.

'Yes, I have.'

'Well, I'll tell you what, Mrs. Stoddard. If any one of them can type, well, there's probably work in the oil field office in Tarrant for her.'

'In the office?'

'Yes,' he said. 'There might be a position there in a few weeks and I would be glad to put in a word for her.'

For a moment she was too surprised to speak. 'That would be my oldest, Mayme.' Men were begging for work and he was saying the Magnolia oil field office might hire a single girl. 'A woman? They would hire a woman?'

Mr. Lacey smiled. 'Yes. I would put in a good word for her.'

'Well, I can't thank you enough.'

'My pleasure.'

She smiled in return and then got up and walked to the door. He hurried to open it for her. A roughneck came up; he was carrying a pressure gauge in one fist and both fists on his hips and his battered, oily fedora drooped around his head.

The connections foreman said, 'Just a minute, Lloyd.' Behind them, in the nearest derrick, the enormous block and tackle called the traveling block was drawing drill pipe from the hole, two hundred feet into the air, a joint at a time.

The roughneck said, 'Tom, I wanted to ask you about one of them cores pulled up. If I could have it. It's got a fish in it. For my fish collection.'

'Yes, just a minute.' He lifted his hat again to Elizabeth. 'Like I said about that well.'

'Thank you, Mr. Lacey,' she said. 'I wouldn't put a penny on a wildcat.'

'Mrs. Stoddard, if you need advice or anything, please call me.'

'I will.'

He stood and watched as she got into the Studebaker and drove away down the road between the derricks and the pumpjacks.

Bea had to go out and sit in the fodder shed, on a discarded old kitchen chair with no back, beside the cane shredder to write in her journal. Her breath poured out in frozen clouds. They had had the first freeze of the year on November 12 and it hadn't let up yet but nonetheless the thirteen-year-old was flushed with a grateful, joyous feeling, like somebody pulled alive out of a collapsing house. They had paid an installment on the taxes and they would not foreclose for now. Life was possible. Bea put an old blanket over her knees and laid her journal on it.

She had to find out how you made a script. Where could she find a radio script? If she wrote to *One Man's Family* would they send her an old one so she could copy it, and see how they did it? And how much did they pay you? It was easy to see how you had to write things up for magazines. Radio scripts were mysterious. They were a hidden, arcane secret.

Bea bit the end of her pencil. The eraser in her other hand was gummy and crumbling. There were spiders in this place. She drew her feet together.

At Gareau's Dairy, Mayme joyfully tore off her head scarf and said good-bye to Mr. Gareau. She would wait until she actually went into town to apply for the office job to tell him she was quitting, but in the meantime they all said she seemed so happy. Whistling when she scalded the separator vat and forked chopped cane to the Holsteins in the foggy atmosphere of the cowhouse. Their breath and the manure and the hot milk made a constant lifting mist in the place. Her auburn hair was in spirals when she walked into the front door of the old Tolliver house.

Jeanine bent over the cookstove, drying her own short hair in the rising heat. Their mother was sitting at the kitchen table, worrying over some papers. She had decided to make herself a little desk. Her own desk. Elizabeth's mother's old enamel worktable was on the back porch and she could bring it in and *call* it a desk. Nobody would remember her mother cutting up chickens on it.

'You said you were going to keep house while I made the money,' said Mayme. She sponged off her shiny old gabardine coat and blew the dust from her little cloche hat. 'When are you going to fix the roof?'

'I need help,' said Jeanine. 'There's got to be two of us do it.' Her light-brown hair whipped and crackled through the bristles.

'And you can't just turn those chickens loose in the barn. Varmints will get them. And that's my brush, sister.' Mayme pointed accusingly and then beat on the hat with a dishtowel.

'I'm doing it! I'm closing in one of the old stalls.' Jeanine put the brush down.

'You need chicken wire for a run, Jeanine, and

150

a dog. We need a dog to kill the varmints. Whoever heard of a farm without a dog?'

'Will you let me do the work, Mayme? Who asked you to supervise?'

'Well it's got to get done!' Mayme slapped the hat down on the safe counter. 'And you can't hang colored clothes out in the sun!' Her voice was rising. 'They fade, you faded my only good dress!' She turned to the laundry basket and jerked the dress out in an explosion of cloth, making Albert bolt out of the basket and across the room. Loud voices made him afraid of getting his nose smashed again. Mayme threw the print dress, now faded from navy and green to the color of old denim, at Jeanine. 'Look at that!'

'It's only faded a little!' Jeanine was yelling as well. They were yelling because they were afraid of taxes and drought, afraid of being reduced to taking relief in town, of being alone without their father to help them and it had come upon them suddenly, like a little hot dust devil full of field debris, stinging them. Jeanine's hands shook. 'They wouldn't hire you if you walked in there stark naked with your hair on fire so shut up about it!' She wadded the dress into a tight ball and threw it back at Mayme and it hit the sugar canister and knocked the canister over. Sugar spilled out onto the floor, a rare and precious treasure pouring through the cracks of the floorboards.

'Stop it!' Elizabeth stood up and banged the hairbrush on the table. 'Clean that up.'

Mayme and Jeanine got down on their knees

151

with a spatula and a box top and began to scoop up the sugar. They were rigidly, furiously polite with each other. Jeanine knew she should say she would hang out the colored clothes overnight from now on. She should say *Sorry*. But she was too mad and also hurt and so she didn't. Sugar clung to her fingers.

Mayme caught a ride on Gareau's milk truck to the high school library in Tarrant and returned with an instruction book on typing. She made herself a piece of cardboard covered with rows of circles that said QWERTYUIOP and ASDFG-HJKL and ZXCVBNM and she pressed these imaginary keys with her eyes on the ceiling with great fervor for hour after hour while Jeanine brought in wood and bleached out the tea towels and Bea sat with her homework, her small cat on her lap. The lithograph of the small girl in the forest turned in the rising heat from the stove and the glass flashed and it seemed to Bea the bird's song had turned into fragments of light to enchant the solitary child. Then she sighed and forced herself back to the gray printed page and facts about the produce of the state of Texas. Cotton. Cattle. Oil. Peanuts.

'Try to stay friends with Mr. Gareau,' said Elizabeth. 'We are going to need rides to town in the milk truck to save gas.'

Jeanine heard Smoky calling down in the field. It was a kind of scream. She pulled on her jacket and ran with the halter in her hand across the graveyard, through the peach orchard, then into the field with the seedling cedar. Smoky stood on one side of the fence line and old Mr. Crowser's Jo-Jo on the other. Smoky was trying to paw the fence down to get at him. He wanted to kill him and then he would have the lovely Sheba all to himself. Sheba stood off to one side. She was a dark half-Percheron and very elderly and at this moment, coy. Jeanine saw old Mr. Crowser coming down in a stiff and jerky run. He was also carrying a halter and lead rope.

'Get away, Miss Stoddard,' he said. 'You're going to get hurt. Don't get between them.' He put the halter on Jo-Jo to lead him away. Smoky shifted with tense, small movements, darting back and forth, his two front legs stiff as fence posts and squatting on his hind legs. He wanted to go over the fence and couldn't make up his mind whether he would or not.

'I can handle him,' she said. But she was afraid of him. She held the halter in her left hand and put her right hand on his neck. His neck muscles were so tense they had the feel of warm iron. She slipped the halter over his nose and buckled it and jerked at the lead rope. 'Pay attention to me,' she said. 'Here, look here.' Her hair flew into her eyes.

'I'll repair this fence line,' Mr. Crowser said. 'But you've got to do something with that stallion.'

'Yes, sir,' she said. She took the slack of the lead rope in her left hand and lifted it. 'He'll mind me.'

Smoky flung his head against the lead rope and suddenly darted his head at her with all his teeth exposed. She struck him across the nose with the end of the lead rope and he reared. She held on and pulled him down.

'Young woman, you are going to get yourself killed,' said Mr. Crowser. He turned back to the barn with Jo-Jo following. 'Keep him in the barn for a couple of days while I repair this fence.'

It took a long time to get Smoky back to the old sugar barn. It was like fighting with a tornado on the end of a rope. He circled her and once stood very still, watching her, as if he would charge. He was thinking about it. By the time Jeanine coaxed him into the barn she was sweating and shaking.

She rested for a while and then got up and warmed water to wash out the juniper green silk. She had to do something about Smoky Joe. When he got near a mare he became some other creature. He became volcanic. He was no longer her friend. He was nobody's friend. She plunged the silk into lukewarm water and chipped soap into the tub. She handled it very carefully. She would make a pretty dress for Mayme from it and then they wouldn't be mad at each other anymore. When she was done it hung on the line with the sun behind it sinking into a dust haze, and the material lifted and sank like a pale flag.

Mayme put on her faded good dress and the shiny gabardine coat, and drove the Ford truck with its balding tires into Tarrant to apply at the oil field office. They hired her.

CHAPTER THIRTEEN

It was as if he were pulling the calf out of a cave and some great force that had nothing to do with the cow had hold of the other end of it, and would not let it go.

Everett had a piggin string wrapped around the calf's front feet for a handhold. He tore the calf out of its mother with all the strength of his back and arm muscles. The cow struggled to get up, her tongue thrust out of her mouth. His boots made crackling sounds as he slid around in the crisp, dusty soil. His horse stood tied to a little persimmon tree and the dog lay at his feet, both of them staring at this difficult birth with a kind of dread interest.

The calf slid out in a rush of fluid and with it came the entire uterus, flowing out of the cow and turning inside out, prolapsing, a sliding sack of flesh the size of a sleeping bag, shedding its red lining. The cow made a gasping noise and she lay in a great mound, lifting her head again and again.

He tied the umbilical cord in two places, four inches apart, with twine. He cut between the knots with his penknife. He threw his slicker over the calf and pegged it down around it with rocks. It was a bull calf. He fished around for the roll of gauze bandage in his saddlebags and found it. He knelt down and began to wind it around and around the prolapsed uterus, now stuck all over with twigs and the small leaves of the Texas persimmon. There was blood all over his coat. He was smeared with fluids. Every predator within miles would be lifting its head, opening nostrils, licking its muzzle.

The bovine uterus was a great unwieldy bag that weighed more than thirty pounds. It began to take on a manageable shape as he wound the gauze bandage around it until it was the shape of a column. His hands seemed very old, older than the rest of him. They were spotted with white scars. They were difficult to operate. He got to his feet.

'Get up,' he said. She made a mawing, blatting sound. 'Get up, goddamn it.' Her big hooves scrabbled and made grooves in the dust and ripping up the shiny, elastic stems of the leather plant. He knelt at her head and held her muzzle in one hand, clamping her mouth shut and with his other hand shut her nostrils and cut off her wind.

She fought with the last of her strength against suffocation and suddenly plunged to her feet, back end up first and then the front and Ross jumped to get out of her way. She swung her head and knocked his hat off. He kicked it aside and kept one hand on her. She was swaying. 'Good girl,' he said.

The prolapsed uterus, bound into a long column, hung from her rear end. He pushed it back into her, unwinding the bandage as he fed the internal organ back into the cave of her body. The smell of birth and its detritus all around him in the crisp and burning drought lands. He put his hat back on after he wiped his bloody fingers on his shirt. He stripped the slicker from the newborn bull calf, and got it on its feet, and milked the cow of some of the birth milk. He opened the calf's mouth and thrust it in. He stroked his hard fingers over the calf's eyes and dug matter out of its nostrils and wiped the matter on his cracked chaps.

'Come on, baby.' He held the calf between his legs, and pressed the teat at his mouth. 'Come on, sport, I been waiting for you a long time.'

The calf sucked one suck and turned his head up to the empty blue sky as the heavy cream rolled down its throat. It opened its perfectly fitted mouth and closed it again and sucked again, and the stuff of the new world poured into its body and with a sort of finality it sucked again and was committed.

He waited for a while. Then he untied his horse and held the rein with one hand and picked up the calf with the other. He threw the off-rein over the horse's neck and stepped up into the saddle. It was a clumsy thing to do with the little brush carbine sticking up out of the scabbard and the loose-limbed bull calf slipping under his arm.

The horse took in a deep breath of the wind to see what information might be riding down on it. Then he turned his head quickly to a clump of little live oaks and cedar. His ears were stiff as buckram. Something had come along already, probably a coyote or a fox, but nothing to challenge a man on a horse. The dog started off across the stony ground toward whatever it was, but Ross whistled him back. Then he lifted the reins and they moved off, downhill, the cow trailing after, bawling for her calf. He wanted her to walk very slowly or she would come apart again. They passed by the ravine where the government men had buried his shot cattle. Some of the skulls and bones were exposed, scoured by the dry wind.

At the barn he put the cow into a stall and the calf in the straw beside her. His son helped to hold the cow while he took a jerrican and poured five gallons of water down into her uterus. The weight of the water would settle it and hold it in place until the tissues reattached themselves. He led the bay gelding into the fairway and shucked off the saddle and the rifle scabbard and the blankets and carried it all into the tack room and shoved it onto a saddle tree. He hung the bridle over the horn and turned the bay out into the lot. The bay had had a hard ride with double weight and wouldn't be worth a crying dime for two days. He put his hand on the boy's shoulder and they turned toward the house, where it drowsed under the bare limbs of the mesquite and the pinwheel of the windmill fan sailing stationary with its long blades. His gray stud Kat Tracks ran down the fence line and lifted his muzzle in the air with a feline curiosity to take in the smell of the new calf.

The cook came into the kitchen in his rubber apron.

'Yo, Jugs,' said Ross.

Jugs said, 'What is it?'

'Bull calf.' Ross picked up a scrap of paper from the kitchen table. It had columns of figures on it and he smeared the paper with cow blood.

'Is that it?'

Ross tried to wipe off the paper. 'That's it.'

'No branding crew this year.'

'Nope. We can do it ourselves. Me, you, and the boy.'

He laid down the paper and then went upstairs to Miriam's room. He searched through the drawers of her vanity for a little three-minute sand glass he had given her years ago. Brought it back from a trip to San Antonio. He found it in the second drawer along with a hank of ribbon. *The Magic of Old San Antonio,* the glass said. He blew the dust from it and took it downstairs and sat it on the kerosene stove and lit a burner. He filled a shallow pan with milk from yesterday's milking and then broke three eggs into the pan and turned over the three-minute glass.

He heard shots from the barn; a twenty-two. Innis was shooting rats. They nested in the four-hundred-pound mohair bags, chewed holes in them and made themselves comfortable in the world's most expensive fiber. There was at present no place to sell it except in the East. He turned to the kitchen table and again went over his figures. So much for the shearing crews and so much for the shipping and so much for a train ticket to Woonsocket, Rhode Island, where most of the mills were shut down by strikes. Several people had been shot dead by the police. He would keep taking whatever he could get and storing it if he could keep the rats from

159

establishing entire rat cities and rat undernations in it. This was called betting on the come. He had lost all his cattle except seven breeding cows and out of them he had got the bull calf in the barn and four other heifer calves.

Someday the grass would come back, someday there would be a market for angora coats and sweaters, and the military would need mohair for uniforms and flight suits. If they got into a war the four-hundred-pound bags would move quickly. In the meantime he had a match for Kat Tracks and that should bring in some money. He smelled something burning and the cook ran in the door.

'Shit, boss, it's boiled over and them's the last eggs.'

Ross took the pan by the handle and walked to the back door and threw the smoking eggs and burnt milk into the hardpan dirt of the backyard. He said, 'Well, at least I still got my whiskey.'

His son walked up with five rats by the tails. He stepped around the mess of burnt eggs and milk.

'Was that my breakfast?' he said.

'Yes.' Ross kicked the pan. 'There's grits.'

CHAPTER FOURTEEN

Jeanine sat in Abel and Alice Crowser's kitchen and laid out the map she had drawn of the 150 acres of Tolliver land and where she would begin clearing scrub cedar, which acres she could rent.

But he knew the fields as well as she did. He had been neighbors to the Tollivers all his life, and friends with her grandfather for many years and Jeanine understood that he had stood as guardian and steward to the lower fields all the years of their abandonment and kept them clear. He placed his square forefinger on the map and explained to her that all the properties along the Brazos River were in the main smaller acreages, for farming, while those away from the river and in the other parts of Palo Pinto and Comanche County were much larger and held for ranching. If there were some way to pump water to the fields from the river, and if people could afford it, why, they would snap their fingers at the drought.

He would lease the lower seventy-five acres from them for ten dollars a month and she could drive their tractor. His own land would lie fallow and recover. It was an old John Deere and she couldn't wait to get her hands on it. Alice said Abel wanted to plow with the horses anyway and if she could afford the gas for it then it was all right with her. Alice's white hair sprang up in loops. She leaned over and patted Jeanine on top of her head.

'We never had a girl,' she said. 'It's a wonder I ain't dead from the washing. Couldn't get the boys to help. Your mother said you are a great hand to sew.'

'Yes, ma'am,' said Jeanine. 'I can sew.' She folded up her map.

'Better go see Mrs. Joplin at the Strawn store. Her grandson is marrying Martha Jane Arm-

161

strong and they have some silk they need made into a wedding dress.'

Jeanine bit her lip. 'That's quite a job,' she said. 'A wedding dress.'

'It was some old silk Martha Jane's grandfather got in New Orleans,' said Alice. 'When he went down there and shot somebody and went bankrupt. Now she's getting married to Tim Joplin and they got a use for it. After all these years.'

The John Deere exploded in backfires and smoke when Abel started it up. Jeanine rode on the drawbar behind him, holding to the edge of the perforated seat until she could understand the gears and the line to the lever that lowered and raised the cultivator blades. The clutch was operated by hand and there were two brakes, one for each foot and each wheel. It was confusing. Then Jeanine climbed into the seat and started it up and jammed the gearshift down. The tractor charged forward into the Crowsers' garden fence. She forgot where all the levers were and so roared on and churned up two plowed rows and took down the six-foot deer fence with the fender while nails shrieked as they were ripped out of the posts. Alice put a dishtowel up to her face and turned back into the house.

'Never mind, I'll fix it,' said Abel. 'Back her up.'

Jeanine wrapped her scarf carefully around her neck and shoved the left-hand stick shift backward. There were two stick shifts. She had to remember which was the reverse and what foot went with it. She stared at her feet for a minute as to fix in her mind which was on the right brake and the left brake. She backed up. Abel attached the cultivator to the drawbar and she made it out to the road.

She drove it at ten miles an hour from the Crowsers' place to their own, the cultivator on behind, carried six inches above the road. The great steel wheels banged along on their rigid cleats. She wanted to wave at people passing by, to be jaunty and lighthearted and important, a slight girl in charge of a huge machine, but then they might want to stop and give her advice. So she ignored passing cars and gripped the bucking wheel and crashed through the front yard, through the gate at the sugar barn and then started up the hill toward the orchard.

The brochures from Texas A&M said the grass and weeds would drink up all the nutrients from the soil and she would have nothing but sour peaches the size of marbles if she didn't rip them up and that was what she was going to do, starting today. Big sweet lamps of fruit would shine from the limbs in August. Wasn't that what they had longed for all those years in the oil field towns?

She let go the line that dropped the cultivator blades but it was hung up on something she couldn't see. She got down, climbing over all the levers and gears. She bent over the square links of the chain drive. The engine was still running and she suddenly found she couldn't move her head. Both ends of her wool scarf were caught in the chain drive.

She fought with the scarf with both hands and the John Deere started to move forward into the peach trees. Jeanine was dragged along with it. The square links drew the woolen fabric in their teeth in a slow, regular progression as if it were something very good to eat and they were going to eat it all and her head along with it. The tractor lumbered forward and caught one wheel on a twisted small peach tree and tore the limbs with a shrieking sound. It spun around to the left and stopped and then tore on again. Jeanine began to choke and her head was drawn farther down until it looked as if she were bowing to the cultivator blades and she realized she was going to die in the most horrible way right here in the peach orchard, or at least lose some portion of her face or her scalp. With the cold noise of the gears in her face she came to the edge of a bottomless knowledge of how people could be torn into pieces. The chain chewed and spun and finally ripped the scarf in half. She tore loose and flung herself backward with all her strength.

Bright round spots drifted through the black peach trees. They blanked out her vision wherever she turned, but she reached with one hand to where she knew the spark lever was and she turned it down and the engine died.

Jeanine waited until the luminous round spots diminished into red sparks and faded. She sat for a long time on the steel seat with her hands around her throbbing neck. Water trembled in minute drops on the points of the graveyard fence and on the bayonets of the sotol. She felt very small under the awning of the universe; her life was a pale and insignificant spark, easily extinguished. She swallowed over and over again,

164

trying to open her throat. I must have something to do in life, she thought. *And the Lord said, Jeanine, build me a peach orchard ten cubits by fifteen cubits.* Then she wiped the cold sweat from her eyes and turned the spark lever until the engine started up again and shook all the metal of the engine block and the tall exhaust pipe. She was taken unaware by an overwhelming feeling of gratitude. It was like a warm flood and it flushed the blood into her face and limbs again. Jeanine slowly began to drag the clawed cultivator through the beautiful bare trees even though her hands were shaking. She must never let her mother know this had happened.

That night she ran through the cold hall with the torn woolen muffler in her hands. She could see the marks on her neck in the old mirror with the beveled edges that took up the light in strange prisms all along its edges, as if saying that beyond the ordinary light of day there were other worlds. Behind her, the front double doors shut tight against the weather leaked a suffused gray luminosity into the hall. Her Tolliver grandparents sat beside each other in their ornate frame and stared down into her very thoughts. *It's all right,* they said, *we've seen worse.*

Elizabeth, Lillian, and Violet stood wrapped in their winter coats, in their worn and carefully polished shoes, among the crowd of people who came to watch the driller and his machine arrive. They were in a hayfield that had been sheared off to stubble on a farm north of Mineral Wells. They were at the edge of the Jacksboro field. Elizabeth kicked at the stubble. The farmer hadn't got much in the haying. He and his wife stood on their back porch, looking down the gravel road as if they were watching for mounted enemies or the Second Coming.

The three women stood close together against the wind. Elizabeth felt very widowed, like something unshelled. But inside her there must be some small riverine pearl, however misshapen. She was comforted, standing close to Lillian and Violet. They could all throw their money away together. It was something to keep her mind off things.

The ancient steam boiler sat waiting for the drilling rig. Its chimney rose twenty feet into the air and stared with a metallic hauteur out over the stubble. Nearby were three storage tanks and a separator and a string of used pipe stacked neatly with sawmill sidings as headers. The crowd waited like a theater audience. Cars were parked all around the windmill. Milton Brown scrambled up a pile of dirt to see better and began to scribble notes. He had a photographer with him, but the photographer did not open up his camera.

The promoter was a tall, square-shouldered man in a worn gabardine suit from the early 1930s. He wore a wide tie patterned with art deco zigzags. He had a thick head of curly hair and a broad white smile. He waved his hands at the crowd, he paced up and down on the uneven ground.

'You see!' he said. 'I told you he would make it.'

In the distance a convoy of trucks approached,

raising a cloud of pale dust. At the head of the convoy a flatbed truck carried the drilling rig. It seemed like something from the Iron Age. Its ancient wooden Sampson post waved back and forth as if it were poorly secured. The enormous bull wheel wobbled on its axle. It was made of wood and shod with steel. Most of the metal parts of the machine were rusted, and what was not rusted was covered with flaking dark-red paint, and to power this unsteady rig they had the prehistoric steam boiler. Behind the flatbed was an overloaded 1918 Nash two-ton truck, and following the Nash was a Model A. In this manner apparently the rig and the trucks and the men had traveled all the way from Ruston, Louisiana, to Central Texas towing this parachute of dust behind them over every mile.

'But it's made out of wood,' Violet said. Her voice was high and alarmed.

'I can see that,' said Lillian.

'It's like it was from *Alley Oop*.' Violet wouldn't quiet down. People glared at her and then turned back nervously to watching the machine arrive.

'They can still drill with it,' said Elizabeth. But it was worrisome. It was an old cable-tool rig, and what was needed was something better. A rotary. They had tried a cable-tool here before and nothing came of it but a dry hole.

Lillian shifted her cold feet and watched the outfit come crashing into the field. 'I bet it was put together out of scrap,' she said.

They held their purses in front of them. Violet Keener's coat was tweed with a fox fur collar. Elizabeth's was a worn, dark maroon tabby-weave with square wooden buttons that let the wind through. Her sister-in-law Lillian was wrapped in a man's canvas chore coat and stood in her saddle shoes with a dismal expression and shifted her feet with crushing noises on the frozen rank pasture grasses.

'I don't know what my husband will say when he finds out,' said Violet. 'He'll get that look on his face.' She took hold of the sleeve of Elizabeth's coat. 'Have you told the girls?'

'I told them,' said Elizabeth. 'Jeanine screamed. Mayme sat down and said Oh, Mother. Bea ran off to the bedroom to write it all down.' Elizabeth lifted her chin. 'I can decide can't I?' But her heart was speeding up, now that the machine was here and it was an old cable-tool rig, with a wooden derrick, and she could see plainly before her a slow hole being driven for months and months with no return and Bea going to school in beat-up tennis shoes and more than two hundred dollars owed in back taxes. She suddenly found herself arguing in her head with Jack, who always said she could never handle money.

The crowd of fifty or so people stood with their eyes fixed on the approaching machine. They were farmers and farmwives, several more women without men who might be housewives from town, and clerks and a waiter from the Baker Hotel. People who should have known better.

Milton Brown came over and took off his hat. Elizabeth remembered him. She felt sorry for him with his stutter and his thick glasses. She had heard the Mineral Wells *Star* was paying their

168

reporters in scrip or even produce that farmers brought in to pay for their subscriptions and the reporters and editor had the eggs and beans for dinner. Elizabeth smiled at him and said hello. Milton said he was coming out to visit them one of these better days if there were any better d-d-days now that we are all reduced to a b-b-barter economy like cavemen paying for ax heads with turnips and fish.

Elizabeth looked up at the farmhouse; smoke wavered out of a metal chimney and a long-eared dog lay curled up in the rocking chair while the farm couple stood on the steps. The flatbed bullied its way through the front yard and then through the gate into the pasture. It slewed to one side and took out one of the gateposts with a raw, splintering noise and then the convoy rumbled across the stubble. The men were leaning out of the windows of their vehicles shouting directions at one another.

The producer held up one hand and announced to the crowd the present circumstances. He cleared his throat.

He said his name was Albert Spanner. He said, You all know me, you all have trusted my vision here. And in the oil business, vision is what counts. He told them that another outfit had driven the first well here five years before because there was water in the pasture windmill nearby to make a slush pit and a promising formation below. He spoke in a loud voice so they could all hear; the first crew had shot the well in a spectacular explosion with 135 quarts of nitro and half a ton of ball bearings but it hadn't shaken anything loose.

I am telling you everything here, because Beatty-Orviel is an honest outfit. They gave up because they ran out of money. What was left of the first drilling was the cased hole, and the corrugated steel engine shed, two redwood tanks and a separator, some empty forty-two-gallon drums, a broken reel that had held the bailer line.

'Now listen; that first crew said they could not get down any farther unless they used a rotary rig and a rotary rig was a machine for millionaires or for the big oil companies, it was the latest technology and not for independents like themselves running an old cable-tool rig. That was their excuse! Excuses? You've all heard about excuses? And so after one thousand eight hundred feet they pulled up their drill string and off they went. They had no gumption. No stick-to-it-iveness.

'And now the Beatty-Orviel Oil Company has again put together a block of leases and we are going to drill the same hole. But! Beatty-Orviel is going to *win through* where the others failed! All it takes is confidence. Belief. You know when you can smell oil. Remember Dad Joiner. Remember H. L. Hunt.'

The drilling rig sat on its wide iron wheels on the flatbed truck, a 1929 Ford with a stubby nose. On the door panel was a crude but jovial painting of Pluto, the cartoon dog. Pluto's scarlet tongue poured out of his mouth. Two men bounced on the edge of the flatbed as the entire rigging crashed and wobbled its way toward the waiting crowd. The two crewmen riding on the

170

flatbed were singing.

Old Joe Clark had a yellow cat,
could neither sing nor pray,
stuck his head in the buttermilk jar
and washed his sins away...

The convoy arrived at the engine shed and separator, and came to a halt. The driver shut his engine off and got out. The producer walked toward the rig with his hands clasped behind his back and his loud tie waving. The wind drove past and like a pickpocket lifted anything that was loose in its cold and biting rush. The two crewmen on the flatbed stopped singing and stared at the crowd.

The driver of the vehicle walked forward to the producer, and stuck out his hand.

'I am the driller, Cornelius Crowninshield. Captain is what they call me, like Captain Marvel. We had a hard journey but we come through all right. Just took her slow.'

They shook hands. Captain Crowninshield lifted his bowler hat briefly and wiped his skull with one hand. His laced boots were brand-new. So were his hat and overalls. He must have just been paid off his last job, thought Elizabeth, and now he was starting another. A gypsy driller.

The producer said, 'Well, I am glad you're here!' He was performing on an open-air stage for the investors, he was Mr. Interlocutor and the Captain was Mr. Bones. He turned his head up to the drilling rig and portable derrick on the flatbed. 'What year *is* this thing?'

171

Elizabeth and Violet and Lillian and others in the crowd pressed in more closely to hear. Elizabeth was jammed up against an older woman who seemed to be a waitress with her hair in a net and an apron of heavy material. How they dreamed of food and shoes; of bread, made with flour, rising hot and browned inside the cookstove and filling the house with the smell of yeast, and the slick hard shine of brand-new sole leather.

'This here thing was put together in Fort Worth by hand in nineteen and double aught. It was made by hand.' Captain Crowninshield walked over and slapped the metal-shod wooden bull wheel with a theatrical smack. 'Appearances deceive. This here spudder made two thousand feet of hole back there in Louisiana in less than a *month.*'

Elizabeth watched as the farmer who owned the field stepped forward.

The farmer said, 'Well, the fellows that started this well some years ago said they couldn't get down any farther with a cable-tool rig. They said it needed one of those new rotary rigs.'

'Aw hell no,' said Captain. 'They must have been new at cable-tool drilling, either that or they ran out of money.' He hooked his thumbs in the side pockets of his new canvas coveralls as if he were surveying the audience. 'Now, what have we got here for hole?'

'Over here, Captain,' Spanner said. 'Eighteen hundred feet. They capped it about five years ago. I guess the casing pipe is good, but you'll have to see about that.'

At this, the two men on the flatbed jumped down to the ground, as hounds leap to their feet when they hear the word *hunt*, and even spelling the word out has never been known to work. At the mention of *hole* and *drill* and *casing pipe* the two cable-tool men came to stand behind the captain, looking about themselves eagerly. Captain Crowninshield walked over to the wellhead and the producer came after him along with the impoverished investors and the rest of the crew.

Crowninshield said, 'If it's been cased and it's broken up down there, we may have to jack it out. That ain't going to be easy. I guess we could get hold of Erle Halliburton, borrow a casing jack. We'd be ripping out near two thousand feet of pipe in busted-up sections. But if we're lucky it's all there.'

He squatted down on his heels and pried the cap off the five inches of pipe that stuck up above the brown stubble. He stood up and got a dime out of his pocket and lay down again with his ear to the borehole.

He said, 'It's silver that will give you the feel of the thing. A penny won't tell you the truth. Silver has the true ring.' He held up the coin for all to see.

Then Crowninshield dropped the dime down the hole. The ten-cent piece flew into a spiral and sang down the casing. It spun down the walls of the pipe, deeper and deeper, and the long thin whine built and built and then finally the sound whistled into infinity and disappeared at 1,800 feet in a final fluted whisper. Oil lay down there somewhere, if he could only drive this abandoned hole a little farther. Maybe it lay in a pinch-out trap or an anticline trap, poured up against a subterranean wall of impermeable rock salt, dyked in a wide bay below human sight. It had to be felt for blind. Drillers were like blind men in a deep cave, feeling their way along the walls, sightless bandits searching for treasure in the earth's unseen heart.

Crowninshield held his ear to the pipe until the sound gave out and then said, 'It ain't broke, it's all there. It's continuous and it's solid.' He stood up. 'Looks like the slush pit's still good. All right, Andy, Otto, set up the ramp and let's get her off.'

He strolled past the crowd with both hands in his pockets and took no notice of them. The producer trailed behind.

'Go on, Elizabeth,' said Lillian. 'Go on now.'

Violet gave her a little shove. 'Go talk to him now.'

Elizabeth took a deep breath and pulled her gray gloves tight and then walked over to the promoter.

'Mr. Spanner?'

'Yes.'

He turned to her, to her mild and pleasant face, her wide smile. His loud tie beat on his shirtfront in the wind like a single hand clapping.

'Um, the driller there, that Mr. Crowninshield, owes my husband fifty dollars.' She held out the note. Spanner took it and examined it carefully. She said, 'For hauling this boiler up to here this last September.'

'Well, he is going to have to wait a little longer to be paid,' he said. 'But it won't be for very long,

174

madam, not very long!'

'Well, my husband has passed away, Mr. Spanner.'

'Madam! I am so very sorry!' He lifted his hat to her. 'But this well is going to produce, madam, and you will be proud of having lent money to this enterprise. Proud. There is oil down there and it's going to deliver itself into our hands.' He also lifted his porkpie hat to Lillian and Violet, up and down, up and down. 'Now here are two ladies with faith in this well. Mrs. Keener, the other Mrs. Stoddard. They are trusting the Beatty-Orviel Oil Company with their hard-earned dollars. Y'all are in for...?'

'Seventy-five each,' said Violet.

Elizabeth said, 'Well, what I thought was, I would exchange this note for shares. Fifty dollars' worth of shares.'

'Madam! You have made an extremely wise choice!' He turned to another small grayish man sitting with a bored expression in the front seat of his car. 'Let's do the paperwork!'

They rolled the strange machine off the flatbed. Both crewmen and the captain and several volunteers all began to shove. It rolled down the ramps and struck the ground with its iron wheels. Then Crowninshield hooked a chain between it and the 1918 Nash and pulled it into place.

Elizabeth and Lillian and Violet stood for a while, watching them haul wooden boxes and suitcases out of the Nash truck, pack them into the engine shed and set up house. They even had a small cook-stove and a chuck box. The farmer's wife came up to the crew, her full dress skirts were ballooning and her hair sprang out from under a slat bonnet.

'Ma'am,' they all said. 'Howdy, ma'am.'

'Do you-all eat hominy?' she asked. 'Black-eyed peas?'

The men nodded eagerly.

The captain said, 'They'll eat anything you send over, ma'am. Andy here, he used to be a geek in a carnival. He bit heads off chickens and then he got religion and joined a drilling crew.'

Andy lifted his hat again.

'I've eat chicken before,' he said. 'Fried.'

'Tastes just like armadillo,' said Otto.

CHAPTER FIFTEEN

Prince Albert sat on the old well curb and made nervous mewing noises. He was watching the sparrows that lived up in the well cover in their trashy little nests. It was in early December and the entire world of the Brazos valley was crisp and dry and burnt out. Bea had decided to pray that morning that her mother would not throw away all their money on the oil well certificates. She didn't know what else to do. Her mother was going to lose all they had, and then they would take the house for the taxes still owed and this time there would be no rent house to go to. She had wished her father dead and then he had died. But it didn't work the other way around. She could not wish him back again alive out of his jail cell, out of his lonely grave in Wharton. They would be evicted from their own land and house and then they would go and live in a tent under the bridge in Fort Worth. That was where Bonnie Parker and her family lived when Bonnie Parker was a little girl, before she had taken up a life of shooting policemen. When her father was arrested Bea understood that there were unknown depths to which people could fall, when all the structures of the world came loose, the framework gave way. When, like the king, you abdicated.

Bea came out of the back door of the house with a lard pail full of cracked corn for the chickens, in her ragged housedress and tennis shoes without socks. She saw the cat reaching out over the empty space of the well toward the little roof and the sparrows' nest.

'Albert, get away!'

His tail lashed and he gathered himself for a jump. Bea threw down the lard pail, and the bits of corn scattered over the hard dirt. She ran for the well.

'Albert, no!'

He saw her and jumped straight up into the construction of the roof over the well, and when Bea leaned on the well curb to reach for him the entire curb gave way. The mortar that had been dried out by seven years of drought shattered and Bea went down into the well along with the blocks of limestone. They fell alongside her and before her. She fell twenty feet in an endless cascade of rock and showering mortar. She struck the projecting stones of the bottom where the well narrowed and several rocks the size of bread loaves fell onto her head and her legs. There was four feet of water at the bottom. Her head was above water and one arm was jammed between fallen stones and the wall. Far above her was the narrow eye of light from the upper world. She was not entirely conscious. She couldn't tell whether the dripping from her ear and jaw was water or blood. She couldn't make her mouth work.

The water was very cold. She heard Prince Albert making strange noises far above at the edge of the well. Bea could feel a distant sort of panic overtaking her but she seemed to look on her overwhelming fear of being buried alive at the bottom of the well from a faraway place. The well cover was twisted; after a few moments a board fell from it and came turning over and over down the well shaft and struck her foot, but her foot seemed to be connected to some other body. She was drifting in deep December water. She was in the terrible underground. She was in another world, which was deadly, and above her was the old house and the warm stove and Albert.

Mayme jumped out of the Gareau's milk delivery truck at six o'clock and ran inside to turn on the radio so she could hear *One Man's Family* and the evening news. The sun was melting red and flat on the horizon of tabled hills. She beat up corn bread batter and put the pan into the oven. She washed the greens. They would have a good supper that night. In her purse she carried five pounds of bacon. She unwrapped it and cut it into thick slices and put them in the skillet.

Jeanine came in from the fields carrying her borrowed saw. Her wrists above the old leather gloves were torn by cedar. She stood in front of the stove and lifted her head to listen to a distant noise. It was very peculiar. An animal noise, a sort of low hoarse crying. There were things out there in the Brazos Valley she knew nothing about.

She said, 'Should I make a fire in the parlor?'

'Not with that cedar,' said Mayme. 'You'll set the chimney afire. When are you going to get somebody to cut up that dead oak?'

Elizabeth had just come back from Mineral Wells with more of the oil-well certificates; she turned from her desk and asked where Bea was.

Nobody knew.

She might be with the Miller kids staying late at school, she might be hidden away in the house somewhere, reading. They searched through all the rooms but Bea wasn't anywhere reading or writing. Still the low crying went on outside, behind the house. Elizabeth stood up and tried to think if there had been any strangers walking down the road during the day. The Lindbergh kidnapping was always on her mind.

'Go to the school,' she said to Jeanine. 'Maybe she's stayed after school with the teacher.'

Jeanine ran most of the mile to the Old Valley Road schoolhouse, but it was closed up and dark. She stopped by the Crowsers' but they had not seen Bea either. The old couple were worried by her breathless question and stood watching her run out the door and down the road standing side by side in a portrait of Gothic alarm.

'Well, where is she?' Elizabeth got up and went to the back porch and they all called her *Bea! Bea!*

'That well curb has given way,' said Jeanine. Prince Albert sat on an upturned lard can beside the well and was making a noise that was not very much like a cat at all. He was howling in a sort of deep singing. His eyes were wide and he cried and cried to them in a low hoarse voice. The chicken feed, a yellow scattering of shorts, was strewn all around him. The cat was staring at them in an odd and disconcerting way.

Elizabeth clapped both hands to her face. 'My Lord he has rabies!' she said. 'He's bitten Bea! She's laying sick and she's in convulsions somewhere!'

Mayme turned and ran back to the porch and stood staring at Albert, as if to keep the porch rail between herself and the cat.

'Do you think?' she said. 'I never saw anything with rabies before.'

'Get the shotgun,' said Elizabeth. 'He is, he's rabid, he's bitten Bea.'

Jeanine said, 'No, Mother. He's not rabid.' She held out her hand and walked toward the cat and called to him but he evaded her and stared at her and called out again. Jeanine stopped. 'When did the well curb fall in?'

It was growing dark. It was the time of evening when the sun set the low hills afire and the shadow of the old sugar barn poured in a tide of darkness over the house and the back porch and the well and the twisted cedar that guarded the well.

'Push it all in,' said Elizabeth. 'We need to just collapse it completely and stop that well up. Bea could come wandering back here in the dark and fall in it.' She stepped down the three steps to the bare dusty yard. 'Then I'll go to the Millers and you girls get down to the barn and look there.'

They all three went out to shove the rest of the stones of the well curb into the well. Albert stopped his terrible calling and began to mew. He darted around their legs. They bent over the opening and heard a long exaggerated voice from deep in the well. *Mother Mother Mother.*

They drove Bea to the hospital in Mineral Wells. It seemed to take years to drive the twisted road. Jeanine drove. Mayme and her mother sat holding Bea, laid in the bed of the truck on as many quilts and pillows as they could rip off the beds, her left leg bent at an acute angle, as if there were a new joint in the middle of her shin. Jeanine's hands and legs and coat were covered with mud and torn by the rope they had lowered into the well. Mayme had run to the Crowsers', but by the time Abel got there Elizabeth and Jeanine had rigged the rope to the cedar tree and Jeanine had gone down into the well. She didn't know if she had torn or broken Bea's legs any worse getting her out. Bea's face was covered in blood so that it looked as if somebody had thrown red paint in her face. Her skin was pale blue and splattered with random blood splashes.

Mayme and Abel Crowser put blankets to the stove to heat them and wrapped Bea in them and so they appeared in the emergency room at the

Mineral Wells hospital. The nurse asked if anyone else was hurt. Jeanine's clothes were in such a state it seemed that she had fallen in herself. She was covered in well slime and her shoulders smeared with blood from Bea's head wound, but she told the nurse no. They took Bea away on a gurney. At one in the morning the doctor came to them in the waiting room and said the left lower leg was broken in several places, very badly broken, for them to go somewhere and get some sleep and we'll see in the morning how things are.

They slept at Violet Keener's house, on the floor, in the blankets they had wrapped Bea in.

The next morning all three of the women walked to the hospital from Violet's. They ate biscuits as they walked. Violet could not make them sit and eat breakfast nor could she let them go without food so they carried the biscuits with them. The streets were full of people going to work, men in suits going to the oil company offices, the boys selling the Mineral Wells *Star* and *Grit* and the Dallas papers.

'That cat of hers was trying to tell us,' said Jeanine. She started to cry again.

'Yes, but I don't speak cat,' said Mayme. 'Hush, Jeanine, don't cry in front of the doctor. They don't like it.'

The doctor was a short man with a fringe of hair around his head and a loose lower lip that he constantly caught up with his upper teeth. He walked on rubber-soled shoes and wore a white coat with a stethoscope looping out of his pocket. A nurse brought them coffee and said these kinds of accidents happened and we never know when they are going to happen, things are peaceful one minute and then, you know. Elizabeth nodded. *Yes,* she said, *yes yes.*

'Mrs. Stoddard, she's going to be fine.' They waited. 'She's had a scalp laceration. Not serious. Sewed it up. We've taken X-rays and her pelvis is most likely slightly fractured, but there's nothing to be done about that, except lying quietly for a month. Now her left lower leg is broken in several places, both bones of the lower leg. That's a problem.'

Elizabeth said, 'I see.' He was talking about money. This was now a money problem. Bea was alive and her skull hadn't been broken and she was in her right mind, she had her wits, and now the problem was money. They didn't have it. She, Elizabeth, her mother, had thrown away almost all they had on a wild gamble and there was no getting it back.

'She needs extensive work if she is not to have one leg shorter than the other.' He clasped his hands together and sat down across from them with the knot of his pale, clean hands between his knees. 'We can cast it now as it is but it will end up shorter.' He cleared his throat. 'Several inches.'

'Please just tell us what she needs,' said Elizabeth.

'I'll send her home now to save you the cost of the hospital,' the doctor said. 'But the leg needs a bone specialist. It needs surgery. I wouldn't

183

attempt it myself. It needs a specialist who will insert pins and who knows how to set the right sort of cast. That's how it is.'

'Where?' said Elizabeth.

'We can do it here, but we'll have to have a specialist come from Dallas.'

'Get him,' said Jeanine.

Her mother turned to her for a moment and then looked at the doctor.

'What kind of arrangements can we make?' she said.

He hesitated. How many farm accidents had come in here, mangled arms and legs, tractor accidents, children kicked in the head by horses, unloaded guns going off, not to speak of tuberculosis and cancer and pellegra, and the loved ones asking what kind of arrangements they could make.

'I'm going to sell Smoky Joe,' said Jeanine. 'I know where I can sell him.'

Elizabeth thought for a moment and then she said to the doctor, 'Just let me know when you have some kind of estimate.'

'I will,' said the doctor.

'We can do it,' said Mayme. 'Whatever it is.'

They spent the morning fussing over Bea, who lay on a narrow cot in a ward with a great many other people. It was a pauper's ward, thought Jeanine. And we're paupers. Bea had a large bandage around her head, and her leg was cast in a light plaster-and-webbing cast because it would soon have to be broken off again. She sobbed and swallowed repeatedly because of the pain and then she wanted a mirror so she could see her head bandage and when the nurse brought one she said in a shaking voice that it was very dramatic and the nurse laughed and patted her shoulder.

Bea smiled when they lied and told her that Prince Albert had led them to her. He had rushed into the kitchen and then to the door, leading them outside, he had done everything but point his paw down the well. They would wait until later to tell her that Elizabeth had come near shooting him, or maybe they would never tell her. Maybe they would never tell her how they had almost shoved the rest of the well curb down onto her. For now Bea was made very happy by the fact that her cat had cried out, and galloped around their legs, and had dashed back and forth between them and the well. It was important that she be happy. Her mother would not distress her by crying, thinking of her youngest daughter lying crushed and dying of the cold at the bottom of the well while they made supper and listened to the radio. Elizabeth would not say *My baby, my baby, we almost lost you.* Would you buy him some liver? Bea asked. And they said they would. The nurse stood by and listened. She liked to hear this. Times were hard. Very hard, and once in a while people like to hear stories with happy endings, pets saving their owners, for instance; stories of courage and hope. Or just go to a Busby Berkeley movie and watch a lot of people dancing.

Jeanine walked into the Baker Hotel. She approached the telephone on its stand, a new

185

rotary telephone. She did not know how it worked. The clerk dialed the rotary phone for her and the operator said a call to Comanche would cost fifteen cents and she paid it, and took the heavy receiver in her hand.

She heard Mr. Everett's voice on the other end of the line. Long bars of noon sunlight shone on the glossy black-and-white tiles. Men sat in the leather chairs of the lobby and smoked and read their Fort Worth and Dallas newspapers. A paper cut-out of a Thanksgiving turkey was pasted to the restaurant entrance and behind the desk the clerk's radio said Hitler was sending thirty thousand Jews to resettlement camps. His voice startled her.

'Hello,' he said.

'Mr. Everett, this is Jeanine Stoddard.'

'What can I do for you, Jeanine?'

'Mr. Everett, Daddy said you once offered three hundred dollars for Smoky Joe Hancock. Do you still want him?'

She spoke very loudly in order to cast her voice all the way to his ranch in Comanche County, until she saw that the hotel clerk was putting his finger to his lips. She said *All right, all right,* and then listened carefully. He sounded like one of the thin electric voices on the radio.

'Maybe. I have to ask you, what's wrong with him that you're selling him now?'

'Nothing's wrong with him, he's as fast as ever.' She considered for a moment what she should say. 'Bea's been injured and we need to pay for a specialist to come out from Dallas.'

There was a considering pause. She waited

through it. People were looking at her and she needed to go to the bathroom.

'Well, I'm sorry to hear it, Jeanine.'

'Daddy said you'd offered three hundred.'

'I did say three hundred, but that was a year ago and I wasn't tied to it.'

Jeanine felt another wave of anxiety come over her and so she cleared her throat and pretended to be firm. She stepped back and forth as far as the telephone cord would allow.

'Mr. Everett, you don't really have me over a barrel like you think you do. I have another offer for him, and rather than go to the trouble of hauling him all the way over to you I'd just as soon sell him to somebody closer to here. I wouldn't have to pay so much for gas.'

'Who made you an offer?'

'Charles Findlay told me he was interested. I just called him.' She didn't know what made her tell such an outrageous lie. It was panic. He could easily call old man Findlay and find out for himself.

'He is?'

'Yes, sir. You know he has those Buck Thomas mares there and he is real partial to the Hancock line.'

'When did you race him last?'

Jeanine lifted her head and breathed out through her nostrils slowly so he could not hear how nervous she was.

'He did three hundred and fifty yards in eighteen seconds at Kingsville last year. Me and Daddy took him there. He was matched against Chimney Sweep and beat him by a long head.

You can call Bill Solwell and ask him yourself.'

She said nothing during the long silence as Ross Everett considered things. Finally he said, 'All right. But I have to ask you to haul him here to my place.'

'What about gas and everything?'

'That's not my problem.'

'All right, Mr. Everett. All right.'

'I once told you to call me Ross. For all the good it does.'

'All right, Ross.'

'I got my gray stud matched against a fellow on the fifth, maybe he'll show up and maybe he won't. There at the sale barn in Stillwater. Here's how you get to it. Do you have a pencil and paper?'

She felt around in her purse with the receiver caught up between her shoulder and her ear. She wrote down the directions.

'All right. How will I know if you're there?'

'Ask people, sweetheart.'

CHAPTER SIXTEEN

The nurses helped them load Bea in the back of the truck on the stretcher as if she were a pallet of grain sacks and gave them an entire list of rules they had to mind very carefully if they were not to injure her leg any further, and let them take the stretcher with them, and stroked Bea's hair and said Good-bye now, honey, we'll see you in a week or so. Another nurse said she wanted Bea to get well soon so she could sit up at a desk and write all her stories and sell them to magazines.

'Oh Bea,' said Elizabeth, and smiled at her fondly and stroked her cheek.

They were given the name of a home visiting nurse. She was employed by the county health department, and it wouldn't cost them anything. Her name was Winifred Beasley, she was very efficient and had a degree in nutrition as well as nursing and was just the most concerned person in the world. She would be out there in a few days to give them a hand.

Jeanine drove so her mother could cry all she wanted on the way home, in the truck cab, where Bea couldn't hear her. When they arrived at the house Elizabeth blew her nose and Jeanine and Mayme carried Bea in on the stretcher, and lifted her onto the bed they had prepared for her in the parlor. She would have the fire in the fireplace and a view out to the front yard.

Abel and Alice came over in their old Model T roadster. Abel volunteered to fill in the well, but Bea heard him and called out, Please don't. Please just fix the curb. She loved the well. It was the most important terrible thing that had ever happened to her.

Abel and Alice walked into the parlor and took Bea's hand; Alice touched the temporary cast and then Bea's head bandage. They shook their heads.

'By golly, girl, we about lost you,' Abel said. 'You've put about ten years on your sisters' and mother's life.'

'But don't fill it in,' said Bea. Her voice was weak and she shifted back and forth as much as she could. She had begun to look like a little old woman, with the pain lines in her face deepening, it seemed, every hour.

Abel said he wouldn't. Instead he and Jeanine mixed mortar and reset the stones, and then tore down the tipped and twisted well roof. Then they covered the opening with hog wire and cemented another row of stones on top. When they were done she and the old man stood with their hands caked with cement watching Smoky gallop across the lower field with his tail in the air, calling out to Sheba. He had worn a path along the fence line as if it were his own private racetrack, he had pounded it smooth with his unshod hooves and raced along it because someday it would lead him somewhere and something important would happen to him. Dust rose up in a cold cloud behind him.

Winifred Beasley came driving into their driveway at five in the afternoon two days later in a dark blue Chevrolet. It was a good car, only two years old. She stepped out in a careful way. She opened the double doors to the house as if the doors were disjointed and she was fearful of them coming apart. She walked into the hallway without a word and then into the kitchen; she gave them a brief, curt bob of her head and asked where Bea was.

'I'm Elizabeth Stoddard.' Their mother turned away from her small desk, and laid down a seed catalog. She stood and faced Winifred.

'Good to meet you, Mrs. Stoddard.' Winifred put her purse on the table. 'And you are Bea's sister?' She regarded Jeanine with a cool stare but didn't wait for an answer. 'My concern is with the child. Where is she?'

Jeanine laid down the load of wood she had just brought in and said, 'In here.'

Winifred walked into the parlor, and as she did she turned one way and then another to see what they had in the house, and what sort of furniture they sat on and the dishes they ate on, whether there were pictures on the wall or a cloth on the table and proper washing facilities. She glanced down at the braided rug made of flesh-colored hosiery and up at the dancing orange pigs of the feed-sack curtains and sideways to the back window with the outhouse beyond.

She stood by Bea's bed and smiled. Her smile was drawn and it made her mouth look square.

'Well, Miss Bea,' she said. 'We're here to make you well and healthy.'

'Good,' said Bea. 'I'm happy to meet you.' Bea went back to staring at the wall and counting the willow leaves on the stained wallpaper. She moved her mouth as she counted in a whisper. She counted between pain pills.

'I am sure you are. I am the county health nurse and I visit lots and lots of families.' She reached down and pulled the blankets up around Bea's throat. 'You must stay warm. How do you use the facilities?'

'The facilities?'

Elizabeth was standing at the door. 'She is lifted

onto a chamber pot,' she said.

'It must be cleansed after every use,' said Winifred. 'And disinfected with bleach or Lysol.' She leaned down and patted Bea's head and parted a lock of hair above the bandage. Bea shrank away and lifted a hand to her head bandage. Winifred grasped her hand and laid it firmly down on the blanket. 'Do not touch that bandage,' she said. 'An infection would be disastrous.' She straightened up. 'Now I must speak with your mother and sister. Is this all you are?' She turned to Elizabeth. 'Just the three of you?'

'No, I have another daughter. My oldest.'

'Are any of you employed?'

'Yes, my oldest is employed.' Elizabeth pressed her lips together and clasped both hands together in front of her, as if she had Winifred Beasley's neck between them. 'Are we to pay you? Is that why you're asking?' She turned her head. Mayme came in the door in a blooming shaft of cold air with a jug of skim milk in one hand and called out to Bea.

'No, you are not to pay me. The government provides this service.' She turned and walked past Elizabeth and into the kitchen and sat down at the table. 'We need to lay out some ground rules here,' she said. Mayme stood and stared at her. 'You're the oldest daughter? Stop staring at me. I am the county health nurse. Sit down.'

Elizabeth and her two daughters glanced at one another but they sat down.

Winifred looked around the kitchen. 'Do you have pencil and paper? I want you to take notes.' Elizabeth got up and stalked into the parlor and came back with Bea's Big Chief tablet and pencil. She sharpened the pencil with the kitchen knife and bent her head to the task so Winifred would not see how furious she was, and would not go away and leave them without help.

'I have in my car relief rations,' said Winifred. 'They are to be used by the injured child. No one else. I will bring in canned milk, beef, beef stock, malted milk tablets, cod liver oil, powdered eggs, and calcium tablets. She needs a nutritious diet in order for the bones to knit. These are strictly, I repeat, for the injured child.'

'We heard you the first time,' said Jeanine. She held up a forefinger. 'The first time.'

'Jeanine, hush up,' said her mother.

'There's a dairy just down the road. I used to work at there,' said Mayme. Her eyes were sparkling with malice. 'I bring home lots of milk every evening. We have milk.'

'Skim?' said Winifred.

'Well, what of it?' Mayme said. Albert slipped in through the window and hurried to sit beside the stove. He stared at Winifred and then walked into the parlor.

'Won't do.' Winifred had little expression on her face. Her repertoire of emotions was clearly very limited, she seemed to vary between contempt and disapproval. Maybe she went to a Charlie Chaplin movie once in a while and laughed but Mayme doubted it. 'Whole milk. Contains butterfat. Our patient in there is below normal weight. But who isn't these days? At any rate, I see you have a cat. The cat is to be kept away from the patient. Also, I congratulate you that she does not have head lice. Do any of you?'

'No!' said Elizabeth. Her pencil point broke. 'Really!'

Winifred stared at her calmly. 'It's very prevalent. Now. I know the cost of the surgery and the specialist will be very expensive. So you are going to be in financial straits.'

'We are not,' said Jeanine. 'We have a horse we can sell, and that's going to pay for it.'

'A horse?' Winifred's eyes widened and she smiled slightly. 'A horse?'

'He's a racehorse,' said Jeanine.

'I see.' Winifred for the first time seemed somewhat interested. 'Why do you have a racehorse?'

Elizabeth said, 'My late husband liked to match race. And when he died we were left with the horse.'

'What happened to your husband?' Winifred said. 'I am used to being nosy. I have no reluctance about being intrusive. My concern is with the patient and the entire emotional and social environment that affects the patient. Was it a communicable disease?'

'No, sour gas,' said Elizabeth.

'And he gambled. On horses.'

'Yes.'

Winifred pressed her thin lips together. She was taking mental notes. 'Why did Bea fall down the well?'

'Well, she was leaning over the well curb and it gave way.'

'Is that your water source?'

'No, we're using the windmill water.'

Winifred stood up. 'You two.' She pointed to

Jeanine and Mayme. 'Come and help me bring in the supplies.' She pulled on her gloves. 'I must tell you that you are three women and a seriously injured child with little income on an isolated farm. I want you to keep in mind that there is a very good home established for dependent and neglected children who are not orphans but whose parents are unable to care for them. Buckner's Home for Children in Dallas is known worldwide. If and when you find yourselves out of money and out of food supplies, and in need of yet another operation for Bea, you will keep that in mind. Were they to take her in, the operations would be paid for.'

They went out to Winifred's blue Chevrolet and packed in the relief supplies, cans and sacks and a gallon tin of Lysol. Jeanine felt obligated to place it in a stack beneath the window away from the Hamilton safe. She hated herself for being submissive, for not grasping Winifred by her jacket lapels and flinging her out of the house.

CHAPTER SEVENTEEN

The next morning very early Mayme opened the cookstove door to check on the corn bread and then took it out and left it on the sink to cool. It sent up steam against the window and the winter stars. Jeanine carried a lamp downstairs, the light bobbing down the steps. Her clothes hung on the back of a chair in front of the stove to warm. She

195

pulled on a shirt and her Levi's and then her tweed jacket. She scraped a bit of her lipstick from the tube with a hairpin. It was almost gone. She sat the dark green fedora on her head as if it were armor, a miner's helmet. In the kitchen she took a wedge of hot corn bread and spread butter on it, wrapped it in a piece of newspaper, and gave her sister a hug for good-bye. Then she went out to back the truck up to the trailer, and then to catch Smoky.

He seemed to know he was leaving. He read her intentions in her hands and her nervous walk, the strain in her voice. She could not catch him for an hour, he bolted from the graveyard fence through the peach orchard, he roared through the little grove of live oaks and darted into one end of the barn and out the other. Finally he stood beside the gate, trembling and breathing hard, watching her come for him with the halter.

Then it took her another thirty minutes to get him loaded. He balked and fought the lead rope. He didn't want the hubcap full of oats that sat inside the trailer. It was only after she sat down on the trailer fender in despair to think what to do that he became quiet. Jeanine rubbed her rough hands together and asked why he had to make it so hard for her. She didn't know who she was asking. After a moment he cocked his ears and stretched out his nose toward her.

She got to her feet slowly and threw the lead rope over his neck and said, *Load.* And he gave up and walked into the trailer. It took her another fifteen minutes to start the truck. She didn't get away until noon.

She left Highway 80 at Rising Star and drove into Comanche County. It was the time of year when deer came into rut, and a large stag bearing his antlers like a troublesome crown stood staring at her truck before he sprang over the roadside fence. She drove with the cracked window rolled down. People were burning cedar and the smoke stung her eyes.

She stopped at a gas station and asked for directions and then went on toward the sale barn. It was nearing sundown. The sale barn was empty; outside a crowd of men in the unlit grounds, their faces shadowed by hats, their horses tied to trailer slats.

Jeanine got out of the truck. She brushed out her short hair and stood before the side mirror to tie on her silk scarf, with the point down in front, clipped on the round gold-colored earrings. In the mirror she saw a man standing behind her, his hat down and his coat collar standing up. She turned around.

'Mr. Everett?' she said. She walked toward him.

He lifted his hat. 'You're talking to him.' His chore coat was made of a heavy, wooden canvas. 'Do you have that horse?'

'Yes, sir. He's right here. In the trailer.'

'Let's get him into a pen.'

The bulked shadow of the auction barn flooded outward over the gravel, reaching out to the stock pens. He walked up to the horse in the trailer. He regarded Smoky's blunt, prehistoric head and the wired stand of mane, his thick neck.

'This is Smoky Joe Hancock?'

'Yes, sir.'

Smoky lifted his blunt nose to take in the news that the wind brought to him. Jeanine slipped the halter on him.

She said, 'How are your wife and little boy?'

'She's dead.' Ross Everett pushed his hat back by the brim. 'He's alive. He's over there with the men.'

'Oh, Mr. Everett.' Her mouth opened and she put her hand to her lips. Her heart seemed to stop for a moment and she tried to think of something to say, but he seemed to be made of a kind of private granite. Jeanine finally said, 'She's *dead?*'

'She died of pneumonia during that dust storm in '35. They called it dust pneumonia.' Everett turned to watch a horse being unloaded from a long stock trailer. 'And she had asthma.'

Jeanine was silent for a space of time. He searched his coat pocket for his truck keys. 'Well, that's terrible, Mr. Everett. I'm so sorry.'

He nodded. 'Let's see about your horse.' She shrugged up her jacket around her shoulders. The wind slapped the silk scarf against her collar with small rippling sounds. 'Get him unloaded and let him buck it out.'

Ross Everett and two other men stood watching her swing up onto the trailer fender. She untied the horse where he stood, riding backward. One of the men came forward to offer to help but Ross Everett motioned to him to leave her alone. He watched as she shoved the gate open, and Jeanine and the horse both jumped down from the trailer at the same time, side by side. She took firm hold of his halter rope as the dark horse charged around against it.

Everett said, 'All right,' and then walked straight on past her toward the livestock pens. She hurried to catch up.

Smoky Joe galloped around the small pen in short rushes. He stopped for a moment and stood stiff-legged and called to the mares in a violent shivering whinny. He bucked himself into the air with all four hooves off the ground and landed and hurled himself into the air again, shaking off all the hard miles.

Jeanine shook out the leather halter to straighten it. 'I guess you still want him?'

Everett stood with his hands in his pockets and watched the horse.

'We got a match race going here, Miss Stoddard. Let's see how he does.' His voice was hoarse from smoking.

'You said three hundred.' She reached out and grasped the canvas sleeve of his chore coat.

He glanced down at her hand. 'I know I did. I also said I wasn't tied to it.'

'Mr. Everett, you didn't tell me I would have to race him.' Jeanine began to roll up the lead rope in loops.

'Well, girl, I didn't tell you to come or not come.' He seemed preoccupied. 'Have you got a flat saddle?'

'No, I don't.'

'Borrow one.'

Jeanine went back and stood resting against the door of the truck, her hat in her hand. She didn't know what to do, here at the point of handing the horse over to somebody else, or not. In this dark auction yard, the empty livestock pens like a construction of mazes and the sun going down in Comanche County; abandon him in this unknown place to strangers.

Ross Everett came and sat down on the running board. Jeanine listened to the rasp as he struck a match to his cigarette. She lifted her head. The flame lit his face for three seconds and then he shook it out.

Jeanine bit her lower lip. 'He hasn't been warmed up.'

Ross Everett sat without saying anything for a while and then took off his hat and turned it in his hands. As if he were searching out holes in the felt or maybe wondering if it were time to buy a new one.

'Jeanine, I know you need the money.'

'Maybe I changed my mind,' she said.

'Maybe.'

'But you want to see what he can do,' said Jeanine.

'That's about it.'

Jeanine regarded the low hills sliding off into the horizon and the dark coming on. She was the only woman at this gathering of men, their trucks and trailers and horses and saddles, in the unlighted spread of buildings and pens. The rails and bars threw crisscross shadows against one another in faint grids.

'Who are all these people?' said Jeanine.

'Some fellows got up a match race. My gray stud against a Midnight colt. Fellow that owns him is from Abilene.'

'Are other people going to race?'

'Depends.' He sat with his forearms on his thighs and watched the other men and their horses intently. 'On what the competition looks like.' He stood up. 'There's a flat place out there where they run. Ride with me. I'll get a kid to ride your horse out there. That will warm him up.'

A procession of trucks and trailers and horses moved away from the auction barn. Dust sifted up into the air. It was right at sundown and the sparse grasses of the open field were lit at the tips by the level rays. Whoever owned the field was burning piles of cedar bulldozed out of the pastures, and in the distance, black shadows moved around the great fires.

He said, 'Don't get attached to a horse, Jeanine.'

'You can say that. He's the only one I got.'

'We always outlive them. Except the last one.'

On the seat of Everett's Dodge truck things slid forward onto the floorboard and she reached out to catch them; a thermometer case and a pair of pliers and a work glove and a brown bottle that said SULFONATE. A 1932 license plate. Welding bills for a calf chute, a bill for Perpetual Care from the Comanche Cemetery Association. The radio talked on and on in a dim murmur.

'Just throw that stuff on the floor,' he said, but she placed them all back on the seat beside her and held them as the truck crashed over ruts and stones. He drove with one hand. His large body took up all of his seat and part of hers. He reached up and turned the radio off. The light of the flames shone on the flat planes of his face and his dark blue eyes. He stared straight ahead.

They came to a plowed straightaway. On either side of the track midwinter mesquite trees twisted black and leafless in the last rich remains of the sun and the burning brush-piles of cedar blazed up in volcanic reds. The burnt needles drifted in small ashy fragments like soft hail. He parked, and they both got out.

Everett shook out a bag of hydrated lime into a long score line. A man in a plaid coat paced off the 440 yards of the track with the other two men beside him. They hung flags from mesquite branches at the 200-, the 220-, and 440-yard points.

'What's his name?' she asked Everett. His frantic, dancing gray stallion was up against a dark stallion from Abilene.

'Kat Tracks,' he said. 'You remember his mother from when I raced in East Texas. She Kitty. That's her colt.'

Everett turned and took the reins of his gray horse. The dappled stallion was edgy with the crackling flames and the prospect of a race and the noisy trucks.

The man from Abilene came up to Everett. In his bow tie, he had the appearance of a banker. He said, 'What will you agree to?'

'Quarter mile,' said Everett. 'And a dollar a yard.'

They lined up the two stallions at the score line. Cactus pads shone like red plates out in the brush. Everett slapped the jockey's butt and told him to just stay aboard and don't do anything cute. Don't pull him down at the end, run him in a circle or you'll get your head taken off on a mesquite. A man dropped his hat. A loud shout of men's deep voices sent the horses out into the burning fields. The jockeys were carried into the weaving shadows at thirty miles an hour, balanced on out-of-control horses, tearing through the mesquite and pasture grasses afire with the sunset light. They charged through the blue smoke from the cedar fires and in the last stretch Kat Tracks caught up and passed the brown and flew through the flagger's arc a length ahead.

Jeanine listened to the talk around her, saw a great amount of money counted out in twenties and fifties. Everett collected his money from the man in the suit and bright yellow bow tie. He rolled the four one-hundred-dollar bills and four tens into a tube and shoved them into his watch pocket. He walked back to her. 'Are you racing that horse or not?'

'Yes.' In the distance she heard the frail whistling of blue quail scattering over the pasture, disturbed by the burning cedar and the noise of the race. The flames had risen so high that they detached at the top, sending off red scarves that evaporated against the night sky. 'I'll match up against you.'

'What will you agree to?'

'Quarter mile. Four hundred and forty yards,' she said. She hesitated. 'And a hundred dollars.'

'That's a hundred dollars you don't have.'

'If I lose, take it off Smoky's price.'

He thought about it for a moment. 'If I buy him.'

Smoky Joe became nearly uncontrollable when he saw the track in front of him. He danced and lashed out. Jeanine stood with her hand out, as if to help, or to ward him off. Ross Everett threw a borrowed saddlecloth and racing saddle on Smoky Joe and cinched up tight, both the undergirth and the overgirth. He held out his hand, down low, to the jockey. He said, 'Up you go.' The jockey cocked one leg behind him and Everett took hold of his ankle and threw him up into the saddle, lightly, as if he were releasing a bird into the air.

'Just bust him loose with all you got,' said Jeanine. She danced back and forth with Smoky's erratic plunging. She held out her hand against his shoulder. 'I think he'll outlast Everett's horse. He's run already. And only use that bat once. He won't stand for it a second time. He'll put you on the ground. You get one hit and that's all.'

Down at the far end the flagger stood with a white flour sack in his hand. A truck caught him in its bright flood lamps.

'Lap and tap,' said Everett. 'Cola y cola.'

Jeanine left Smoky Joe and his jockey at the score line and ran past the line of pickups and cars parked along the track until she was two-thirds of the way down. She scrambled up onto the running board of a Chevrolet pickup.

She watched as the two horses were ridden away from the track. Their shadows poured away from their bodies and their legs danced in the headlights. As soon as their tails were even at the starting line, the man at the score line dropped his hat on the ground for the go signal, the horses were wrenched around to face the track just as Smoky Joe reared, losing seconds, and Kat Tracks burst away with his jockey nearly up between his ears.

Smoky leaped forward like a trout and sprang after him with his heavy dark legs reaching and striking and reaching again, as if he would snatch the dirt track up under him and then fling it away behind.

He stretched out his heavy neck and caught up to Kat Tracks within five seconds, his nose at the gray's tail. The men among the twisted cast-iron limbs of the mesquites began to shout. Jeanine held on to her hat as if it would fly away. The horses tore through the angular beams of headlights, between ranks of yelling men. They flew through the light of the brushfires. Dust foamed up behind them and the great engines of their bodies.

Smoky streaked past the eighth-of-a-mile flag; the gray had now used up his sprint and didn't have much left in him. Smoky came boring through the air, his nostrils wide open. He passed the gray and poured himself down the dusty brown track, hurling up dirt and gravel into Kat Tracks's face and his head pounded up and down like a walking beam.

Kat Tracks's jockey swung his bat, and even though the gray stallion had used up his air he reached out and gave it more, and within three long seconds he was again at Smoky's tail and crowding him and then he passed him.

They streaked past Jeanine with Smoky's pounding head at the gray stallion's stirrup and the jockey brought the bat down once again, for the second time, and instead of pitching his jockey into the air, Smoky poured out yet more speed as if he possessed an endless reservoir of it. He flattened out. Jeanine's entire life narrowed and reduced itself to one horse flying runaway down a dirt track carrying a hundred dollars on a wild bet. It seemed to Jeanine she could hear the percussion of his enormous heart. He was born to run, under any name and on any track whatever.

Smoky Joe caught up to the gray stallion, and then passed him, running through the flaggers streaming arc. The jockey stood up in the stirrups and Jeanine realized they had won. She sat down heavily on the truck's running board with her head in her hands.

The jockey ran Smoky Joe straight on, into the dark field. After a while the jockey managed to get him turned back. Smoky began to slow and pitched one or two bucks out of triumph and joy. The jockey jumped to the ground and landed on his feet while men crowded around to grab Smoky's reins.

Everett came up to her with a pocket watch in his hand. It was a big old nickel-plated railroad ticker.

He said, 'He did it in twenty-three point five seconds.'

'Twenty-three five?'

'Near as I can tell.'

The businessman from Abilene, with his suit and yellow bow tie, came up. He held up his stopwatch.

'Twenty-three two,' he said. 'Miss, I heard that horse was for sale.'

'Yes, he is,' said Ross. 'And I'm buying him.'

Jeanine stepped forward to take Smoky's reins. 'Ain't you a rocket?' she said. She patted his neck and he stared around eagerly, with both ears cocked up, and his eyes were bright. He lashed his tail and bounced at the ends of the reins, his great heated body streaked with sweat.

Everett took his wallet from his rear pocket and opened it and handed her a hundred-dollar bill. She had won it in twenty-three seconds. She reached out for the sweet, easy money. She took the bill and folded it over with one hand and tucked it into the watch pocket of her jeans.

'He's all right,' said Everett. Jeanine smiled up at him and gripped Smoky's reins. 'Will you run him again?' He looked down at her and said, 'The man with that Midnight colt will take you on.'

'No,' said Jeanine. She smoothed her hands over Smoky Joe's eyes, but he was in no mood to be petted. He threw his heavy, hard-boned head and the eggbutt snaffle bit jangled and flashed. 'No, I'll stay with what I have. I can't afford to lose.'

At the sale barn Jeanine walked Smoky Joe out of his sweat. She walked him back and forth in the stockyard. She held his lead rope and they paced between the sale barn and the pens. The dark horse's breath slowed and he stepped along lightly. He tried to take Jeanine's hat from her head and she took it back from him and patted him on his great round jaw. Jeanine kept on walking Smoky Joe long after he cooled out.

A man came past her. 'Miss, there's a stock tank there in back of the auction barn. There's a pole light on.'

She watched Smoky Joe drink his fill. The horse's ears flicked slightly with every swallow, as if they were part of some tiny, hidden, intricate pumping system in his head. Then she led him back to the trailer. Truck motors started up, headlights made a long snaking line out of the stockyards.

Ross came toward her.

'Load him up,' Everett said. 'And follow me back to my place. I'll write you out a bill of sale.'

CHAPTER EIGHTEEN

He drove his truck and trailer at top speed, the gray stallion's tail streaming over the trailer gate and glowing bright red in the taillights. At the top of one of the great rises she saw the lights of Comanche in the distance and the faint sparks of distant houses. After a good many miles she saw him turn into a ranch gate. She slowed and turned in. After a mile or a mile and a half she came to a stone house shaded by two massive live oaks. Behind the house was a large barn and a shearing platform with a fire burning on its level concrete table. Several men sat around the fire and threw chunks of wood into it. The fan of the windmill rolled with a continual knocking clank where one of the blades was missing.

He came out to greet her, closing the doors of the house behind him. He walked out from beneath the shadow of the galleria with his canvas coat collar turned up. A loose spur rang on the stony ground.

She said, 'I got to turn Smoky out.'

'My boy will do that.' He turned toward the house and shouted, 'Innis? Innis? Get out here and turn this woman's horse in the lot.' He sat and watched as his young son held on to Joe's lead rope and walked him toward the barn and the corrals. 'Come in.' He stood up. 'I got a wind-mill crew here. I guess they already ate. The cook's here.'

She followed him to the house and they walked across the galleria floor and its veined limestones and through a set of double doors. It was hard to shut the doors. He had to slam them twice.

'Sit down,' he said. 'While I get this fire going. What can I offer you?' Jeanine sat on a hard-backed chair in front of the fire. Everett sat down and unbuckled his spurs and pulled them from his boots. He dropped them on the telephone stand. Jeanine realized he was not wearing his spurs in the house as a gesture of politeness, and that if there wasn't a woman around he and his son and the cook and the boys probably wore their spurs at the dining room table and hooked them on the chair rungs and caught them in the curtains. They probably wore them in the bathtub and in bed as far as she knew.

'You know, I think I would drink a bottle of beer.'

Everett said, 'All right.' He went to the kitchen door and called to the cook.

'Yes, sir.'

'Get this young woman a bottle of beer.'

The cook came out again with the beer. His face sparkled with a week's growth of red beard and he was covered with a heavy rubber apron as if he had been scalding turkeys.

He said, 'Them boys is finished up and ate. I guess I'll go on back.'

'Well, tell them I'd come out but I got business.'

The cook rubbed his whiskery chin. 'I'll do it,' he said. Then he went back in the kitchen.

Everett found a bottle of whiskey inside a glass-fronted bookcase. He took up a coffee cup from the dining room table and blew the dust out of it and then poured two fingers of whiskey into it. He opened her beer bottle on his belt buckle and handed it to her. He sat down again. He tipped up the coffee cup to drink his whiskey and then stood up and quietly choked and threw the rest of the whiskey into the fire. He threw the cup after it and it smashed against the grate. He went and took the bottle out of the bookcase and dropped it into a wastebasket.

'I'll find out who did that,' he said. Jeanine moved her earrings from one hand to another. She heard voices outside; men laughing. The broken cup was full of blue flames where it held some dangerous, low-grade fuel.

'I'm not afraid of you, Mr. Everett,' she said.

'I know you're not. Where are you staying tonight?'

'Here,' Jeanine said. 'You've got to have a spare

room around here somewhere. Unless that whole windmill crew is coming in here. I know you got a spare room.'

'You'd better drive on into Ranger. To save your reputation.' He sat back and took in her short, thatched hair of various sunburnt colors and her slight body and her nervous hands.

'I don't have one,' she said.

'I'd be happy to tell you the name of a tourist court in Ranger. I'll give you five dollars to go there and get a cabin.'

'No. Why should I drive on tonight? I'm wore out.'

He said, 'You're a hard woman, Jeanine.'

'Make it ten and I'll think about it.'

He bit his lower lip to keep from laughing at her. 'You're out of my price range.' He held out a callused hand. 'Let's see your paper.'

She handed him the bill of sale from her tweed jacket pocket and he sat down at a long dining room table with it. Jeanine walked around the room. On the walls were photographs of him and his wife at about the time Jeanine had seen her last, it must have been five or six years ago. His wife wore a sheer dress with a tiny collar and a straw hat. The picture had been taken in the bright daylight so that the shadows were very black and her eyes were squinted against the sun. Ross Everett and his wife stood at a train station with suitcases around them and a freight wagon behind them. It was the San Angelo station because Jeanine could see the sign. They were going somewhere and they were happy and they smiled at whoever was taking the picture. Jeanine turned away.

'Your paper is good,' he said.

He laid the bill of sale in front of him that said Smoky Joe Hancock, a two-year-old stallion, had been sold by Manuel Benavides to John C. Stoddard March 9, 1935. Height 15.2 hands. Color: seal. Markings: none. By Joe Hancock by John Wilkins by Peter McCue. Out of a Rainy Day mare on the Waggoner ranch.

He took another cigarette and set it on fire with a metal lighter. He squinted at her over the smoke.

'You don't want to sell him.'

'I don't know, I've kind of got to like him.' She sat down on the other side of the long table and crossed one blue-jean leg over the other, then uncrossed them again and nervously twisted her hands on her bony kneecaps. 'Now all of a sudden.'

'I told you,' he said. 'Don't get all wrapped around the axle about a horse.'

She went to stand once again in front of the hooded fireplace. The place was a mess. There was a saddle turned up on its fork against the wall and a stack of old *Farm and Ranch* magazines beside it, and *Time* and the *Providence Journal*, which seemed to be a newspaper from the East somewhere. A plate with half a dried-out sandwich on a chair. Trophies for prize cattle, championship Angora goats. The ageless contradictions of ranch life where creatures were cherished against storms and against sickness and other creatures, sometimes at the risk of a person's health and even life, and then

212

slaughtered. There was a stuffed, dusty javelina head with a red plaster tongue sticking out between the teeth and a spur hanging from one of the curved tusks.

'Did you kill all this stuff?'

'Yes. I did.'

She untied her scarf and let it drape around her neck. It was getting warm; the fire had surrounded two large sections of live oak logs and lit up the zoo of taxidermy animals on the walls. She put the heel of her hand to her forehead and thrust her fingers into her hair.

'Tell me about Bea,' he said. She told him. As she spoke she saw Bea at the bottom of the well in the dim light like a cracked and discarded Skippy doll and the loose, fainting feeling of horror that had come over her when she saw her little sister and the blood. Of the doctor with his loose mouth and the smell of Lysol in the hospital.

'And she's all right except for that leg?'

'Yes. She just needs a specialist. A surgeon. That's how come I'm selling Smoky Joe to you.'

He stared at the fire for a moment. 'And how are y'all holding out on that farm?'

'All right.'

'Lots of people are moving back to the country. At least you can raise chickens. Do y'all have chickens?'

'Yes. And Mayme got a job at the Magnolia office in Tarrant.'

He stared at the fire. 'It seemed like things were going to get better for a while. In '35. But the economy has cratered again.'

213

'That's when I saw you last,' she said. 'In Conroe. I mean before Tarrant last month. Last time I talked to you was in Conroe.'

'Yes.'

'Do you remember me when I was fifteen?'

He started to say what it was he remembered and then he changed his mind. He got up and crossed the room, slamming storage doors and then he opened the gun cabinet. He found a bottle of Irish whiskey behind the stock of a shotgun. He poured some into a dusty wineglass that said SAN ANGELO CLASS OF '26.

'Well, let's give this a try,' he said. 'Yes, I remember you very well. I remember you very well.'

Jeanine wrapped her arms around herself. 'I guess you read it in the papers.'

'Are you cold?'

'No, I'm nervous.'

'Yes, I read about it. I read about his arrest.'

Jeanine considered her bitten nails. 'For gambling.'

He sat for a long time in silence; the fire erupted in sparks and the sparks winked out on the tile floor.

'No, Jeanine. For statutory rape.' The whiskey charged into his bloodstream. Jeanine held her beer bottle wrapped in her fingers, as if she would break it. His cigarette burned and smoked out of the folded architecture of his two hands and the smoke drifted toward the fireplace and its draft. Finally he asked her, 'Did you know the girl?'

She took up a stick of kindling and shoved

fiercely at the coals on the edge of the fireplace. 'How would I know somebody like that?'

'Jeanine, I'm sorry. I'm very sorry.'

Jeanine felt her throat tighten and an odd, blocked feeling in her ears and realized that tears were rising to her eyes like mercury in a thermometer.

He said, 'You're about to break out crying.'

'I know it. I don't want to.' If she started crying it would never stop. 'Why?' she said. She lifted her head to him in search of an answer. 'Why did he have to do that to us?'

Everett took a long breath and blew it out his nose, along with smoke. He said, 'I'm not the person to ask, sweetheart, but then you're not asking me.' He got up and walked over to the fireplace beside her and threw his cigarette butt into it. The flames shone across the tiled floor and she heard footsteps in the kitchen, the low voices of children being very quiet and very intent. Then a slashing, sprung noise and the pinging sound of broken crockery.

He turned toward the kitchen and said, 'Innis!'

Jeanine wiped at her eyes firmly. Ross reached to his back pocket and brought out a handkerchief, shook it out of its folds and handed it to her. She took it and scrubbed at her eyes and blew her nose.

The door from the kitchen opened. The boy stood there, his face spotted with large freckles, the doorknob in his hand. He wore a very dirty small Stetson and a stained sweater that zipped up the front. Behind him another boy kicked pieces of a china plate under the kitchen table.

'Yes, sir?'

'What are you doing?'

'Well, me and Aaron were going to get something to eat.' He had a slingshot in his hand cut from the Y crotch of a branch. It was made with strips of inner tube for slings and a leather pocket made of an old shoe tongue.

'You were going to get something to eat with a slingshot?'

Innis glanced down at the primitive weapon in his hand. 'Kind of.' He stuck it into his coat pocket. 'We were shooting at rats and Aaron broke one of those Spodes.'

Another smash. Jeanine saw chips of china spray across the kitchen floor.

Ross stood up. 'Damn it!'

'Well, we were going to sit up and wait for that coon.' The boy had fair hair cut short with a whirled cowlick in the middle of his forehead. 'Since I can't use the twenty-two on him. Can Aaron stay all night?' He turned and said, 'Aaron, stop shooting.'

'Not tonight.'

The boy stood silent in the doorway. He glanced at Jeanine and pressed his lips together and regarded his boot toes.

'Why not?'

Ross said, 'Somebody is going to get snatched bald-headed in a minute. Aaron's dad is going home. Aaron is going with him.'

'Yes, sir.'

The door closed.

Jeanine set her beer bottle down on the tiles beside the fireplace.

'I'll drink another beer,' she said.

'No.' He said it in an absentminded sort of way. He crooked his forefinger over the bridge of his nose. 'You'll be up all night peeing.' He stood beside her, watching the fire. 'The bathroom is behind the kitchen.' He lit another cigarette. Flaming bits of paper fell to the floor and he stepped on them. She watched the smoke wander into the bars of light and out again. 'I'll make you out a bill of sale,' he said.

She got up and walked from one end of his dining room to the other while he wrote. He used it for an office. His desk was the long dark dining table, made in the fashion of the 1920s, when people liked that spare straight look, and it was scarred with cigarette burns and lamp rings. Apparently he and the boy ate in the kitchen, probably living on tamales and chili and mutton or whatever the cook made up for them.

'It's hard to give him up,' she said.

'You don't have the money to campaign him properly. He needs to run on the good tracks in New Mexico and Arizona. He needs to get used to a starting gate, he needs to be exercised the right way, consistently.' Everett saw how spare she was, not big enough to hold the horse to a working gallop. Not much bigger than his son. 'He'll go down on one of these brush tracks before long and break a leg and you don't even have the money for vet bills.'

'You saw him run today.' She had a stubborn edge to her voice. 'He's worth more than three hundred.'

'Then try to get it somewhere else.'

217

Jeanine sat and listened to footsteps coming down a hall somewhere. A door opened and then the sound of running water.

'How do I know you'll treat him well?' It was the last objection she could think of.

'Look at my other horses,' he said. 'I beat them regularly. I use a hammer.'

Jeanine lifted her shoulders. 'I guess I've got to.'

He thought about it for a moment. Then he said, 'I'll pay you two hundred and you can have a percentage in his winnings. Ten percent.'

Jeanine paused and then whispered the math to herself.

'But how would I get it?'

'I'll hand it to you, sweetheart.' He drank up his whiskey. 'I hate to take a good horse away from an ignoramus like you.'

'That sounds like a deal.' She didn't smile. 'I promised my mother I wouldn't ever bet any-more.'

'You're not. I'll do it.'

'Well here, then.' She handed him back a ten-dollar bill. 'Put it on Smoky whenever you race him.'

'All right.'

'Well, write it out,' said Jeanine. 'And sign it.'

He opened a drawer beneath the table edge, one of those drawers where people used to keep the silver. In it were a metal cash box and a revolver. He opened the cash box and took two one-hundred-dollar bills. He found a sheet of paper and a pen. He wrote out a new bill of sale and a percentage agreement. He handed it to her. She paused and read it over. He waved away the drifting veils of cigarette smoke. The lamp sat between them on the table and shone on their faces and hands and they were reflected in the black windows like some old portrait of conspirators or highwaymen, their treasure before them, dividing the spoils. She signed her name to the paper.

She shoved the bills and her winnings into her jacket pocket. Everett drew their chairs closer to the fire and they sat side by side, for the night was growing intensely cold and the cold crept through the walls of the old house, slipped under the warped baseboards. The fire was collapsing into crumbling red coals.

He turned his dark blue eyes to her and then away again. He listened for any new damages going on in the kitchen. 'If that kid breaks something else I'll kill him.' He swirled the final drops of whiskey in his glass. 'He does this when I have somebody to visit.'

'Like who?' said Jeanine. She didn't know why she asked it.

'Women.' Everett shoved at a log with his boot. 'Find yourself a room. Make sure it's the one with the window looking out at the shearing platform. So the windmill crew can see you and you can scandalize the place. Try upstairs. There's blankets somewhere.'

Jeanine found her way through the kitchen and then opened a door to one side of it. It was a boy's room. *Archie* comics and the Red Ryder puppet and balsa wood airplanes. Faded small jeans on the floor. Old-fashioned square wooden stirrups and boxes of twenty-two ammunition.

The boy was probably still outside with his slingshot, waiting up for the midnight visit of a raccoon or a ringtailed wildcat. They all thirsted for the blood of chickens and the yolks of eggs.

She opened another door; a room jammed full of old-style folded canvas cowboy beds and cooking pots. It was camping gear, roundup gear. It had all come back from the fall works unwashed and it stank of campfire smoke and bacon grease. Unlucky the woman who had to clean that mess up. Jeanine closed the door and climbed a flight of stairs and walked down a hallway. The old wooden floor creaked beneath her feet.

She knew she was not going to be able to sleep. She saw framed photographs on the hallway walls, people in 1920s clothes. She didn't stop to see who they were, they were frightening, they might be of his dead wife. At the end of the hall was a tall window framed in stone like the door to another world. Jeanine saw outside a sudden graininess to the night air and realized snow was failing. She put her face to the glass. Out beside the shearing platform a fire still burnt and snow fell into its lit red heart, like moths drawn to light.

She opened the last door in the hallway and in that room found a bed with bright pillow shams. Three mirrors at a vanity reflected her dark figure in the doorway, wavering like a trinity of selves. She reached for the light chain and pulled it and sat on the bed. He was crazy to keep her room like this. Jeanine wished she hadn't found it. She couldn't make herself turn off the light but lay back, wrapped in blankets that she found in a trunk at the foot of the bed.

She saw a wardrobe built into a corner and its shut door was worrisome to her. As to what might be in it. Her clothes. Some part of a person always remained in their clothes somehow. Snow pinged at the window, it came sweeping down out of the Texas Panhandle unobstructed. He didn't want anybody here. Except some sort of women; casual women. That's why he kept her room like this. And he blamed it on the boy.

At last she pulled the light chain. She knew she would not sleep. She got up again and drew a chair to the window. She leaned her forehead against the pane to watch the mysterious and rare sight of a fall of snow.

The fire outside died and the last of the windmill crew left in a trailing glitter of red taillights that winked out in the restless foaming of the snowstorm.

She saw Ross Everett walk out of the house, moving through the dark. Snow settled on the shoulders of his canvas coat. He sat down beside the still water of the windmill tank. He sat and smoked and watched the surface of the water twilled by the grainy fall of the snow, a rough and luminous weave. The fan of the windmill turned, clanking, in the hard wind. He threw his cigarette into the water. A sudden gust of wind shook the window, the old glass panes vaulted in their frames and Jeanine's dim reflection moved in strange angles.

CHAPTER NINETEEN

After a long time he went into the house and in the bathroom shoved a handful of kindling in the hot-water heater and poured kerosene on it and fired it up. He lay back in the hot water and listened to the wind. There was no sound of the tailpin shifting; it meant the wind was fixed. It's going to bring more hard weather behind this front. He dried off and pulled on his jeans and walked barefoot and shirtless into the dining room and stood in front of the dying fire. Garish colors of magazines in the chair. Miriam's book on cave art. Early humans, twenty thousand years of stalking aurochs and wild horses, painting the horses on cave walls in their beautiful calligraphy. I love you, I love you, I want to kill you. Events come about in chains. People die without warning. Droughts settle on the country and become fixed and will not move on. Without warning a boy starts turning into a man. Nothing you yourself did or failed to do. He stared into the design of the fire. The wind fluted at the edges of the roof and at the windowpanes in a wandering series of tones. In the stanzas of the wind's singing he could hear voices from a past time, and they were hard voices, for this was a hard country and they were living in a hard time.

The people who had built the stone house were still here. Like the imprints of fish and shells he

222

had seen in the tumbled blocks of fossil hash on the San Saba River. They were still here and had not gone away. In some other dimension their songs and words and passionate loves and hatred and violence and gestures of selflessness had not gone away. Made some permanent petrified record. Her father for instance. It was so easy to be cruel to people who trusted you. First they had to trust you.

He opened the drawer in the dining room table. He lifted out a ledger that had been used as a diary for decades, with weather records written in it from 1886. He wrote in the date and the fall of snow. He noted two hundred dollars paid out for a Joe Hancock stallion and a hundred dollars lost on a match race. He went to his room and stripped off his Levi's and fell into bed under cold quilts, heavy with batts of compressed wool. He stared into the black-and-white night; into unbidden images of horses with the power of speech and the clock at his bedside paying out, with its light-boned hands, the hours in gold earrings one after another.

The moon was now dimmed by the cloud cover and the snow fell, glazing the hills and the pastures.

In the morning Jeanine sat up in her stiff pile of blankets. She threw them to one side quickly and pulled on the chilled socks and jeans and shirt and her tweed jacket. She hurried down the stairs and into the warm kitchen.

The boy and his father were already at their breakfast. They sat and ate and their movements and their low voices were very like one another. The boy took up a spoonful of oatmeal and, seeing her, plopped it down again. Remnants of what had once been a woman's kitchen were still visible in the red and white checkered curtains, the clock with a sun face, a shelf of Spode china plates in the Italian Blue pattern, now with two empty holders. They were eating with the good silver. Wedding silver.

'I thought you left,' the boy said.

'Innis.' His father stood up out of his chair.

'What?'

'You're on thin ice, son.'

Ross went to the stove and poured a cup of coffee and handed it to her.

'I don't want any breakfast,' she said. Her hair was tousled and uncombed. 'I better get going.'

'Good,' Innis said.

Ross reached across the table and took the boy by the collar and the belt and lifted him out of his chair. He turned him around and walked him toward the back kitchen door.

'Wait for the bus outside,' he said. 'And if you are still in that mood when you come home, don't bother coming in the house.' He turned to her. 'Get your coat,' he said. 'Say good-bye to your horse.'

'Oh, tell him to come back in,' she said. 'Where's his coat?'

'Let's go.'

Jeanine pulled on her muffler and hat and hurried out the back door after him. The snow had brushed up the dusty world of corrals and bare trees like new paint. It was still coming down in winking columns of drift. She caught up to him and they both left black prints behind them in the snow that led backward into 1935 and even farther, to a vanished blacksmith shop in Mexia and the blind man who sends us all off on some journey through a night lit only by gas flares.

She said, 'I'm sorry, Ross. I shouldn't have stayed.'

'He doesn't get to say who stays.'

They walked across the littered yard to the barn, and the gate open to the pasture beyond. The dead fire of the windmill crew was a pile of blackened stubs covered lightly with snow like some aboriginal tartan in whites and blacks.

'Don't bawl,' he said.

'All right.'

Jeanine watched the dark brown stallion as he trotted among the cattle. Everett was holding some calves and their mothers in a fifty-acre trap and Smoky Joe was trotting among them very like a great landowner checking on his herds. He had a dashing little pouffe of snow on his forelock. He lifted his boxy head. His frizzy forelock stood out like a broom, spangled with snowflakes. He came to see what she had in her hand and then tried to take her hat from her head.

'Give that back,' she said in a quavering voice. She patted him. 'Ain't you a rocket?'

Jeannine drove out of Comanche County into headwinds and snow. When she pulled out of the drive she saw Everett's son standing at the mailbox to wait for the bus, thrown out into the snow, his hands in his pockets and his feet shifting. As she came onto the gravel she heard a heavy chunk and realized the boy had hit the trailer fender with something, probably a slug of double O buck from his slingshot.

But she had two hundred dollars from Smoky and a hundred in winnings and so let him do whatever he wanted. She drove on. The trailer no longer lugged heavily at the scissors hitch, she could feel it bouncing along the uneven blacktop surface with no horse in it, no nothing. She had only sixty miles to go.

She crossed the spidery steel bridges over the Leon River and then Jim Ned Creek. The water ran between snowy banks, the flakes pouring onto the disturbed surfaces of the current. Just past the highway bridge over Jim Ned Creek, in a misted, snow-clouded pasture she saw four old horses. They were like ghosts, ancient and drawn, standing under a live oak, coated with white. Maybe it was Maisie and Jeff and Big Man and Little Man with their heads together, comforting one another in their old age. The last of the snow skittered in small waves down the black surface of the Bankhead highway.

CHAPTER TWENTY

Bea dreamed that they were sawing her leg off. Her new leg would be made of a large metal spring from a Model T with a round plate like a waffle iron for a foot so she would be able to

226

print tracks like a tennis racket wherever she walked. She asked them not to. Nobody listened. Bea could hear the grating noise as they sawed and sawed. The surgeon raised his head and said afterward he would get to her arms. He would trade her arms and her leg for eternal life and a bushel of peaches. Bea felt that all her blood had drained out and that she was transparent and full of sunlight. She sat up and asked what they had done with her leg. She was in a beautiful white room with a knocking radiator and white curtains. The nurse said her leg was where it always was, and here were her mother and sisters.

Bea looked at her sisters. They seemed so coarse and normal but then she became transparent again when her mother laid her hand on Bea's forehead and said the surgeon was very happy with the operation. Bea wanted to see her leg in its white bandages and then she drank a cup of smoking broth and ate cherry Jell-O and fell asleep again.

Winifred came and organized Bea's sickroom in the parlor, and opened the windows for fresh air. She recommended that Jeanine wear a dust mask whenever she was working outside and could see haze in the air, especially if another dust storm came at them from Oklahoma. This was to prevent dust pneumonia. They did not need more sickness if Bea was to be taken care of and recover the use of her leg after that very, very expensive operation.

Bea was in intense pain, and the pain was dulled only by the bottle of brown liquid at her bedside. Winifred brought a package of yellow crepe paper and pipe cleaners for Bea to make yellow roses with, so she could contribute to the celebration for Texas Independence Day at the Old Valley Road schoolhouse and forget that her shinbone was a rod of intensely painful fire. Winifred sat down to look at what food they normally ate and wrote out, in a small square hand, recipes for nutritious meals that could be made from white beans and soup bones and a jelly from agarita berries, and admonitions about prudent spending.

She brought more books for Bea and some pamphlets about chickens for Elizabeth on raising productive layers. She read Bea's journal when Bea was asleep. She went through Elizabeth's reports on the oil-well investment when Elizabeth was not in the house and read some of her other papers – Jack Stoddard's death certificate and the lawyer's report on the charges. She was interested in the charges. It was too late to do anything about removing the child from the home but you never knew. There was so much in the world a wonderful child like Bea had a right to. Music lessons and a plentitude of good books and new shoes. Stimulating friends, art museums. Winifred rolled up *Savage Western Tales* to shove the magazine into the cookstove fire but changed her mind. They probably needed it for toilet paper.

Mayme and Jeannie climbed up on the roof with hammers and tin cans that had been sheared open and flattened out with bricks. It was the Sunday before Christmas. They tore up shingles looking for the leak and their breath smoked out in front of them and their hands were bent and white with cold. They could see down the slope to the river.

'Here the damn thing is, Jeanine. Help me with this.'

They crawled forward on hands and knees to the chimney to tear out the shingles. Next to the brick they found the rotted laths and ripped them out and replaced them with the slats from a set of wooden window blinds. Nothing but old composite shingles tacked over cedar shakes stood between them and the dust and the wind. The grit ground into their knees as they worked side by side. They nailed the flattened tin cans over the hole and watched more dust-haze come up over Shinnery Mountain. Mayme lifted her head and stared out across the valley when she heard the sound of hen turkeys yelping, anxious after their broods that all came shifting and hurrying in curious gliding motions far down the slope, at the edge of the Brazos.

'I wish we had one of those for Christmas dinner,' said Mayme. Her head was wrapped in the white kerchief and she was working barehanded. There was only one pair of gloves and she let Jeanine have them.

'Maybe I could shoot us one,' said Jeanine.

'You need to let both barrels go on that damn nurse. Winifred the Almighty.'

'Too bad we covered the well over with hog wire. They'd never find her body.' Jeanine mentally threw Winifred off the Brazos River Bridge and watched her float away, screaming, amid tangles of driftwood.

Mayme sat back and wiped her nose with her sleeve. She turned up her collar against the wind. 'Why do we let that witch talk to us like that?'

'Because we need the relief food, that's why,' said Jeanine. 'We're letting ourselves be insulted for food. When are you getting paid?'

'They say it's a month. Two weeks' probation and then another two weeks and I get my paycheck.'

'Do they pay you for the probation?'

'Yes, but only half.' Mayme placed another set of shingles with her bare hands, which had become raw with the asphalted grit. 'And so when is Ross Everett going to be out here looking for you with a bouquet of roses?'

Jeanine laughed. 'Mayme, you should see how they live. Him and that boy. It's a mess. And the kid is as mean...' She searched for the right sort of thing he was as mean as, but couldn't think of a comparison.

'He's hunting for a wife to clean the place up. You can bet on that.'

'He better not be hunting for me.' Jeanine tapped in finishing nails to hold the laths in place. She sat back and regarded the horizon of hills, a column of smoke from the Crowsers' cookstove beyond the Spanish oak. 'Sometimes I wish Dad could know we were doing all right here. That we're getting by on our own.'

Mayme paused with her hammer in the air. Then she laid it down and put both arms around her sister's neck and held her for a moment and then picked up the hammer again.

'If we'd have lost Bea too,' she said. 'Well, I don't know what.'

'But we didn't,' said Jeanine.

'I remember one time he said I had Orphan Annie hair. I don't have Orphan Annie hair but at least he said something to me.' She fished around in her coat pocket for a nail. 'He only talked to you and Mother.'

'I know it.'

Mayme laid her hammer down and sat back to rest. 'How much is left over?'

'From the surgery? About fifty dollars.'

'Hide it, Jeanine. Don't let Mother know you have it.'

'Because she'll buy more shares in that well.'

'Yes.'

'All right. It's got to go for the tax bill anyway.'

They laid their thin fingers crisscross over the old shingles to hold them there, over the heads of their mother and their little sister to protect them from the crawling dust and whatever else might come upon them from the four corners of the world. Jeanine positioned a nail.

'Sock it in, Mayme,' she said. 'Don't smash my finger.'

A dry norther boomed in and the temperature fell to eighteen. Cold dust surged up and hissed in wind-thrown horizontal lines. Jeanine fought through it and into the kitchen with armloads of wood. She built up the parlor fire; Bea could at least be kept warm. She was asleep when Jeanine came in, fragments of yellow crepe paper in her fingers. She was so pale.

231

Jeanine put on three splits and tiptoed out again. Her hair was gritty and she dreamed of a bath in a six-foot tub, with something foamy in it, big thick towels. She wanted the shiny look people had when they owned a house with a bathroom. And a good-looking man with a suit and a country estate held a bouquet of roses, waiting to take her to dinner at the Baker Hotel. She wished she knew something about hot-water heaters.

Tomorrow Abel Crowser was going to start bedding in with the sulky plow. The Tolliver farm had 150 acres according to the title. Fifteen was in orchard, twenty in a thick cedar brake with trunks the size of stovepipe. Fifty acres were completely clear. The rest was studded with cedar seedlings and sotol. She could cut that by hand. She would get hold of Ross Everett and ask when he was running Smoky Joe. If she owned 10 percent of him and he was 100 percent horse she hoped her part was that on the forward end, the square head with the toilet-brush forelock that would stretch out and win by a nose.

And the days went on through the last week of December with a high-velocity wind that would not stop. There was no end to the flat sunshine and dry skies, and the wind, the endless river of sandpaper wind.

Winifred Beasley drove up and walked into the house without a word to anyone. She bent over the stack of tin cans and bags in front of the window, and brought out a notebook and wrote things down and checked off a list. Elizabeth came in from the parlor and screamed when she saw Winifred in her stout gray suit and bird's-nest hat.

'Well! I didn't even know you were here!'

'I like to surprise people,' said Winifred. 'Test of character.' Then she went straight to Bea's room and said, 'Well, how is our patient today?'

'Good.' Bea stared at her with wide eyes. 'Why don't you knock?'

'Ha ha ha!' Winifred laughed and smiled her stiff rectangular smile. 'Oh I like to surprise people.' She sat down on the chair beside Bea's bed and checked her hair.

'I don't have any lice,' Bea said. 'None of us have ever had lice.'

'There's an outbreak in the school here,' said Winifred. 'The law requires that I check. When I go to the Buckner's Home for Children in Dallas, we have lists of things we have to check.'

'Do you work for them?' said Bea.

'No no no! I work for the county!' Winifred was very cheerful. 'But I have been associated with them formerly and I have the greatest respect for them. The children are happy and well cared for. They have an enormous library, Bea.'

Jeanine boiled water for the dishes and listened. She wondered if somehow Winifred Beasley were paid for every child she spirited off to the orphans' home. Jeanine thought she would, in a few more moments, be tempted to pour scalding water on the county health nurse. She turned away and took a long breath when Winifred came back into the kitchen with a ticktock noise of her polished shoes.

She said, 'Does the Buckner Home get money

233

from the government for each child?'

'Of course,' said Winifred. 'But in the main it is the generosity of the good people of Texas, churches and so on.' She waved one hand out toward the world, full of generous people. 'And so you sold your horse. What a great sacrifice you made for your sister.'

'Yes,' said Jeanine. 'Sold him to Ross Everett over in Comanche County. And paid for the surgery.' She pressed her front teeth together and told herself to shut up. It didn't do her any good. 'Everett's going to run him on the official tracks. He's very fast.'

Winifred raised her eyebrows to express surprise in a wooden, polite way. Then she said, 'Come and help me bring in the supplies,' she said. 'I have asked for twice the amount of canned milk. Make her drink it down. Condensed milk is not pleasant but a glass a day of condensed milk and the malt tablets are desperately needed.' She started toward the door where wavy lines of blown dust crossed the floorboards. 'I know Ross Everett,' she said. 'I used to be the county nurse for Comanche County. He killed his wife.'

Jeanine pulled on her coat. She followed Winifred out the door and across the flat dirt of their front yard. There was almost no grass, just the dead matts of Indian grass flattened into circles. She held out her arms for the canned beef and condensed milk. Finally she said, 'Oh, he killed her.'

'He killed her with overwork. She was delicate. She had asthma. I told him she was not to get up from bed. A week later I came in and she was in the stock pens keeping up the branding fire. I did my best to point out the inadvisability of this. After she died I recommended his boy be moved somewhere for his education and his own health. Mr. Everett was rude.'

'She was helping with the branding fire?' Jeanine balanced a load of tinned goods. 'And she had dust pneumonia?'

'I wish it weren't true.'

Mayme came home a week later, riding in Gareau's milk truck, with a paycheck from the Magnolia Oil Corporation offices in Tarrant and laid it on the table. Seventy-five dollars. Bea could now sit up at the kitchen table, and the pain had subsided. Bea held the check between her two hands and looked at it intently. Her leg in its cast stuck out straight with a sock over the toes.

Bea said, 'I need some more western romance magazines. They have emotionally charged story lines.' She thought for a moment and her toes writhed at the end of the cast. 'Women tied to stakes. Rattlers crawling down out of the attic. Dropping in the beans. Jeanine could be struck by lightning, Mayme could be kidnapped, Mother could drive off a cliff in the dark or end up in Mexico with the white slavers.' She reached for her notebook. 'The road could disappear, it could turn into a great chasm in the desert. I was taken away, screaming, to the Buckner Children's Home.' Bea knew that she said these things because she was inventing dramatic stories in her head and she, couldn't stop herself from saying them aloud as if they were true. 'I thrust my arms out the window, screaming, "Mother! Mother!"

Jeanine put down the bottle of hot sauce and sat without eating, watching Bea writing and writing it all down.

'If a magazine were to pay me for something I wrote, would the check have my name on it like that?' Bea lifted a hopeful face to her mother.

'Yes, Bea darling,' said Elizabeth. 'It would say your name, and the date, and the amount, and then somebody signs it. An authorizing person.'

'I could do it,' Bea said to herself. 'Why not?' She lay in her cot beside the stove. Albert slept stretched out alongside her legs. 'Why not?'

Nobody answered her. Beyond the back door they heard coyotes. One sang in a warbling soprano and the others barked in high yips; they were young coyote pups who had not yet learned to howl. It was a mother and her family. In the barn the hens flew up to the high beams because there had not yet been enough money to buy chicken wire until the check for seventy-five dollars was on the table. Everything had a family to feed, it was just a matter of who ate who and devil take the hindmost.

CHAPTER TWENTY-ONE

The day before Christmas, Abel Crowser appeared at the door with a fat cock turkey held upside down by its scaly feet. Bea cried out in her usual exclamation points that she would cook the turkey as her present to them all, but she was not allowed to, she was not even allowed on crutches. Jeanine set about roasting the bird with great care.

On Christmas morning they each woke up in their own beds and made silent promises to themselves to be cheerful. Their gifts to one another were things they could make; a tin star for the tree and the juniper green silk dress for Mayme, Lepp cookies for Elizabeth, and the promise of a new coat for Bea. They remembered the Christmas of '29 in far West Texas, and of '32 when they sang for their parents, and the worst one in '35 when they had only exchanged promises. It seemed that Jack Stoddard was still alive in those places, driving nitro and saltwater pumpers, gambling in a back room, calling out for Red Buck to win, drifting transparently over the vast distances of the Permian or through the snow that sifted over the gas flares that Christmas of '32 in Kilgore. He had always been a shape changer who could talk the legs off an iron stove, and imagined worlds of beauty and chance and drink, and desired these worlds so ardently it seemed impossible he should not still be here in some glassy apparition carrying transparent jelly beans or throwing a pair of invisible dice with stars for dots. Jeanine missed him. They all missed him and nobody would say so. The sisters needed him to drive nails and change the tires and to tell them what kind of men to look for in life, to say *Don't marry somebody like me*. To explain why Roosevelt had stored all the gold in Fort Knox. But he was so irrevocably gone.

That afternoon Jeanine cut up what was left of the turkey and put it in jars. She heard a car's tires crackling on the gravel. It was the school-teacher, Miss Callaway, a young woman with a pompadour hairdo. She called out *Hello! Hello!* and jumped out of the car with a paper sack full of handmade Christmas cards from Bea's schoolmates, and all of Bea's schoolbooks and lesson plans. Miss Callaway had only been paid in scrip from the county, those official and optimistic IOUs, but she somehow contrived to be nicely dressed, with a long wraparound coat. She had an eastern accent and very deep, round brown eyes. She wouldn't have any coffee, she was in a hurry. Many more homes to visit.

'I'm from Pennsylvania,' said Miss Callaway. 'The Keystone state!'

Elizabeth smiled. 'I thought it was the Quaker state.' She put a cup of coffee in front of the teacher anyway and Miss Callaway lifted the cup and blew on it.

'Keystone!' shouted Bea, from the parlor. She eagerly read through all twenty-five of the crayoned Christmas cards.

'And don't you tease me about being a Yankee,' said Miss Callaway. She had a very wide smile and good teeth. Jeanine cringed as the teacher poured a great deal of sugar and Bea's condensed milk into her cup. 'You Texans wouldn't ever have got a drop of oil if it hadn't been for us Penn-sylvanians, we came down here and taught you how to drill.' She put the cup down. 'Bea is so talented,' she said. 'Wonderful stories about horse

238

races and nitroglycerin and hobo jungles. How does she make all that up? What an imagination.'

'I know,' said Elizabeth.

Jeanine walked the fields on Christmas Day from the seventy-five acres on the slope of the ridge, bristly with little cedars, to the heavy cedar brakes beyond the graveyard and then to the orchard. She came back and drew a map and thought about where to start.

Her Christmas present from Bea was a brochure from Texas A&M on the care of peach orchards. Peaches named Springold and Texstar. After a while she laid it down and fell asleep in the chair in front of the cookstove.

CHAPTER TWENTY-TWO

In late January Milton left a telephone message for Jeanine at Strawn's store. She said thank you to Mrs. Joplin and read the words printed on the back of a wanted poster as the tall woman wrote up the beans and cornmeal and half a pound of salt pork and garden seeds. He was coming to visit her. Jeanine was pleased and cautiously happy. She felt she had become a permanent farm girl who drove tractors and hewed down cedar, and that personage had little to do with being attractive for young men.

Jeanine carefully counted out the coins. Maybe she should buy something else, something to present to Milton when he came. The cold display case held thick steaks and liverwurst; in the back, cages of chickens talked to one another. There was a steel barrel full of rakes and hoes but it seemed very few people were buying any of these things. What about gingersnaps? She turned a box of Mrs. Baird's gingersnaps over in her hand in the grip of indecision and then with a sudden gesture laid them on top of the beans. There went another dime.

She paid Mrs. Joplin an extra nickel for the message and walked home into the fist of the glassy, hard wind. The haze at the edge of the world was yellow with Kansas dust. She pulled down her hat and held her purchases against her chest and bent her head. If the wind got under the brim of her little fedora it would throw it into the fields and she would be climbing through barbed wire to run after it. She might drop the gingersnaps.

She passed the Crowsers'. She could smell bread baking. In the distance Abel called out to his team. The hills were brown from drought, and even though they were approaching spring, some of the smaller live oaks were yellowing. The tabled tops of the far hills were held up against the sky like great sere altars.

As she came around the curve she could see the Spanish oaks beside the house that held on to only their topmost rusty leaves, the ones that would not give up or be torn loose. The repaired roof with its tin patches gave her a good feeling. Milton's message had said he would drive up this afternoon in the newspaper's car. And there he was, pulling a rooster tail of dust after him in a Model A. She ran into her own driveway.

'Why are you here now?' she said. 'I was going to straighten the house, I was going to have coffee on the stove!' She held the packages against her plaid jacket.

He slammed the car door behind him and held on to the brim of his hat with one hand and her elbow with the other. Something live was leaping up and down in the backseat of the Model A. It was ripping up paper and flinging it around the backseat of the Ford.

'Let's get in the house. It's like being b-b-beat up,' he said. He had a newspaper rolled up in his hand.

Bea was singing along with the radio in the parlor across the hall. It was Bob Wills and the Light Crust Doughboys on WBAP. They were broadcasting out of a furniture store in Fort Worth and Bea knew the lemon oil commercial by heart. *Lemon fresh, lemon bright, try Dickson's Lemon Oyuuuuuul.*

'Hello, Bea!' Milton shouted. He threw his hat across the room and it landed on a chair back. 'Are you decent? Are you presentable for receiving g-g-guests? A handsome and dashing rep-p-porter?' He crossed the hall and stuck his head in Bea's open bedroom door. 'Crushed at the bottom of a well,' he said. 'Left for dead.'

Bea pushed herself upright. 'Don't you take Jeanine anywhere,' she said. 'Don't run off and get married. She's got to stay here until I can walk.'

'Oh, sweetpea Bea,' he said and sat down on

241

her bed. She pulled at her feed-sack dress and tried to smooth down her fuzzy braid. 'You look like you've combed your hair with a skillet, girl.' The hair on either side of her scar stuck up in bristles. Her cast lay on the bed like a section of pipeline and her toes stuck out of the end. She didn't feel dressed without her sock over the toes but what could she do. 'Look here what I brought for you. *Grit* newspaper. Look here. They pay two dollars for a poem. Feast on this, my wounded butterfly.'

Jeanine put the kettle on and hid their hosiery in the cornmeal bin and snatched up a brassiere and a pair of underpants that were drying in front of the stove and shoved them into the woodbox and put kindling over them. She wiped the table off in one long swipe, scattering loose beans and corn bread crumbs onto the floor and swept it all under the cookstove. There were wavy lines of dust in front of the door but she would have to leave that. Sweeping it would only fill the air of the kitchen with Kansas topsoil. She slammed down a fruit jar and stuck one of the yellow paper roses in it. Then she took off her coat and the fedora and ran a brush through her hair. She set out two cups and took a handful of ground coffee from the bin in the grinder. She dropped it into the coffeepot and poured boiling water over it. Prince Albert watched her from the top of the old Hamilton safe and yawned and rolled over.

'What poems?' Bea flipped over the pages of the newspaper. 'What kind do they want? Two dollars?'

Milton bent over the paper with her. His

magnified blue eyes shifted unsteadily behind his thick spectacles. 'There,' he said. 'There's one, d-d-dripping with unctuous sentiments and garb-led rhymes.' He stood up. 'Read it and weep.'

'Thanks, Mr. Milton.' She smiled up at him. 'Maybe I'll try. If I can figure out what they want.'

'Milt,' he said. 'M-m-milt to you, cruel charmer. They want your abject obedience and total conformity. What else do you need before I go into the kitchen and sweep your sister off her worn-out shoes?'

'Would you put my sock on my cast?' She held the sock up to him.

'Darling toes,' he said. 'There.'

Bea settled down with the newspaper poems as if they were a puzzle that needed decoding, and when she had discovered their secret the reward would be two dollars. Her name written out on a check. *Here, Jeanine, go and buy us cocoa and sugar and butter and liver for my minion.* She heard a loud thud. Albert had gone to sleep on top of the safe and had fallen off. He did it all the time. The wind hooted and blew at the edges of the parlor windows, and the dancing orange pig curtains in the kitchen fluttered.

'Ah, the old hand-c-c-c-colored lithograph of the lost child in the forest,' said Milton. He stood before the framed picture and nodded. 'The b-b-bird is singing to her, the bird is symbolic of a hernia truss, which is symbolic, Jeanine, of dread, which is symbolic–'

'Oh, Milton.' Jeanine poured coffee.

'Of feet. Bea looks wonderful, rosy cheeks,' he said.

'How did you know about Bea?' Jeanine said. She set out a plate with gingersnaps on it. She had carefully counted out three for each of them and the rest were for her sisters and her mother.

'Reporters are sick and twisted people,' he said. 'We haunt emergency wards, we always have hopes somebody might, might have been, ah, dismembered by a passenger t-train, preferably the Sunset Limited carrying a politician, po- police reports, Baker Hotel, famous or desperate cinema stars drying out in the Crazy Water baaaths. Drying out in a bath.' He laboriously slapped his knee. 'That's the kind of sophisti- cated reporter jokes we make in the newsroom. Beautiful Jeanine. What are these?'

'My seed packages.' She managed to stop laughing.

They sat down with the Burke's seed packages. Enormous vegetables in violent colors glowed on the stiff paper. Sexual-looking beets and radishes, poisonous rutabagas, sweet potatoes and lettuces swarming in swamp greens.

'Are you going to raise this stuff?' He pulled off his topcoat. A threadbare Chesterfield, a formal evening coat, that was about fifteen years old with worn velvet on the collar and threads netted and loose around each cuff. 'These things look like they could crawl out of the g-g-garden at night and f-f-fasten themselves on your faces.' He clawed his hand over his face. 'Ahhhhhhhh, Ma! Ma! Get it off me!'

Jeanine grasped his hand and pulled it away from his face. 'This is food,' she said. 'I'm Jolly Jeanine the Texas farmer girl.'

'Don't bend over in the garden, Grandma, you know them taters got eyes.' He slammed his hand on the tabletop and made the coffee cups jump. 'By God, there's a poem for Bea. That'll get her t-t-ten dollars. What rhymes with eyes? Lots of things rhyme with eyes.' He poured some of Bea's condensed milk into his coffee. 'I regard coffee as a food,' he said. Jeanine handed him the sugar and watched as he shoveled two heaping teaspoons full into the cup and stirred it. 'Come with me,' he said. For the first time since he had walked into the house he looked at her. Her short flyaway brown hair and deep gray eyes, her thin shoulders, her hands around the coffee cup for warmth and the worn plaid jacket over her shoulders. 'Come with me to Glen Rose. They have let me loose with the newspaper automobile. You could sit in the p-passenger seat and be whisked along Texas highways, paved with taxpayer dollars.'

'Why are you going to Glen Rose?' Jeanine smiled and wished she had put on her gold clip earrings.

'I must commune with a concrete dinosaur. It looms over the courthouse. Ponder, darling, these busted statues. I must solicit advertisements for Dr. T-Tabler's Buckeye Pile Cure. This is the life I am leading.' He lifted the smoking coffee cup to his mouth, blew on it and drank. 'Jeanine, it's cold in here. Let me throw on some k-kindling for you to prove my manliness.'

'No no!' She jumped up and stood between him and the woodbox and the hidden wet underpants and brassiere; she threw out both arms. 'I'll get some splits from outside. We have to save the kindling.'

'Y'all are st-st-starving out here and perishing of the cold,' he said. She came back in from the back porch where they had stacked the day's wood. Her breath smoked.

'I can't go to Glen Rose with you, I can't leave Bea,' she said. She threw in two splits of live oak and slammed the cookstove door shut. 'I would love to see the concrete dinosaur. My mother said I had to have a social life, and a concrete dinosaur would be just the thing. Would it?'

'No, the better thing would be to come to that benefit d-d-dance they're having on Valentine's Day. It's for poor p-p-people. I mean it's for *the* poor people.' He fanned himself with the seed catalog as if he were fanning air toward her. 'Can you smell my new aftershave? I was hoping you would swoon.'

Jeanine closed her eyes and took a deep breath. 'No. Yes. It's Clubman's, isn't it?'

'In exchange for an aaaad, ahem, ad, from Horton's Men's Store.'

'And so the dance is for poor people. And?' She opened both hands and raised her colorless eyebrows.

'Yes. That doesn't include you-all because you-all are wearing clothes. The really poor people are up in the Panhandle b-b-buried stark naked in dust storms. They have shoes made out of bark and gravel. They eat asphalt.'

'Fill me in, Milt,' she said. 'Are you asking me to the dance?' She leaned close to him and took the Chesterfield from the back of his chair. 'I

246

should turn these cuffs for you. Then you wouldn't look like you're selling apples on a street corner. Where did you get this coat?' Jeanine's life had been a chain that had come unlinked and left connections broken and scattered and she had a pleased, sort of loose feeling of comfort that here was somebody who remembered her from second grade when she wore a yellow bonnet. She wanted to fix whatever was wrong with him. His buttons, for instance. They were of three different kinds all down his shirt.

'The mortuary supply.' He put another spoonful of sugar into his cup. 'Ask you to the d-d-dance!' He turned up his coffee cup and drained it of the last sugary drops. 'I am haaaaard to get, Jeanine. I am not somebody who thu-throws myself at the first girl that asks me to a poor-people dance. I am not desperate for flattery and attention. No, no indeed.' He stood up and took the coat from her. 'It's the Red C-c-cross and the Tarrant County Relief Committee. You bring a box of something. Food somethings, any old lumpy foodish articles you happen to have, on the theory that giving to charity makes people feel less poverty-stricken.' He put on the coat and took off his glasses. He pulled out his shirttail and wiped them and then put them back on and smiled at her. 'Grinding. That's what poverty always is. Grinding.'

Jeanine said, 'Why are you telling me this, Milt?' She crossed her arms.

'Because I have to be there and write about it. And if you're there too, well, *voilà*, girl, I take you in my arms and we d-d-d-dance. And if your mother wants you to get a social life, tell her social lives aren't laying around on the street like hamburger papers. You're too old for the high school crowd and you're not going to college and the CCC won't take you because of your g-g-gender and so the answer is...' He held up a forefinger.

'Good works!' said Jeanine.

'Ding!'

He went out to the car and threw open the door and a black-and-tan rat terrier left off tearing a magazine into pieces and sprang out as if it had been shot from a popgun. Jeanine put her arms in the sleeves of the plaid jacket and squinted in the glaring hard sun. Cold and rainless, every day was the same, blue and dry and a perfectly clear sky. It was weatherless weather in which nothing ever happened from one month to the next. She peered into the window of the Model A.

'This,' said Milton, 'is Biggety the rat killer. The chicken protector, the security alarm. Go get 'em, Rats.' The dog darted from the Spanish oak to the flower beds to the veranda. He seemed to be operating on a different level of time. He was in a speeded-up dimension where entire days went by in minutes. By the time Jeanine said she didn't know if they really needed a dog, Biggety, or Rats, had shot into the house through the half-open door and was pursuing Albert from one room to another. They seemed to cover every room in the downstairs within a minute and a half. Bea screamed. She tried to get out of bed. Albert tore up the stairs with Biggety immediately behind. Jeanine laid hold of the garden mattock with its short handle and went after them. She decided to brain the dog.

Then Biggety yelped and came running back down the stairs with Albert behind him clawing at his male parts. Again they went through all the downstairs rooms in reverse order and Albert kept pressing his advantage and both shot out into the yard. Biggety jumped back into Milton's newspaper car and would not come out. Albert was puffed out to twice his original size and strolled up and down in front of the door with an arched back, making very deep terrible noises.

'Now now,' said Milt. 'You really need this dog. G-g-g-get out of there, you flaming coward.' He grabbed Biggety by the neck and threw him out again. Biggety ran under the front veranda. Albert sat down and kept watch on the hole he had run into. Everybody was in for a long day.

Jeanine stood at the door with her hand over her eyes against the hard cold sunshine and watched Milton drive away. She didn't mind about the dog. But he could have asked her to the dance.

CHAPTER TWENTY-THREE

The newspaper came. A subscription, a gift from Milton. It was thrown from the back of an old Model TT Ford truck. The truck was loaded with the Mineral Wells *Star* and the *Dallas Morning*

249

News in tight folds. Two little boys in the back hurled the newspapers out to the mailboxes. The boys had neither shoes nor coats but kept themselves warm with hectic energy, flinging the newspapers and getting in one another's way and arguing. Jeanine shook out the *Star* and read Milton's story on the Texas Health Festival in Mineral Wells, with a parade featuring the Queen of Health and her court and tours to the sulfur-water baths at the Baker and Crazy Hotels. There were floods in California that drowned 144 people and a hurricane in New England where 628 people died. Jeanine was envious. How were both coasts getting all that rain and not a drop in Texas?

Shinnery Mountain was gray with forests of mesquite that had lost their leaves and turned the color of winter smoke; studded throughout the cloudy color were the dark greens of live oak and cedar. Jeanine finished cutting cedar seedlings out of another five acres and started a second cultivation of the peach orchard. If only she could get water to it somehow. Every evening her hands hurt; the bucking steering wheel of the tractor fought against her like a live thing. But she soaked her hands in hot water and then sat down at the Singer. She ripped out a secondhand man's gabardine suit jacket and turned it inside out, cut it once again, lined it with Quadriga cloth, and put in windowpane pockets and a bagged hem. She cut into the squirrel-fur coat and managed a good collar. Bea was allowed on crutches now, and she put the coat on and then propped herself up in front of the hall mirror.

She was so happy and grateful it made Jeanine feel terrible. It was nothing but a remade coat with a little fur collar, but Bea turned in front of the mirror and admired herself so. She took Bea to school in the truck. Her younger sister was anxious to show off both her coat and her cast to Miss Callaway and the Miller kids. With the exception of the wet snow in early December, it had not rained in over a year.

She eased the silver horse ring from her finger and opened and closed her hands, put it back on.

'Mayme, when you're in town look at the junkman's for paint. Any kind of paint.'

'I'll find something,' said Mayme. She shook out the Mineral Wells newspaper. 'Wow. Fresh paint.'

The next day Mayme came back from town with ten gallons of mint green paint left over from when they built the hospital, so old the labels were gone. She had got them for ten cents apiece.

Dust clouded the windowpanes. Jeanine washed them and then spent three days ripping off the old wallpaper and began painting. The day after it was done she walked again and again through the hall and the parlor to see her shadow thrown on the pale, mint green walls in the pure color and the silence.

President Roosevelt spoke over the radio. The newspapers had said he would give a fireside chat, if people had a fire, if they were willing to listen to chats. Bea's face was shining with hope as she listened.

Happiness lies not in the mere possession of money,

it lies in the joy of achievement, in the thrill of creative effort. The joy and moral stimulation of work no longer must be forgotten in the mad chase of evanescent profits. These dark days will be worth what they have cost us if they teach us that our true destiny is not to be ministered to, but to minister to ourselves and our fellow men.

'Does anybody know what he's talking about?' asked Elizabeth.

'Beats me,' said Jeanine and discarded; she and Mayme played Crazy Eights in the winter evening, chasing the elusive one-eyed Jack that would change the suit from clubs to hearts.

Jeanine walked toward the entrance of St. Stephen's church hall in the remade garnet silk dress and jacket and makeup and her last pair of silk stockings. She felt synthetic, like a mannequin made of pressed sawdust and paint. She and Mayme walked through the pool of light at the entrance, while down the street in front of the squat Romanesque church two boys rode double on an uncurried ranch horse singing *Show me the way to go home.*

'Over there,' a lady said. 'They're taking the boxes over there.'

Jeanine laid her box down on the long table in front of a stout woman in a pie-tin hat. There were stacks of boxes on the floor beside her.

'Name? We just want to know who to thank for contributing.'

'Jeanine Stoddard.'

'Contents?'

Jeanine held out the list. Her hand thrust out of

her stiff new jacket-sleeve ringless except for the little silver horse ring jammed onto her little finger. A blunt, small, inelegant hand.

The trumpet player on the bandstand blew out a long flat note and a clarinet responded. Mayme's auburn hair drifted in slow, pretty waves as she took off her coat. Underneath she wore her new dress in the juniper-colored silk.

'There's the band!' She turned toward the bandstand as if greeting an old friend. Her skirt flared and settled. 'Jeanine, I'll see you over at that table.'

Minutes later Jeanine saw her sister stepping out onto the floor of the church hall in the arms of a short man to 'Stormy Weather.'

'Stormy weather,' said an elderly man. 'Don't we all wish.' He stood and held his hand out to his elderly wife. 'Let's get out amongst them, Mother. It's a rain dance.'

And then the dance floor was crowded with couples drawn into a two-step by the clarinet's reedy, sensual tones. Jeanine sat at one of the small tables against the wall and watched her sister swinging around the sanded hardwood floor with the short boy in saddle shoes. There was no sign of Milton Brown. She was sitting alone among the potted palms and tinsel in her new clothes. Trying to have a social life.

'There she is.' Milton took hold of the back of her chair and cleared his throat. 'Boys in the band. A little drink or two.' She turned around and smiled up at him with relief. 'Hate social lives. They're no good. I have nine social lives and a drink always makes things a little easier.' He

253

took off his glasses and wiped them on the tablecloth. 'My speech becomes faultless. My accent moves into second gear, which is mid-Atlantic.' He put the glasses on again. 'And how do you like your blue-eyed boy now, Mister Death?' He sat beside her and handed her a drink. Jeanine laughed and then drank down the paper cup of rum and Coke and it hit her as if she had been gassed.

'Fancy meeting you here,' he said. He turned up his own drink. 'I don't know if you want to dance or not but consider it as taking your life in your hands.'

Milton stood up again and smiled at her. He had been pressed at one time but now he was all wrinkled and his tie seemed to be too tight and it was making his face red.

Jeanine said, 'Oh, Milton.' She took hold of his coat sleeve.

'Oh, Milton nothing. Shall we dance?'

He led her onto the dance floor. Jeanine moved with him to help him keep his balance.

'How are you Jennie? How are you?'

'I'm fine,' she said. 'How are you?'

'Drunk. It helps. Never good at social things. I remember you in second grade, Jennie. In a yellow dress.'

'And a yellow sunbonnet,' Jeanine said. 'You forgot the sunbonnet.'

'My memory is going. Next I'll forget the dress and then where I am and then where my feet are. How is little Bea?'

A glittering ball beamed revolving fragments of light over potted palms, and a board with the increasing numbers of contributed boxes, that was marked out and rewritten as more and more people came in, and a map of the areas hardest hit by the dust storms, and red paper hearts were plastered up on the walls. They danced unsteadily in the fugitive illumination.

'Bea is up, and on crutches. She goes to school two times a week now.' Jeanine tried to smile.

'Darling girl.'

'Milton.'

'Jeanine,' he said. 'Help me. Repair my ragged coat, feed me, listen to me, clean my glasses, carry me home in a wheelbarrow.'

Jeanine stood still and took his hand. 'Let's sit down.'

They sat down and Jeanine waved to her cousin Betty. Betty and her friend Leona lifted their paper cups and shouted as the band played 'We're in the Money.' Jeanine refused somebody who asked her to dance. Her drink was half-empty and she wondered if her cup leaked. But the Episcopalians didn't particularly care if anybody drank. When she turned back to Milton her drink had been refilled and he half smiled at her as if he had been caught at something. A man in an Army Air Corps uniform came to their table.

'Do you mind?' he said.

'No, no, not at all.' Milt invited him with an open hand to dance with Jeanine.

She danced briefly with him. Then he said thank you and excused himself when he saw Mayme and her satiny auburn hair. Her sister was dancing with a young man in a bow tie and the airman tapped the young man on the shoulder and cut in. Mayme and the Air Corps fellow stepped gracefully across the sanded floor to 'San Antonio Rose' and then they came to sit at the table and he shook hands with Milt and it seemed he could not stop smiling at Mayme.

He said he was home in Tarrant visiting, he had come all the way from Randolph Army Air Field in San Antonio. They had just finished grading off a four-thousand-foot strip before those new AT-6 trainers were taking off.

'Are you flying them?' asked Mayme.

'Nope. Maintenance. Single-engine.'

Milt said, 'Jeanine, your face isn't as long as it was a while ago.'

'How would I know,' Jeanine said. 'I didn't make my own face.' She put her hand to her chin surreptitiously, and then reached for her drink again.

Mayme and her Air Corps fellow with the wing-and-star patch on his shoulder were in a musical conversation as they danced a two-step to 'You Are My Lucky Star.' Jeanine turned up her drink and emptied it.

Milton turned to her to say something, and then closed his eyes. He woke up in a moment and stared around himself, as if he expected to find he had disappeared from the dance and then maybe reappeared on some other planet. Then he fell asleep again sitting up. Jeanine fanned him with one of the bulletins and went and got a glass of water and sat it in front of him. He woke up and drank it all and shut one eye. Behind his thick glasses the one open eye wandered from one side of the hall to another. Jeanine wasn't feeling all that great herself. Then two men came up behind Milton and stood there, looking at him for a few moments.

'Do you mind if we take him home?' said one of them. They seemed old enough to be his father and/or uncle. Their nails were stained very black. 'We're printers,' the other one said. 'We've got to set type tonight.'

'He works too hard,' said the other. 'Six days a week, ten hours a day.'

'One drink and he's a vegetable.'

'A turnip,' said the other one.

'Almost never drinks.'

'He's a doper. We take his needles away all the time.'

'So don't judge him harshly,' said the other one. 'Just because he's knee-walking drunk.'

'He's going to be talking to Beulah, the Queen of Porcelain.'

They chortled. Then they each took him under an arm on either side and walked backward as Milt's heels dragged two lines on the dance floor and his thick glasses slid forward on his nose. They disappeared into the swinging kitchen doors that snapped shut with a brief flash of light and steam. Jeanine sat turned around in her chair, watching the door flap open and shut for a few times. They had done that before. She started to pull on her gloves. She would go outside and walk around in the fresh air rather than sit here looking like a Kewpie doll that nobody wanted to buy. She was angry and humiliated. It seemed that people were glancing at her in secretive ways so she stared straight ahead stiff as a hammer wanting to knock somebody on the head.

She had a hard time getting her gloves on. A big red pasteboard heart came loose from the wall and fell down onto the table and knocked over what was left of her drink. The rum and Coke ran off the edge of the tablecloth and splattered on her pumps and stockings. *I am so mad,* she said. She probably said it aloud. The rum and Coke smelled like something from hell. She wadded up the deceitful pasteboard heart and its fake paper lace and threw it on the floor. Her sister and the Army Air Corps man could hardly stop talking to each other. Her cousin Betty and Si were badgering the band for some swing music so they could jitterbug, and the dancing couples were all absorbed in one another, turning like planets in their own private courses. Jeanine thought about walking all fifteen miles home. Everybody else was having a good time; Mayme was clumsily trying to smoke a cigarette and laughing, fumes enveloped her hair, she looked both happy and flammable.

Jeanine turned to see Ross Everett sitting beside her.

He held his hat in one hand and in the other a cigarette glowed. He had apparently just skinned his knuckles. Jeanine tried to focus on him.

'Well, what brings you here?' She delicately lifted her hair away from her forehead, afraid she would poke herself in the eye.

'I volunteered to carry all the Red Cross boxes to Fort Worth,' he said. 'To the Red Cross distribution depot.' He leaned back in his chair and crossed his legs at the ankles. His boots were shined.

'How's my horse?'

'Good. I've plowed out an exercise track.'

'How's the ranch? Meanwhile.'

'Meanwhile, back at the ranch.' The low light behind him lit up all his wool edges and his short-cropped hair. 'Getting ready to buy up the mohair shear crop. Store it. Wait it out.' He drank from a small glass. 'I'm throwing a tenant out of one of my tenant houses. That takes up a lot of time and yelling.'

'That's cruel.' She sat up in a wave of indignation and then found herself unable to sustain it and fell back in the chair again. 'That's not fair.'

'No,' he said. 'It's not.'

'You're throwing children out into the snow.'

'Throwing them out into the dust is probably just as good.' He reached across the table and picked up her hat, inspected it, and then put it down again. 'I'm trying to think of a compliment. I love that ratty squirrel fur collar.' He thought again. 'And the color of your dress is very good for you. A kind of furious bloody purple.'

'I've been abandoned right here in front of strangers.'

'You have your sister and your cousin here, I see.'

'And you got Smoky Joe,' she said. 'My horse. I could have raced him myself.'

'You have a ten percent interest in him.'

'And you took Maisie and Jeff and Big Man and Little Man too, and you sold them.' She couldn't stop herself. Anger rose up like smoke out of her ruined heart. Ross Everett gazed back at her. He wore the same worn three-piece herringbone suit, and a white muffler of rough silk was draped over his shoulders. It made him look like a man in a magazine advertisement, or as if he were about to offer communion. She wondered where he got it. Probably his dead wife. Jeanine's hand drifted to her eyes. She brushed away a small accumulation of tears.

'You're drunk.'

'No, I'm not.'

'You could at least not be drunk in public. Stay home and drink Lydia Pinkham in the barn.'

'I'm sober as anything,' she said. 'As whatever things are sober.'

'And you're about to get mean.' He drew on the cigarette.

'You're just dying to ask me out, aren't you?'

She was indeed drunk or she wouldn't have said it.

'No.' He took the cigarette from his mouth and turned in his chair to shove it into the dirt of a potted palm.

'Why not?'

'My boy runs them all off.'

'Children need discipline.'

'I'm taking you home.'

He got up and went away and then came back, put her coat over her shoulders and helped her get her arms into the sleeves. She suddenly seemed to have four arms but he managed. They crossed the street in the cool night air and he lifted her into his two-tone Dodge pickup in the parking lot of the men's store.

They pulled up in front of the old Tolliver farmhouse where the lamps were on and the second storey stared into the winter night from blind windows. The light from the parlor lamp spilled out onto the long front veranda through the thick Virginia creeper vine, and their five-leaved clusters threw spider shadows. She trod on a saucer of milk and bread crusts. There was milk all over her pumps.

'Let's sit on the porch a minute,' he said. 'Until you sober up.'

'My mother will jerk a knot in my tail,' she said. 'If she knew I'd been drinking.'

'Well, just sit here for a minute.'

They sat for a while as the sky cleared over the Brazos valley in scudding small clouds. He put his left boot up on his knee and ran his hand over it. The stars turned on their immense and distant wheels and Orion stood out in blazing winter jewels.

He turned his hat in his hands. 'Here's the plan, Jeanine. You choose Smoky's colors. Racing colors. And come with me when we cash in at the official tracks.'

'That means we're dating. That means your kid is going to put a hole in my truck with double O buckshot.'

'I'll break his arm. We're not dating. We're business partners.'

From inside they heard the radio laughter from *Fibber McGee and Mollie*. Milton said their names were really Jim and Marian Jordan, that they had tried out for the Crazy Water radio program but they got turned down. So they went to New York

261

and said to hell with you, Texas. Jeanine listened for a moment, staring at the spur marks on his boots and then lifted her wobbly head and said, 'Ross, don't say anything to my mother about my percentage.' She put her hand on his coat sleeve.

He ignored her hand and her sudden alarmed expression and sat sturdy as a post in his heavy wool suit and the odor of cigarette smoke and Lysol. Inside the kitchen Bea and her mother had turned off the radio and were singing 'We Are Marching to Zion.' Their voices poured out of the kitchen into the halls and rooms and out onto the veranda of the old house. Jeanine closed her eyes for a minute and still behind her eyelids Orion swarmed with stars on his shoulders. She suddenly felt ill and bent forward.

'Are you going to throw up?'

'No. Not yet.' She opened her dress collar for air. He reached over and pulled it back gently and saw the blue bruises around her neck.

'Have you tried to hang yourself, Jeanine?'

'No. Don't tell Mother.'

'Don't tell Mother what?'

He waited a moment. He contained his exasperation by drumming his fingers on the chair arm.

'I got my scarf hung up in the drive chain of the cultivator. Both ends. It finally ripped loose.'

He took a pack of Lucky Strikes from his coat pocket and shook one out.

'Is this going to bother you?'

'No.' She fell against the chair back again.

'You'd probably feel better if you threw up.'

'I don't want to throw up.'

'You may not have any choice.'

Jeanine drew in another deep breath through her nose. 'Don't talk about it and I won't.'

Sparks from his cigarette sprayed into the dark. 'Is there some kind of gear cover on it?'

'No.'

'All right. I'll see what I can do.'

He saw headlights in the distance turning off on the farm-to-market road. It would probably be her sister in a car full of revelers, all reveled out. He laid his arm along her shoulder, on the back of her chair, and turned his face up to stare at the sky. Several long moments passed.

'And now what?'

She said, 'I wish I could drive nitro like my dad used to.'

He nodded. 'I see.'

'I think I could get to like driving nitro.'

'You probably could. But you need to be fashionable and have a career as a secretary. Then you can find a man and get married.'

'My dad told me I'd never get a man.'

'What a goddamned shitty thing to say.'

'Excuse your language.'

'Thank you.'

'It gets worse.'

'Worse how?'

Jeanine hesitated. Then she said, 'My mother has invested everything we had in some phony oil-well scheme. Everything left over from when Dad died. And we owe a lot in county taxes and there's no money for milk and malt tablets for Bea. A horrible county nurse comes and brings us relief supplies and she is a hateful witch and she insults everybody. She's always checking Bea's hair for lice.' Jeanine took in a sobbing breath. 'I keep thinking about killing her.'

'Really.'

'Yes.'

'Which oil well?'

'It's a wildcat company called Beatty-Orviel up there in Jacksboro. I forgot the promoter's name. Anyway I'll think of it later. I can't think right now.'

Ross drummed his fingers on the chair back. 'We can never get our parents to act right, Jeanine. I know. I've tried. So has my boy.'

This was lost on Jeanine. She was lost in inebriated thoughts of her difficulties. 'They all blame me for covering up for Dad all those years,' she said, and hiccuped.

'Yes, well, as I remember, you did. In fact.'

Jeanine started to say something. Probably something in her own defense but he laid his blunt forefinger on her mouth and said, 'You were caught between them.' He put his hand back into his lap. 'Do you miss him?'

'We all do but nobody will say it.'

'How is Bea?'

She fell back into the crook of his arm. Might as well. He was big and he loomed and she had known him forever. It was cold. She slipped her hand into his coat pocket and pressed against the warmth of his body.

'Jeanine, you are messing with me.'

She smiled up at him. 'I know it.'

'I asked you about Bea.'

'Good. She's doing everything the doctor says.

264

And that hound Winifred. The county nurse.'

He smiled. 'I know her. Tough it out.'

She realized she was not going to throw up after all and she could say something about food.

'You know what? I've never been out to dinner in my life.'

He turned to her and thought about it for a minute. He pushed his hat to the back of his head. 'You mean with a waiter standing around. Dressed up. At the Baker Hotel. Wine in an ice bucket. And so on. A string quartet.'

'Yes. I've never been. I'm an oil field child, raised on bread heels and beans. I've heard they give you two forks. You could take me.'

He smiled and said, 'You know, somewhere under that hard varnish, Jeanine, you are a really awful person.'

'I do my best,' she said.

He said, 'Other than a string quartet and nitro, is there anything you need?'

'We need tires. I wish I knew where I could find good used ones.'

Ross thought for a moment. 'All right. I can do that.'

They sat in silence for so long that Jeanine fell asleep. Ross held her with one arm until his shoulder joint began to ache and at last he woke her up and said good night. She managed to make it up the stairs and fell asleep with her clothes on.

CHAPTER TWENTY-FOUR

Martha Jane Armstrong was twenty years old with bright red hair and freckles. She was an only child and had a room by herself and that room was littered with letters from Tim Joplin, who was having a great time out with the CCC boys in Big Spring. Jeanine drove to the Armstrong house with her measuring tape and her suit and Bea's coat. The Armstrongs were kidding out. Two minute Angora goat babies just born into a harsh world of coyotes and neglectful mothers lay beside the kitchen stove, folded in straw-filled washtubs making the kitchen a hell of noise and goat odor.

Martha Jane said they kept the silk upstairs in the loft because if they left it downstairs it would take up the smell of goats, as did everything else, including her hair and school clothes. It was the same heathen mess every year but her father and a lot of people were betting that the market would come back. When Daddy said he was quitting cattle and going to goats and sheep Martha Jane had about died. But the screw-worms had driven them to this necessity and so the two newborn dogie goats with their strange horizontal pupils and soft, triangular cat mouths lay curled in washtubs and sobbed for attention.

Martha Jane and her mother and Jeanine went up a precarious set of stairs to see the silk there in the loft by the light of a kerosene lamp. Around them on the walls were varmint traps with carnivorous, rusty jaws. The silk shone like rare treasure in the lamplight, a faint eggshell color. It was brocaded with a shamrock or ace of clubs pattern that stood out when the material was tilted this way and that in the light. There were fifteen yards of it. No, it didn't come from New Orleans, no matter what Alice Crowser told you, Mrs. Armstrong said. Their grandfather had brought it from New York in 1922, where he had also gone looking for somebody who not only owed him a great deal of money but who had also insulted him in ways no gentleman could endure. He saw it in some store and bought it to calm himself down. It has sat up here in the loft ever since.

Jeanine laid out Bea's coat and her garnet silk dress and jacket to show them her work. She turned them inside out and held the careful seams and the linings and the windowpane pockets to the light. Martha Jane said she wished she could do work like that but when God was handing out patience and he said *Martha Jane Armstrong!* she must have been asleep. She was so sad to hear about Jeanine's father. But wasn't he in jail for something?

Jeanine said, 'Malfeasance and walking disorderly. Homicide in a no-homicide zone.'

Martha Jane said *Hmmmm* and chewed gum. She said, 'I kind of remember when y'all buried your grandparents there at the Tolliver place.'

'We came,' said her mother. 'When they were laid in the all-enveloping grave.'

'Oh, you were the redheaded girl,' said Jeanine. 'They kept you and Bea in the house and y'all got up on the table and ate all the bread and butter.'

'I know it.'

Then Mrs. Armstrong started telling Jeanine about the visions she'd been having about Tim, and Martha said Mother, be quiet. Martha Jane found the *Vogue* pattern in its envelope and they wrapped the material again in its old sheet. Mrs. Armstrong said a lot of people had visions. She herself had talked to Amelia Earhart on the Ouija board. Jeanine turned to her and wanted to hear what it was that Amelia Earhart said on the Ouija board but Martha said that Timmy was perfectly safe and he had not been bitten by a rattlesnake. Martha handed Jeanine the *Vogue* pattern and said, 'Jeanine let us give you five dollars before-hand.'

'That would be fine,' said Jeanine. 'Because I'll have to buy thread and lining and buttons.'

On their way out Mr. Armstrong sat half asleep by the fireplace, exhausted and stained with blood and manure. He was short and balding; he struggled up out of the chair and said good evening to them.

'Y'all leasing your fields?'

'Yes, sir, to Abel Crowser.'

'Good, good.'

Jeanine said, 'Well, are you finding a good market for your shear crop?'

'Oh Lord yes, fellow from Comanche County, Ross Everett, buying it all up. Has his own shear crews, electric shears, brings his own generator.' He sat back down again and folded his hands in

268

his lap. They seemed to be made from wood and horsehide. 'He's a hard dealer, that man. Hard to bargain with.'

'But he's good-looking,' said Martha Jane. 'He's got a cute butt.'

'Martha, you are headed for the lakes of fire,' said her mother. Mr. Armstrong ran a hand over his balding head and said he knew folks who were cedar choppers. In fact they lived on one of Ross Everett's tenant farms. They'd do it for the posts. But stay away from them if they come. The way they cuss it would make your nose bleed.

Jeanine sat down to work at the Singer in her upstairs sewing room. It was late February; the shingles were in place on the roof so that dust would not leak in and stain the beautiful silk and sift into the machine gears. The room was dark because they had nailed cardboard over the missing panes but she would deal with that later. She laid out the silk and the tissues of the *Vogue* pattern and thought about where to make the first cut. She marked it with her chalk. Then she went downstairs to start the pinto beans and bread dough. With Mayme's paycheck they could afford flour now, and the kitchen smelled of baking bread.

Abel sank the nose of his sulky plow into the dry soil to terrace the field against the slope. The two workhorses bent into the job until the back band stood up off their spines and the muscles of their thighs were knotted and coiled. The sharp edge of the turning plow threw the earth to one side

269

with a ripping noise. The layer of root matt was torn loose and turned over. He went over the field three times and then he would let it lie until early April to take in rain, which had not come for seven years but maybe it would come this year.

Mayme brought in the mail. Church bulletins from the First Baptist and Third Presbyterian and a postcard from Vernon Galbraith, who was in the Army Air Corps and had danced with her the night of the Valentine's Day dance to 'You Are My Lucky Star' and had fallen in love with her auburn hair, and her unsinkable good cheer, and her kind heart that stood open to the world like a door painted in Chinese red.

On a Monday in the first week of March Jeanine put the John Deere into gear and made her way up the slope with long divots flying up off the wheel cleats like birds made of dirt. It was midmorning on a late March day, and cool, and foggy. She could barely see Abel Crowser on the sulky plow with the rein ends thrown across his left shoulder; Jo-Jo and Sheba bent nearly to the ground, trying to haul the blade through the dry red soil. The fog rose up out of the Brazos River bottoms to the trees below Jeanine and then she watched Abel and the team disappear into it. It was a very still mist without wind, it seemed to develop of its own accord and suddenly she was in the middle of it and the air was heavy and wet.

She shut off the engine. The tall exhaust pipe was hot and steam curled around it. She heard something overhead like a freight train passing but it was a sustained sound that reverberated in millisecond waves, like immensely amplified radio static, so loud she could not think. It was the strangest thunder she had ever heard. It was hostile and full of incoherent buzzes and it went on and on and on. She sat stock-still on the John Deere, listening.

Ross walked across the field to her, with long strides across turned earth. He appeared out of the dense fog, indistinct at first and then solid, with edges. She lifted one hand to him with the other resting on the metal steering wheel. He touched his hat brim and then lifted a hand in return. And then as he walked he bent down and picked up something from the ground and then came on.

He came up to her and shoved his hands in his canvas coat pockets. He regarded the tractor. 'What are you paying for gas for that thing?'

She smiled at him and tipped her floppy hat. 'Thirteen cents a gallon, just like everybody.'

'You need to go fill out forms for an agricultural exemption.' He handed her an envelope. 'Ten percent of a match race.'

'Hey!' She opened the envelope and took out three twenty-dollar bills. 'Sixty dollars!' She stared at it for a moment and with a feeling of great joy realized they could pay off this year's taxes entirely. She waved the bills in the wet air. 'Ross, I am a betting fool. Who did he run against?'

'Little Badger. After this he's going to qualify on the official tracks.' He watched her count the money over twice, and then stuff it into her jacket pocket and turn her face to him with a wide smile. 'Let's get this tractor into the barn,' he said. 'It's looking strange. The weather looks strange.' He reached for her hand. 'Let me drive.'

Jeanine rode behind him on the drawbar and held to his waist as they banged over the rocky ground, through the fog. She turned her head to one side and laid her cheek on his back, her arms around him. He drove uphill in the general direction of the house; they could not see far through the fog and things came at them in blurs and then with details out of the circumscribed world. Then small bits of ice began to fall through the mist and ping on the metal surfaces of the tractor. They were no bigger than a pinhead and perfectly square. The strange thunder sounded again. She felt as if the hair were rising on her arms.

'Damn, what is this?' he said.

'I don't know,' said Jeanine.

'You should have had sense enough to get in, Jeanine,' he said.

He drove straight into the barn fairway and turned off the engine and they both got down. Just beyond the barn entrance the fog turned and swirled, the tiny ice grains pinged. Far away Jeanine could hear a car on the farm-to-market road. They sat and watched out the opened bay doors to the draining sky and the fields in their long descending slopes to the Brazos River disappearing now in stacked planes. She watched a flight of pigeons tilting through the barn; they came to rest on a crossbeam and settled their wings with a clattering sound. The buzzing thunder sounded again and again. They listened with lifted faces.

'What is it?' she said.

'I don't know. But you should have gotten out of the field.'

'I wanted to get it all cleared, Ross. For hay.' Jeanine spread her hands wide, as if a crop of coastal hay would grow up between them. 'Abel could get a hay crop out of it if I cleared the seedlings.'

'You worry a lot, Jeanine.' He rested his forearms on his thighs. He was not much more than thirty years old and he was worn already by the nature of his work and all the work he had in front of him every day when the sun came up. The thought of clearing a field for a hay crop seemed to be too much at the moment. He smiled at her. 'It will wear you out. That tractor is hard to drive.'

'There's plenty to worry about,' she said. 'Ain't there?' They sat down on the old sugar-mill grinding stone and the fall of tiny ice grains stopped suddenly, and then the strange thunder faded away. 'I wish there wasn't.'

'What was the best time of your life, Jeanine?' Ross turned over a white object in his hand. 'When you weren't worrying. Or getting strangled.'

She pulled off the old hat and ran her fingers through her hair. 'Well, let me see.' She could think about it, now that she had sixty dollars in her hands. She lifted her head to the path to the house where it turned through the gate, up to the well. She was six or seven, they had come on a visit to her grandparents. She walked down with her grandfather and her father and uncle to the barn lot in the evening, this very barn. The warm, breezy dark was full of the sound of chuckwill's-widows calling over and over, the men leaned on the mesquite rails and talked about the plow team; she wanted to stay with them forever and hear their talk of horses. How they loved their animals. She was holding her father's hand and the whole night sky and the air had a deep scent of horses and grass, of large warm animals and cedar. Back in the house her sisters and cousin cut out paper dolls from the catalog by the light of the coal-oil lamp but she was with the men in the beautiful darkness and it seemed to her then that the men were strong and harmless, they held the world of the Brazos valley in careful possession. This was some vanished fantasy world that children inhabit the way remote stars inhabit the night sky and form mythic figures, so immortal, so primitive. So she told him about that evening, that brief moment, as best she could although she could hardly put into words why it was so deeply moving to her. He listened with a serious expression, without speaking.

Then he opened her hand and put into it a white porcelain doll's head. 'I found that in your field,' he said.

'Where did this come from?' Jeanine turned it over between her fingers; a face of exaggerated femininity with faded black hair and red lips, broken off at the neck.

'Ask your mother. Maybe she lost it. A doll's

head.' He stood up. Then he bent down and kissed her on the mouth, his hand on her neck. It felt very good to her, sitting there on the sugar-mill grinding stone with its scent of old sweetness and his body so close. He put the fedora on her head. 'Are you done for the day?'

She looked up at him for a moment and then she said, 'I guess I'd better wait and see what the weather does.'

'Good idea.' His hand slid down her cheek and he hesitated but then turned to the house. 'I'll be back to rig you a chain guard.'

She walked with him to his truck, and when he drove away she ran into the house with a feeling that very bad weather was coming. She hunted around for something to eat. She sat in her dusty jeans in the empty house and ate bread and beans. Her mother was in town with Bea for a doctor's appointment. Soon Bea's cast could come off. She took the doll's head to her sewing room and set it on the windowsill thinking someday she would make a body and a dress for it. She brushed out her wet hair and thought about Ross, and then want to the hall mirror, and wished she had looked a little better when he drove up. Then she realized she had not asked Ross what was the best time of his own life. It would probably have been a time with Miriam, she thought. She had a hateful thought that she could end up in a competition with a dead woman and did not like herself for thinking it.

The next day a hailstorm came out of the northeast. Solid-looking clouds the color of ice and irises peered at the Brazos Valley over the range of Shinnery and Blanco and Crawford Mountains, full of the immense voice of thunder and stitched with lightning. Bea was sitting up at the kitchen table, studying the odd habits of other nations for her social studies class. Hitler occupied Austria without resistance, and in the distant hiss of radio static CBS set up a thing called a news roundup with an announcer named Edward R. Murrow reporting from London.

The thunderheads erupted into the dry air with flat, circular mists crowning their tops. They blossomed upward in leisurely explosions, closed in the sky over the valley until the sky was full of thunderheads and could hold no more. The world turned a dark marine blue. The first blast of wind turned up a section of their newly repaired shingles like cat fur and ripped them off, layer after layer, and spun them off into the driveway and all over the yard, their work gone for nothing. Then the hail came down, a wild, tympanic hammering. It smashed two great galactic stars into the truck's windshield. It beat down the clothes that were out on the clothesline, and brained one of the hens, which became confused and darted in a snaky, erratic motion for several minutes, unable to remember where the barn was. The terrier and Albert found themselves hiding under the same bed but neither one would move. They all began to cry out the names of things that would be smashed and ruined, *The garden! It's hitting the windows! The truck!*

They could not do without the truck, they

could not drive it with its windshield a mass of blued craters, and Jeanine ran for the door with such urgency she slammed into the kitchen table, and the coal-oil lamp tipped and roiled. If it fell and shattered, it would have sent out its flaming oil all over the floor. But Bea threw herself forward to catch it and grasped the hot glass chimney and set it back upright and burnt her hand severely.

Jeanine snatched up a quilt from the back porch and then the washtub, and held it over her head. She jumped down the three steps onto the grass; the barn and all the darkened world was being obscured by jumping spangled eyes the size of golf balls, beating on the galvanized metal of the washtub with an indescribable noise so that she could not hear the shouting inside the house as the lamp tipped and was taken up by its scalding chimney by Bea, in her bare hand.

Jeanine flung the quilt over the windshield of the truck. It had already been struck twice. The truck sat under the Spanish oak and the hail was bringing down small limbs and the new green leaves with their hanging pendants of tiny blooms and last year's acorns. She then turned and ran back into the house under her washtub helmet with hail striking her on the bare legs and shoe tops and her unprotected knuckles grasping the handles.

When she got back inside Bea was sitting with a handful of hailstones in her burnt hand and a tea towel wrapped around it and the sound upstairs of glass smashing.

'My silk!'

277

Jeanine ran through the sudden darkness of the hallway and to the upstairs room where the wedding dress was laid out in all its complicated parts. The wind had blown out the cardboard. Jeanine threw a sheet over the silk, scattering button cards and spools of eggshell-colored thread. Her own room was also a mass of disorder as she had left her window open to the bright spring air of that morning. The window was smashed completely and hail was jumping inside. The wind had thrown the curtains and the rod with them onto her orange-crate dressing table, knocking down everything that sat on a level surface.

That night she and her sisters and mother sat at the kitchen table, over the luxury of fried chicken, eating the hail-bruised drumsticks. They went over the damage. Rain fell quietly outside, with a weeping noise. They had lost three windowpanes entirely, some were cracked, but the windshield of the truck had been hit only twice. The old house stood at the edge of ruin and for a moment Jeanine felt it was more than she could bear or care about. Bea, with her wrapped hand, glowed when Mayme and her mother exclaimed over her heroic snatch at the falling lamp and Jeanine smiled and said she was very brave. Her mother said the garden would come back, to leave it alone, even though the rows were still filled with the marbled, melting hail that by morning would be gone. It would come back.

The next morning they cleaned up. Elizabeth said, 'What would I have done if it were just me and Bea?' They crept about in the upstairs hall, bent over to pick up splinters of glass. 'If I just hadn't spent that fifty dollars on shares in that well we could buy new panes.'

'Why don't we just move in town?' said Mayme. 'Let's give it up.' She straightened up and glanced out the window into the yard, which was a mess of litter beaten down from the oaks. Her hair was twisted up in bobby pins.

Jeanine said, 'No, listen, I know, I know how we can fix it. I am going to call Ross Everett. He has that empty tenant farm, he said he was tearing it down. I am going to ask him to give us the shingles and the windowpanes if he hasn't been hit by this same storm.'

She forgot her objections to Ross throwing the tenants out into the snow. Too bad for them. She pressed her tangled hair from her face and her gray eyes were wide and anxious.

'We can't pay him, Jeanine,' said her mother.

Jeanine said, 'Maybe we could all dance and sing for him?'

'Oh there's Vernon!' Mayme screamed and threw down her paper sack of broken glass. A car had driven up, it was the young airman from the Valentine's Day dance. He got out of the old Model A carrying a limp bouquet of carnations and daisies that had suffered from the long drive in a borrowed car and stared around at all the storm damage. Mayme took the stairs two at a time, ripping the bobby pins from her hair.

By the time Mayme had brushed out her hair and put on lipstick Vernon had shed his jacket and rolled up his sleeves. Mayme said, oh don't, Vernon, you don't have to help. Hush, Mayme,

279

he said. Then he peeled potatoes for supper and said he had peeled many a one in basic training. That evening before he left he and Mayme sat for an hour out on the veranda. What musical voices they seemed to have, what light tones of speech. Jeanine polished her oxfords with brown polish and tried not to hear them. Then Vernon came in to say good-bye and drew an airplane on Bea's cast and drove away.

That evening as Jeanine was making the fire in the fireplace for Bea, Mayme crept up to her sewing room and picked up the silk wedding dress. The bodice was still in two halves. She held the front half up against herself, tucked the long skirt into her waistband. She saw herself in the black window, night behind it, the lamp in front.

The spring rushed past them to somewhere else, some other dimension. The house was weathered to the color of burnished steel. It shut itself down every night as coals crumbled in the stove and the old well stood outside like a throat that would speak or sing from the underworld when it was dark and everyone was asleep. Every morning the windows gazed at the weather no matter if it were a spotless blue sky or great clouds that roared and tumbled overhead in fugitive waterless balloons while Jeanine's immaculate laundry snapped on the line. Below, the Brazos drained out of the high plains and cut its way through the red earth and every month it was lower and lower until now there were only separated holes of water and it was possible the river would go dry for the first time in human memory.

CHAPTER TWENTY-FIVE

Mrs Joplin wrote down the occurrence of Jack Stoddard's death in her book of the Brazos Valley Genealogies. It was a thick ledger in which somebody had started to enter the accounts of the old Strawn cotton gin and then quit after August 21, 1929; ten bales, six hundred pounds apiece. After that Mrs. Joplin set down intricate genealogies and random gossip. She gave the book to Bea to read. She said that she had heard that Bea's father had once found a Comanche skull and if Bea knew anything about it or any of his memories she was free to write it down and it would give her some interesting thing to do while she was confined to crutches. Mrs. Joplin had heard that Bea was quite the little writer. These stories should be written down before they turned into folktales. She gave Bea a book on the Comanche and one on the history of Palo Pinto County. Bea kept on writing in this book for many years and in it the folds, or perhaps valves, of time were pressed together like the bellows of an accordion.

In times past, before the Tollivers had built the house, before Europeans had come, before there were horses, the spring air was choked with smoke as the Lipan Apache set fire to the grass in the valleys. After the fire, small sprouts grew up for the buffalo who every year came out of caves in the far south. The ridges were left wooded where men could sit in the shade and become invisible to the buffalo down below. Where they could watch them with the intense pleasure the predator has in watching its prey. The creatures they hunted were not only animals but also the representatives of animals to come, they were the protagonists of stories.

Then the *Nermernah* came down from the Rocky Mountains, from the remote north. They came on horses of all colors, out of the plains of alkali water. The *Nermernah* scattered before them the Apaches, the Mexicans, the Texans, the Tonkawas, and the Caddos, and took what they wanted: captives and guns and horses and women's petticoats and mattress ticking and watches and chamber pots and kegs of tobacco. The few Lipan Apache who were left alive went away to the east, and were not heard from anymore. Their name among the Mescalero Apache and the Jicarilla Apache was a variation of the word for *lost,* for *disappeared,* for *remnant.*

By their enemies, the *Nermernah* were called *Komantcia,* Comanche. It meant someone who wants to fight all the time. Long ago they lived in the far north. They were a tribe on foot who were driven into the mountains by stronger people. They lived hungry lives and were always in fear of other tribes. They hid in the Wind River Mountains that stand like a wall of snow in northern Wyoming. They seemed to be inept, they were good at nothing. Their own cousins, the Utes, called them snakes and dirt eaters. They had messy hair and wore unclean skins.

Their language had only vague names for colors. They had no ceremonies and they were too proud to eat dog. Other tribes ate dog but the Comanche would not, even if they were starving. And so the dogs that nodded and ragged at the edges of their campfires were grateful, and after many centuries of arrogant starvation and suffering on the part of the Comanche, the dogs brought to them a gift: horses.

The horse spread across the plains sometime after the Pueblo Rebellion of 1680. The dogs came harrying them through the deep snows, up a ravine. They waited and turned in the snow and stared expectantly at the people around the campfires. And when the Comanche were mounted, they found that they were more than themselves. They discovered something in themselves that had been there all along. They possessed a genius for war and horsemanship beyond all other people. They sank onto the horses' backs in the knowledge that they had acquired the other half of their bodies, that they were now complete. They turned on those who had disdained them. They were a moving wall of fatality. Their cavalry charges swept the plains clean. They could not be unhorsed nor outrun. Nothing could equal their joy in riding at suicidal speeds toward the terrified enemy.

They raided and set fire to Mexican settlements in South Texas and New Mexico, and if the women and children survived they were ransomed back or sold as slaves. They ranged up to the Black Hills to batter the Sioux and the Cheyenne. Their war cry was *Rah! Rah! Rah!*

283

They grew rich in horses. They loved their horses beyond anything and they bred them carefully for splashy three-colored paints. They rode these unflinching horses into war and then came home in triumph wearing corsets and top hats and other people's hair.

For two hundred years they were the lords of the southern plains. Nothing could stand before them except the slow tidal wave of people who came from the East. This was because the Europeans divided the land into pieces, and recorded everything they did in writing, which was a form of distilled speech. And that was the end of the story of the wars of the Comanche. The grinning, treacherous dogs trotted up in the night, gray as bullets, and took back their gift of horses.

The house was built in 1873, the year the last person in Palo Pinto County was killed by the Comanche. Jesse Veale's horse threw him as he tried to escape, near Ioni Creek. They found him dead and pale, leaning back against a tree, shot through many times. His hat and his gun were gone, but he still had his hair. By that time Samuel Tolliver had bought land including the ridge overlooking the Brazos, and with his two brothers he laid the sandstone foundations of the house, and lifted the balloon frame over it and dug the well. They nailed on cedar shingles and placed glass in each window.

In 1883 Nannie and Samuel Tolliver lost their two children in a diphtheria epidemic. That year Mussolini was born in the village of Predappio in Emilia-Romagna, and in 1884 Isoroku Yamamoto was born in Niigata on Honshu Island in Japan. In early January of 1887 a norther struck the Brazos River valley, dropping the temperatures to eight degrees Fahrenheit. By the fifteenth of January the temperature had climbed to eighty-six degrees. Then on the sixteenth of January a second norther blew in at four-thirty in the afternoon, driving the temperature down to forty-two. By the thirty-first of that same January the temperature was ninety degrees in the shade.

In 1889 Adolph Schickelgruber was born in Braunau-am-Inn, Austria, and the great Union Stockyards were open for business in Fort Worth, with a capacity for 5,000 head of cattle per day. In the spring of 1892 Israel C. Everett, a cattleman of Comanche County, drove into the nearby town of DeLeon with his wife and two sons. They were on their way to attend the funeral of Reverend Cyrus Campbell, one of the oldest settlers of the area. The two boys were told to look carefully at the face of the dead man, because in his youth he had been paid five dollars by the Republic of Texas to forge the leg irons for Santa Ana after the battle of San Jacinto. In 1897 John Cardwell Stoddard was born at the remains of the Stoddard ranch west of Mineral Wells while his father and grandfather drank themselves blind in the corn crib. In 1900, Samuel and Nannie's last and only surviving child was born, a late baby that they named Elizabeth.

The Tolliver house was built in the southern style, with a fireplace and chimney at each end and a long cool hall in the middle. The house was alive in a stubborn and silent way and within its walls people were born and died and bread rose in its wooden tray. The wearings of use patterned the house; the beaten path to the well, the grapevines that grew in profusion near the wash-house where soapy water was thrown out, a trench dug by the front hooves of horses at the hitch rack. Men left their spurs at the back porch rail. Visiting cousins hid in the sugar barn to attempt smoking cigarette butts and watched in nauseated fascination as the world revolved slowly around them. Men left for the oil fields and broke their marriage vows and marriages were contracted again and broke apart and re-formed and somewhere a woman wept with her face to the window glass.

Two hundred miles to the north, where the rolling hills of Central Texas flattened out to the plains, the XIT ranch was broken up because of the drought and financial depression of the late 1880s. The owners began to sell most of its million acres in farm-size lots. The Slaughter ranch did the same. Families came for cheap land, thirteen dollars an acre, and gang plows tore up the grama buffalo grass and the wire grass. They planted wheat and dismembered the root matts of the short-grass plains and for a while the dry-land farmers made money with wheat, but it didn't last long. The Great Depression and the great drought began in 1930. On April 14, 1935, the largest dust storm ever recorded foamed across the skinned land and in three states buried whole towns, railroads, cars, trucks, people, cattle, and houses. Miriam

Everett died of dust pneumonia.

The Milky Way moved through its summer and winter journeys. The Comanche do not believe in a succession of numbered years. That the year 1873 will progress on to 1883 and then to 1889, and finally to 1937, and on into an infinity of numbers. They believe it is always the same year, unchanging, moving in a steady circle and within the circle of the year we are born and strive upward toward something and then we wilt and fade away. Within the year's wheel different people rise to power and then are defeated and their names are a variation for the word *lost,* for *disappeared,* for *remnant.* And in the meantime in the center of the wheel the people charge forward in a glorious manner toward the places where their enemies dwell.

Jeanine bent down to pick up the arrowhead at the edge of the graveyard. She lay down her tools to hold it in both hands and look at it. It was a dark rose flint. The edge was still sharp. Flint never dulls. No matter how old an arrowhead might be it is still edged with ancient wars and bloodletting. She put it in her pocket and went on to the peach orchard with her borrowed pruning shears and the booklet from Texas A&M in hand. It was a pale, dry day and the peach orchard was raining a few pink petals, which lifted and fell on the traveling wind like snow from distant mountains. The directions were complicated. She had to remove all hanger shoots, rootstock suckers, and water sprouts from the center of the tree. Leave one-year-old, red, eighteen- to twenty-four-inch bearing shoots. Peach trees, it said, bear fruit only on one-year-old branches. She would make all this happen and it would leave her with a deep feeling of being more than herself.

She began to sculpt and carve the old trees and take away the imprisoning scale and opened the door for the new fruit. As she stood with a flowering branch in her hand it occurred to her that the round of the year would go on forever, the peach trees would bloom and then it would be hay time and cotton harvest and branding time all up and down the valley, and then winter again. This was work that she loved, the work that it took to keep the house alive, looking out of its shivery glass, its heart the beating small thunder of a good fire in the cookstove, and its voice the radio; Bob Wills singing 'Time Changes Everything.'

CHAPTER TWENTY-SIX

The gang of cedar choppers came rattling down the road in a wagon. They hewed down acre after acre of cedar. They brought down the great mature cedars of the brake in perfumed chips and laid them in rows. Two mules towed the old wagon through the brush and out the barn gate. They swore in a conversational way, as if their sentences would be incomplete if they did not salt them with rich and graphic images. After one visit Jeanine stayed away. *That goddamned Ross*

288

Everett can kiss my ass, they said. *I should have burnt down his asshole house, cheap son of a bitch.*

Milton stalked behind her as she unrolled the chicken wire.

'But I want you to say s-s-something like "Everybody gets drunk at bub-benefit dances!" I want you to understand me. Look deep into my soul, ragged as it is, a mere unraveled thing.'

The wire caught on everything. Jeanine jerked at it. She was dressed in the same dress she had worn when the sheriff had come to them in Wharton and had told them that their father had been arrested. She should burn it, tear it up for rags, its loud tiger stripes were faded and apologetic. Mayme called it her Barnum & Bailey dress.

'Just help me, why don't you?' she said. 'All right, all right, here I am looking deep into your soul. Everybody gets drunk at benefit dances.' She wiped her face with the hem of her skirt. The flat sunlight stoked up the barn like a furnace even though it was only mid-March.

'Oh, Jeanine, you have released me from a hell of self-condemn-n-nation,' he said. 'The nights I have sat awake listening to the St. St-St-Stephen's Episcopaaaaal Church ringing the hours of one, two in the morning and reliving the dreadful scene as much as I could remember of it.' He reached out for the edge of the chicken wire and helped her pull it over the stall. He stuck himself with one of the ends and put his bleeding finger in his mouth and then took out a handkerchief and wrapped it around his finger. 'I waited a whole month before d-daring to creep in here, wringing my hands. Ap-pologizing.' Biggity the rat terrier sped past them with a large, thrashing rat in his mouth. Since they would not allow him to kill the cat he took it out on the rodent population. He would bring Mayme the rat's head because Mayme loved him.

'I hope you stayed awake until your eyes dried out,' said Jeanine. 'You didn't even ask me to the dance. It wasn't even a date, and I was supposed to put up with you drunk?'

'I know it, I know, I know myself,' Milton said. He handed her nails. She slammed them in over the wire. 'I know myself and every smoky b-b-backroom corner of my gelatinous mind. Who could c-c-care for me, Jeanine?' He caught his coat sleeve on the ends of the wire and tore loose more threads. 'Every time I fall for a girl, I think, "I would never go out on a d-d-d-date with somebody like me." Take a girl with really really thick glasses, for instance, and a speech impediment, and twenty dollars a week at the local rag. I wouldn't go out with her.'

Jeanine laughed and bent her head down on the chicken wire. 'Stop, stop, stop,' she said.

'Here,' he said. 'I am risking my mental health t-to offer this.' He reached in his jacket pocket and held up a small box covered with red satin. 'The only thing a g-g-gentleman offers a lady is candy and flowers, and it was this or a set of new underwear. Do you need some underwear?'

Jeanine stared at the box and finally understood it was some sort of candy or chocolates.

'You're breaking my heart,' she said.

'Kiss me,' he said, and closed his eyes. He

tapped his lips with an inky forefinger. 'Right here.'

Jeanine paused for a moment and saw his closed eyes behind the thick glasses, saw every eyelash and the darting movements of his eyes behind the lids. She leaned forward and kissed him. The wind was starting up again and old straw drifted down from overhead and landed on them.

'Again,' he said. His eyes were still closed. Jeanine reached out and took the box from him. She held the hammer in the other hand. She kissed him again, because he needed kissing. Maybe it would, like sticky tape, lift some of the stutter from his lips, and then they would say honest and heartfelt things to each other and his incessant light irony would crackle and drift off like onionskin.

He opened his eyes and smiled at her and put both his arms around her neck and pressed his forehead against hers. 'No underwear?'

'Hush,' she said. She heard Bea calling from the back porch. She was calling Albert. She wanted to make sure the dog had not killed him. The wind increased and started tearing at the sheet iron of the barn roof. One of these days it was going to tear it off and send it flying across the pasture. Jeanine let out a long sigh and dropped the hammer. 'No underwear.'

They walked back to the house against the hot wind, their arms around each other. The Spanish oak leaves were uncurling in tiny green fists and pushing off the tassels. He bent down his head against the wind and laid his hand flat on top of his hat to hold it on. He held the back door for her and dust followed them. Milton made himself at home in a kitchen chair, stretched out his legs. Biggety lay in the middle of the kitchen floor with half a rat body.

'Oh get it out of here!' said Jeanine. She found a paper sack and threw it in by the tail. She wadded up the sack and went outside and dropped it into the burn barrel. Biggety went after it. She came back in. 'I'm making coffee,' she said. 'Where are you going today?'

He put his chin on both hands and watched her fill the coffeepot and set it on the stove. She opened the box and looked at the chocolates, chose one. He chose another. They tapped them together as if they were champagne glasses and tossed them down. Then she found her sewing box and took his coat and turned it inside out and began to separate the lining from the sleeves. 'This one is as bad as the overcoat.' She smiled at him and held up the needle. 'Miss Fixer-upper.'

'Where to today? To the sulfur springs at Arlington. People drink the stuff for their health. Vile. I am inured to all the d-d-depravities of human nature. Why do they not do stories of the families living under the Trinity bridge in Dallas? People in tents, little children sleeping in the dirt. Living on stuff from garbage cans.' He slumped back in his chair, watching Jeanine fix his coat. It made him feel quiet and unstuttering. The chair creaked. The dry air had shrunk up the glue and it was about to fall apart. 'I drift around the country looking at drought and the soil is like concrete, abandoned farms taken over by cedar,

292

and all they want to hear about is all these people trying to attract t-t-tourism with concrete dinosaurs and rotten-egg water.'

'I would pay a dime to see dinosaur tracks,' said Jeanine. She turned back the cuffs an inch and snipped off the ragged threads and began to stitch them back to the lining.

'Then, my dear, you would love the town of Fairy.' He bent forward to watch her sew his sleeves up again as if she were neatly repairing his very self. 'Named for some railroad owner's daughter. What's interesting about it is the cemetery. The Fairy Cemetery. I told them to put up some tombstones for Snow White and her dwarf entourage but d-d-do they listen to me? No. Then there are the weddings of all the rich oil people. Murchisons, Hunts.'

'What about ordinary people?' she said. 'The ones who haven't hit oil.'

'Ordinary people getting married?' He laughed heavily. Ha. Ha. Ha. 'They have to pay to get their notices in the paper. Irish potatoes, chickens, eggs, and sometimes b-b-banknotes.' He lifted one clasped hand to his eye and peered through it. 'Fifty cents to the photographer. We get to go to the big weddings sometimes.'

'Because you get free party favors. Free chocolates.' She threw his coat at him and he caught it up.

'N-no! Oh cold and r-r-rejecting one! Rife with suspicion!' He stood up and put on the coat and shot out his wrists, admiring the sleeves.

'You did! You didn't buy them, you got them at some Dallas society wedding.'

'You don't trust men, Jeanine. C-c-common psychological problem. Your father b-b-betrayed you, all men are suspect.'

She got up and crossed her arms. 'What is this about my dad?' she said.

He was blank for a moment. 'I'm trying to think what I just said. Mouth running but brain not engaged.' He put his finger to his lips. 'Ah, your dad was arrested and unfortunately died in, in, ah jail.' He walked over to her and took her hand. She pulled it away. 'They never said what for. Wasn't reported in *my* paper.' He stared at the floor. Then at her. 'I always wondered what for.'

Jeanine didn't know what to think or what to say. The chocolates suddenly had a dismal and dusty look to them scattered in their brown paper cups. She listened to Bea's light humming in the parlor across the hall. The wind made the back screen door open and shut, open and shut, bang bang bang.

'For gambling,' she said, finally, and stabbed the needle into her pincushion.

'There!' He snapped his fingers. 'They didn't even give him any medical care, I would bet. Scandalous, the way p-p-people are treated by Texas justice is scandalous. No good making a complaint, either, not with James Allred running things.' She watched as he struggled with himself to say something serious, to utter some genuine and sincere sympathy, some condolence. He made little waving motions as he fought without much conviction against the incessant stream of irony, and silliness, and derision. It was an affliction. He loved it. 'Terrible loss,' he said. 'Sad. Bitter.'

'I'm not sad and bitter, Milton,' she said. She marched back and forth across the kitchen twice and took an enormous breath of air, slapped both hands on the table and smiled. 'See?'

'No, stupid thing to say. Always saying something stupid.' He took her hand again. 'I am on the outside of everything, Jenny, and I like it. I am not g-g-good for much else. I am the perfect newspaperman. I would love to be K-K-Kaltenborn, I would love to intone in a deep clear voice that the Reichstag has burnt down or the Hindenburg exploded– Oh the humanity! – that was Herb Morrison. It was spontaneous. He said it on the spot. That will go down through the ages.'

'Milton, you know, maybe you'd better give up on radio.' She smiled at him once more.

'I work the buttons, though. I give airtime to hog callers. But no airtime for me.' He pushed a chair toward her and she sat down again. 'How's that for stimulating the economy? He may sound like a soul tortured in hell but he's only c-calling hogs and making six bits for doing it on air.'

'Can't you do anything about your stutter?' Jeanine didn't know what caused stuttering but she could ask, couldn't she?

'Yes.' He took another chocolate. 'A school in Chicago. Excellent. Costs a lot of money. Saving every penny.' He ate the pecan creme and swallowed. His pale unweathered skin glowed in the dusty evening light and Jeanine heard her mother and Mayme drive up outside. His pinwheel cowlick made it seem as if his face were topped by a kind of toy. 'And by God I will go there. And I am going to make it in radio. W-w-wait and see.' He stood up and put on his hat and walked to the door, waved at her mother and sister, turned back and took her by the shoulders and kissed her. 'What if I asked you to go to the movies with me?'

'Try me,' she said. 'See what happens.'

'What if I inquired about your interest in Fred Astaire and urm, let's see, we could bring our own popcorn?'

'Ask and ye shall receive.'

'What if I p-pressed myself upon you with insistence?'

'I would melt in your arms, Milton.'

In the little parlor Bea lay in a haze of liquid morphine; the pain that radiated from the pin in her broken leg was moderating and she dreamed of going to school again. Where the pretty teacher Miss Callaway would ask her about her day. Would lay out new books for her to read.

CHAPTER TWENTY-SEVEN

At breakfast they looked out at the ridges to the north; the flats below drifted with an early haze like thin smoke. Mingus bluffs rose behind them topped out with oak and cedar and the smoke of the breakfast fire climbed straight into the sky. Everything they said came back to them in a hollow repetition. 'Hey!' shouted the boy. The bluffs said hey.

'Hush,' said Everett. He blew smoke away from himself and listened. Then he spit on the end of his cigarette and dropped it.

'Any of them you want particular, Ross?' said Homer.

Ross said, 'Yes. She's a red mare. All red. I want her. She must have got loose from somewhere.'

'Could have,' said Nolan. 'Up at Lubbock the dust is drifted so high the stock is walking right over the fences.'

'Try not to hit her,' said Ross.

'All right.'

'I hear them,' Ross said. 'Let's get along.'

The pasture was two thousand acres. It had been recently fenced off with four strands of good wire, cedar posts nine strides apart. The band of feral horses had been there for two years and he had tolerated them but there had been no rain and they had increased more than the grass could bear and the hooves of horses were bad for the soil, tamping and compacting it. They had been joined by loose stock that wandered in from other places. Some of them had the weight and the appearance of Percherons or army remount Thoroughbreds. The April landscape was deceptively green along the slopes because of the cedar and live oak but in the valleys the grass stood in stiff clumps spaced farther and farther apart with every month, with hard dirt in between. The live oaks along the creek banks had lost limbs from drought. They shattered when they struck the ground. The same with the pecans. Another high wind and he would lose half the trees in the pecan flats.

The tips of Spanish dagger and the sotol held up their needled tips in blazing points of light. The sudden sunrise heat made the land smoke, a haze of thin evaporation lifted and moved slightly. To the north another battleship of red dust was building. They came down one of the long rolling ridges of Comanche County. It was a country of vastly separated ridges of limestone, and the country in between them held in place by a drying cover of grass that was not going to be there much longer if the horses grazed it out. They figured on being able to shoot about thirty head of horses that morning. They had run them away from the water for three days now.

Ross Everett and three of his neighbors rode to a bluff overlooking Upshaw's Creek. There was one pool of water left in it. Wave after wave of scaled quail flushed up and flew, singing their high one-note song, and settled again and then flew again as they rode through the coveys once more.

The pool was twenty feet long, an eye drinking in light, the first light of the morning. The smell of dust and the peppery smell of cedar lay close to the ground. Everett sat his horse with ease, loose at the waist, his canvas jacket hung open from his shoulders. The lines of his face were graven deep, and he seemed ten years older than he was. The small rain had passed and the weather turned the world back over to the drought. Low, nebulous clouds bowled past at a low altitude, loose, glowing banks of traveling mist.

Nolan Simms and his two sons moved away to another angle. They tied up in a cramped stand of live oaks that were no more than ten feet tall and all twisted into one another, and got out their rifles and lay down on the ground and sighted on the pool. Everett and Innis tied up and lay down as well. Ross took a box of 30-30 shells and opened it and placed it on the ground between himself and his son. Homer Fletcher and the two men who worked for him moved away to the right. Everett didn't like the two men who worked for old man Fletcher but what could you do.

'I want you to think and shoot carefully,' Everett said. His son slipped in one shell after another. He was being asked to do a man's job with a man's rifle and it made his hands slick with sweat.

'Yes, sir,' he said. He wiped his hands on his shirt.

'I don't want to see any wounded animals thrashing around suffering.'

'No, sir.'

They came in with an old mare leading them. The oldest mare always led the herd. The boss stallion came behind and some younger stallions darted around the outer edges of the herd, desperate for water and afraid of the boss stallion. They were all thin; it was painful to look at them. They seemed to be nothing more than bones moving inside horsehide and eaten by internal worms and wounded by the larvae of the insatiable screw fly that ripped at tissue and feasted on fresh blood. They knew there were men above them on the ridge and hidden in the stiffened dry brush but they could no longer go without water. Suddenly Simms's boy stood up in his excitement and fired. Then Nolan Simms and his other boy started firing.

Everett sighted on the old mare and brought her down. She seized up and stiffened as if she had suddenly been fired in pottery and then dropped with her head and flying mane falling last. She lay there and other horses ran over her. He shot and worked the lever and shot again. The red mare ran, low and graceful, in a panicked circle around and around the pool. She couldn't keep on much longer. There was a festering, ragged wound on the inside of her right foreleg. One of the young stallions slammed into her and knocked her onto her side, but she fought to get on her feet again. Everett's rifle barrel followed the young stallion for a few seconds and then he shot. It was a little bay stallion so thin a person would think it couldn't still be alive and when he collapsed he looked like he had been dead for a month.

Dead horses lay unmoving around the glittering surface of the pool and at last you could hear the musical sound of falling water as it ran over a lip of rock and into a smaller pool. After that the water went underground. The only ones left standing were the red mare and a foal several months old that ran calling from one carcass to another.

'Anybody want him?' Everett yelled. He stood up. So did his son. The ammunition box was empty.

'I do.'

300

Everett turned and put his hand on the boy's shoulder. 'That's what I get for taking you to see *Bambi,*' he said. 'No more Walt Disney for you.'

'I want him,' the boy said.

Everett called out, 'Leave the foal!'

They walked down to the gravel of Upshaw's Creek. The red mare thrust her muzzle into the water and drank and drank. When Everett came toward her she stepped back with a dripping muzzle and nodded to him. She took one step toward him and then two. She was begging for her life. He had seen other horses do it. It was a strange thing. He turned his back to her and crossed his arms and stood very still. She came toward him and he could hear her sucking ragged breath. She touched his shoulder with her muzzle and stood there shaking.

Old man Fletcher walked among the dead horses. 'We need that goddamned Gene Autry to come here and sing "Home on the Range" for us,' he said. 'Happy days are here again.'

On the way back home they passed by the tenants' houses on Grape Creek. The fields had not been turned that winter. There was no point. The tenants loaded a buckboard with their possessions and children and went to chop cedar. They would trim them down to fence posts and make five cents a post. They had paid him what they owed him in cedar posts for the new pasture fence. Everett would cannibalize the houses, strip them of glass and shingles. Then probably the best thing to do would be to set them on fire.

Smoky Joe was galloping from one end of the horse barn lot to the other. His hair was all turned up, he galloped in wild short rushes and stared out over the top of the mesquite palings with his nostrils wide and white around his eyes. He was shod now and worked hard every morning on the bull's-eye track behind the storage shed. It was strange how he could tell what had happened, miles away. But he knew. Then he called out to the red mare in a low murmur.

Everett turned her into the sick corral and watched her. She stood in the center of the half-acre lot, very still, her red tail blowing around her hocks. It was a solid pen made with sucker rod pipe and casing pipe for the uprights and it would hold her well enough. She carried a Rafter S brand and he did not know where it was from. Nolan would know, he had the brand registries for the Texas and Southwestern Cattle Raisers' Association and it was possible an owner would claim her, but he hoped not because she was a handsome girl, even drawn down by parasites and her hooves split out by drought. He carried a feed pan made of an old tire out to her and hung it over one of the uprights and filled it with feed. He could smell the rotting flesh from screwworm larvae but they could get to that later.

The foal was turned into the lot with the white-face and her bull calf. Innis stood and watched as both of them nursed from the cow and she was patient and chewed and ran her tongue up her nose holes. The foal sucked furiously and his short brush tail thrashed like a machine. Foam leaked out of the sides of his mouth.

Innis found the creosote paste in the bunkhouse. It was now used for saddle storage and medicines and number three cans of hominy and tomatoes, the anvil and horseshoes. They could no longer afford to pay help. Old pieces of latigo and wooden stirrups were thrown on the beds. They would have to tie the mare down to dig out the screwworms and pour creosote into the meaty wound. He wanted the red mare to be well, and take up with the stud foal and mother him. If he were mothered, then the foal would thrive. Innis poured out the creosote into an empty tin can and swirled a brush around in it.

Ross went into the house and climbed the stairs. From the window of Miriam's room he could see Innis walking out to the sick corral with the creosote. He began to fold the possessions of the boy's mother into boxes. The bedspread, the curtains, the doilies on the vanity and the things from the drawers. Outside, another relentless and bitterly clear day. The sky was blue from one horizon to the other and shaded only by a light marking of dust from the east, from Kansas, where topsoil lingered airborne in the lofting winds. Ross knew he had to do it sooner or later and the time had come because of Jeanine. He had made up his mind. He opened the closet and took out Miriam's dresses. He folded those as well. They would go to the Baptist church and be sent somewhere. He would ask them to pack it all off to a Baptist church somewhere out of the area. Some woman headed for California, in a Model T with mattresses on top, with a washtub and blankets strapped to the back, would wear them.

303

CHAPTER TWENTY-EIGHT

Mayme said, 'Mother, go talk to Violet and Joe about a telephone. He works for the phone company. Get him to see how much it would cost to lay a line out here.' Mayme carried a bucket full of dead leaves from under the broad live oak and dumped them onto the dry earth around the zinnias. It helped keep the roots cool. Jeanine and Mayme had decided the zinnias and sunflowers were Mayme's job, and in trade Jeanine would whitewash the rocks bordering the walk.

Elizabeth sat in the shade of the veranda watching her daughters work and then said no to the telephone. She was afflicted with nervousness in waves. But she sat on a kitchen chair and appeared very calm in the light breeze, turning the little porcelain doll's head over in her fingers. She was afraid for all the money she had poured into the drilling, money that was gone forever and herself a mother depriving Bea of the things she needed, condensed milk and subscriptions to *Far West Stories*. But the well might come in, it might come in. Elizabeth fanned herself with a piece of cardboard and said that before they spent money on a telephone, Mayme should buy herself clothes for work. Mayme brought in their only cash, and she should have new clothes and a good hat.

Mayme sighed and said Yes, Mother. She could

have had a new spring straw hat months ago but she had instead given her mother ten dollars and then ten again, to buy more Beatty-Orviel stock certificates. What could she say? It made her mother happy. Elizabeth liked to sit with Lillian and Violet and go over the seismograph reports, talk about torsion balance technology, they visited the site with potato salad for the men. They were like schoolgirls. Mayme went inside, thinking up patterns for summer dresses. They could not afford new ones but Jeanine could put something together.

Jeanine pumped water from the kitchen sink pump over a colander of beans. 'Get me the material, Mayme, I'll make whatever you want.'

'I thought you were busy with Ross's racing sheet. For Smoky Joe.'

'I can do that racing sheet in an afternoon.'

'Well, then.' Mayme brightened up and opened a magazine and flipped through the pages and then held it up. 'Can you do something like this? I found some dotted swiss curtains at the church basement. There's about ten yards.'

'Easy.' Jeanine took the magazine in her wet hand. 'Cross-tabs on a standing collar. Sure. Easy.'

'What did Ross Everett say about the shingles and stuff?'

'He's bringing them.'

Jeanine's garden had burnt out. There was no rain and she could not carry enough water to keep it alive. But on the other hand she had collected so many agarita berries that she had filled ten jars with the rose-colored jelly. Mrs. Crowser showed her how to spread a sheet on the ground around the thorny bushes and then beat the agarita with a hoe handle until the berries fell into the sheet. Before long they would have a secure roof and then whole milk from the dairy in trade for eggs and then maybe a telephone from Mayme's pay. They would talk to their cousin from their own kitchen, dressed in beautiful smart clothes like the women in the WPA posters, the annoying posters plastered everywhere that said you were to brush your teeth, take care of your hands, and save waste fats. What waste fats? Jeanine wondered who made up the damned posters. Didn't they know everybody was eating their fats and it wasn't waste?

Jeanine sat down and wrote out their budget for May. They were in the main living on Mayme's seventy-five a month. They spent twenty a month for groceries and her Smoky Joe bet money went to pay off this year's taxes, but still they owed over two hundred dollars for the years past and now they needed another fifty dollars for 1938 taxes. If only Smoky Joe would bring in a little more. Then she could buy luxuries like new dress material unrolled fresh and smelling of crisp sizing from a bolt in a store. Then the telephone. She put the paper aside. The rat terrier lay at the back screen door, on the outside, with his nose against the frame, blinking. Albert sat opposite him on the inside of the screen. He stared back and didn't blink.

Ross sat on a cane-bottomed chair in Jeanine's room. He stretched out his long legs. He listened while Jeanine told him of her first cut into the silk. She had comforted herself with the thought that if she ruined it, she would have borrowed the money from him to replace it. Then the hailstorm. It was one thing after another.

Ross thought of how his grandfather or even his father would have shot themselves in the foot with a large-caliber weapon rather than step into a young woman's bedroom, but times had changed. He smelled of mohair and sweat and cigarettes. He had a train ticket in his pocket, a coach seat all the way to Washington, D.C., where he would change trains for Woonsocket, Rhode Island. The American Wool Company was presently not on strike, but by the time he got there anything could happen.

He said, 'Do you understand about the shingles? Can you do it?'

'Yes.' She lifted her face to him and smiled at him because she knew his face would change. He would flush a little at his cheekbones, he would smile back, slightly, at one corner of his mouth. 'First, I smash Mayme's thumb. She screams. We fall off the roof.' Then she opened her hand and dropped an imaginary hammer and said *Thud*. Ross smiled just as she thought he would and watched her pick up the wedding dress bodice and there was indeed a slight flush along his cheekbones, under the sunburnt skin.

In the kitchen Ross heard her mother and sisters talking, their quiet laughter. They had all looked on as if they were mildly astonished when he drove up and stripped off his tie and coat and vest, rolled up his white shirtsleeves and changed

307

all four tires on their truck for four good used ones, and shook his head at the hail craters in the windshield. All the time her mother saying he would get grease and tire marks all over his suit and himself saying it was all right, he'd changed many a tire in a suit and tie before now. The glass panes were packed in straw and laid in long ammunition crates left over from the Great War and they would keep safe until Jeanine and Mayme could putty them into the frames. He carried a chain guard to the barn and fixed it over the chain drive on the cultivator.

They regarded him washing at the sink as if he were some strange official male come to deliver a telegram or inspect the property or lead them in prayer. His broad thick wrists, the way he took up the embroidered tea towel and dried his callused hands. He searched for someplace to put his hat and finally laid it on the safe counter upside down. They inquired about Smoky Joe and he assured them that the stallion was about to enter the official tracks. He had to qualify in Lubbock. Up north in the plains country. He would like for Jeanine to go with him. They would get there and back in a day.

Elizabeth handed her oldest daughter the tray with coffee cups. 'That's a hundred and fifty miles from here. Up where they have all those dust storms.'

'I would really like to go,' said Jeanine.

'Promise me you won't bet,' she said.

'I'll make sure she doesn't,' said Ross. 'It's illegal.'

'Oh, Ross,' said Elizabeth. 'Really.'

'He has to what?' said Mayme. 'Are they going to run all the way around the track?'

'Qualify,' said Jeanine.

'Qualify for what?'

'For an A rating. If he does four hundred and forty yards in twenty-four seconds or less he's rated A, and then he can race on all these official quarter-horse tracks. Against other A horses. The prize money is good.'

Ross said that Mayme should come too. But she was going with Vernon to the baseball game in Eastland on that same date, and she said, 'Y'all will have to go by yourselves.'

Ross said, 'The boy is coming.'

Jeanine frowned. She shoved her hair out of her face. 'His boy is coming, Mother,' she said.

Ross glanced at her. He decided to ignore it. He said, 'I see you made something out of that doll's head, Jeanine.'

The porcelain head with its black hair and red lips stared out with a stiff hieratic face from the mantelpiece, given new life with a stuffed body and a dress made from scraps of the eggshell-colored wedding silk.

'Oh yes!' said Elizabeth. 'It was my mother's! I don't know how you ever found it. Strange how things turn up.' She smiled. To Elizabeth she seemed to have come back out of the earth to take her place in the house again, after years of loss and neglect. 'I was so happy.'

Then they had played gin rummy for an hour in the newly painted parlor. There was the silent knowledge that he had come to be with Jeanine. Everything was proper and quiet inside the clean mint-colored walls. He saw how pleased Mrs. Stoddard was, that she radiated a lighthearted, even slightly apprehensive gladness that her daughters and herself had a house where they could receive, as people used to say; where they could offer a new-painted parlor and coffee, laugh and shriek over their triumphs at gin rummy. Ross remembered the board-and-batten shack in which they had existed in Conroe, with the washtubs out in back on the bare dirt and the front yard no more than eight hundred square feet littered with jacks and wheel hubs. The loud public battles in the ravaged tar paper shack next to them between a man and wife and innumerable children in some unrecognizable language. Pure squalor. And Jack Stoddard leaking money at every pocket in the gambling joints.

Ross expressed admiration and astonishment at the way Prince Albert had personally rescued Bea from the well. He listened while they told him of Bea's heroic grab for the falling lamp. When Bea cried out in her customary exclamation points that next year was high school, and she would be allowed to cut her hair! And she would have an English teacher! Just for English! he shook his head in amazement and whistled.

'My, my. Just for English.'

'But you knew that already, you graduated from high school,' said Bea, darkly.

'And also from Texas A&M,' said Ross. 'I learned just enough to come back and tell my old man how to run the ranch.'

'Are your parents still with us?' asked Elizabeth. Jeanine spun out the cards to each in turn

310

and then picked up her hand and gasped in amazement at what she had and Ross laughed at her transparency.

They were very much alive, he told her, living in San Angelo. They started out as cross-timbers ranchers with cattle running loose and a couple hundred acres saved aside for cotton and hay. And three boys. His father got desperate and tried sheep and poured a shearing platform and then gave up on sheep. Then somebody hit that Fry field, it came in good in 1926, Pure Oil bought out our leases. Daddy made money on it. He never liked ranching anyhow, and his brothers didn't either. His father was an odd man, Ross was fully prepared to admit it, involved with inventions, one of which was a pecan-shelling machine that had thrown shattered pecan shells all over the old stone ranch house where Jeanine had spent the night, until he finally perfected it, and so he had made a great deal of money. He and Ross's mother garnered their oil-lease and shelling machine profits and at long last fled the Comanche County ranch and its six thousand acres for life in town. Now his father was working on the hydraulics of irrigation pumps. The Depression had not affected them all that much. He asked if he could smoke. Bea hurried to bring him a saucer and watched with a kind of helpless, hypnotized fascination as he lit up. His mother, he said, was nearly six feet tall and could sing like an angel, alto, and when she was in a full cry on 'Faith of Our Fathers' you could hear her from Brownwood to Rising Star. Ross's two brothers had joined them in San Angelo to work with his father in the engine shed

311

full of machines and parts of machines, with his mother inside the house practicing for a choir, shattering glass. Ross snorted out smoke and shuffled again. And so during the drought, with the dust storms and the falling cattle prices, they had signed over the ranch to him and he abjured any part in the profits from their noisy and malodorous inventions.

Then after a while her mother and sisters yawned and laid down their cards. They drifted in vague, diplomatic movements away to the kitchen and Ross followed Jeanine up the stairs to her room to see the wedding dress. Elizabeth and Bea and Mayme were now sitting in the kitchen, in steamy domestic peace, to knit and read and listen to the news.

'What are you doing other than running around with a washtub on your head?' he said.

'Driving that tractor,' she said. 'Sewing. How's your boy? The gunslinger.'

'I had a serious talk with him. I don't want him hitting people with slingshots. I told him before long he's going to get a new mother. Sooner or later. He's not allowed to kill her. He's exercising Smoky and doing pretty well with him. When he qualifies, the money will come in by the cotton sack.'

'You're going to tell him that I'm going to be his new mother!' She dropped a card of buttons and grabbed his shirtsleeve. 'Don't you dare.'

He picked up the card. They were little mother-of-pearl knobs. There would be twenty-five of them up the back of the dress, he figured. 'I'll tell him you're going to be my mistress, my

312

paramour, my secret valentine.'

'Oh stop it.'

'I told him we were going to have wild, un-inhibited sex in the barn and he should turn Catholic and pray for our souls.'

Jeanine kicked at the baseboard. 'You're going to go to hell, Ross.' She crossed her arms. 'You're going to go to hell and shovel ashes.'

'I know it,' he said, calmly. 'Are you coming to Lubbock?'

'Yes. We can get there and back in a day?'

'Yes.'

She got up and threw a window open, the one that looked out over the valley where harmless cottony clouds crept over Blanco Mountain, shadow by shadow, and behind them stars lit themselves. The light made her seem almost transparent. The evening wind swept into the room like a guest from the horizon of tabled hills and rippled the fringes of her bedspread.

She smiled at him and he looked away from her sweet mouth and sunburnt skin. He rolled down his sleeves and buttoned them. Desire had taken hold of him like a mugger. It was beating him up. Many small evasive plans came to him, of stopping off at the Bluebird's Rest Tourist Courts near Lubbock, where that transparency would dissolve in his hands. He jiggled his foot.

Jeanine sat down on her bed and started laying the piecings of silk one on top of the other, her long legs knobby at the knee, her hair cut at a pageboy length and curling at the edge of her square jaw.

'I don't know how to thank you for all this stuff,

Ross, shingles and glass and tires.' She turned to her closet and brought out the racing sheet and the saddlecloth folded together. 'How about these colors? Dark blue and kind of brick red.'

'That will do.' He took the packet from her. 'It looks very good.'

'I thought it would show off his color.'

'It will.' He touched her shoulder. 'Walk me to the truck,' he said. 'I have a train to catch.'

They walked out to his truck. There was a long silence and both of them rested in the cool night, in the new-minted springtime of Central Texas.

'When will you be back?' she said.

'Two weeks, three weeks. Then when I've made my contracts, I'm going to be involved in buying up the June shear crop, getting my shearing crews from one place to another.' He laid the folded racing sheet and saddlecloth on the seat.

She put her hand on his arm. Sometimes he seemed like a large older brother or uncle and other times, like now, in the dry clean darkness there was something so powerfully private and sexual between them. He might touch her body, he would lay himself alongside her. He would hear whatever she had to say. He would bend down and listen with that grave, considering expression on his face and so she said, 'Ross, we're all going in different directions.' She took hold of his white shirtsleeve.

'Who?'

'Us. Us here.'

He thought about it for a while. He reached out and put his hand on her shoulder and felt the articulation of bones beneath his hand and the

314

light material of her dress. He looked down at her square face and her long gray eyes. He tightened his hand on her shoulder and then he turned away from his thoughts. He said, 'Yes. You're wondering what will become of this place.' He cleared his throat. 'Mayme's very caught up with that Air Force fellow. And your mother is spending a lot of her time in town.'

Jeanine said, 'Yes,' and turned to look at the rising moon, which was a dark yellow sickle lifting over the top of Shinnery Mountain. The old barn had held out against gale winds despite its missing boards. The house seemed white and lofty in the dark, pinioned between the two chimneys. She wondered where they had got the stones. If the house were abandoned once again that would be the end of it. She tried to see forward into the time to come. It seemed they all kept turning into other people, that there was no one germ of self held in reserve against all that shifted and changed and blew at them from some remote source. They had wanted so much to come here, this place where she had walked down in the soft darkness with her father and grandfather to listen to the breathing of the work team. And in not too many years they would all go away.

He turned his back to the door of the truck and leaned against it. He put his arm around her shoulders and she came to him and lay her cheek on his shirt.

'Nobody has to get married, Jeanine,' he said. 'You can live here the rest of your life if you wanted.'

315

'I can't do it by myself.'

'No.' He thought about it for a moment and then said, 'No, not alone.' The rat terrier came softly padding across the lawn. He came near them and ducked his head several times and then sat down and tucked his tail around his front legs and blinked. 'Be good to that dog, Jeanine. He's begging you.'

'I don't like him.'

'That's not the point. He runs off the things that get chickens. He kills rats.'

Jeanine shifted away from his arms and bent down and ran her hand over the little bony skull, and the terrier's tail whipped back and forth. Ross watched her. The dog sat and stared at them with his ears standing up.

'I guess someday we might have to rent the place out,' she said.

'Renters move,' he said. 'Three renters is as bad as a fire. You never know what will happen, sweetheart.'

'Then what?'

'Then you just keep trying.' He bent down and kissed her, lightly. 'There's no alternative.' He opened the car door. 'I've got three days sitting up in coach looking at me.'

Jeanine held the door handle. 'Do you have something to eat?'

'Yes.' He slid into the seat and she shut the door. 'A lot.' There was a cardboard box beside him on the seat. Probably full of hardboiled eggs and biscuits and other things that would crumble all over his coach seat. He was going to meet the Yankee capitalists of the Rhode Island mills with his worn suit and a box full of homemade food and a Stetson hat. 'Good-bye, Jeanine.'

When his taillights had disappeared she walked down to the barn in the dark with Biggety at her heels. She circled the barn and checked the hens shut up in the stall behind chicken wire. They would do this every night. It was to show Biggety that she was on his side and between them they would guard against predators and change and mischance. Then she sat for a long time on the veranda, listening to the familiar dark.

CHAPTER TWENTY-NINE

Cap and the men lived like trolls in the engine shed. They set up a table made of a cable spool and they put a coal-oil lamp in the middle and sat around it on empty wooden liquor boxes and dynamite boxes. They cooked in their tiny cast-iron stove and slept on the floor. One late, hot evening George Lacey drove in and walked in the door of the engine shed and said good evening and sat down with them.

'I'm snooping,' he said. He reached for a deck of cards. 'And looking for something to do of an evening.' He shuffled the cards. 'I'll deal you a hand.'

'I don't play,' said the captain. He lay back on his bedroll, on the floor beside the stove, with a candle stuck in a sardine can. 'I quit.'

'Quit what?'

'Shooting dice and playing poker. I don't wager.' The wind sang in disjointed hoots at the edge of the tin roof and Captain Crowninshield squinted at the Magnolia field connections foreman in the dim light.

'Well what do you do for entertainment, Mr. Crowninshield?'

'I'm reading a book.'

'What's it about?' Lacey spun the cards out from man to man and laid a handful of pennies on the table.

'It's a detective in Los Angeles that's mixed up with fast women and gangsters.'

'Leave him read,' said Andy. 'You just have to leave him read.'

The driller figured Lacey was going to ask him when they were going to give it up. All the core samples were dry as fossils and no sign of sand. In fact Andy had pulled up a sample with a strange birdlike skeleton in it, like a print, something beached in a waterless limestone sea. Both Andy and Otto laid down their cards and yawned until their jaws cracked.

'You play dominoes?' said Lacey.

'Hell yes.' Crowninshield emptied a box of black dominoes out onto the cable spool.

'You got the old well log?' said Lacey. 'From when they drilled here before?'

Crowninshield tried to think what business George Lacey had in this wildcat well, and thought for a moment. He should just ask him. When they had reached three thousand feet, Captain Crowninshield asked the shabby producer if he still had the old well log from fifteen years ago, and the producer said he probably did, that he might be able to find it somewhere in his papers. Tells you what kind of outfit Beatty-Orviel was. And he did find it, the long thin strip of paper with mysterious seismograph markings on it, and in some parts the markings were thick with spikes and in others they were so tight as to form a solid bar. Crowninshield had stuffed it into a cardboard box somewhere, he wasn't sure where. But he left his dominoes and went searching through his piles of papers in the Carnation box. He found it. He flipped through the log by the light of the kerosene lamp. Ran his finger down the jittering black lines indicating strata.

'What does that tell you?' Lacey said. He scraped up his pennies and put them in his coat pocket.

Andy and Otto lay in their blankets beside the stove and snored.

Crowninshield said, 'Not much. In the five years since they drilled here, there's been a lot of oil pulled out of the field. All over the Woodbine field. Lot of oil, lot of gas.'

'I know it,' said Lacey.

Crowninshield sat down again and shoved the well log at Lacey.

'It means the pressure in the entire field is reduced. The law says now if you hit salt water you got to pump it back in, keep the pressure up. They learned that in the big East Texas strike. In '31. They haven't been pumping back salt water like they should, law or no law. So when the pressure changes, gets lower, that means the oil all over the field has probably shifted. It ain't in the

319

same places it was when they first drilled this hole here, fifteen years ago. So everbody's guessing.'

'There's two wells over at Apache where they hit salt water,' said Mr. Lacey. 'They're just letting them blow.' He set up his dominoes.

'I know it.'

'I personally don't think it ever stops shifting,' said Lacey. 'It is my personal theory that something is making more of it down there. Making it all the time.'

The wind sliced through the leaky sills and blew a spider across the floor. It trod with sticky legs across the remains of a shepherd's pie.

'What's your interest in this, George?' Crowninshield set up his own line of dominoes.

'A lady has invested in this well that...' He paused. 'Somebody I know.'

'Hmmm.'

'Jack Stoddard's widow.'

'Hmmm.' Crowninshield wiped his hand over his bald head. 'I knew Jack Stoddard. The less said the better.'

Andy sat up in his blanket and said, 'Judas priest, when is that wind going to quit?' He flopped down again.

'I'll bring some tow sacks you can stuff under those sills,' said Lacey. He folded up the well log.

Otto turned in his blankets and said, in the strangled, low tone that comes out of a dream, 'The wages of sin is death.' Then he kicked his feet out straight and began to snore.

'So are the wages of virtue.' Crowninshield considered his dominoes. 'And wages is plural.'

CHAPTER THIRTY

Tarrant's streets were full on a hot Saturday evening. Jeanine and Milton each paid for their own tickets to the Lyric Theater to see *Bringing Up Baby,* where large overhead fans sucked out the stale air. It made Jeanine feel as if her hair was standing on end. The Movietone News shorts zoomed over a globe that looked as if it were made of plaster but the audience sat and ate popcorn and were entranced with the illusion of being in outer space and regarding their home planet at a distance. Then the newsreel brought them back to earth. There was Mussolini in a uniform and high boots and then the prime minister of Finland. They both seemed of equal importance simply because they were walking and talking through the grainy atmosphere of newsreel films. Then sports. People like Babe Didrikson and Lou Gehrig did not seem to have any stories about them, Jeanine thought; they were sort of human sporting goods.

Dust sifted beneath the double doors and past the concession stand and then drained down the carpeted aisles and settled at the edge of the proscenium. Amelia Earhart had disappeared in the Pacific and the search had finally been given up. King George was perfectly happy now that his weak and silly brother was married to an American divorcée, and the newest bathing suits

321

were demonstrated on a California beach. Jeanine never saw moving pictures from one month to the next and so was completely absorbed. Milton watched her and laughed when she was so moved by the opening scene of *Bringing Up Baby* that she paused with popcorn halfway to her open mouth to watch Cary Grant, the paleontologist, fit bones onto a brontosaurus skeleton. Katharine Hepburn was impossibly bold and outspoken. Jeanine sank down in her seat in seizures of laughter. She clutched her red-and-white-striped box of popcorn with both hands. Other people in the theater were calling out *Hey shut it up* and *Pipe down.*

'They snatched m-m-my idea,' said Milton. 'Dinosaur skeletons! J-jeanine, they are thieves, shameless thieves!'

'What dinosaur idea?'

'You and I st-standing in the Fairy dinosaur tracks, hunting d-d-down the leaping tyrannosaurus...'

Their voices were loud and people called out, *Pipe down, hey, go outside!*

Jeanine whispered, 'Into a lost world, I get to wear a kind of suede bathing suit and a rock necklace. You wear one of those jungle hats.'

'Yes, yes!'

And at the end Katharine Hepburn, who was a society girl, and Cary Grant, who was a paleontologist, fell in love after one day of insanity, and leopards, and being jailed. It seemed perfectly logical. Jeanine was completely caught up in the hypnotic sequences, the beautiful interiors. It seized her mind.

They walked out onto Main Street, and as they stood on the curb all the streetlights came on. People on the sidewalks glanced up into the electric glare and then went on in the warm night air, as if they were people on a stage set. The Movietone News and the soft brilliance of the black-and-white film dazed her and she could not shift her mind away from it. Tarrant's main street seemed like some kind of background to Jeanine, a street full of people hired to wander around, to dance to a jukebox in the drugstore across the street, an empty wagon coming down the street, driven by an actor posing as a tired man who had sold all his produce at the Saturday farmers' market. So was she, she was some kind of a body in a crowd scene. She was to stay all night with Betty and go to the MacComber House the next day for volunteer work with the Red Cross. Now she and Betty were going to act in some movie scene about aspiring secretaries who roomed together and traded lipsticks.

She took hold of his shirtsleeve. 'I feel like an extra, Milton,' she said. 'Help me, help me, my mind is stuck in that movie.'

He stood back and blinked at her from behind his thick glasses. 'I see. Well, Jenny, the way you can tell if you're an extra or not is if they p-p-pay you.' He grasped her hand and strode on down the street. They were to go to his apartment over the shoe store and see his radio. He said it was not as seductive as going up to see his etchings but his radio appealed to the mind and not the sweaty, lugubrious body. Milton led her through the crowded street. It still seemed to her they were all people on a stage or a movie set, speaking dialogue. They went up some back stairs in the alley behind the shoe shop and he suggested that he and she escape the fictional world of Tarrant, Texas, the picturesque but desiccated cattle herds of Palo Pinto County, the starving cotton farmers in their costumes of rags, and go to the big city. He said he was smitten with her, devastated, his heart was being crushed like foil in her small, elegant hands and she said for him to give it a rest but she laughed and held his arm.

His apartment was one room with a bathroom over the shoe store, next to Betty's little room. Long panels of typewritten pages were pasted to the walls. Wires came through the window and fed themselves into the back of a huge radio. His clothes, what there were of them, were flung over a cot and a pair of shoes turned up with socks spilling out of them, as if they were crawling out and about to begin speaking in tongues. In the corner was a wooden crate of cabbages and potatoes. An icebox dripped. The hot night air poured in through the open window.

He pulled out a chair for her. 'I get free ice,' he said. 'I get free milk and formal wear from the f-f-funeral home, and fifteen dollars a week. These riches can all be yours if you pledge your troth to mine.'

'What's a troth?' said Jeanine.

'They bear l-l-live young and lurk under bridges.' He then turned to the big Philco console radio and held his hand out to it. 'Jeanine, this is Philco console radio. Philco, this

324

is Jeanine Stoddard.'

'Charmed,' she said. 'Crushed, devastated. Slaughtered.' She sat down and crossed her feet at the ankles.

'I sold the family cow for that thing. L-l-look, Jeanine.' He turned the fan toward her and the long strips of newspaper copy fluttered. He gestured out the window. She got up and came to lean out the window frame beside him. 'I've strung antenna wire in a *hu-u-u-u-uge* c-circle, from the top of the saddle store to the peanut-shelling outfit, warehouse, whatever the hell they call it, to the harness-making place and b-b-back here. I can get anywhere, I can get goddamned *Mars.*' He turned the radio on. A glow appeared from behind its fabric front panel. 'It's on KMOX, St.-Louis,' he said. 'Listen. NBC.' He sang along with the tones; bong, *bong,* bong. The announcer's voice came on. *In twenty minutes we will have a report from H. V Kaltenborn. Kaltenborn has spent the last eight days in Munich reporting on these momentous events, barely taking time to eat or sleep.* Milton sat down in a chair beside her and his hair seemed to spike up in yet wilder shocks of internal electricity, his excitement made his glasses sparkle. 'J-Jeanine, Jenny, come to Chicago with me. This is a proposal. We could guh-get married. Lots of people get married. You and I could marry one another, shamelessly, openly. Scandalize everybody.'

'Stop it,' said Jeanine, but she was laughing. 'I like where I am.'

'But then we would move back! I promise. Little boys on the st-street would say "That's Jeanine

and Milton, used to live in Chi-Chicago!"' He
jumped up. Big-band music came through the
speaker. 'But this is the modern world, Jeanine.
Modern! Moving forward, p-pretty soon nobody
will be from anywhere. Archaic ties. Ancient tribal
deadwood.' He turned down the volume. 'I have
a favorite d-d-dish, here, saved it just for you.' She
bent forward in the chair to watch him unscrew a
jar of preserved blackberries, fling them in a dish,
crush two peppermint candy canes with a
hammer and sweep the crushings into the bowl.
Then he took an ice pick and hewed mightily at a
block of ice in the icebox and threw in cool,
glittering pieces.

They bent over the single bowl with two spoons
on his scarred and rickety table while the fan
blasted them with hot air.

'You propose to everybody,' said Jeanine. She
reached for a dish-towel and wiped her lips.

'No, n-no,' he said. 'Just two or three in the past
month. A m-month has fled past me during
which t-time I have proposed nothin' to nobody,
not nohow.' He bent forward and kissed her. His
breath was fragrant with mint and blackberries.
'If I could ever get over my stutter I would duh-
drop all this cynicism. It's flat and shallow isn't
it? It's the fashion.' He dipped into the bowl
again. 'Just through these copper wires, imagine,
the voice and, uh, words have more power and
import than they ever have in human history.' He
waved his spoon. Jeanine stopped eating the mint
and blackberries and listened. '*Never* has the
human language been so imp-p-portant and
that's because far away things are now reaching

out t-t-t-to us, we aren't protected anymore here behind the Continental shelf. We can saturate people with words. They believe them. It's lovely. I want to do that. Come with me to Chicago, Jenny. Sweet Jenny.'

'You're going to some school for elocution,' she said. 'In Chicago.'

He nodded and put one hand to his mouth, briefly. 'Learn to speak at will. You don't know...' He paused and his eyes had a watery brightness. 'What a weight it is. Like every w-w-word is weighted or ch-chained.' He took up a triangular piece of ice in the bowl of his spoon. 'I have a talent, Jeanine. A g-gift, and it is languishing in chains. So unfair!' He breathed out a long breath and swallowed. 'It's so unfair. And I don't know why.' He wiped his forehead and then became himself again. 'We could make p-plans,' he said. 'Plots. I like plotting better than p-planning.'

'You don't have any money, Milton,' she said. 'Are you going to go to school in Chicago on cabbages?'

'Wait and see,' he said. 'Juuu-just wait.' He spooned up the last bite, deep purple berries and syrup and bits of candy cane, and put it to her lips and she swallowed it. 'Move in town,' he said. 'B-b-beautiful Jeanine, of the gray eyes. Town is b-better. Even your cousin has running water. Even I have running water. Why not?'

'I don't know,' she said. 'If I said I just loved being out there, would that sound crazy?'

'Yes. Everybody wants to get off the d-d-damn farm, Jeanine.'

They sat together on his cot and listened to

Kaltenborn's report from Munich. Jeanine closed her eyes and lay back with Milton's arm over her shoulder. They were trading countries with one another, chopping off pieces here and there and handing them around. She thought about moving into town. And then to a bigger town, the excitement of Chicago or St. Louis. They were all moving someplace else anyway, weren't they? This thought made her heart constrict, briefly, and an image came into her mind of the old house empty once again. She could hear the sound of a T&P freight going through Tarrant, such a small place in the middle of Central Texas with the power plant on the Leon River and the farm and ranch stores, the town swimming pool and the doctor with his cactus growing in the front yard and the hotel where oil leases were sold and marriages betrayed, the rodeo grounds swirling with dust. And beyond the electric lights, the dark hills. Radio waves passed through all these things and were invisible as speech. The Tolliver house and the town of Tarrant suddenly seemed unimportant and common. Jeanine found herself in an anxious dream, walking behind several black-and-white people who were dressed in glossy stylish clothes; she was saying something that nobody was listening to. They would not listen to her. She and Milton were slumped against each other and sound asleep when Betty hammered on the door, yelling for them to wake up.

Jeanine wadded herself up on Betty's couch in a nightgown. Betty's face was hot and sweaty, she twisted up her hair and said she'd been smooching with Si, and then they got into an argument, right there in the China Moon dance palace, and then they made up and the smooching went on unabated until she tore herself away and ran up the stairs to find Jeanine and Milton asleep and the big Philco radio blasting out Hawaiian dance music. Betty was covered in a yellow nightgown as big as a parachute. Her dark Stoddard hair snarled up in a tangle of pin curls. Lights from a passing car washed across the ceiling and the music of a radio from somewhere down at street level came to them. Betty frowned at her fingernails. She reached for an emery board on her nightstand. 'Come on, Jeanine, go to work somewhere in Fort Worth. You could get a good job somewhere. Buy some nice clothes, you could be a receptionist. You could go to work in a flower shop or Montgomery Ward. There's decent jobs around.'

'I couldn't stand it,' said Jeanine. The thought of dressing up every day and living in a town and hurrying to please people was enough to freeze her blood. She could never manage to please people and especially not for five dollars a week. 'I like to dress in rags and make chicken coops. I'm my own boss.'

Betty didn't laugh. 'Get a dull stupid job,' she said. 'Like me. And go out dancing or something in the evenings. Ross Everett is very *serious* about you.' Betty got up and poked in her little cupboard and found a waxed-paper sleeve of Saltines and jumped back in her bed and threw some to Jeanine. 'Ross'd just *love* you in a playsuit. Can't you just *picture* yourself spraying cows with tick dip and wearing a playsuit?' They ate Saltines and scattered crumbs on the sheets.

'I like being at our place. I don't want a playsuit. Why doesn't anybody listen to me?' Jeanine found she had dribbled cracker crumbs into the neck of her nightgown and she tried to slap them away. 'Why am I eating these things?'

'And now Milton Brown, you buy yourself a satin dress for dancing in, and those little open-toed numbers I showed you, and he's a dead man. *Dead.* Just get a job for a while and buy yourself some nice clothes, Jeanine. It ain't forever.' Betty sighed with a big *Ooof* sound. She was exhausted from all the arguing and smooching with Si. 'You're seeing two different men! Now that's what I call a social life. You got to nail down Milton, though. That's the kind of guy he is. You got to nail his shoes to the floor.'

'You're not listening to me, Betty. This is like a nightmare.' Jeanine stared out the window. Then sleep nearly overcame her. She lifted her head and searched in her straw purse for her handkerchief and blew her nose. 'When you talk and people don't hear anything you say.'

'Si keeps wanting to get married,' Betty said. 'But I'm having too much fun right now. I ain't ready for kids and housework.' Betty watched another car crawl by on the street below. 'And we're going to have some oil well money coming in.'

'Betty, there ain't going to be any oil well money.'

'Yes there is. That well is going to come in.'

330

'Come in what? Sour gas and salt water probably.'

'Mama says it's good.'

'Good for what?' Jeanine yawned until tears ran, and then flopped back on the pillow.

'She says it's going to come in, girl.' Betty stared out the window into the faintly lit night of the small town. Then her eyes slid shut. 'Going to be high-gravity and under pressure.'

'You tell me how you know that,' said Jeanine. 'But you ain't going to answer, you're going to sleep.'

'No I am not, I'm just checking my eyelids for holes.'

In a minute Betty fell into a light snoring. Jeanine thrashed around on the narrow couch and could not sleep; she looked out into the street where trees bent like hair, brushed by the wind that had come up out of the southeast as if there might be a hurricane down in the Gulf, as if this wind might reach all the way to Palo Pinto County bearing rain. Jeanine thought that if she lived in a big city it would no longer matter if it rained or not.

CHAPTER THIRTY-ONE

The stores and offices on the main streets of Tarrant were bright with posters declaring we must all work together to bring America out of the economic emergency. At the MacComber

House soup kitchen Jeanine made coffee and cut up donated, stringy beef for the soup. She washed her hands and sat down at a table with five other girls and threaded a needle. It was hard to hold all the material down with pieces of scrap iron and cut pipe rings but they could not do without the fan blowing on them. The streets outside wavered with heat distortion. They were piecing together dust masks to be sent to other Red Cross centers. Most would go up to the Panhandle hospitals, to Lubbock and Amarillo, where the dust storms were the worst. The streets were filled with train noises and crowds. Martha Jane Armstrong showed up to help make decorations for the Fourth of July benefit dance and Betty came with a box of linen scraps. Uncertain, ragged families strung themselves one by one through the door and stood silently, waiting to be told, to be offered something and too proud to ask.

Jeanine told Martha about the drive chain on the cultivator grabbing her scarf and Martha said she'd better carry a knife, she didn't know how many people had caught their clothes in machinery and got killed. You need to cut yourself loose and if all else fails you can jam the blade in the gears.

A stout woman named Bricey was the democratically elected head of the Mineral Wells Relief Committee and she had a voice like a sawmill whistle. Jeanine remembered her from the Valentine's Day dance, where she had sat behind a table and took in the boxes, gray as cast iron and completely unmoved by the traveling light-spots that rained on her pie-tin hat, sorting the small gifts for poor people given by other poor people.

Now Bricey cut sandwiches with a big carving knife, and laid them out in stacks. A family of four sat down on the unsprung couch and the mother handed the sandwiches to her husband and two small children. Jeanine glanced at them and away again. *Like we used to be,* she thought. *On their way to something better.*

'You girls just think I am a stodgy old lady,' said Bricey. She turned the key on another can of Spam. 'But I have a secret life.'

'Well, tell us,' said Betty. 'Don't hold back.'

'I am an astronomer.'

They all said, No! Bricey smiled.

'Does that mean stars?' somebody asked in a whisper.

'Tell us,' said Martha Jane.

So Bricey told them about the telescope on the roof of her house and how she went out on clear nights to see the rings of Saturn, and the canals of Mars, light-years from this town, so slack and depressed. The stillness afflicted her. The rising dust storms. So she went up to her roof and gazed out into the limitless Great Otherwise and worlds upon worlds.

'So there. My secret life.'

Jeanine smiled at Bricey, surprised. Bricey sat up on the roof and drank in the light of the stars like a little old nocturnal hummingbird. She had her own secret life there. And she dressed in dumpy dresses and her awful gray hat in the daytime. Jeanine realized she knew so little about

333

people; that she and her family had moved around so much they had always depended only on each other and she in truth knew as little about the world as a nun. Jeanine's big stitches galloped across a square of layered gauze.

Bricey had a small round mouth and never wore lipstick and when she smiled it showed her gold tooth.

'And I knew your mother, Jeanine. I think it's marvelous that she bought into that oil well.'

'You knew my mother?'

'You were born here, Jeanine. Y'all weren't brought up on a desert island.' Bricey took her hairbrush from her purse and brushed back Jeanine's hair. 'You should let your hair grow out, honey, and do it in one of those pompadours. It would make you look older.'

Jeanine sat carefully still while Bricey drew her short hair back and thought about the effect and then let it spring back to its brief waves.

'How did you know my mother?'

'Why, we went to high school together! She was a freshman and I was graduating. Oh she was so pretty. She's still pretty. And that oil well is just the thing for her. She can busy herself to death with that thing and it'll never come in and so she can buy into another one. She should have done something like that years ago.' She smiled and ruffled Jeanine's flyaway hair. 'I'm glad y'all are back, Jeanine,' she said. 'Y'all have had your troubles but I'm glad you're back.'

'Thank you,' said Jeanine, and wished she knew how to say more; something more of the sudden rush of gratitude for such simple words.

'And how is Bea?'

'She's going to have that cast off pretty soon.'

'Is Mrs. Beasley taking good care of her?'

'Yes,' said Jeanine, and her good feelings evaporated at the image of Winifred Beasley and her bird's-nest hat. She went to stand in front of the electric fan. 'But if she keeps on ordering us around she isn't going to live out the summer. I swear I'll throw her down the well.'

'Jeanine!' Bricey jammed the hairbrush back into her purse and shut it up hard. 'I didn't know you were like that.' She closed her mouth over the gold tooth. 'Winifred has dedicated her life to rural nursing. She is selfless. She has worked without cease.'

Betty stared at her cousin and put a finger to her lips.

'Well excuse me,' said Jeanine. 'I didn't know you knew her.' Jeanine sat down and started stitching quickly.

Bricey sat down with pinking shears and began cutting out linen squares. 'Absolutely selfless,' she said. Jeanine felt like she ought to leave but Ross was supposed to come in on the afternoon train and she wanted to meet him and hear if he got a contract or not. She wondered if they would remain friends if Milton Brown presented her with an engagement ring and declared his undying love and set a date to m-m-marry her and they would stroll among the dinosaur tracks and kiss beside the drying bed of the Brazos where catfish swam in circles in the shrinking holes of water. Then they would get on a train to Chicago with everybody throwing shoes and rice and then herself and Milton in a Pullman bed. She turned toward the door as the Old Valley Road teacher, Miss Callaway, hurried inside with a box containing jars of red, white, and blue poster paint and a tube of sparkles. She wore a light pink printed cotton dress and she was crying. She stopped and put the box down and shook out a handkerchief and wiped her eyes.

'Why, Lou-Ann!' said Bricey. 'What is it?'

Lou-Ann Callaway motioned toward the back room and Bricey got up and followed her. They all listened intently; they heard the kind of pressured noise people make when they are whispering at top volume. It was something about a young man. Martha raised her eyebrows and kept sewing. Who was seeing someone else, she had just discovered. Betty thumped her heart with a fist and rolled her eyes. Martha Jane placed her wrist against her forehead and pretended to faint. Jeanine heard the faraway noise of the train whistle as it crossed the Brazos River Bridge coming into Mineral Wells, and said she would be back later. She knew that sooner or later Bricey was going to have a long chat with Winifred Beasley and that something would come of it; something unpleasant.

Through the heat waves and engine steam she saw Ross Everett stepping off the westbound passenger train. He took off his hat and came walking toward her. 'I figured I would find you here. This is one of your days at the Red Cross.'

She came to him and took his coat sleeve in her hand. He laid his hand over hers and bent down to kiss her hot face. The smell of his body and skin was very intimate; tobacco, train, sweat, himself. He said they would go somewhere cool, the drugstore, and have something cold, and he would tell her about his contract if she were interested, and then he would drive her home when the temperature had cooled down. He told her about the rain he had seen in the East. Sheets of it. The feel and air of the world when it was drenched and running with water. One beautiful rain after another.

They drove back out to the Tolliver farm in the blue evening, listening to his car radio. She bent forward and turned it up when she heard the first strains of 'Stormy Weather.'

CHAPTER THIRTY-TWO

It was toward the end of July that they got the telephone. Joe Keener backed toward the house, unreeling telephone line from a large spool. He bored holes in the wall and ran the line in and tested it with a kick meter that registered things called megohms. The next day the phone rang and Mayme screamed.

'What was that??'

Her mother said calmly, 'The telephone.'

Jeanine lifted her head with the scissors in her hand.

Mayme said, 'How many times does it ring?'

'Just answer it!' Elizabeth said.

'Maybe it's Vernon!' Mayme clapped the large receiver to her head. 'Hello!' she shouted. 'Hello!'

'Don't shout,' said Elizabeth.

Mayme carefully laid the receiver down. 'It's for you, Mother. There's a shareholders' meeting.'

The shareholders and others with the certificates of interest met in St. Stephen's church hall. Elizabeth told people how she had learned about the meeting from a *telephone* call. Their own telephone in their own parlor. She sat with her purse on her lap and a feeling of desperation. The producer wore his loudest tie, an orange and blue fish pattern, and held up charts and graphs while they all shouted at him. He said they had reached two thousand feet at very little cost, why, it had hardly cost six thousand to drill that far and that was cheaper than he had ever imagined. All they needed was to drive it a little farther. It was down there. Elizabeth stood up and spoke at a public meeting for the first time in her life. Mr. Lacey the connections foreman sat in the back row unnoticed and listened to her. She pulled at her gray cotton gloves nervously and her voice shook but she asked the producer if he was slant drilling and he swore he was not and wondered how this woman knew about slant drilling. Then she asked if he had tried acid, and he said they couldn't afford acid, all they needed was a few more hundred feet. Oil wants to migrate. Oil always wants to go somewhere else, it wants to be on top, it wants to wander. It is wanton and unfaithful, it's almost always riding on salt water, looking for better company. It ain't lying down there in a big pool. It's in the pores in sandstone. Smashed into the pores among sand grains and under pressure if we're lucky. In another five hundred feet, we should hit the sand.

George Lacey stood up. Elizabeth turned to see who was speaking. He said, 'And when and if it comes in, it could be oil, it could be oil and gas, it could be oil and salt water or gas and salt water. If it comes in gas you stand a good chance of blowing yourself up along with the derrick if there's a live flame anywhere. If it's H_2S it will kill the whole crew. And if you live through that, if you get oil, you got to lay production pipeline to get it somewhere.'

'We all know that, Mr. Lacey,' said Spanner. 'There will be enough to pay off everybody and lay the pipelines. You ought to know, Mr. Lacey. Your company's field isn't ten miles away, and if Magnolia has ten producing wells there, then, you see.'

Elizabeth Stoddard remained standing, and did not sit down, and was not comforted. She said she wanted to see the old well log, the one from when they had drilled there five years before. Mr. Spanner laughed and said of course but well logs are hard to read.

'I can read one, Mr. Spanner,' she said. 'I would like for it to be made available.'

Mr. Spanner said he would have it at the next meeting, in a week's time.

At the end of the meeting Mr. Lacey pushed his way through the crowd. He made a gesture with his hat at her in lieu of tipping it and then put it on his head. He asked Elizabeth if he could be of any service and if she needed a ride home.

'Well, no,' she said. 'I, well, no thank you, Mr. Lacey.'

'I have the old well log,' he said.

'You do?' People pushed past them in the hallway. The school seemed abandoned and bereft of children's voices in the summer night; the closed rooms seemed dead.

'Yes.' He took her elbow and with the other hand gestured toward his car. 'You know, the City Lights Café has good big tables where we could sit and look at it. Have something cool to drink.'

She paused and then said, 'That sounds very nice.'

The Armstrong house and headquarters was a lunatic asylum with hundreds of Angoras jammed into the pens and the scorching sound of electric shears and the howling engine of the generator, the Mexican crew singing 'Los Caminos de Guanajuato' on the shearing platform. They peeled the silky mohair from the soft, baggy bodies like onionskin. The goats were then carried to another pen and by this time they were silent and stupid, their thin-boned bodies hung in a man's arms like a grain sack. Mrs. Armstrong sprayed gentian violet on the shear cuts and then the mature does were run into one pen and the yearlings into another. Ross Everett leaned on the pen rails, watching. Men loaded the four-hundred-pound bags of mohair onto Everett's two-ton trucks as soon as it was bagged, pounded down, and the burlap sewn shut and tagged.

Jeanine and Martha Jane were in the bunk-

340

house trying on the wedding dress. They were both stripped down to their underwear. Every room in the Armstrong house was jammed with equipment and cartons of medicines and men walking in and out and so they had come out to the bunkhouse. Like everybody else, the Armstrongs had had to let their help go, so now the bunkhouse was a sort of tack room and toolshed, made of corrugated steel. Saddles were piled one on top of another and bridles and halters hung from nails in the beams and every metal surface gleamed with heat.

Martha Jane wanted to see how it looked on, and so Jeanine pulled the dress on over her head and Martha pinned her up in back. Jeanine tried to walk gracefully in the long skirts but she stumbled over cans of sheep dip chemical and the long hoses of a cactus burner. The steel walls made cracking noises from the heat. Outside the thermometer said 100 and inside the bunkhouse it had to be at least 105.

Jeanine picked up her marking chalk from a table full of paper shotgun shells beside the pellet-loading device. She handed it to Martha. 'Here, mark where the shoulder pads go,' she said. 'Why don't y'all have a mirror?'

'Soon as I sell my ram.' Martha Jane's hands were wet with sweat as she laid quick white stripes on the shoulder with the chalk. 'I got a good ram out of those dogies.' She stepped back. 'You're thinner than me.' She took a fistful of waist. 'But it looks good. Turn around.'

'Okay, but get your sweaty hands off it, Martha.' Jeanine turned in a slow spin and the yards of skirt floated out and snagged on the iron bedstead legs. She clutched up the material and said, 'I'm going to pass out.'

'Don't,' said Martha Jane.

'Martha, you've got to get this thing off of me.'

'Wait, wait.' Martha chalked the buttonhole lines and then Jeanine pulled off the supple yardage of the wedding dress and took up an enamel pitcher of water and poured it over her head. She stood skinny and soaked in her underpants and brassiere with water dripping from her elbows and ears. It ran into her cotton socks. She wiped at her face with a towel and gasped.

'It's going to fit you,' she said.

'We got to get out of here,' said Martha Jane. 'I don't care when he gets back, we are getting married in December.' Martha took the pitcher from Jeanine and dipped the towel in it to wipe her face. Sweat ran into her eyes and burned until she could hardly see. 'I got to go help Mother, Jeanine.' She pulled on her jeans and an old shirt of her father's. 'Stay and eat with us and the crew.'

'I've got work at home,' said Jeanine. In reality she was afraid they would be eating goat. Goat babies. She wrapped the dress in its sheet, stuck straight pins in it to hold it together. 'I can't believe I am going to fire up that cookstove.'

'Have y'all got electricity yet?'

'Soon as y'all pay me.'

'Get it from Daddy now,' said Martha Jane. 'Before he spends it on does. He'll blow it on does.'

342

'Okay.'

'God, I tell you, I'd about rather go be a missionary in Borneo than go through another shearing.' Martha pulled a comb through her hair. Jeanine put her chalk and scissors and spools of thread into an old purse she used for a kit. Martha pulled on her boots. She stood up and stamped her feet to jam her heels into the boots. She stamped again and walked out into a yellow blaze that seemed to swallow her up.

Jeanine stepped out of the bunkhouse. At the door she gasped at the inferno radiating from the corrugated steel wall. She ran for the back porch of the Armstrong house, to the water bucket that hung from a spike nail, and under it a lusty growth of peppermint where the water was thrown by exhausted men whose shirts and underwear stuck to their bodies in the unvarying heat. She came upon Ross Everett with his pants undone, his belt hanging loose, his shirt open. His shorts were striped blue and hung from his hip bones. She screamed in a faint, hoarse noise. It was all she could manage.

'Hello,' he said.

'Why don't you just strip naked?' said Jeanine. She turned her back.

'You're a virgin, Jeanine,' he said. 'I can tell.'

He took off his hat and poured a dipper of water over his head, and then began to stuff his shirt into his waistband.

She felt dizzy with the heat and so she took a firm hold of the porch rail. 'Can you say it a little louder?' she said. 'They can't hear you in the kitchen.'

He zipped up his pants and buckled his belt.

'Are you about to pass out?'

'Yes.' She liked his voice, it was a strong voice with that sliding West Texas accent. 'Just about.'

He took hold of the collar of her shirt, touching her hot skin with his fingertips. He pulled it away from her neck and with the other hand scooped up a dipper of water from the bucket. He poured the water down into her shirt, flooding her breasts and ribs. Jeanine closed her eyes and he poured another over her head. 'Hold out your hands.' He poured another dipperful into her cupped hands and she splashed it into her face. 'How's the dress?'

'Ross, it's beautiful.'

He took the bucket from the giant nail and emptied it over her head and then set it beneath the pump. He filled it and hung it up again.

'Good.'

Jeanine said, 'I could throw myself into the stock tank.'

He shifted his hat to the back of his head. She was good to look at; drops sparkled in her eyebrows and on small tips of hair that hung against her cheeks. He handed her the towel and watched her wipe her face with it.

'Come and see the shearing.'

'Couldn't you just tell me about it?'

'No.' She followed him in her soaked shirt and overlong Levi's, her hands over her ears because the violent noise of hundreds of distraught Angoras had risen to a deafening level. With his broad hand he gently turned back the fleece of a pinioned goat. The hair grew from the skin with a slight wave to it, it had the sheen of mother-of-pearl. 'They're taking it raw at the mill in Rhode Island, sticks and goat shit excuse me and lice and all. A few bags at a time.'

'Why do they take it raw?'

'Because they want to handle it themselves.' He stood back and two men chivvied the doe toward the shearing shed. 'You need perfectly pure water, a neutral pH, to wash it and workers with great patience to comb the staple out or you end up with something that looks like mattress stuffing and will never be untangled in our lifetime. The water in Rhode Island comes from granite wells. Our water is alkaline, with this limestone. It's very delicate fiber.'

He walked at the edge of the frantic activity, for he was the buyer and the manager of the shearing and he would not get in the men's way once they had begun. Two of the Mexican shear crew did not get a gate shut quickly enough and goats began to pour through it, suddenly becoming liquid, a dusty current of suds foaming out.

Jeanine laid down the sheeted package of dress and ran forward. She grasped one of the goats by the horns and a man yelled at her, *No por las cuernas!* The goat twisted its head around so that it seemed it had a rubber neck. She was in the middle of four men all laying hands on the goats, gripping them by the shaggy hair.

'Let go,' said Ross. He had a full-grown doe in his arms and waded through the noise and the dust. 'You'll bust those horns.'

She let go of the horns and seized the doe up in her arms and carried her toward the shearing

345

shed. The animal was baggy and loose in all its bones. They were bred for hair and for nothing else, not brains or hardiness or bone or color or flesh. The goat dropped pellets all down her jeans. A man took the doe from her and the gate was shut. Ross wiped his shirtsleeve across his face and streaked it with sweat and dust. She turned at the sound of shouts, men harried more goats into the hands of Mrs. Armstrong and now Martha Jane, who jabbed each Angora with a syringe of sore-mouth vaccination.

Jeanine wiped her face on her sleeve. 'It's hard to believe Mr. Armstrong took up goats without somebody putting a pistol to his head,' said Jeanine.

'It's ranching life, honey.'

'You should see their bedroom, Ross. It's not a bedroom. It's full of goat medicine and clippers and dirty Levi's. What kind of a married life is this?'

Ross turned and rested both elbows on the rails of the pen. 'Good question,' he said. He lifted his head to the view away from the headquarters; a rising slope of mountain, complicated by limestone bluffs and fallen square boulders. The grass had shrunk into disparate clumps and was as crisp as paper. Prickly pear climbed up the slope with lifted round bats. He turned to watch the shearing crew fleecing off great sheaves of silky mohair in the suspended dust of the shearing shed. The gasoline engine thudded heavily. It was running on kerosene, which was cheaper than gas, but its smell was oily and hot. The shearer finished with a doe and dropped a red mountain laurel bean into a can as a counter.

'I'd never live like this,' Jeanine said. She drooped on the fence and held to an upright.

He nodded. 'Mrs. Armstrong probably said the same thing.'

She shoved the heels of her hands against her eyes to wipe away the running salty sweat. He took off his hat and ran his finger around the sweat band. The generator choked and failed. There were shouts and recriminations over who had not brought more kerosene, and then a man came lugging a jerrican. Ross fished in his shirt pocket for a cigarette. The generator sparked and snorted and started again.

For some reason she couldn't figure out herself she took his lighter from his hand and lit his cigarette for him and he drew on it. She dropped the old Zippo into his palm. He was silent for a few moments; smoke drifted around his fist.

'Jeanine, you're just always messing with me.'

'I know it.'

Over the shouts and baaing and noise of the generator, a loud and splintering crunch. One of Ross's drivers had backed a haulage truck into the feed shed and smashed the rain gutter into a V. The truck sat in the driveway fully loaded and ready to go to the warehouse in Comanche and the kid had smashed up the rain gutter and part of the stock racks.

'Well kiss my ass,' he said. He threw down the cigarette and stepped on it.

Jeanine watched with interest. He would lose his temper and do something spectacular. He would commit some violence upon the sweating

347

teenage driver. He left her and vaulted over a low fence made of railroad ties, and jerked open the truck door and said, Get out. She waited to see if he would lay his enormous hand on the boy's collar and snatch him out into the dirt. The boy beat him to it. He turned and jumped to the ground.

'Sorry, Mr. Everett!'

'Shut up.'

Ross climbed in and began the long process of shifting, moving an inch forward so as not to take the rain gutter with the truck, turning, backing. He spun the wheel and she saw his lips moving, he was swearing.

'Mr. Everett, I didn't see–'

'Shut the hell up.' He got the truck clear and got out again, slammed the door, went to look at the gutter. 'Don't talk to me when I'm busy.'

'Yes, sir.'

'You'll fix that when you get back from the warehouse,' he said. 'First you're dropping Jeanine off at her house.'

'Yes sir, Mr. Everett.'

'You're lucky I didn't kill you.'

'I know it.'

After she said good-bye to the Armstrongs he handed her into the cab of the truck. She held the silk dress safely wrapped in the sheet. She had the fifty dollars in her jeans pocket.

'What if it had been me that smashed up that gutter?' she said.

The young driver turned quickly and walked over to the feed shed and pretended a deep interest in the twisted convolutions of the tin

348

gutter. Ross cleared his throat and hitched up his pants. He stared at the goat pens with a blank face for several seconds.

'I understand what you're saying.' He reached up to the windshield wiper and pressed back a loose edge. 'Would you like some kind of promise that I would never lose my temper with you?'

Although no particular words came to Jeanine's mind she knew that she stood at the very thin edge of a commitment, of binding promises exchanged. Which might lead to hot, stiff wedding dresses that shut around your waist like a clamp, a bedroom full of blackleg medicines in boxes and piled horse blankets, and if they were both worn out, to arguments and broken vows. And leaving the Tolliver farm where she had worked so hard, and had made the place her own with nobody to account to. How could she just trust in words? Words words words.

'No, Ross, don't make any promises.' But still she reached out to him and laid her hand on his neck, beneath the collar. She didn't care if the Armstrongs saw her. She loved the touch of him. Still she wavered and drew her hand away and laid it on the sheeted packet of silk. 'You just carry on all you want.'

He smiled, and slapped his hand on the door and stood back. 'See you in a week.'

She held the packet carefully all the way home. The dress now only needed the skirt lining and twenty-five buttons up the back. And Tim Joplin, who was three hundred miles away.

She made up her bed neatly with the chenille bedspread, and the satin pillow with the sprayed-on legend, EL PASO LAND OF SUNSHINE. The cool air of the early morning rolled in through the tall windows and katydids sang in the oaks outside with their long, crawling noise. She dressed in an ironed blouse and clean Levi's, brushed her hair and clipped on the earrings, looked in the mirror and was pleased with herself. The cotton had opened into its four leaves each and Abel was drawing the cultivator through the rows. Jeanine herself was turning and leaving out in some kind of interior rain, washed and wet and bright, despite the drought. Despite anything and everything an image of herself reaching out toward Ross came into her mind again and again, and she understood, all by herself, without reading it in a novel or hearing it on a radio program, that falling passionately in love with someone, without reservation or holding back, was good for the heart. For its valves and its arteries and that invisible shadow of the heart called the soul. Falling in love was good for the soul. However. And Jeanine felt herself stuck in the However.

A letter, or rather a sort of announcement, came from Winifred Beasley that stated it had come to her notice that Mrs. Stoddard was investing in an oil well, and if that were the case they certainly were not justified in taking relief supplies and in fact there could be an examination of the possibility that Mrs. Stoddard was involved in welfare fraud. If Mrs. Stoddard wished to continue to receive relief supplies for her daughter, to wit Bea Stoddard, would she please present herself to the county relief committee. Many other families were in need and it was unconscionable of her to take supplies that others were so in need of yours truly Winifred Beasley County Health Nurse, R.N.

'Oh this makes me feel terrible!' Elizabeth slapped the letter down. 'I feel like a thief!'

'We're well rid of her,' said Jeanine. 'Let it go, Mother.' She was cutting up sweet potatoes with an eye in each piece in order to try for a fall garden. She was not going to quit on the garden. They might get rain.

'If my parents ever knew we were even on relief, much less accused of fraud...' Elizabeth pressed her lips together in a thin line. She smashed up the letter into a wadded missile that she shot into the cookstove. Mayme and Jeanine had never seen her so upset. She was furious.

'Let it go, Mother,' said Mayme.

Bea spread out her schoolwork on the location and products and peoples of New Guinea to read it aloud to their mother, who quickly put away her rage over Winifred Beasley so that Bea would not ask what was the matter, and said *My gracious.* Elizabeth looked at the *National Geographic* illustrations Bea had pasted in, grimy dark photos of the people of New Guinea. She said, *Why do people do those things to themselves?*

Mayme read through the brochures of Galveston. It was where all the officers went to take their leave. If Vernon got leave they would meet there. Elizabeth had to come too so that it would all be above board and Vernon's parents wouldn't think she was a redheaded stepchild. Jeanine laid out *Vogue* patterns on the table and then pinned the tissues to her sister's shoulders.

Jeanine sat up late that night and listened to Kaltenborn. He said that Chancellor Adolph Hitler was meeting with Chamberlain and there was going to be peace in our time. Then WBAP started to fade, a star fading at the horizon of radio time, and the voices and music from WLS Chicago, a place unimaginable to Jeanine, arrived transparent in the thin night air of the Brazos Valley. Then the WLS signal diminished and slipped away as if it had something to do elsewhere, some other people to entrance, and the music abandoned her to the night and the dry wind.

CHAPTER THIRTY-THREE

Jeanine carried the kitchen table out to the veranda by herself and one leg jammed up on the doorframe and knocked her backward but she caught her balance and trundled on with it like a doodlebug.

She threw their one linen tablecloth over it and straightened the edges. It was her August birthday. Her peaches birthday. She was twenty-one years old and now she could vote for President Roosevelt herself. Mayme had saved up sugar for two weeks and made a white cake with frosting. They sat on the front porch with the new peaches sliced up on plates in front of them and a basketful sitting beside the table. Bea bit down on a slice and bit again. Jeanine spooned out another helping.

'Aren't they good? This is what we came for.' She poured more of their precious sugar onto her peach slices. 'Jeez, they're like shoe leather.' She swallowed. 'Use more sugar, y'all.'

Mayme said, 'Maybe next year they'll be better.'

They chewed industriously at the hard slices. The peaches had dark spots, and near the pit the flesh was pale green. They ate them anyway. They sat out on the front veranda in the shade, waiting for the evening wind to come up out of the earth's shadow. Curtains streamed out of the open windows. The posts on the veranda were painted white, the passionflower vine was in bloom. It was very hot. Biggety came trotting up from the cedar brake. He had just eaten the lunch of one of the cedar choppers, a thick braunschweiger sandwich, and rolled in a dead armadillo. Life was good.

'Where are you going to be next year, Mayme?' asked Jeanine. 'On my next birthday?'

Her sister laid her spoon on the plate.

'I don't know,' she said. She said it in an apologetic voice and pushed her red hair out of her eyes. There was a long silence and Jeanine held the hot basket of fruit in her hands like a load of failed hopes.

Bea ran into the driveway, with the purchases from Strawn's store. She carried the flour and pork chops in the school satchel on her back and it slammed against her shoulder blades as she ran at top speed, on the tips of her toes. She was being pursued by Comanches. They appeared like wraiths out of the Texas earth, from the green matrix of the cotton field. She was Katie McLauren, Cynthia Parker, the Kelsay girl, and in the final yards to the door of the house she called out *My God, Mother, they are killing me!* She was full of arrows.

'Bea, there's a letter or something for you,' said her mother. It was from *True Western Stories*. Bea unloaded her groceries and sat down to read the letter. Her left leg was marked with deep red scars but she no longer needed the crutches. The letter said although hers was a commendable effort she needed more polish and whoever wrote the letter said in a cheerful tone that it was a sure bet that Miss Stoddard would attain that polish in the years ahead. Bea threw it away and ran to find her Big Chief. The world was full of ignorant people and one of them had just written to her. She went out to the back porch to sit on her busted old chair, found her book on the shelf under the washing buckets, and opened it to her place.

Jeanine backed into the kitchen unrolling loops of fabric-covered wire.

'Just leave it there,' said Mr. Miller. Upstairs another man thumped in the halls and through the rooms. In the kitchen Mr. Miller and his brother Deemie, who was generally useless but was occasionally browbeaten by his brother into some form of short-term work, shouted out instructions to each other as they threaded electrical wires up through the ceiling. They

354

would be paid, when they had finished, with the wedding dress money. Jeanine turned her head up to the ceiling as the thick wire rose into the hole like a snake. Bea ignored it all for the seductive pleasures of *The Yearling*. She sat on the back steps bent over the book, imprinting sweaty fingerprints on the margins as she held it in a rigid grip because she could see it coming, she knew they were going to shoot that little deer. If the house caught fire she would not have been able to put it down.

'What are you reading, Bea?' said Jeanine.

'*The Yearling*. Miss Callaway,' said Bea. 'She gave it to me to read.' Bea turned a page. 'Oh no,' she groaned.

Jeanine said, 'I thought Miss Callaway went back to Pennsylvania for the summer.'

Bea stood up and kept her finger in her place. 'No, she's staying in town, Milton Brown carried her stuff into Tarrant, suitcases.' Bea found herself speaking disjointedly in her desire to go hide somewhere and finish the story. 'She just adores Milton. I hate love stories. Oh what does it *matter?* They're going to shoot him anyway.' She stalked off to the barn with Prince Albert trailing after her, his tail held up in a slight curve like a question mark. In the hot amber air of the barn she would be able to sob in peace.

Elizabeth and Violet and Lillian sat on the fenders of somebody's car. They didn't speak about what might happen because it would be bad luck. People who could get away from work came with their children and wives and lunches of thick homemade bread and bologna. Local ranchers came, and also the young people who had never seen a well come in but had heard the stories. Several well-dressed men from the other oil company offices in Fort Worth drove up. They were scouts and lease hounds and seismograph men, and they had heard through the invisible oil field telegraph that Crowninshield had hit sand.

Oilfield Willy came to call out the demonic names of the geological strata, to preach on the text of the seismograph charts and he walked back and forth as he preached. His ancient suit of shiny gabardine hung on him like a theatrical draping and once in a while someone would hand him a dime or a quarter, and he nodded and kept on. *The Lord only knows where it all lies in His deep dominions,* he shouted. *And what shall be done with it and where it shall go. This is the blood of the earth in its veins and its arteries and he created it and so it belongs to the earth's heart and not to mankind.*

Captain Crowninshield strode about the drilling platform. It was a shaky structure that had been nailed together out of mesquite poles and mill sidings. The long, twisted cable lifted and fell, lifted and fell. His hand rode up and down with it as if he were playing an immense stringed instrument. It rose and fell out of the borehole and the thumping of the great drill string went on long into the blue evening when the whitewing doves came to water, and it went on when the sky turned madonna blue and the first stars came out, late summer stars, clear and icy.

Elizabeth said she had to go home. 'Nothing's

going to happen,' she said. 'Just because he hit the pay horizon doesn't mean anything.' It was a hot night, hazed over with fine dust carried high among the contrail clouds that made stars seem blurry, even the great yellow Arcturus. She and Lillian and Violet climbed into the Studebaker.

More and more people started up their engines and went home, the ones with children to put to bed. Others stayed on, perhaps fifty or sixty people. The men in good suits stood leaning against the car fenders, their ties pulled loose from around their necks, listening and watching. They had not always worn good suits nor had they always driven comfortable passenger cars. They knew the sound of a cable-tool rig, they knew what it was doing and what it was saying and they didn't talk very much but listened intently. There was a light wind and the temperature fell slightly. The cartoon dog Pluto, painted on the flatbed truck door, grinned at everybody. Pluto, god of precious metals and of the underworld.

Andy said, 'I'll build us a fire for coffee.'

'No, don't,' said the captain. He was filthy with drilling mud, and Otto and Andy stood ready at the forge fire and the bailer, if either were needed. Crowninshield held his hand on the cable, rising and falling two feet six inches. He bent toward it, intent, as if it were speaking to him.

He said, 'Otto, put that forge fire out.'

Steam rose from the extinguished embers. The men all around noted this and turned to one another. *He's putting the damn forge fire out.* A couple of cars started up and turned on the headlights to provide Cap with illumination. Several men crowded into a big Dodge to listen to the baseball game.

Otto and Andy were smoking homemades, sitting at the cable spool they used for a table on the drill platform, where they kept swivels and hooks and pieces of lead for bushing and a box of dominoes. Otto laid out a hand of dominoes. As he reached for a piece it danced oddly across the surface in a strange clattering jig and away from his hand. He frowned and grabbed at it. The rest of the dominoes started to rattle. They fell over and began to jitter about the surface like live things. Otto clasped them together in his hand and lifted his head with an alarmed look. Andy spread his hand out on the cable spool and felt it vibrating. The vibration grew stronger each second.

The entire drilling platform was shaking.

The engine began to rattle in its mounts and the Sampson post swayed weirdly sideways instead of up and down.

'Put out those cigarettes!' screamed Crownin-shield. He jumped up on the platform and came running at them. 'Kill the damn boiler fire, Otto! Now!' He snatched the cigarettes from their hands. 'Put out the boiler fire, she's coming in!'

Otto jumped to his feet and crashed through a pile of bailers and slammed the boiler door shut and cranked on the damper.

'Get the hell off the platform!'

Crowninshield and Otto and Andy all came off the platform at the same time. They struck the dirt and fell and got up again. They ran toward the engine shed. It was the only cover available. They heard the deep and sinister roar coming from the borehole as if something down there was calling out to them in a rage at being awakened from a million-year sleep. Andy's hair rose all over his body.

Then he turned and saw the most amazing thing. He saw casing pipe rising up out of the borehole as if it were self-propelled, joints of pipe that weighed more than two hundred pounds apiece, flying up one after another, in a spray of white salt water that was as thick and hard as a sycamore trunk. And then more pipe was blown out by a great fountain of sand, enclosed in a foaming mist of gas that expanded like a geyser, sideways, snaking low and wild over the ground.

Then the massive drill bit rose up out of the hole, twenty feet long and weighing two tons, spewing straight up through the derrick and taking out the crown block along with it. Spars and shattered planks flew upward in ballistic fragments.

Within moments the pieces of lumber were raining down on the roof of the engine shed. Andy yelled, 'Ooooh! Ooooh! Shit! There went the derrick!' Cap was on his hands and knees looking for the flashlight. They dared not strike a match to the lamp.

Then the oil came in, under great pressure, a standing column of jet that erupted with a deafening roar. The entire derrick blew away, leaving only the footings and twisted masses of metal.

The people who had gathered to watch were

either huddling in their cars, or running, or driving away. Cap heard their engines, some of them growing more and more distant while overhead the tornado of pure oil wavered and shrieked and lunged snakelike into the night sky.

Crowninshield shouted, 'Andy, Otto, we got to get help to get that thing shut down!' He had to yell over the noise of oil beating on the engine-shed roof. He sat crouched over as crude oil rained on the ground and the noise of the blow-out sounded like some beast roaring and looking for prey.

'Okay, boss,' said Andy. His voice was faint and very calm in the most peculiar way. He sat on Cap's bed among the detective novels and the sardine cans. 'But I think we ought to hang in here and wait in case any more of that casing pipe gets blown out, you know, because if it lands on somebody, that's all she wrote. They'll ship you home in a shoe box.'

'I know it.' They hunched their shoulders up around their ears, as if they were being struck, and the flashlight shone on their anxious faces.

'We're lucky something ain't come through the roof already.'

Cap said, 'I think we can make a run for it.'

'I never thought I'd live to see it,' said Andy. 'A blowout like this.'

'You might not yet,' said Otto.

Jeanine stood at the front door and counted the cars. There were five or six automobiles parked in their driveway. The telephone rang every five minutes.

'Oh, I don't think we're going to be rich,' Elizabeth said. 'And if they don't get it shut down they'll lose pressure and they'll junk the well. And there's too many people to share the money with, but what the heck!' She hung up the telephone and turned to her daughters. 'Who was I just talking to?'

There was laughter and shouts as more people drove in. Jeanine said hello to Betty, and Aunt Lillian, and a man named Mr. Lacey from the Magnolia field, all of them with congratulations and advice and cautions and recent figures on price per barrel.

'Elizabeth.' Mr. Lacey carried his hat in his hand. 'I was never happier to be wrong in my life. And I'm just going to be rude here and insist on advising you. Beatty-Orviel is going to be made an offer and it could be by my company.' He turned his hat by the brim. 'I can get you a volunteer blowout crew. From our company.'

Elizabeth turned to him with an interested expression and before long Mr. Lacey had to bring up the dreaded name of Harold Ickes and the attendant suggestion of dark cabals in Washington.

'We are going to have to tell the Texas Railroad Commission that what we have here is an eleven-thousand-foot well in order to increase your allowables.'

Elizabeth said, 'Texas Railroad Commission?' She paused and touched his arm. 'Allowables? Harold Ickes?'

Mr. Lacey said he would explain. He stood very still so she wouldn't take her hand away, and his heart was drowned in a sweet, high-gravity sensation.

Lillian and Violet started making plans for a big dinner, and an entire turkey for the crew. Jeanine and Mayme brewed coffee and slammed cups on the kitchen table and sang snatches of songs; *That old black magic has me in its spell...*

CHAPTER THIRTY-FOUR

The skies in the summer of 1938 were gravid with rain clouds that passed over the Brazos valley dryshod and spilled their rain up against the wall of the Rocky Mountains or the Sangre de Cristos in New Mexico. Hurricane season turned the Gulf of Mexico into a tormented cauldron of wind and rain, and people said that this time the season would bring rain into north-central Texas and there would be grass again. Elizabeth and her daughters lived under an atmosphere that shifted its higher winds in a different direction throughout the remote strata miles above the earth. Some change was taking place. Droughts come and stay for seven years and in those seven years the weak are driven away; mistakes and miscalculations grow into catastrophes, there is no margin for error. Drought is a lack of something, a vacuum, an empty place in danger of implosion.

Jeanine stood in the stands with Innis at the

Lubbock South Plains Livestock Show and Rodeo race grounds under the metal roof where people were packed together as if the limits of shade were an invisible fence. The national anthem ended and Innis and a thousand other men raised their hands to replace their hats on their heads. It looked like a broad shore of birds taking flight. Innis and Jeanine were uneasy with each other and so they showed great politeness and Innis said *Yes, ma'am* to everything she said or happened to mention. Sometimes he said *Yes, ma'am* before she even finished a sentence and so it made her forget what it was she was saying. Jeanine wore a straw hat with the brim turned up in front, a silk rose pinned to the hatband, and a cool print dress in the new style. Everything was changing. Fashions were changing. Her dress had sharp padded shoulders and a Peter Pan collar. All the styles were sharper now; there was less of a feeling of stylish lassitude, drooping hems, no more sagging necklines that lolled like tongues.

Jeanine had been raised with sisters and Innis had been brought up around adult men and every day of his life he wished to be like them, to be a grown man instead of a child, and grown men did not sit in the bleachers with women when there was a horse race in the works. A grown man was down in the shedrow, among the horse trailers and the manure and the nervous horses, they made obscure references to women and livestock, in brief sentences. It was a love of language, never to waste a word.

He knew his father's regard had undergone some great shift, toward this woman who was

363

very mature, with lipstick and high heels and a rose in her hat. He wondered if he had to do whatever she said and just who was the enforcer around here. But there was nothing to be done about it except to say Yes, ma'am to whatever she said. He ran his hands along his hat brim to bring it down in front like Randolph Scott's hat. His cheeks were bright red in the heat. Far away he heard one of the high school bands that had come to play for the evening rodeo tooting and blowing spit out spit-valves. They began on 'Mexicali Rose.'

Jeanine beat the hot, still air with the racing program. Innis sat in his white shirt and tie, his Stetson pulled down over his eyes, with both hands knotted between his knees. Down behind the starting gates Smoky Joe was held by two boys, one on each side of his halter. The jockey was worried. Smoky Joe Hancock was a hard case. Everybody knew he was a hard case. Smoky opened his nostrils wide and struck out at the horses around him. Horses that were springy two-year-olds and hot with energy lay in wait for him. But Smoky was seven years old and he would be running in a pack of other horses for the first time. It was an oval track with grandstands newly painted, with an official clock and a camera at the finish line whose eye was infallible and settled all arguments about nose-to-nose races. The two boys released him. The saddling area was a flaming white blur, and across it, Smoky Joe came at his lunging trot, with his navy and red saddlecloth, his coat shining brilliant as some vital, dark metal. They had done something with his mane; it lay down on his neck, tamed and silky. His tail streamed out in one solid banner.

Behind the stands the noise of the livestock show made a heated tangle of incoherent sounds; the noise and confusion of men grappling with prize sheep and goats, a very small girl speaking in sweet tones to an overheated rabbit in a cage, two boys riding double on a cow pony, the noise of horses and cattle being unloaded from trailers, engines starting up. Jeanine felt in the distance, far beyond the visible horizon, a bass sound of gathering wind and the knotted heart of a storm that could have been weather or maybe it was the life she saw opening in front of her.

Maybe she should begin her sentences with *Tell Me*, instead of *How Is*. Such as, tell me about your new foal, the red mare, and the ringtailed cats, about how you shot horses. Tell me what the cook, Jugs, said about something. She had ten dollars in her purse, saved out of the household money. Maybe instead of saying *Tell Me* she should say *Don't Tell*. She had been raised in a household of sisters and an absent father and the thing that had drawn them together into talk, spilled talk unreeling late into the night, was secrets.

She leaned closer to Innis and said, 'Don't tell your dad.'

'Yes, ma'am.' Then he glanced at her. 'Don't tell my dad what?'

'I'm going down to the shedrow and find a bet.' She settled her hat firmly on her head.

'Yes, ma'am.' He thought about it and then unknotted his hands. 'Dang! I want to come too.'

'No. You got to stay here and hold the fort. I'm going to leave my purse, and with this crowd, it could get stolen.' She took out the ten dollars from her purse and set the purse on the bleacher seat. 'Your dad is going to look up here and if we're both gone he won't know what to think.'

'Well dang,' he said. 'Ma'am.'

'And don't tell him unless he asks. You don't have to lie.'

Innis thought about it for a long time. Then he made a sort of gesture with his right hand, an off-hand drift toward her purse with a curled forefinger.

'You go on and make your bet,' he said. 'I'll keep an eye on that purse.' When she hurried off down the bleacher's wide concrete steps he folded his arms and sat back and surveyed the crowd like a Pinkerton man.

Jeanine walked along the shedrow confidently and saw a man she knew, Tom Baker, from Seguin.

'Anybody taking bets?' she said. Baker lifted his hat and smiled. 'Right here they are, little lady.'

'Who are you running, Tom?'

'Soldier Boy. Out of Gonzales Joe Bailey.'

Baker and a man from Abilene and two men from the King ranch were amused by her, and smiled, and asked who she was putting her money on and she said Smoky Joe Hancock. Ross Everett was running him to qualify and she had five dollars that said he would break twenty-three seconds and five that he would daylight Soldier Boy out of the gate. Baker and the King ranch man took her bets, and she ran back up the

366

bleacher steps to find Innis.

At the starting gate Smoky Joe was being backed in. All the gates shut in a sharp clang and he snaked his head to one side with his teeth showing in a white row like piano keys. The horse next to him screamed and tossed his head in a feeble, apologetic warning. Smoky's narrow little jockey said, 'Here! Here now!'

And so Smoky straightened out again and cocked his ears toward the track because he was satisfied with the other horse's weak reaction. He wanted to run badly, not even to win, but to beat up and humiliate the other horses in the gates around him. Ross Everett climbed up on the rear bars behind Smoky's starting gate and pulled off his belt.

'Ross, don't hit him,' said the jockey. 'Come on, don't hit him.' His red and navy-blue silks shone in the dulled sunlight.

Ross said, 'The son of a bitch is going to qualify or I'll shoot him and drag him out to the pasture for the coyotes.'

'He'll rear,' said the jockey. 'He'll bash my brains out in this gate.'

At the end of the line of gates an old man stepped up on a steel ladder and laid his hand on a heavy metal lever, When he pulled it down it would throw all the gates open. The other horses heard the ringing footsteps and began to dance. Smoky threw his head from side to side against the bit and slavered at the horses on both sides of him. He did not understand about the noise of the man's footsteps.

Ross Everett watched the old man place himself on the top rung and pull the lever. All the gates clanged open and he brought the belt and buckle down on Smoky Joe's rear end with all his strength. The dark stallion bolted straight out of the open gate and left a length of daylight between himself and Soldier Boy. Smoky Joe ran toward the magic, otherworldly feeling that would overcome him in a short distance, where the other horses would fall behind him and disappear, shamed. Tenths of seconds splintered and broke up into fragments like sparks from cedar fires, they floated in his wake and burnt the eyes and nostrils of his enemies.

He had never had such clean ground underfoot, it was as level and unmarked as the first day of the world and he broke through the invisible line of the photo finish beam so far ahead of the others that the track steward lost sight of him.

The track steward saw only the horses bunched up five lengths behind Smoky and declared the foremost among them the winner. This was a horse from San Angelo named Yellow Buck. A man stood at the rail with a stopwatch held high in one hand and facing the steward. He was yelling. It was the banker from Abilene with the yellow bow tie and a derby who had wanted to buy Smoky. A lot of people were yelling and Jeanine scrambled up to stand on her bleacher seat to look at the time. The electric clock said 22.9. Smoky Joe was pitching his way around the unused far side of the track, trying to throw his jockey into the rails. Another man raced up the bleacher steps toward the steward's tower.

'Where do we go?' asked Jeanine. She was

hurrying down the steps behind Innis as fast as she could in her high heels. 'Will he get a plate?'

'Yes, ma'am,' said Innis. 'Listen.'

The steward had so many men yelling at him to check the film that when he did and realized Smoky had been five lengths ahead, he simply threw the film out the observation post window and somebody caught it and carried it to Ross Everett.

'Does he want me to autograph it?' Everett said. He laughed and handed it to a boy and gave the boy a dime and said to carry it back to the steward and tell him to make a copy for Everett. The PA system coughed and said there was a correction, that Smoky Joe Hancock had won in 22.9 seconds. There were low whistles. Smoky had won on two different bets; he had broken 23 seconds and he'd daylighted Soldier Boy out of the gate.

Innis took off his hat and brushed it, set it back on his head.

'I've got to lead him into the winner's circle, Miss Jeanine.'

'Oh good for you!' Jeanine said. Innis was clearing his throat and tucking in his shirt. This was to be his first public appearance other than reciting Kipling's 'Tommy' at the end-of-the-year school program. She said, 'Go look for your dad. I'll go this way.'

Innis said Yes, ma'am and went around the end of the bleachers toward the place where they were unsaddling the horses. Jeanine walked quickly back toward the jockeys' rooms and saw Tom Baker standing with the man in the yellow bow tie. Baker shook his head ruefully and opened his wallet and handed her two ten-dollar bills. A jockey slouched by, near to fainting with heat and anorexia, carrying his saddlecloth and racing saddle.

The King ranch man lifted his hat. 'Do I get a kiss? Loser's privilege.'

'In your dreams,' said Jeanine and jammed the money in her purse. They lifted their hats again and watched her walk away. One of them sang *Hold tight, baby, hold tight.*

She walked quickly toward the winner's circle. She stepped through old dried horse manure; the twenty dollars meant luxuries for herself. Her mother's oil money had paid all the back taxes, and she had bought an electric fan for the kitchen and a kerosene refrigerator. The sweaty wadded bills in her hand could now be spent on a bathtub and perfumed soap. She had to figure out how to tell her mother she came by it.

In the winner's circle Jeanine turned in the wind in her new summer dress. She held out her hand to Smoky Joe. He was staring around, looking for other horses, the lowly geldings, a stallion to challenge, the sweet and lovely mares. Jeanine patted him on the neck and laughed with delight. He was the brave horse that lived in a trash yard, the thin underfed horse that ran his heart out on the brush tracks, and she did not remember the hard times but only his springing step and his courage and his bright, irrepressible gallantry. She said, 'Ain't you a rocket?'

Innis held up the championship silver plate and a man took his picture with his face glowing in

370

the hot air. Ross put his hand on Jeanine's shoulder and said, 'Another one, please. Send me a copy and the bill.'

The sparkling silver plate ran its reflection of the intense sun across the crowd. Ross stood beside her wearing a summer jacket and tie, lace-up cordovan shoes and his good Stetson. She felt his hand on her elbow, it steadied her. The brim of her hat made flying motions in the breeze. It was a breeze that seemed to come out of the mouth of a furnace.

'Dad?'

'Yes.' Ross turned to his son and when he did his full attention was on the boy. He faced his son in a direct manner with his hands clasped behind his back, and in the intense sun his face was dark under the shadow of his hat.

'Do you want me to load him?' Innis stood holding the halter line, and his hand was on Smoky's shoulder. He was an undersize replica of his father and he could not stop smiling in the joy of a clean win and a silver plate.

'No, not right now. Get him back in the stall.' He reached out to take the boy's hat from his head and wiped the sweat from his forehead. 'Go stick your head in the horse tank, son. You're overheated.' The boy's face was alight with un-spoiled pleasure. Ross put his son's hat back on his head and tapped the crown. 'You and Jugs take him to a stall. Y'all are staying the night here. It would be too dark by the time you got him home. Me and Jeanine are going on. I have to get her back.' He turned to Jeanine. 'Word gets around,' he said.

'It was only a ten-dollar bet,' she said. She kept her voice low. 'It's bathtub money.' She smiled up at him and thought of a bathtub full of cool water.

'You were ruined for a normal life.'

'No I wasn't!' She fanned herself with the race program. 'I'm more normal than anybody. More than Mayme.'

He nodded. 'The purse was two thousand.'

'Oh my God, you didn't tell me!'

'It would have been too nerve-wracking,' he said. 'My nerves were wracked enough as it was.' He took off his hat and wiped his forehead and put it back on. 'Let's get you a cold drink and get home.'

They waded through the hot sand toward the run-out, and she took hold of his arm to keep her balance. She was proud of him and proud to be seen with him. From the perspective of Baker and the man from the King ranch, who were both lounging in the shade of the runout, she and Ross would seem to be wavering in the heat distortion. Her hand on his coat sleeve for balance, shifting closer and then slipping away, unsure, her hat shimmering in planes, holding on to his sleeve with an iron grip.

CHAPTER THIRTY-FIVE

Ross and Jeanine drove out onto Highway 84 south of Lubbock, into the flat country. The earth was the color of brick and cream. An increasing wind ruffled the roadside dust. The daylight dimmed to a faint gray. There was nothing to see but distant oil rigs, the braced, orthodontic structures of the expansion joints, and the small variations of slope and erosion dotted with blackbrush, and as they drove long flatbeds loaded with oil field equipment appeared on the diminishing black line of the highway and the drivers waved as they passed.

They were following the old Burlington Northern tracks and in the distance a train called out. It was coming toward them and it went past with a rush of dust and Russian thistles dried out to barbed wads flying away from the cowcatcher on both sides. Jeanine turned the window wing toward her face and closed her eyes against the blast and her hair streamed out away from her forehead.

'I'm taking you to dinner in Abilene.'

Jeanine stuck out her lower lip. 'I didn't know we were going to dinner in Abilene.'

'I know it.'

'Why didn't Innis come too?'

'Because I want to talk to you.' He leaned back in the seat and pulled his tie loose. They passed a struggling, backfiring bus with peeling paint and missing windows, with children hanging out the window frames and trunks lashed to the top. Their tires sang on the blacktop. A flock of rosy finches, gathering for the fall migration, flashed at the windshield and then tilted away. She thought, not yet, not yet. She felt tears burning her eyelids in the hot wind and she wiped them away with the heel of her hand. The wind roared at the open windows.

'I'm not the person you want to be talking to,' she said. 'You need somebody more cheerful.'

'You have a bright, cheerful, and sunny nature, Jeanine. Happiness is your middle name. You spread joy and cheer wherever you go. Secretly inside you are the Bluebonnet Molasses girl.'

'No I'm not.'

He said, 'I want you to marry me. What object-ions would you have to marrying me?' He stared straight ahead from under the brim of his hat. His hand was dropped easy and relaxed over the top of the steering wheel.

She twisted around on the seat. She loved the old Tolliver house. It was their own house with pale mint green walls and the family graveyard. If she left, it would be a door shut behind her. Someday she would marry somebody, after all, and open another door to her husband and to other lives that devolved one inside the other in an infinite progression of lives. But not yet. And still Jeanine felt she could turn to Ross and put her arms around him and that only with him would her restlessness unwind itself. With him her interior drought would be over. She put her hand on his shoulder for a moment and then turned her face to the hot wind again.

He opened and closed his hard fist. He did not look at her.

'You don't know what to do with your mind, Jeanine,' he said. 'I'm the only man that can save you. I'll marry you and keep you out at the ranch and you can occupy yourself with four-hundred-pound calves at branding and screwworm caustic and Smoky Joe and fighting with the cook. The fun will never end.'

'What a life,' Jeanine said. She smiled at him. 'Being a ranch wife. When does a person get to enjoy themselves?'

'In bed,' he said. 'In the hot hours of the night, sweetheart.'

'I knew that's where this was going.'

'I would guess that you are seeing somebody else.'

'It's not serious.'

'Then what is it?'

'Just fun.' She wiped her eyes on the hem of her skirt.

'And I'm not.'

'Ross, you are a very serious man.'

She thought about Innis and what was fair to him and what was not. There were two men to think about. The boy made this all so much more important. She sat back again in the narrow seat and put her hand over her eyes. 'It's just that I have worked so hard for that place. We saved it. We got out of the oil fields and saved it.' She dropped her hand in her lap and turned the horse ring around and around on her little finger. She shut her hand up into a fist. 'I want my own house.'

'Ah, Jeanine.' He took a deep breath.

'What?'

'Whatever you want, darling, you want it so badly.'

The wind had built up and was pushing the car toward the right, and loose, dried vegetation bowled along the verge, and she could feel that the temperature had dropped. Behind them, from the northwest, a solid front was rolling down over the flat country. Ross glanced in his rearview mirror, and then fixed his eyes on it. He frowned.

'What the hell is that?' he said. Behind them all through the empty countryside the stiff black-brush and stripped cotton stalks and the desert willow were bent over and whipping. Jeanine did not notice it or what he had said. She was thinking of something else. She said, 'You could take up work as a rodeo clown, Ross. That would fix you being too serious.'

'Yes, well, I am being serious here for the moment, Jeanine. Turn around and look out the back.'

Jeanine turned to look out the back window. 'Oh God, Ross, it's a dust storm.' A heavy, solid avalanche of darkness was moving toward them with its vaporous head vanishing in the upper atmosphere. It was a toppling great mountain on the loose, boiling at its front edge.

'I see it.'

Jeanine instinctively pulled her hat down around her ears. She said, 'It's come out of nowhere.'

The wind lifted sheer curtains of sand and flung them along the highway and they seethed like discontented spirits.

'It's come down out of Colorado.'

They were approaching a town called Liberty-ville. The sign said there were fifty people there but it looked like no one had lived there for the last ten years nor would they ever live there again. A small concrete bridge took them over a

376

dry ravine with a sign that said it was the DOUBLE MOUNTAIN FORK OF THE BRAZOS. They came upon a lay-by in the railroad tracks and a water tank where trains took on water and the water tank spout lunged back and forth in the wind. Jeanine turned again to look out the back window. The front of the dust storm was solid, it seemed to be made of a thick substance like Bakelite, and it was swallowing up the landscape as it rolled toward them.

Ross slowed and searched for a place of refuge, a shed or a garage.

A gas station made of scrap boards was disappearing in the frontal winds, its Sinclair sign swinging back and forth. A board wrenched loose and was tilted end over end down the highway. There was a side-tracked passenger car at the water tank. It was a dark red and in yellow letters it said ATCHISON TOPEKA AND SANTA FE. The glass in the windows was muted, scored by sand. Ross drove over the main tracks at the crossing and pulled alongside it.

'Get out,' he said. 'We could get buried in that car.'

She held her straw hat brim down around her ears and got out on the passenger side. He came around the front of the Dodge and took her hand. He shoved at the door of the passenger car and it slid back into its slot as the LIBERTY-VILLE POPULATION 50 sign disappeared. The wind built and built until it seemed solid, like floodwater. It sang at the windows with a flutelike sound, and as it increased it howled through the fence wires along the railroad tracks and blew sand in galloping waves down the highway. The wind drove sand grains into the windows with a quick, peppering noise. The old passenger car was vibrating. Ross fought the door back into place. They stood for a moment and she reached out and took his arm as if he were a fence post or a tree that would prevent her from blowing away.

'It's all right,' he said. 'There's got to be a light here somewhere. They must use this for a crew car.' He went toward the rear of the car. There was a table that folded out from the wall. On the wall was an old sconce that held a kerosene lamp and he lit it just as all the windows went dark. The noise of the wind was so loud Jeanine called out for him and he said it was going to be all right. He carried the lamp toward her, a dim beacon in the darkness. Dust began to pour through a broken window. He took off his hat and jammed it into the cracked and jagged hole.

They waited. He told her not to touch anything because the static electricity could carry enough of a charge to set something on fire. He turned two seats toward each other and set the kerosene lamp on the floor between his boots and held it there. The metal parts of the seats were washed with vagrant streams of blue light. Jeanine felt her hair crackle. The wind seemed to be taking everything left of the plains earth and blowing it into outer space. The passenger car shook on its wheels.

Ross got up and sat down again beside Jeanine and put his arm over her shoulder and she pressed against him and took his hand. The wind screamed at the joints of the door and they could see the dust shifting in the air in front of them as small spouts of wind streamed around Ross's hat, and from under the sliding door and around the edges of the windows. It circled around the lamp's small flame and they were washed in sepia tones from the red dust and the yellow lamplight.

She had only read about things like this. She had seen the photographs but it was the electricity that surprised her, the feeling of being a live wire humming with static. Ross's hair was thick with dust and she knew that hers was as well. His hat blew out of the broken window with a pop, like a cork being pulled, and slammed into the opposite wall. He got up and shoved it in again and took off his jacket. He came down the aisle and sat down and then bent over and blew out the lamp and said it was using too much oxygen.

It was hard to breathe. Hard to find oxygen in all the powdered air. The wind howled at every crevice. The noise began to disturb her. She felt like running somewhere. There had to be a better place than this old passenger car. It was the end of the world, the dry world from which the king had abdicated and had deserted his people. The old car rocked on its wheels. She felt she was going to suffocate. Ross undid his tie and pulled off his shirt and held the shirt over their heads. She put her arm around him and it felt as if they were both naked in the swarming dust and the heat with their skin burning in contact like the two poles of a battery.

She asked him how long did he think it would

last, and he said that it was a cold front coming down off the Rockies and it might last for a day and there might be rain behind it. They had to get out of the passenger car by dark or they would have to spend the night in here. She couldn't stand it, being trapped inside this dusty prison, she was very thirsty and her throat seemed to be closing up. Was there not any water in this car somewhere? Wait, he said. Just wait. Don't get frantic, you'll just use up oxygen and there is not a lot of it. Sit quiet.

Then after an hour the storm passed them by and went south, streaming currents of sand and powder in its wings. It went on into the night, into Central Texas, and it left Jeanine so thirsty she could hardly speak. He pulled on his shirt and jacket and rescued his battered hat from the hole in the window and beat the dust from it on his thigh.

Ross shoved the door open and they went out into the polished air. Sand and dust were still hurrying along in currents at ground level. The pickup was drifted in solid. He needed a shovel. They went out into the dark, down the highway, between the few empty houses. The doors were all shut and locked, as if everyone had left many storms ago. It was a drifted town. Dust stood piled on top of picket fences like a fall of snow, it made crowns over windows and shapes like fan ribs over old concrete foundations. The wind had blasted labels from tin cans, and even now it flowed across the blacktopped highway in light scarves.

'The one day I didn't carry water,' he said.

380

'Ross, if we could just find a tank or some-thing.'

'We will.'

They came to the old filling station. The pumps had lollipop heads and had been shut down a long time ago and from its windows faded advertisements for Nehi soda and Quaker State Oil advertised to the empty plains. Ross rattled the knob but the station door was locked, so he took the tire iron out of the bed of the Dodge and broke the glass and reached inside to turn the knob. He flicked on his lighter and held it up. Jeanine wanted a bottle of Nehi worse than she had ever wanted anything in her life. Dust covered the concrete floor. There was nothing in the interior and so he pulled the door shut again.

They went on among the houses with their broken windows. They opened all the doors that would open. Some of them were locked and some flew open before she even touched the doorknob and some were rusted on their hinges. In each house some family had lived and had hung pictures on the walls and lit fires in the dark against the cold bare plains and the stars in a rainless sky. They had made for themselves these houses like shells and then abandoned them, leaving behind broken bottles and tin cans and two hand-prints in a concrete foundation and beside them an inscription that said MAGGIE AND TOM SEPTEMBER 4 1931.

There was an automobile that was so old it might have been the first one ever made, rusted into a pile of scrap metal with broken square oil lamps. Picket fences had fallen over. On one door was a chalked message: KEY. From it an arrow pointed down toward the sill but the door was open inward and it made no sense. They walked on down the highway and he scooped up a tin can and handed it to her. As the sky cleared to stars and wheeling constellations Ross saw a windmill at the edge of the deserted town and took her arm.

'Let's see if this thing will pump.'

Four or five of the sails were missing and the helmet had been shot full of holes by passing hunters, which would have let the dust into the gears and so it did not look promising. He pulled the stick lever and released the brake. The tailpin shifted and the windmill turned its face sideways to the wind and the sails creaked around on their hub. Ross waited until the upstroke and then gave a sharp rap on the water column with the tire iron and water began to pour out of the pipe and into the rusted tank.

'Wait,' he said. He held out both hands and tasted it, and then said it was all right. Jeanine put her tin can into the stream and drank down two cans full and then handed him the can, gasping, and he drank as well. The water poured out over her hands in hiccuping bolts.

'I meant for us to go someplace where they give you two forks,' he said.

She stood with both arms held out to the water. 'It doesn't matter. I don't think anything could be as good as that tin can full of water.'

He took off his hat and held his head under the spout. He held her by the shoulders and kissed her wet face. She put her arms around his waist and stuck her thumbs in his belt and he reached around and took her hands and said Jeanine, you are always messing with me. They had to find some way to shovel out. He slid his hands down her shoulders again and again and felt that if he could not have her then he wished she would choose some other person and quickly. They could not stay there the night and so she would not take off that light print dress and lie down beside him, not yet.

He shoveled out with a flat piece of tin and the Dodge truck started up after several tries. At nine at night they came into Amarillo and parked outside the Stockman's Hotel. They got out of the truck and she dusted him off as best she could with a tow sack she found in the truck and then herself as well.

They were ushered into the restaurant. The maître d' asked them if they had been caught in that dust storm and Ross asked him if they did not look like it? The waiter came and said a lot of other people had been caught in it and were staying the night at the hotel and did they want a room and then noticed that Jeanine did not have a ring and said excuse me, excuse me.

Jeanine sat down with dreadful precision on the plush-and-mahogany chair when Ross pulled it out for her. She put her hands in her lap and gazed at the ranks of silverware and crockery. Things happened around her in a noiseless, air-conditioned hush. Linen-covered tables stretched in every direction. This was a place where people were very *serious* about eating. The gray-haired waiter impressed her with his willingness to bring her anything she asked for, and to arrange her knives and forks and spoons and pour her a glass of water with ice in it. These were things a woman usually did. He seemed to be quite happy doing it, and Jeanine wondered if he were mentally unfit in some way. He clasped his hands together in front of his white apron and asked if they had kept on driving through the storm and Ross said they had taken refuge in a laid-by passenger car of the Atchison Topeka and Santa Fe and the waiter glanced at Jeanine's tangled flyaway hair and said Lord, Lord.

The waiter came beside Ross's chair to take his hat and then with brisk gestures, bore it away to the hat shelf and said he would get it brushed off.

'Have the steak,' Ross said. 'Don't eat it with your hands.'

'I ought to do it just to embarrass you.'

Ross ran his hand quickly through his hair to relieve the pressure of his hat. He opened the menu and did not read it.

He said, 'I won't quit until I have an answer.'

In the hotel dining room there was a murmuring buzz of voices drifting through the brick arches, but it was hushed and mannerly. Jeanine glanced around herself at all the white linen and silver water pitchers beaded with sweat. Ross reached over the table and took her napkin and shook it out and handed it to her.

'Did you hear me?'

'Yes.'

'Yes what?'

'Ross, life would be hard at your place.' She

384

wrapped the napkin around one hand and unwrapped it. 'There's more to life than making money.' She spread the napkin on her knee and thought of something lighthearted to say. She couldn't think of anything at the moment.

'That's true.' His hand tightened briefly into a fist. 'I figure I'll make it when the war comes and afterwards I'll go to Texas U. in Austin and take courses in harpsichord music. And, let's see.'

'I bet.'

'And watercolors. I'll become a philanthropist. I'll buy free iron lungs for everybody. Even people who don't need them but might need them.'

She started wrapping the napkin around her hand again. She said, 'My dad cheated on my mother all those years. And she put up with it and he finally went off with some fourteen-year-old.'

'I'm not your dad. You're twenty-one, I would think you could tell the difference between one human being and another.'

She leaned her head on her fist. 'I know as much about men as a hog knows about Sunday. But you know what?' she said. 'I love you.'

He shifted his large body in the chair and turned up a fork and looked at the tines. The waiter came bearing a salad with strawberries in it. They were small red hearts crying out to be eaten. At the next table several dusty-haired men were urgently discussing the possibilities of using artillery as a rainmaking device. He put the fork down.

'I love you too,' he said. 'I have for a long time.'

385

She said, 'Are these strawberries just for decoration? Or are they rubber?'

'They look real to me.

When they were done with the steak, she ordered the thickest, sweetest dessert on the menu. The overhead fans shifted her hair in vagrant strands about her head. She smiled up at him over the pound cake and its caramel sauce.

'Last chance, Jeanine,' he said.

'Yes,' she said.

He sat without saying anything for a moment and then asked her when. She said in a year, in the year 1939, well, more than a year, in December of 1939. She thought of the orchard and the graveyard and all her work and the pain of leaving it, but still, she would close the door behind her. After that, she thought, would come 1940 and 1941, and so on, she would become a stepmother and there would be hard work, children, droughts, one year opening into another and herself and Ross Everett in their own bedroom and the circle of the year turning outside like the sails of the windmill unfurled and taking into its wheel any wind that came.

CHAPTER THIRTY-SIX

Jugs and Innis sat on the two beds of the Bluebird's Rest Tourist Court cabin and listened as the sand hammered at the windows. Innis jiggled his knee up and down. He got up and walked to the door and then walked back again. Smoky Joe was safe in a stall at the fairgrounds. The Bluebird's Rest Tourist Court was near the new, bald campus of Texas Technological Institute, on the outskirts of Lubbock. Texas Tech, with its Spanish-style buildings scattered over the hard earth and now the visibility was down to a hundred yards and one building could not be seen from another.

'They're going to be all right,' said Jugs.

'Well, this can give people dust pneumonia,' Innis said.

'I know it,' said Jugs. 'But this is a different person.'

'Well, I guess she doesn't have asthma,' said Innis.

'No,' said Jugs. 'She don't.'

Innis nodded and finally he sat down. He took up the fringes of the chenille bedspread and began twisting them. They couldn't get anything on the radio because of the static. He thought about Smoky Joe getting dust pneumonia but he had never heard of animals coming down with it. They were trapped in this one room while the wind and dust tried to take the tourist cabin apart. The floor was gray concrete, slick from years of footsteps. Innis sat on the bed and listened to the shrieking wind. The pillow smelled of hen feathers.

He stared at the pictures on the wall and listened to Jugs snapping out a hand of solitaire. One picture was a landscape with deer drinking from a pool and the other was a framed print of the Sacred Heart of Jesus. The people who owned the place must be Catholic. Jesus himself looked all right, with his mild countenance and an intense gaze in his blue eyes, but he was holding open his red robe and there was a glowing human heart with a crown of thorns on it and Innis found this disturbing and unfathomable. It seemed to him like some terrible surgery. Then he fell asleep and when he woke up in the middle of the night, from a confused dream of burning food on the stove at home, the picture was still there and still without explanation. But the wind had died. They were enveloped in an exhausted silence. Innis sat and listened to it for a long time. He heard coyotes crying in the surrounding hills. They decanted themselves and their warbling, soprano, unstable voices down the draws, unseen in the distance. After a while he fell asleep again.

After two hours the dust moved on from the southern plains into Fort Worth and then on to Waco, losing material as it went and becoming only a high wind with a fluting noise that called and sang at every window and door in Central Texas. Vernon and Mayme parked in a drive shed in Cisco. The shed was used by the Sinclair oil company and the workmen saw the storm coming and they saw the car with two people in it turn off the main highway and they shoved back the doors for them. Vernon and Mayme got out and sat with the men and shared their big glass jug of iced tea without any ice in it. The men asked them where they were headed, and Mayme said they were going to her home, a farm outside of Mineral Wells. They had been to the baseball game in Eastland, because Vernon got a weekend pass. The Fort Worth Cats had beaten the Coca-Cola team from Eastland and they were just getting into the car when it hit. The dust storm had scattered people, thrown them off the highways and into shelters all over the country in general, sent vehicles and people on foot into odd trajectories. Vernon said his sister-in-law and her fellow were caught out in it somewhere, up by Lubbock, and he was worried about them.

Mayme said, 'Vernon!'

'Well, almost a sister-in-law.' Vernon shifted his garrison cap around in his hand. He was sitting on a toolbox chest. To the men he said, 'I was going to ask her to marry me and if she married me, then her sister would be my sister-in-law.' He pulled at the knot of his mohair tie. 'Both of them.'

Mayme said, 'I'm glad to hear about this.'

This turned the conversation toward marriage in general. They waited out the dust storm that was hammering against the steel sides of the drive shed by giving their opinions on marriage during a time of Depression and drought and dust storms. And a very short man said that no matter what happened in the world people got married. It didn't have anything to do with what the weather was like or if you had any money or not, people just went and got married. Another man said that a war was coming and here this boy was in the service, that was something you had to keep in mind. He could get sent to some

389

aerodrome in a foreign country. But the short man said it didn't matter about wars, either. It was the damnedest thing. He didn't know what would matter, anywise.

Bea and Elizabeth sat in Jeanine's room upstairs. The windows were more tightly fitted up here because they were not used as much, but everything – doors and windows and floorboards and chair rungs – had all shrunk over the years of the drought. The window-lights were tall blanks of windy dust. Sometimes when the wind dropped they could see the well below and the barn, the whipping cotton plants, the places where everything had happened going back forty years in Elizabeth's memory, as if revealing to them one scene after another. The roaring windmill whose blades sliced the wind and threatened to come off the derrick, the water that streamed from the pipe flashing out into wild sprays. How she had climbed that derrick on a dare, and the well her daughter had fallen into, the enormous live oak at the end of the driveway where she had sat with Jack Stoddard eating jelly beans and kissing passionately and planning their wedding. In one sweep the entire field of Abel Crowser's cotton came clear, the cotton blossoms now gone and the boils now forming in squares like green turbans, and disappeared again. The wind carried in another curtain of dust and then it fell again until it died out in the late evening.

Bea said, 'Do you think they're all right?'

'Yes,' said her mother. 'Mayme and Vernon are

in Eastland. And Jeanine is with Ross. She'll be all right with Ross.' She turned from the window and sat down on Jeanine's bed. 'I think it's going to start raining now.'

'How do you know?' Bea sat with Albert on her lap. Biggety lay asleep on the bed in a tight curl with his ears twitching.

'I don't know how I know. I just do.'

Bea thought about it. Her mother had some way of knowing things that Bea didn't understand but that she believed in. Her mother had known the well would come in all along. And so she must in some mysterious way know that the drought had come to an end.

'You mean a lot of rain?' said Bea. 'Or a little?'

'A lot,' said Elizabeth. She stood up. 'Let's go make supper.'

Bea followed her down the stairs and into the gritty kitchen. She still found it miraculous to pull a chain and the clear glass lightbulb illuminated the entire kitchen with glare. She could read the labels on the cans of hominy and tomatoes. 'You mean the drought is over?'

'Yes. I don't know why, I just know. It's over.'

That was the last large dust storm to strike the southern plains. After that it began to rain and the nations of Europe moved toward war and were so heavily weighted with armor that the structures of peace collapsed and would soon take all the other nations with them. Many of the older people remembered the Great War and they said that the artillery expended in millions of tons of shells had caused the incessant rains of that time on the fields of France and that now this was what was happening again. The artillery of Chancellor Hitler and his armies, of the Japanese Imperial Army bombing Shanghai, shook the upper levels of the air and so this brought weather in long streaming columns of rain, the slow kind of rain that fell in very small droplets and soaked in.

Roosevelt came to Amarillo in his only visit to the southern plains, the barren country where all the disasters and dust storms had taken place, where all the news photos had been taken showing mountainous walls of dust falling upon towns, people struggling through wind and dunes. Roosevelt arrived in Amarillo, a town up in the Panhandle, on the presidential train in July of 1938, and it began to rain when the train pulled into the station. Some people said it was a sign from God, that God had forgiven him for trying to pack the Supreme Court and for hiring Harold Ickes. That in fact God had forgiven everybody in a kind of general amnesty and the seven lean years were over.

The rain swept down on President Roosevelt in sheets and he managed despite everything to stand up on his rigid braces and address the great crowd so that people would not see that he was a cripple in a wheelchair and be discouraged or think that a broken man was leading them forward out of the wilderness. He spoke to them with a good wide smile while rain ran down his face, and since nobody could find the umbrellas they had stored away years ago, they stood out in the rain too, and cheered and applauded wildly with wet, spattering hands.

Jeanine pushed kindling into the hot-water heater and lit it. The Millers had put in a gravity-feed tank that filled the commode and the bathtub, and a primitive hot-water heater. Now all the bathroom needed was paint, maybe a pale blue, and little soaps and talcum powder. She heard the newspaper truck backfiring as it struggled down the gravel road, through a faint drizzle, and when the boys threw the folded newspaper at each mailbox it sounded as if they were hurling shot puts. Jeanine ran out and got the paper, and laid it beside the bathtub, ran the tub full and stripped off her clothes. The muddy jeans could nearly stand by themselves. She sank her body into the water. She was going to read the newspaper in the bathtub and spend as much time as she liked soaking herself.

How had they lived without this? How many times had they hung sheets to sit beside the stove, doubled up naked in a number three washtub, and then thrown it out in buckets. Jeanine hooked her heels over the edge of the tub, and shook out the Tarrant newspaper; she ignored the front-page stories. They were always boring. For instance, the Seiberling Latex plant near Akron, Ohio, was three weeks behind in orders making rubber statuettes of Dopey and Doc and Sleepy and the rest of the Seven Dwarves. She went on to the local news with wet hands, and then saw Milton's picture in the society column, just above the obituaries. Milton Brown and Lou-Ann Callaway, former school-teacher, had become engaged. They were smiling, she mooning up at him with a calflike adoring expression, and he gazing manfully at the camera. Milton's cowlick stood out like a pinwheel. After their marriage they planned to live in Chicago where Mr. Brown of this city would take lessons in elocution and prepare for a career in radio broadcasting.

'What!!' She stood up and gushed water all over the bathroom floor. She climbed out of the tub and held the paper in front of her at arm's length and stormed into the kitchen with soapy water pouring from her, the newspaper in one hand and a towel in the other. 'He could have told me!' She threw the paper into the kindling box and began to dry herself. 'He could have *said* something.' She wrapped herself in the towel, and the cat gazed down on her from on top of the Hamilton safe. 'I was going to tell *him*.' She stalked back and forth on the narrow floorboards and into the hall and back again. This was deception, this was unfair, and it didn't matter that she had said she would marry Ross, it was still unfair. She was doomed to be deceived. 'Oh, who cares?' she asked Albert. 'I don't care. J-j-j-ust ask me if I care.'

She walked into her upstairs room and stood before the window to see the slow, light rain. It ran off the eaves in spangles. Everything was dripping, soaked. Wood filled out and doors tightened, the mortar of the well curb thickened and swelled and held. All the peach trees dripped black gum from the water the roots took up. The sky over the Brazos valley had not lifted for weeks. Drawn edges of cloud or mist were carried along the rims of the steep-sided valleys running into the Brazos and then caught and were pulled out like a sheer material.

But then, Jeanine thought, she had not told her mother and sisters of her promise to Ross, either. Six months ago when they were up on the roof she had laughed and told Mayme, *He'd better not be hunting for me.* That was embarrassing. Better to let Mayme tell everyone she and Vernon had got engaged, first. And Jeanine was still wavering. Her ties to this place where she had worked so hard might become frayed and insubstantial. Sometimes during the day she thought of taking the promise back again, as if she had only lent it, and abandoning the entire dubious enterprise of loving and falling in love, its inevitable betrayals; she wondered if maybe it would not be better to stay here forever, smooth and cool and ceramic, like the doll's head.

She dried herself in the wet air and pulled on her old striped dress. She should turn on the radio for the soap operas, she should go in town to a movie. She needed to see some bold, brave young woman defy odds and take a long journey and fall passionately in love. She wanted to see somebody run a plantation single-handed and shoot a Yankee and make dresses out of Mama's portieres. She wanted to sit and eat popcorn and watch somebody with a small dog and impossible companions flee through a magic kingdom. To watch a girl ride National Velvet over the jumps. A story would unfold in which something terrible was at stake, where life and death mattered, where people committed themselves to some course of action without hesitation. Jeanine stood at the window in the parlor, which gave out onto the slope, where the cotton bloomed in tangled fibers out of its hard boils, impelled by a relentless force. She watched Abel Crowser unhitch the cultivator and ride in on Jo-Jo and Sheba with their harnesses and collars still on them, to let them stand in the fairway of the barn, where they stood wet-footed, listening with revolving ears to the rain.

In September the dread cabal in Washington had reduced the allowables on Central Texas wells and increased those in West Texas. Her mother couldn't figure it out. Theirs was much higher-grade oil than the junk out in the Permian, that stuff out there was saturated with sulfur. Mr. Lacey consoled her. It will change, he said. The West Texans have got more influence in the legislature than we have. And besides the pressure is still holding, it's twelve hundred pounds of pressure at the wellhead and they aren't going to need to pump it, it's coming up on its own. Elizabeth sent Mr. Lacey home with casseroles because he was divorced and ate nothing but Spam sandwiches and she had at last been convinced to call him George.

'Vernon's got leave! Vernon's got leave! September fifteenth! Five days!' Mayme skipped around the kitchen and hugged Jeanine and held a geranium flower by her ear. She danced across the room in a sort of tango. 'Rum and Coca-Colaaaa!' A slow rain poured down the windowpanes, and dripped from the tips of the sotol and agarita. Water ran off the edges of the roof in a glittering curtain and the grass was green again.

They would go into Tarrant and stay all night at the Kincaid Hotel and then the next day catch the train to Galveston to meet Vernon. Ross could not go to Galveston because the windmill crew was coming again, they had to pull sucker rods from the water wells in the Upshaw pasture and he had to be there.

But Jeanine and Bea and Mayme were very happy about the hotel, as they had never stayed in one, and could hardly imagine the maids making up a room for them, and cleaning up after them when they left. They would have the whole day in Tarrant, and her mother would talk with Bea's teachers, and she would see the new high school, and she would choose for herself a new pair of beach shoes at the shoe store. Betty would probably urge two pairs on her. After all, Magnolia was making an offer to buy them out. And that Mr. Lacey would be joining them down in Galveston, in a white sharkskin suit, probably with a carnation in his buttonhole and he would take all of them out to dinner. It would be a dinner with daunting and peculiar food such as lobsters and shrimps. Mayme was in a state of anxiety about how to approach these things and what sorts of instruments she would have to use, and Elizabeth said that Mr. Lacey – George – would have a long, serious discussion with Bea about going on to high school. Her mother was happier than Jeanine had ever seen her. Bea ran about the house singing *I used to love you 'til you ate my dog...* It was the Crazy Water Gang's parody of lonesome heartbroke country and western music. *I ain't no cowboy,* she sang. *I just found this hat...*

Bea had lately been reading e.e. cummings, and had taken up an attitude of cynicism and hauteur, but that evaporated when she was mailed a check for five dollars from *Savage Western Tales* for her vivid story of Kitty Kelsay being stabbed repeatedly by a renegade white man during the Comanche attack in Uvalde County and the famous twenty-mile running fight led by the hero horse, Fuzzy Buck. Five dollars had utterly destroyed her desire to go to Paris and write free verse and live on the Rue Chat Noir. If there was such a rue.

Ten girls had come to her freshman party. Some of them were driven out from town in the endless rain. Two were from her eighth-grade class at the Old Valley Road schoolhouse. They snarled into excited knots and spoke in gasps and showed one another the brand names on their saddle shoes. They argued about hillbilly music and Tommy Dorsey. One of the girls said her sister was a junior and all the juniors and seniors loved Tommy Dorsey and so that ended the discussion. They asked about Bea's fall down the well, and her operation, and she showed them the red scars on her leg and said she was going to write about it someday. The kitchen smelled of Evening in Paris cologne and Blue Grass talcum and a fine, soft dampness.

Bea's hair was cut short and curled, she wore a dirndl skirt and peasant blouse and saddle shoes.

There were three more skirts and two dresses in her closet. Her family owned an oil well. They had part interest in a racehorse. They lived in a white-painted two-story house with running water and electricity and a telephone and it was raining everywhere, all over the world.

'I'm going to be an author,' she said. 'I'm published already.' She showed them the check for five dollars with her name on it, and the date and the amount and signature by an authorizing person.

One of the girls from town said, '*Savage Western Tales?* Oh they read that down at the garage. Newton's garage.' The girl stared at Bea for a long moment. 'Well I guess that's nice.'

The party lasted until nearly ten and when Bea lay down to sleep in her own bed, in her own newly painted room, she was suddenly frightened that she had said too much or done too much. Then she was not sleepy at all. She was assaulted with a very clear vision of the town girls in high school coming up to her and repeating Kitty Kelsay's desperate scream, *Oh my God, Mother, they are killing me!* and laughing and laughing. She felt panicked. They would all read it at some garage in Mineral Wells. It was a stupid story, stupid, and it had her name on it, and it would go all over the country. Bea got out of bed and lifted up the sleeping Prince Albert and carried him into the kitchen and began to pace back and forth.

She didn't want to go to high school after all. She would hide at home from her own printed words, hide out forever. Tears came to her eyes as she thought of the horror of it. And then at ten at night she heard Winifred Beasley's voice, metallic and thin. A clear and reasonable Winifred Beasley that spoke to her of the joys of healthful foods, a sweet voice lecturing on the benefits of whole grains and Graham crackers and flaxseed. She was on the radio. Bea stopped pacing to walk over to the old Emerson and turn it up. That was her. After a few moments the announcer said that was the *Home Health Hour* presented by the Humble Oil Company, which would henceforth be aired a half hour every weekday night. They would never get rid of Winifred Beasley. Never.

CHAPTER THIRTY-SEVEN

At four o'clock on the blazing hot afternoon of September 13 Jeanine took the truck down to Strawn's Crossroads store and filled the tires with air, and asked old man Joplin to change the oil for her. He peered into the engine with great interest for a long time and then remembered he said he would change the oil. Jeanine went in to pay. Mrs. Joplin was in the backyard, smoking a cigarette among the cages of live chickens, cooling herself in the shade of the live oak trees that surrounded the old frame building. She exhaled smoke heavily into the damp air, threw the cigarette down, and hurried into the store.

'Now, Jeanine,' said Mrs. Joplin. She slapped a package on the counter. The package was wrapped in a sheet and pinned together. 'I hate to tell you this, but Martha Jane Armstrong is sending this wedding dress back to you.'

Jeanine's mouth dropped open. 'What's wrong with it?' She came up to the counter and laid her hand on the package. 'It was perfect, Martha Jane said so, what's wrong?'

Mrs. Joplin bent her long body over the counter and shifted the package around. 'There isn't anything wrong with it. It's just Martha Jane. They say redheaded people have tempers, and Martha Jane always said she was going to prove otherwise, but she threw that dress down the stairs from that attic of theirs, and then she threw the veil down the stairs too.'

'What happened?'

Mrs. Joplin waved one hand at her. 'Sit down. You are always, always in a hurry, Jeanine. You were in a hurry to be born. I remember it well. Your mother had you in three hours flat from when she was first took to when they cut the cord.' Jeanine sat down on the Jell-O rack. 'Don't sit on the Jell-O rack. Take that old chair seat. Well, my grandson Tim said he was going to work for Pacific Contractors. He made up his mind to. Nothing will change it. He has to see the world, he said. He signed a contract for three years, driving heavy equipment out there in the Pacific Ocean.'

Jeanine took the package and held it in her lap. She still had a blank and amazed look on her face. 'How is he going to drive heavy equipment on top of the Pacific Ocean?'

Mrs. Joplin shook her head. 'On some little island. What they're doing is, they are grading off airstrips for the Army Air Corps. It's called Wake Island. And he's going to be there for three years, and won't be home in all that time, and Martha Jane said it was as good as saying he didn't want to get married, and he could just go to the hot place.'

'Three years,' said Jeanine. She had become acutely aware of the slightest hint of treachery from men, which seemed to operate conjointly in their heads with a tendency to get women to wait for them for indefinite periods, while they went wandering around without reason or limits, but she could not come to any conclusions whether Tim Joplin was actually backing out of his promise or not. 'That's 1941,' she said.

'Yes. And I told her, honey, the Pacific Ocean *is* the hot place.' Mrs. Joplin lifted her thin shoulders in a shrug. 'She's mad enough to eat bees. Her mother said she wasn't fit to see people. Her mother drove this over here and said either hide it or sell it. As if I was supposed to figure out what to do with it. I don't know what I ought to do with it. You better take it back home with you. Need some moth crystals?' The tall old woman turned and began to rummage around in the various poisons she kept underneath the counter. 'Here.' She slapped a blue box down on the solid walnut. 'Those moths just love silk.'

'Didn't she say she would wait for him?' Jeanine reached for the moth crystals. 'It's only...' Then her voice faded and she said in a lower tone, 'Three years.'

'When people are set on getting married they don't like waiting. It is a true fact. They're just thinking, "Well, it's the biggest decision I'll ever make, let's just get on with it." Like somebody that's going to be hanged at dawn. "Why don't you just hang me at midnight and get it over with?" Martha Jane has no patience.' Mrs. Joplin lifted her head as one of the Miller kids came in; it was the youngest one. He carefully laid out a penny on the counter and said he wanted a jawbreaker, a purple one. He went away making sucking sounds, with a frightening bulge in his cheek. His bare feet left dust tracks across the floor. 'She was set to be married and she's going to get married one way or another.' The phone rang and Mrs. Joplin reached up and took the earpiece out of the hook and shouted, 'What?' She listened. 'He's changing somebody's oil. No, he don't want any.' She hung it up again and turned back to Jeanine. 'Now, you've been out visiting at Ross Everett's place. How do you find it?'

Jeanine had been out to the ranch in Comanche County three times now. She had watched as Innis ran Smoky at a slow gallop on the exercise track, standing in the stirrups; had gone with him to the corral to admire his foal and the red mare. The foal was nearly six months old; he had shed out to a light gray and his leg bones had grown sturdy and straight. The red mare's wound was healed to a spiderweb of scar tissue and the mare followed Ross along the fence line and called to him for feed or attention. Innis proudly showed her the wind charger that powered the kitchen and the two clear electric lightbulbs and the electric iron. She had sat down beside Ross as he went over the accounts with her; he explained the shearing costs and how to stay up with the price of mohair in the Dallas newspaper. One evening before she drove home Ross said they needed to do some serious talking, so they sat on the stone-floored veranda and spoke of the future. He wanted her to think clearly about what she would do were anything to happen to him; ranching was a dangerous business. Jeanine found this frightening and she felt like stopping up her ears, but it was a bigger matter than her fright or alarm, and so she sat and read over his will with a still and serious expression as he pointed out the provisions.

The next time she had got through all the roundup gear and the smoke-blackened cooking pots and they had painted the kitchen, and Jugs had helped to move in a new electric refrigerator. Through the tall kitchen window was a view of the branding pens and the long sweeping ridges beyond, now glowing in wet, intense colors. After they married she would look out on this view for many years to come.

Still she had not set a date. *Next time*, she said, *next time*. But people lost patience, she thought. They wanted to be married or hanged without delay once it was decided but still Jeanine had said *Wait, wait*.

'I find it is very well,' said Jeanine. 'The old stone house is beautiful.'

'Well, so does Martha Jane,' said Mrs. Joplin. She turned to look out the back door and saw that Mr. Joplin had sat himself down on an orange crate and was now cleaning the spark plugs. If she didn't say anything he would go on to rebuild the entire engine, but Mrs. Joplin knew it made him happy. 'Martha Jane said to her mother she was going to run over there to Everett's place and ask to see if he was shipping any of her mohair. She said he bought two woolsacks that were hers. I mean separate from her mother and daddy's. Now that don't make sense to me. You know, "Oh I think I'll just drop in and visit with my woolsacks." Like they were people. Woolsacks weigh four hundred pounds and they ain't people. But there it is. Everett's probably lonely out there, has been for years, just him and the boy. And his wife deader than Santa Ana.'

Jeanine listened with a blank face. She shifted the package of wedding dress around on her lap and then stood up. She wanted to ask when it was that Martha Jane had visited, and for how long, but it would be too humiliating. Jeanine had the sudden but familiar feeling of everything going to pieces, despite anything she did, but she was also becoming angry as well as alarmed.

She said she had to get back, she had left beans on the stove. She put the moth crystals and four oranges and a pound of longhorn cheese into her heavy canvas bag and went out to ask Mr. Joplin to put the spark plugs back in so she could start up her engine and go home, and revive her life and her faith in humanity, or at least men.

Mrs. Joplin watched the '29 Ford truck roar off down the road, throwing gravel. Then she walked out to the backyard and sat down beside her elderly husband. She had done what she thought she ought to do. Maybe it was the right thing, maybe not. Mr. Joplin raised his head and then glanced down again.

'Well, Pearl, I guess I got that job done.'

'Yes, you did.' They sat at ease, resting within the spotted, tossing shade.

'What was it?'

'You changed that young woman's oil and cleaned the spark plugs.'

He cleared his throat. He was struggling with the profound shame of knowing that his mind was drifting away; all he had was Pearl to keep him anchored. She watched him sigh heavily and wipe his hands together.

'Pearl, dear,' he said. 'Sometimes I don't know where I am.'

Mrs. Joplin stroked his back. 'It's all right, James,' she said. 'Wherever you are, that's the world.'

Jeanine drove back the one mile to the house with her foot jammed down on the pedal, and the wind came in all the open truck windows in gusts. Behind her the sheet came unwrapped from the silk wedding dress and the whole package began to flounder about in the backseat. The arms of the wedding dress thrashed around, she could see it in the rearview mirror. The skirt billowed up like a dummy turned upside down, the sheet seemed to be pouring out the window, an escapee. She did not know what to do with it. On the other hand, she could save it for Mayme. Mayme wouldn't care if it had been made for somebody else. She was so in love with Vernon she'd get married in a bedspread. Jeanine stamped on the brake and came to a halt under the Spanish oak. What would she do without Ross in her life? It would be terrible, it could not happen.

She called Ross as soon as she got in the house. She threw the wedding dress and the sheet onto the kitchen table and dialed his number. She listened impatiently as the party lines got crossed and two men were discussing some sheep that had got out and were up on Jim Ned Creek. Then finally she heard Ross's voice say, *Hello?*

'Ross, it's Jeanine.'

'Hello, girl,' he said.

'Ross, I want to set a date. And the date is...' She paused. She said the first thing that came into her head. 'December twelfth.'

Faint voices in the background spoke of three head got out and gone up past Ganlin's water gap, they were seen yesterday. Finally he said, 'What brought this on?'

'Martha Jane Armstrong.'

He laughed. 'Jeanine,' he said. 'Jeanine darling.'

'Well?'

There was a long pause. Jeanine sat on the kitchen chair and beat her foot on the floor. You could grow hair in the man's pauses.

'I didn't tell her to come out here, Jenny. I don't like being asked to explain myself.'

'Well, did you ask her to *go?*'

'I did not invite her into the house. When she left, Innis nailed her taillight with a hexagonal nut. He was hiding behind the rock tank.'

'Shame on him,' said Jeanine. 'Ha-ha.'

'Stay friends,' said Ross. 'You could have no worse enemy than Martha Jane Armstrong.'

Then it was Jeanine who fell into the long gap of a wordless pause. She ran her fingers through her tangled hair and finally said, 'All right.'

'Then if you are determined on that date, there is a lot to do.' Her mind vaulted forward to all that there was to do and she banged the toes of her shoes together. 'Your ring came,' he said. Nervously she wrote in the air with her forefinger; r-i-n-g.

'Oh good, Ross!' She listened intently against the distant voices crackling on the crossed party lines about looking for Barkley's merinos as Ross asked her to make lists. Jeanine and her mother and sisters had to present a festive occasion to the world, a celebration that was to be joyful and at the same time corseted with tradition. All the right people had to be invited for fear of offending the wrong people, nothing unlucky must happen, nor could they ignore the dead, who shadowed the event from some other dimension: her father, Ross's first wife. Like fossils printed in stone they sent faint indications of themselves on down the years, admonishing and reminding because they were still very present in memory and because of the children they had introduced, willy-nilly, into the world of the living.

Jeanine did not like talking on the buzzing, public party line; she wanted to hang up, to say that they would talk later, but Ross wanted her to find a pen and paper and write out an announcement now, this very minute, and take it in to the newspaper in Tarrant when they all went in to catch the train to Galveston and have done with it. She bent over a sheet of lined paper with her tongue between her teeth and her hair falling in her face and wrote, *Mrs. Elizabeth Stoddard of Palo Pinto County announces the marriage of her daughter Jeanine ...* and so she was committed.

She put the receiver back into its cradle and looked up at the kitchen. It was somehow a different kitchen. Some shift had taken place. Some alteration in the boards and windows and the kitchen curtains with their jolly orange pigs as she felt her connection to this place suddenly become tenuous and frayed. It was as if she were looking at some memory, already in the past and dearly beloved in each commonplace detail; the braided rug and the old cookstove and Prince Albert asleep on the cool stone of the fireplace hearth.

She folded the paper and put it in her purse and then started the washing to get everyone ready for their weekend in Galveston. She flung clothes into the churning suds of the washing machine and the fumes of the gasoline engine filled the back porch. A strange feeling of being a visitor overcame her; a kind and polite visitor who was helping out with the housework, and who had someplace else to go, someplace exciting.

She sang 'Your Cheating Heart' in a hoarse and wobbling voice as she hung tea towels and underpants and brassieres and sheets on the line as clouds skated overhead like glacial soapsuds. She walked through the garden where the fall harvest of trilobite leaves of sweet potatoes appeared, childlike things toasting brown in their earth beds. Her fields all swept of seedling cedar now seemed to belong to somebody else, and so did the orchard. So she walked through the stones of the family graveyard and pulled up a greenbrier sprout that had sprung up with the new rains and had begun to crawl over her grandmother's headstone. What home had Nannie Tolliver left behind to come here from Northeast Texas, what family graveyards had she abandoned to the greenbrier? You had to wonder. Nannie probably loaded up her trunk with quilts and dishes and the porcelain doll's head and said *Let's go, Samuel.* Jeanine turned away and went into the house, restless, seized by a need for movement.

She threw cold water in her face and then went down into the cotton field. Abel lifted his hat to her; he was on a four-sweep riding cultivator behind Jo-Jo and Sheba. She listened for a moment as he spoke to them, listened to the jingle of the harnesses and the distant sound of the small points slicing through the soil. Tomorrow she would ride the seed drill, which would carry the steel barrels of Paris Green arsenate to kill the weevils and next year when she came back to visit, the new plants would flush out free of infestation. Then she went back into the house again, to stand in front of the electric fan for a moment. In all the valley fields the cotton was expanding into knots of white fiber. It was Tuesday evening; the sky blued with the watercolors of evening. Fibber and Molly burst into the sound waves. *Oh, Molly, how patient and sane you are, with your silly and loving husband, how calm in the make-believe world of radio, in some imaginary town that never changes.* She finally rested on the veranda steps, slouched back against one of the posts, watching the seamless evening fall across the world.

That night she sat in her room while her sisters and mother talked about the suitcases and what if they were lost when they changed trains in Dallas. Whether the Texas Railroad Commission was going to shut down the well, if Clark Gable was going to divorce Rita Langhorn, and did he really pilot the plane in *Test Pilot.* They listened to the radio for an hour and then her mother and sisters went to bed. Jeanine walked restlessly into the hall. A series of selves stood behind her reflection in the beveled mirror, tokens of herself as she grew up from one year to another, from Ranger to Tarrant to Mexia, out to Monahans in the great sea of the Permian Basin, to Arp and Kilgore, to Wharton, where her father had betrayed them so terribly and where he lay in his lonely grave, and finally here, to home, which would soon not be her home anymore. And all the time her heart opening and closing, opening and closing, carrying her through whatever shifts and changes came at her, an unshakable core of self. She pulled on her thin nightgown and went to bed but she could not sleep. The hours went by like scrap metal, rusty and slow. Jeanine got up and went down the stairs and into the kitchen. The moon shone in bars through the windows.

She reached for the drawer with the old photograph album in it. She found herself sitting

411

in front of the lamp with the clear electric light gleaming across the yellowed pictures of herself in her father's arms, of Uncle Reid smiling into the camera with his hands on the great wrenches at the Kelly hose, bound for oblivion. At her father, handsome and still young, before the sour gas, before the arrest, holding Smoky Joe's lead rope and the stallion's blocky dark body a coiled spring from which speed would explode, loosing him down the track into a winner's circle. From across the hall Bea spoke to somebody in a dream and her voice was full of garbled conviction. Jeanine gazed down at the photo of Mayme in her high school graduation dress, Ross Everett sitting on the running board of his truck with his hat pushed back, herself at the edge of the photo in her accidental appearance, in that black-and-white landscape of 1935. And the spectral presence in all these pictures, the one standing behind the camera. The one looking into the lens whose name was soon forgotten or confused in these family albums and so at last remained only as a loving and generous unseen presence.

Jeanine saw that there were four or five pages in the back that were still empty. She ripped out a page from the Sears Roebuck catalog and slipped it in to mark the place where the wedding pictures would go, and postcards from aerodromes in far places, and then photographs of children and all the other lives to come, and shut the old album carefully, and put it back into the tin trunk.

The publishers hope that this book has given you enjoyable reading. Large Print Books are especially designed to be as easy to see and hold as possible. If you wish a complete list of our books please ask at your local library or write directly to:

Magna Large Print Books
Magna House, Long Preston,
Skipton, North Yorkshire.
BD23 4ND

This Large Print Book for the partially sighted, who cannot read normal print, is published under the auspices of

THE ULVERSCROFT FOUNDATION

THE ULVERSCROFT FOUNDATION

... we hope that you have enjoyed this Large Print Book. Please think for a moment about those people who have worse eyesight problems than you ... and are unable to even read or enjoy Large Print, without great difficulty.

You can help them by sending a donation, large or small to:

**The Ulverscroft Foundation,
1, The Green, Bradgate Road,
Anstey, Leicestershire, LE7 7FU,
England.**
or request a copy of our brochure for more details.

The Foundation will use all your help to assist those people who are handicapped by various sight problems and need special attention.

Thank you very much for your help.